Jim O'Brien is a greater Boston native who has lived his entire life with his family in his beloved New England. A graduate of Providence College, Jim has over thirty years of retail experience. He has held positions from entry-level to Director of Sales and Operations where his responsibilities necessitated travel throughout much of the USA. In 2010 Jim was diagnosed with stage three colon cancer. Five years later, he was diagnosed with prostate cancer. He has survived to tell his story to those willing to listen, frequently on a golf course while whacking and swearing at a small, white, dimpled orb.

For Grandpa, Ginny, Domingos, Aunt Alice, Aunt Doris, Minuch, Will, Russ, Doctor Gus, and Alan; some family members and close friends who fought like hell until their last breath.

For my wife and caregiver. Sometimes it's harder to watch the fight than it is to engage in it.

For my two sons. There is nobody on the planet with whom I would rather tee it up.

Jim O'Brien

# CROAKING FROGS

AUSTIN MACAULEY PUBLISHERS™

LONDON • CAMBRIDGE • NEW YORK • SHARJAH

**Ordering Information**
Quantity sales: Special discounts are available on quantity purchases by corporations, associations, and others. For details, contact the publisher at the address below.

**Publisher's Cataloging-in-Publication data**
O'Brien, Jim
Croaking Frogs

ISBN 9781645757191 (Paperback)
ISBN 9781645757207 (Hardback)
ISBN 9781645757214 (ePub e-book)

Library of Congress Control Number: 2020924228

www.austinmacauley.com/us

First Published (2021)
Austin Macauley Publishers LLC
40 Wall Street, 33rd Floor, Suite 3302
New York, NY 10005
USA

mail-usa@austinmacauley.com
+1 (646) 5125767

# 1

Interpretations of a single event by the many are frequently varied.

David pulled to the curb in front of the stately home on Meadow Rd., in the town of Chevon, and sat for a moment before killing the engine of his high-performance sports car. With his right index finger, he pushed his Ray-Ban Chromance Polarized sunglasses up onto the bridge of his nose in order to better shield his glassy, bloodshot eyes from the bright Saturday morning sun. He then tugged on the inside door handle and wobbly stepped away from the warm car as he gathered himself.

David and Gina, his wife, were out to dinner at a local sushi restaurant the night before, minding their own business, when they ran into some close friends from their college years. Since they hadn't seen each other in months, the group had lots of catching up to do. One innocent beer led to another which, in turn, led to a Scotch or two. The second tumbler of Johnnie Walker Blue Label seemed like a really good idea at the time. Especially since it was Friday night, and David knew he had nothing to do the next morning except make it to his ten o'clock tee time at the country club. He figured a little 'hair of the dog' in the form of a Bloody Mary before hitting his first shot would take the edge off if necessary. From there, he had the rest of the day to enjoy a round of golf on what was forecasted to be a beautiful spring morning. However, as Robert Burns penned,

*"The best laid plans o' mice an' men, Gang aft a-gley."*

The azalea bushes lining the driveway leading to the side door of the home were in full bloom, screaming at the recently hatched insects to come over and have a taste of their nectar. In some parts of Turkey, bees are deliberately fed azalea nectar which then produce a mind-altering honey known as 'mad honey.' As he lifted the yellow tape that stretched across the front of the property and stepped under it, David was thinking he could use a little bit of that honey. In fact, he would try anything that could potentially take the edge off from the night before. Glancing at the brilliance of the flowering bushes

7

was adding to the pain in his eyes, and he quickened his pace in order to pass through the gauntlet he created for himself. "I'll never drink again," he said aloud to any bee within voice range that was willing to listen to his plea for mercy. He then grinned while contemplating about the idiot he felt he was for administering his self-inflicted misery and nodded to the man standing guard at the side door of the beautifully landscaped home.

"Nice of you to join us, hot shot," the officer said as David crossed into the foyer of the home and removed his sunglasses, exposing a patriotic pair of red, white, and glassy-blue eyes.

There were two homicide detectives already on the scene, and the coroner was deeply involved in examining the body. David was approached by his older brother, Rick, a police-department computer genius who was often brought into crime scenes in order to gather electronic evidence and other pertinent information that could help solve the crime. The brothers embraced briefly and then went about their business in an extremely efficient, professional manner.

David, or Dave, as his brother frequently called him, was a gifted homicide detective. He began earning his formidable reputation at a relatively young age. Dave had been fresh out the police academy when he helped to solve a high-profile murder case involving a corrupt state official. He had an innate, uncanny ability to process key evidence from seemingly innocuous observations which frequently eluded even the most seasoned detectives. A tenacious competitor, he climbed the ladder quickly and achieved his homicide-detective badge by the time he hit his late 20s. Rick and Dave, who were 'Irish Twins,' kept themselves in top physical condition. Rick stood six-foot three and weighed in at 220 pounds. He appeared to not have even an ounce of fat on his body. Dave was slightly shorter but thicker and more muscular. His body was well-suited to be a linebacker on a football field. They were both even tempered, however, on more than one occasion, an overly aggressive interloper ended up wishing that he had, instead, minded his own business.

"Hey, Rick," Dave said as he approached the family room where the murder victim was being examined and photographed from all angles. "What have we got so far?"

"It appears the murder took place here in the family room," Rick replied. "Not a lot of evidence laying around, either. The guy who did this was pretty neat and clean."

"How do you know that whoever did this to the little lady is a guy?" David asked, staring with a puzzled look on his face in the direction of the body.

"We don't," Rick casually replied. "However, it appears that the murder was committed with the victim lying face down on top of the coffee table. She was alive, kicking, and fighting, until she got to this point. Looks like she put up a bit of a struggle in the kitchen area as well. It's unlikely she just jumped up on the table, strapped her arms and legs together with those kayak straps and said go ahead. The person who did this was strong enough to overpower her and bind her arms and legs together like you see there. As you can also see, she is, how do I put this, big boned. My guess is she weighs about 280-plus. So, the guy or gal, if you insist, who did this would have to be able to deadlift a lot of weight to a height of four feet. You tell me, Dave. I mean, I'm sure there are plenty of women who have the strength to do this. It's just that it would be unusual. Play the odds, right?" he asked, looking for agreement.

David nodded and raised his eyebrows, acknowledging his brother's hypotheses. He moved carefully throughout the scene, looking but not disturbing anything that may turn out to be useful evidence. His eyes silently transmitted minute visual details of the victim to his brain for safe storage. There, the images remained in safe storage for future use. Suddenly, his concentration was broken with sounds coming from a distant room. He looked up and glanced in the general direction of the source. Then, he changed his expression and gazed back toward his brother.

"I'm assuming the wailing coming from over there is the husband?" David asked, pointing toward the source of the disturbance.

"Yeah, he got stuck in San Diego on his business trip yesterday," Rick replied. "So, he flew the red eye all night back to Bradley International. He says he pulled into the driveway at 7:30 this morning. Once he realized what he was walking into, he says he ran back outside and called the emergency line for help. Sorry about the wakeup call, by the way. I know it's supposed to be your day off. Where else would you rather be, though?" Rick chuckled.

"I should be on the second hole already," David quipped. "I did not expect this today," he said, shaking his head and rubbing his brow. "Listen." David held out his right hand, gesturing to his brother to be quiet. "The husband keeps saying she was my best friend ever. How could anyone do such a cruel thing to her? It sounds like they were a loving couple. Either that, or he's a convincing actor. Does everything check out with him claiming to be out of town when she got whacked? Have we ruled him out as a suspect yet?" David asked.

"Yeah, everything checks out as far as him being out of town when the murder happened," Rick confirmed. "The coroner figures she was killed around sunset last night. The husband is not a prime suspect. That's not to say he didn't commission somebody else to do the dirty work. He, however, didn't carry out the deed himself," Rick reported. "You do need to sharpen your observation skills, however." He smirked. "I can tell you are having a rough morning."

David glared at his brother for even suggesting he needed to sharpen anything. The two were close as brothers and friends, but there was much sibling rivalry existing between them. When they played one-on-one basketball, for example, it appeared like there was an all-out bar brawl taking place. Bloody noses were more the rule than the exception. On the golf course, there was nothing given. No liberty with guidelines allowed. Play the ball as it lies. The objective was to win, almost at all cost. However, they had each other's back, always. Never get between a set of Irish twins. Cross one of them, and you will quickly find yourself taking on both.

"What do you mean by that?" David snarled. The leftover alcohol effects from the night before were still taking a toll on his morning mood.

"What I mean is you're assuming that the husband crying over and over about his best friend being killed is talking about his wife," Rick mused, pointing at the victim. "You are still not seeing the whole picture. It's not like you to jump to conclusions like that," he lectured.

Rick allowed his brother to gather his thoughts. He knew David was having a rough morning, but it amused him to be able to contribute to the self-inflicted torture that he was witnessing. Finally, for the sake of time, he offered a little bit of friendly advice to his disjointed younger sibling.

"Why don't you head on over into the living room and see for yourself?" Rick directed. "The husband has been in there all morning, hugging his dead golden retriever like you used to hug your overstuffed teddy bear when we were little. He's devastated about the dog. I don't think he gives two shits about his deceased wife," he surmised, rubbing his chin. "It seems that the murderer killed the dog first, then the wife."

David realized he had made the rookie mistake of assuming something as being fact without fully checking all angles. The recognition caused him to feel a wave of humility sinking into his consciousness. He wasn't as sharp as he usually is, and knew it was because he had one too many drinks last night. The difference between a good detective and the great one that he viewed himself as being was in the details and the preparation. The night before a big game, he always prepared his body and mind for top performance. He was too competitive to allow an opponent to gain even a miniscule amount of advantage due to his lack of preparation. Yet, here he was, his brother rubbing in the fact that he was not totally on top of his game, and it was aggravating him to no end.

"OK, smart guy," David conceded. "What have you found out so far on the hard drives of the computers around here?"

Rick picked up his notepad and gave a quick glance. "Looks like hubby was doing quite a bit of work from home," he reported. "I'll check further once I get the drive copied and back to the lab. She, at first glance, comes off as a bona fide shopaholic. I'm talking about buying all kinds of stuff, and then returning whatever she bought, everywhere. Looks like she spent hours and hours on her hobby. Again, I'll get more info when I get back to the lab and will fill you in after I can do some more digging. I'm supposed to share the information evenly, and at the same with the other detectives, but don't worry. Whatever I turn up is yours right away."

"Thanks, bro. I'll see you before I go." David gave a nod and a smirk as he walked away from his brother and back to where the coroner was studying the body.

"Morning, Neil," David addressed the coroner in a reserved, confident manner. Neil, or Doc, as he was sometimes called, was an experienced investigator and was Mojave Desert dry. No sense toying with any humor while in Doc's presence, ever. If he did get the joke, you'd never know it.

"Morning, David," Doc's voice trailed off in a higher pitch than it started, as if he was dismissing the greeting forever.

"Preliminary cause of death yet, Doc?" David asked, trying to make conversation.

Neil looked at David as if to say, 'what a stupid question.' Before he spoke, however, he caught himself. David's reputation proceeded him. He commanded the same respect in his field as Doc did in his. Realizing this was probably the guy who would, in the end, find the killer, Doc decided it was best to keep his inflated ego in check and play it straight.

"There's a small hole in the base of the skull, large enough to insert a finger directly into the brain, but it's not much bigger around than that," he began speaking as if talking to himself. "I see a significant volume of blood which ran from the wound and down the back of her neck onto the floor. She didn't die instantly. Her heart kept pumping for a short time after being dealt with what amounted to the fatal injury. Interestingly, there is gray matter visible. Not a ton of it, but a noticeable amount just above the collar. Most of her brain is still inside the skull. I'll get a better feel for what condition it is in once I get the body back to the lab. My guess is that it's not intact. For obvious reasons, however, I don't want to get overly involved in making that determination in this setting," he said, staring stone-faced directly into David's eyes.

David looked at Doc, lips pursed and eyebrows together and asked, "Is there an exit wound? The hole in the back of her head would indicate she was perhaps shot execution-style by someone with a .223 caliber rifle, but I don't see any mess on the other end," he observed.

"There is no exit wound," Doc replied. "All I have here is a hole in the back of the head. She was assassinated, for sure, but not with a gun. I'll get more information for you once I get autopsy results, but, for now, you can look, but don't touch," he ordered.

David continued to carefully observe and take his notes on the scene. He knew that Doc needed his space and respected his silent request. David wandered into the kitchen area where it looked like the victim struggled for her life. He wasn't looking for anything special, but he hoped that maybe something was left behind that belonged to the killer. Something that could help him to figure out who did this. As he perused, he caught a glimpse of his brother who was standing in the foyer several feet away. Rick had already gathered everything he needed from the scene and was preparing to say his goodbyes before heading back to his lab.

"Hey, bro," Rick shouted to his younger brother. "You still playing in the morning? I ran into Dad a couple of nights ago at the gym. He was powerlifting with a couple of his buddies. It's hard to believe that guys his age workout the way they do. Anyway, he's really looking forward to our tee time tomorrow. Ten o'clock sharp! We go off at 10:30. Do not disappoint him or me," he ordered.

"Yeah, I'll be there," David warned. "Better bring extra cash. I'm in the mood to take your money," he challenged. "It looks like I'll be here a little while longer. I want to see what I can get out of the husband. From the sound of things, he's still hugging Rover," he whispered. "I'll try to break him away. He must have something interesting that he can tell us. Wish me luck in dragging it out of him."

"Good luck," Rick callously complied. "Enjoy your day off today. You deserve to have a nice day to yourself. Especially knowing how hard you work," he taunted as he closed the front door behind him and stepped into the sunshine of an otherwise beautiful spring day.

## 2

Replace your divots! And always repair your ball marks!

Gerry made a left turn heading toward his destination, stopped, and waited for the oncoming car to pull parallel to his before taking his turn to cross the narrow bridge. The span, built in the early 1900s, crossed a narrow tributary which severed the small island from the mainland. On the far side of the beautifully landscaped island was a mighty river which guarded the relatively meager patch of land from the west. The only way on or off the special island, other than by boat, was via the unassuming, narrow link which Gerry waited patiently for his opportunity to use.

There was only room on the bridge for one car at a time to pass. However, the club members never felt the need to invest in the infrastructure improvements needed to widen it. The fact that the old steel bridge slowed traffic coming in and out added a special charm to the property.

Once an automobile heading onto the island crossed the old bridge, it was imperative for the driver to heed the warning of a subtle sign which was mounted onto the side of a large tree on the right. The bright red letters faced the road and simply stated, 'STOP! Watch Right for Teeing Golfers.'

The ensuing winding road leading from the bridge to the Baracoa clubhouse crossed the first fairway exactly at the landing area of the average player's tee shot. The appropriate etiquette was to wait for the golfers to hit their tee shots before continuing to drive a vehicle along the fairway-crossing roadway. The road was, in fact, a perfect target off the tee, since the player would be rewarded with a tremendous first bounce if they could land their shot on the asphalt. Unfortunately, on occasion, a car driven by someone unfamiliar with the setting would miss the warning sign. Other times, an operator might have the impression that the warning applied to everyone else but them. In either case, the players on the tee would be unwittingly aiming to hit their shot directly at any car which cruised the middle of their fairway. Bounces off a carelessly driven car could come straight back toward the tee, infuriating the player who hit the shot. It would not be a good idea for the driver of any car, sporting a fresh indentation, to approach a golfer who just missed out on the reward of hitting a perfectly placed tee shot. Rarely is a round of golf played at Baracoa Country Club without a copious amount of money riding on every shot. There could be, and probably was, a significant sum of cash wagered on the shot that was interfered with. A careless driver who ruins the opportunity for a golfer to win a hole would not be viewed kindly.

"Good morning, Mr. O'Driscoll," the young man cheerily said as Gerry pulled up to the curb.

Gerry reached for the button to pop open the hatch of his S.U.V., rolled down his window and smiled at the bag attendant. "Morning, Bobby," Gerry greeted. "What a great day for golf! You did an excellent job arranging the weather," he joked. "Have you seen the boys yet?"

"Dave is up at the range, hitting balls," Bobby reported. "Rick is over in the chipping area. He claims that if he practices sand shots all morning, he won't hit a shot into a trap all day on the course," he mentioned as a matter of fact while checking Gerry's bag. "Is it just the three of you, or is someone joining up?"

"Just the three of us this morning, my friend," he proudly replied. Gerry got out of the car and grabbed a couple of clubs from his bag so he could take them over to the practice area. As Bobby pulled the bag forward and lifted it by the handle, Gerry reached over and handed him a crisp ten-dollar bill. "How are your grades, Bobby?" Gerry asked. "This is a good side job, but make sure you stay focused on school. I see big things in your future."

"All As, Mr. O'Driscoll," Bobby robotically replied to the same question Gerry asks him each time they meet. "My grades are good. Thank you, sir," he said respectfully. "I appreciate the tip and the encouragement. It means a lot to me. I hope you have a great round. Hit it straight!" he advised as he shouldered Gerry's golf bag. "There's a lot of wind blowing around up there. Keep your approach shots nice and low. Especially on number 18," he cautioned. "Your boys are going to loft their wedge shots high into the sky, and they're going to get blown all over the place. If you are going to beat them, you are going to have to play it smart." Bobby chuckled at the thought of the experienced father attempting to compete with the athletic youth of his two boys.

Gerry proceeded to park his car in the rear lot, put on his golf shoes, and walked toward the practice range. He was a large man, standing at six-foot four-inches and tipped the scales at 230 pounds. For someone in his late 50s, he kept himself in excellent shape. Although he had a job which demanded that he work a significant number of hours, he made time to frequent the local Y.M.C.A. at least four times a week. His chest and shoulders were rock solid. For fun, he would compete in bench-pressing competitions at the gym.

Competing there against the 20-year-old bodybuilders was a challenge, but he held his own with the 40 and older crowd.

As a young man, Gerry was an excellent athlete. He was fiercely competitive but had the ability to completely mask his emotions. This quality gave him an advantage over his rivals, as his frame of mind was extremely difficult for others to read. He used this natural ability in his business dealings as well. Even in highly charged emotional situations, when he was seething on the inside, he could maintain a calm and deadpan demeanor on the outside. Adversaries frequently had no idea what was going on inside Gerry's mind. Just the way he liked it.

David glanced to his left and saw Gerry lumbering up the hill to the practice area and gave a wave. Rick had finished working on his chipping and was also making his way over to greet his father. The boys were obviously physically cut from the same cloth as their dad. The three men greeted each other with fist pumps and broad smiles. It had been a while since they last played a round of golf together. The O'Driscoll family was a close-knit family, and each was grateful for the opportunity to get together in such a beautiful setting. Gerry had been a member at Baracoa Country Club for over 20 years. He always felt that the club would, over the years, be a magnet for the family to spend time with each other. He taught Rick and David to play golf when they were young boys. Both were eternally grateful to their father for having the foresight to do so.

Gerry's wife, Mary, loved playing tennis with her friends and hanging at the pool with a good book in hand. This afternoon, she would arrive at the club and entertain the boys' wives at the pool. It was too early in the season for swimming, but the sun was warm on the deck. Once the guys finished their round, the six of them would share stories and enjoy a sandwich and a cold drink in the bar area. Spending time on a Sunday with the whole family was something to be cherished. In Gerry's line of work, this was not an occasion that could be counted on as a weekly occurrence.

"How you hitting them, Dad?" David casually asked Gerry as he bent over and teed one up.

"Not bad," Gerry deadpanned. "I think I can break a hundred if I can get a couple of breaks. You two probably will have to give me a shot a hole if we're going to play skins," he reasoned. "By the way, I took the liberty to tip Bobby at the clubhouse. I know how tight with a nickel you two guys are."

"Neither of us can comment on our tipping habits," Rick embarrassingly replied. "There isn't a snowball's chance in hell, though, that we're giving you a shot a hole. You'll get a shot on the number-one through number-four stroke holes. That's it! Dave and I will play it straight up. Do you think we just fell off the turnip truck or something?" he protested. "A shot a hole. Yeah, right."

Gerry gave a wry smile as he drilled a practice shot 250 yards dead on the target. "OK, let's get going," Gerry ordered. "We should be going off in about 20 minutes. I suggest you make a couple of putts on the practice green. They are playing extremely fast from what I hear."

Gerry and the boys gathered the clubs they had been using on the practice range and made their way down the hill toward the first tee. In proximity to the first tee was the practice green. There, the three continued their conversation and got a feel for the greens. Finally, after a few minutes, it was their turn to begin their highly anticipated round.

"O'Driscoll party of three," the starter barked as if he was having difficulty fighting off complete and total boredom. "You are next on the tee."

Gerry, Rick, and David moseyed on over to their carts which were parked adjacent to the first tee. Normally, when David and Rick played, they preferred to walk the course. On weekends, however, electric riding carts were required in order to speed play as much as possible. The brothers would place their clubs in the same cart, however, once on the course, each player would jump in whichever ride was most convenient to their ball. Since Dave liked to hit a draw or move the ball right to left, and Rick hit a fade or left to right, it wasn't all that uncommon for them to be on opposite sides of the fairway. The player closest to Gerry would frequently grab a club or two from their bag and hop in with him.

"We're playing dollar skins," Gerry announced. "I don't want to take too much of your money."

The O'Driscoll clan would usually play a simple version of skins when it was just the three of them. Each player would put in 18 dollars or a dollar per hole. The first hole would be worth three dollars to the player who beat the other two outright. If one of them carded a three and the other two not better than a four, the player scoring a three would win the three dollars. If nobody won the hole outright, the three dollars would carry forward to the next hole, making it worth six dollars. And so forth. Since Dave and Rick were so evenly matched, it wasn't unusual for the skin to build up. If nobody won a hole outright after the fourth hole, the fifth would be worth 15 dollars. Nobody was going to get rich or lose their shirt the way Gerry set the match. It wasn't about the money. The three of them could have been playing for pennies or marbles. The fact of the matter was that someone, at some point, would make a great shot to win a skin. Settling the bets and bragging about the winnings at dinner later at the bar was all part of the fun.

"Dad," David said loud enough for anyone in the general vicinity to hear. "Since you're a year older now, do you still hit from the blue tees, or do you play from the ladies' tees now?" he teased.

Gerry pretended not to hear the question. He suppressed his laughter at the thought and issued a blank stare in the general direction of the chuckling brothers. "I get to hit first and, Rick, since you're ten months older than your smart-ass brother, you go second," Gerry announced. "After that, win the honors," he declared.

Gerry teed one up and striped a low liner 250 yards right down the middle of the fairway. The ball landed squarely on the paved road, which crossed the fairway, and took a huge member's bounce, adding another 25 yards to the shot. He casually bent over, picked up his tee and, without saying a word, put his driver back in his bag.

"Be that way, Dad," Rick muttered to himself. Being next, he placed his ball on the tee and took a long, fluid swing at the brand-new Titleist. The ball sailed down the left side, barely missed the overhanging tree branches, and faded back to the fairway, landing 20 yards beyond the access road. There, the ball took one short bounce and, due to the softness of the morning fairway, it checked up. He outdrove his father in the air but didn't take advantage of the road bounce like Gerry did. Therefore, he came up a little short comparatively in net yards. Still, he left himself an easy approach shot to the green. The fact that he was outdistanced by Gerry didn't go unnoticed, however.

"Nice shot, Sally," Gerry teased. He knew he wouldn't get many opportunities to outdrive either of the boys today, so he had to take advantage when he could.

David was next on the tee. He was known at the club as a big hitter. Players warming up on the practice green knew he was up and many casually leaned on their putters to watch him hit. He has a swing that could best be described as violent. It was as if he was trying to break the ball when he swung at it. When David played a tournament and there was a longest drive hole, the only question was whether he would keep it in the fairway. He was as long, off the tee, as anyone.

"Dave, I got five bucks that says you miss the fairway," his brother challenged.

"You are on, brother," David accepted. "I feel like I'm in a winning zone already." He placed a shiny ProV1 ball on a tee and attacked. The sound of the club striking the ball echoed loud enough to startle nearby peacefully perched birds into flight. Squirrels scrambled for cover. The ball started out low to the ground, along the right side of the fairway, and then rose into the sky like a fighter jet. The spin applied on contact made it draw slightly toward the center of the fairway as it flew against the bright blue sky. Eventually, gravity took over, and it reentered the Earth's atmosphere, landing 50 yards beyond Gerry's ball. His shot finally rolled to a stop, smack dab in the middle of the fairway. David left himself a mere 50 yards to the front of the green on a 400-yard par four hole. There were a couple of gasps heard coming from the practice green along with a few head-shaking chuckles. David had the ability to hit the ball so hard that it was almost funny to watch. He did not disappoint those who stopped what they were doing to have a look at his first shot of the day.

"OK, we're off," Gerry announced. The three jumped into their carts and drove to their ball, sporting broad smiles. All the while, they taunted each other along the way, attempting to get inside each other's head. This was going to be a great day.

The course was in exquisite shape for this time of the year. Trees were blooming, filling the air with the wonderful scent of nature springing back to life. Birds were cheerily chirping to one another as if every one of them wanted to contribute to the conversation at hand. Woodpeckers were banging their beaks into dead trees, searching for a meaty meal. The fairways were a brilliant green contrasting the white sand of the strategically placed bunkers and the brilliant blue sky. 70-degree temperatures with a north-northeast breeze made the conditions almost perfect. Gerry and his two boys were playing each hole like it would be their last. They were enjoying every second of the day and treasured the opportunity to take every shot. More than the golf, each of them appreciated the chance to be able to share the day together. Gerry was in the stage of his life where he had the sense of time being a finite commodity. He yearned for the long-ago days when the four of them traveled together for a family vacation. He missed watching the boys play little league-baseball games and youth soccer. There were so many fond memories of the family of four captured on video or in pictures tucked away in the hallway closet of Gerry and Mary's home. He knew that most of his allotted time on this planet was in the past. Days spent like this one were meant to be cherished. This too would be a fond memory one day, he thought. In the metaphor of life, Gerry felt like he was walking up the 16th fairway. Holes one through 15 already being carded and in the past. Gerry also realized that in his metaphor, he could be unaware of the possibility that he was now walking up the 18th fairway. Who knows what tomorrow might bring? In the present, however, he was extremely proud of the boys and what they were accomplishing in their lives. Each was his own man. Independent thinkers with individual goals and aspirations. The boys had their whole lives ahead of them, and Gerry couldn't be happier for them.

The threesome finished the first 11 holes with no skins being won. After placing their putters back into their bags, they loaded themselves into their respective cart and drove the path to the next tee. Number 12 was a long 220-yard par three which was well-protected by large bunkers on each side of the green. Because of the difficulty of the hole, there, frequently, was a backup on the tee. Today was no exception. There were two groups ahead of Gerry and the boys, waiting to hit the difficult tee shot. One of the groups ahead of those who waited on the tee had significantly slowed play, drawing the ire of the golf marshal.

Since nobody in the O'Driscoll group, to this point, had won a hole outright, the skin was up to 36 dollars. The competition and camaraderie were making the day a special one. Each knew that eventually someone would make a great shot to win a hole. Either that, or two of the three would fold under the pressure and hand the skin to the player with the steady hand. The speculation was the source of tremendous amusement among the three. Still, it was their lot in life, in this moment, to be patient and watch the groups ahead of them play the hole at hand.

While the three sat and waited for their turn to hit their shot, the conversation suddenly turned to the events of the previous day.

"Anything of interest from the hard drives, Rick?" David asked out of the blue.

"No smoking gun," Rick pensively replied. "The victim, Melinda Grayson, spent a lot of time on retailer websites. She had the habit of buying and returning product, almost obsessively. Actually, I think she was able to make a profit on the transactions. I hacked into her email account and found some interesting correspondences. From the tone of some of her emails, it seems she could be unpleasant at times."

"What about the husband?" David asked. "Anthony is his name. I finally got him to calm down about the dog thing. We spoke for a while, but I was wondering if anything turned up with his use of electronics."

"Dead end there," Rick shot back. "He travelled quite a bit as a computer-software salesman. For the most part, what I saw looking into him involved his job or his travel. He makes real good money, so why the wife was so preoccupied with making a few dollars here and there by committing retail fraud is a mystery," he conceded. "Hey, Dad," Rick shouted toward Gerry, who was sitting alone in his golf cart, staring off into the distance. "One of this woman's emails was to your corporate office. Do you remember her?" he asked.

Gerry looked over at the boys. He was barely paying attention to the conversation they were having. Gerry was far more concerned with what club he needed to use on his next shot. "Who is it? What happened? Refresh me," he replied.

"This woman, Melinda Grayson, from Chevon, was murdered on Friday night in her home," Rick stated directly. "I got into her computer and began looking at what she was up to. It helps us to get a better picture of the victim. Sometimes, the profile can lead us to a motive for the murder. Anyway, I found that she spends a lot of time messing around with various retailers. She has numerous complaint emails saved in her archives that were sent back and forth to almost every major store you can think of. It seems her practice was to complain about something until she, in turn, was given something of value from the company. You know, like a token of apology from the company's executives. One of her letters of complaint was to the C.E.O. of Jimbo's. She mentioned something about the staff being rude to her when she tried to return a parka. She claims she paid 300 dollars and the manager would only give her credit for ten dollars. The corporate response was accompanied by a 100-dollar gift card and a sincere apology for her inconvenience. Does it ring a bell?" Rick asked.

"There was a woman a couple of weeks ago," Gerry replied, suddenly engaged in the conversation. "I don't remember her name, but I do remember that she was from Chevon," Gerry recalled. "You want to know something? I think they give potential residents of that town a special test before they allow them to buy a house and move in." He laughed. "Anyway, the woman came in to return an old North Face ski parka. The thing had to be ten years old. Smelled awful. It looked like she picked it up at some consignment shop. The associates at my return desk didn't recognize it. The woman started pitching a fit and asked to see the store manager, so I got called in. The two associates behind the service desk looked visibly shaken when I got there. The customer was extremely abusive from what they later told me. Clare and Sydney were the service desk associates on that day. Clare is a sweetheart, working her way through college and just as pleasant as could be. Syd is a quirky, pudgy, 23-year-old who has an extremely timid personality. He knows the systems inside and out, so if there's a way to find product or product history, he'll find it. He is the go-to guy when a customer wants to special order something we don't have in stock. Sometimes, those orders can get tricky, and he gets it right every time. Great guy, extremely helpful to our customers. He has this odd speech impediment that kicks in to high gear when he gets nervous. The S sound turns into TH. I knew he was upset when I got there because when I asked him if he could find the customer's purchase transaction so we could process the return, he responded with a loud 'NO THUR.' Clare handed me the parka, and I remember telling the customer that I didn't recognize it. I handed the parka back to the woman and told her I'd give her ten dollars for it toward the purchase of something else if she wanted. Otherwise, she could either keep it or come back to the store with the sales receipt so we could better research the purchase date and price. That solution set her off like a rocket ship. She started swearing and calling me every name in the book." Gerry laughed while pounding the steering wheel of the golf cart with his right palm. "Next, she rolled up the parka into a ball and threw it at Clare, demanding we get her the ten-dollar credit immediately. I will say that part got under my skin, but I did my best to not let her know how much it pissed me off. I had Syd process a miscellaneous return for her. I ended up giving her the ten-dollar credit voucher and she left in a tizzy. Nice lady, huh?" He nodded toward the two boys, seeking their affirmation. "We were all hoping she would have a bird shit on her head on the way to her car, but no such luck. I don't know if that's the same woman you are talking about, but I guess it's possible."

"Dad, how often does stuff like that happen?" David looked like he had just seen a ghost.

"Not all that often," Gerry mused. "On average, we get one a day." He chuckled. "You know, 80 percent of all the people we deal with are great people. They're just out to enjoy the shopping experience and pick up something they need. The other 20 percent are not so nice. Of the not-so-nice 20 percent, 95 percent of them, who shop where I work, are from Chevon. I don't know what it is about that town, but there sure are a lot of assholes living in it. When we hear a code nine, which usually means there is a customer problem for the manager on duty to deal with, in most instances, we find that the customer is a proud resident of Chevon. It doesn't matter what part of the store either. MOD, we have a code nine in team sports, fishing, hunting, furniture, customer care, anywhere. When someone is making a ruckus, we usually know exactly which town the complainant resides in."

The three O'Driscolls finally emerged from their carts. Each did some basic stretching to get the blood flowing again in their stiffened muscles. The boys limbered up quickly. Gerry, at his age, was not so fortunate. He took a couple of clubs and made exaggerated swings in a feeble attempt to loosen up. The group ahead of them was finally in the process of putting out. The tallest of the foursome was placing the pin back into the hole, indicating that they were finished.

"OK, finally, we can hit," Gerry announced. "Dave, I think you still have the honors."

David figured he needed a four iron, with the wind conditions as they were, and teed his ball just barely off the turf. His mind was racing in high gear, and he battled to suppress some of the thoughts that were popping up. He was not focused on hitting his shot, and, when he struck the ball, he immediately groaned.

"Hey, Dave. Better get your swimsuit. It looks like you landed in the beach on the left," Gerry mused. "You had a little too much right-to-left spin on that one. Sometimes that draw gets you in trouble," he advised.

Rick was equally unfocused and sliced his ball into the sand trap on the right. The green was wide open for Gerry, but the distance was problematic for him. He pulled out a hybrid and hit his shot straight to the front apron of the green. Short of the hole, but safe from the hazards lurking along the perimeter of the target. The threesome jumped into their carts and drove up to the green to see what kind of approach shot each one had. Gerry was away, but he was pleased to discover that he had a great lie with a nice slight uphill chip to the pin. He took his seven iron, put his weight on his left leg and chipped the ball one-third of the distance to the hole in the air. The ball rolled the remaining two-thirds and settled two inches from the cup. He casually marked his ball, lifted it, and dropped it in his pocket. There were no conceded putts at this point. Especially since it may result in a skin.

The boys were next and, with the soft sand protecting the green, each had been served what is referred to as a fried egg. The balls struck the sand somewhat like a meteor strikes the moon, resulting in a mini crater with the ball centered. The image created closely resembling a fried egg. Each had no choice but to blast or strike the sand, not the ball, creating an intentional explosion of flying sand and ball. Both executed the shot nicely. Rick settled 15 feet from the pin, and David had rolled 12 feet past his target. Both knew they were in trouble. Gerry had a tap in for par, and they each had tricky putts greater than ten feet. They knew that if Gerry won this skin, they would never hear the end of it. Dave was doing all he could to help Rick read the green and make his putt. He was hoping against hope that his brother would make the par which would tie Gerry's impending par, resulting in no skin being won. 'Two tie all tie' is the rule of the game. One of the boys would have to make a putt to tie Gerry, or the hole would be lost for them. Victory for their father. Unfortunately, for the boys, Rick pulled his putt, and he ended up six inches to the left of the hole.

"That one is good," Gerry deadpanned, conceding the short putt. "No need to putt it. I'll give you the bogey."

David now had the pressure of needing to make the tricky 12-footer in order to halve the hole with Gerry. He carefully placed the ball on the green in front of his marker, removed the marker, squatted behind the ball, and studied. The younger brother was laser focused on reading the subtle contours of the green. He was determined to make this putt. He couldn't fathom losing this hole and totally blocked the thought of doing so from his brain.

"Dave, I have that one breaking two balls to the left," Gerry offered, interrupting David's concentration.

"Dad, this putt is not going left, and you know it. If anything, it breaks one ball to the right," Dave sneered as he walked to the hole to take a better look at the last couple of feet.

"OK, no problem, Dave," Gerry capitulated. "I'm just trying to be helpful. I still think it goes left, though," he advised. "Don't give up the hole," Gerry said. By that, he meant that Dave should play his ball directly at the target. Gerry was letting him know that in his faux opinion, even though the ball might break slightly, it wouldn't bend enough, that he should aim the putt outside of the hole. Dave, on the other hand, knew that his father was simply trying to get into his head. Gerry was not so subtly attempting to get him to lose all confidence in making this putt. He was planting seeds of doubt. Rick stood to the side, leaning on his putter with a subdued smile on his face, watching his father mess with his younger brother. He had seen it all before. To Rick, it never got old. Cool, calm Dad getting into high-strung David's head.

"Hey, Dave, I have a question that I've always wanted to ask you about putting," Gerry interrupted unexpectedly. "When you begin your putting stroke and bring the putter back, do you inhale or exhale just before bringing it forward to strike the ball?"

"Dad, I have no freaking clue if I inhale or exhale. I never thought about it," Dave shot back.

"Oh, I was just wondering because I always inhale when I bring the club back, and then exhale when I hit it," Gerry said instructively. "I can't explain why. The first putt I ever made, I did it that way. The last putt that I take, I'm sure will be struck the same way," he said.

"Don't leave it short!" Gerry encouraged. "This one should roll a little slow."

Rick was standing 20 feet away, staring off into the distance, shaking his head. He knew, at this point, that his brother had no chance of making the putt and was almost ready to concede the hole.

Dave walked to his ball, took a couple of practice strokes, and prepared to hit the putt. He wanted to make this one badly but was distracted with swirling thoughts in his head. The conversation on the tee a few minutes ago was still on his mind. As much as he tried to suppress the thought, he was having difficulty blocking it out.

Concerning the immediate task at hand, he had other thoughts whirling. Was Dad messing with him or did this putt go left as he claims? It was a difficult read, but David was convinced it breaks slightly to the right. All he could think of, as he got ready to hit his ball, was his breathing. Inhale? Exhale? No breathing at all? His head was a complete disaster, but the time had come for him to make his attempt. He brought his putter back, struck the ball squarely, and left it two-feet short.

"Nice try, Dave," Gerry said with encouragement. "I think you had the line, but it just needed a little more oomph. I'll give you the four. Is my putt good for the three?"

"Dad, just tap it in," Rick replied. "Enough torture on this hole. Good par, nice skin."

The final holes were fairly uneventful, with no further skins being won. On the 18th green, the three embraced and promised to do it again as soon as possible. Gerry had to work the next five Sundays, so the three planned six weeks from now. Rick and Dave jumped into their cart for the ride back to the clubhouse where they could shower and freshen up before meeting the ladies for dinner. Gerry would meet them there, but he first had to stop off at the pool to let the girls know they were finished and would be in the bar shortly. He made sure they knew he had won the only skin of the day and embellished on the shot he hit to win it.

"Rick, are you thinking what I'm thinking?" Dave asked his brother as they drove the cart back to the clubhouse.

"Thinking about what?" Rick asked as he stopped and waited for a passing car to clear out of the way.

"That the victim interacted with Dad," David replied. "And that it wasn't a pleasant interaction," he said.

"Get the thought out of your head," Rick replied. "I know what you might be thinking, but don't go there," he cautioned. "There is one other detail, however, that I didn't tell you about Melinda Grayson's email to Jimbo's C.E.O. She specifically mentions Dad as the employee who was rude to her at the return desk. She misspelled his name, but says it was Manager Jerry who treated her rudely. I think Dad got into trouble for it. Mom said Dad was all ticked off last week because he got written up at work. She brought it up to me when I was talking to her on the phone the other day. Something about a customer situation that the corporate big-shots said he should have been able to better handle. If it happens again in a three-month period, he goes on a final warning. If it happens again after that, he could lose his job. He hides his emotions well, doesn't he?"

"He has that ability," Dave confirmed. "Dad is one heck of a poker player," he distantly stated. "How about if we forget all that?" he changed subjects. "I'm starved. What do you say we go and get a bite to eat?"

# 3

We should consider a merger.

Gerry pulled into the employee parking lot of Jimbo's Furniture and Firearms at precisely 5:45 in the morning. The overnight crew punches out to go home at seven o'clock, and he wanted to see how much progress they had made in setting the new fishing layout. He figured he could walk the store and then meet with the overnight manager and key associates at 6:30. He also wanted to pass along his feedback and encouragement to the crew. The overnight-stocking job is extremely labor intensive, and the crew gets very few thanks from those who work the day shift. Gerry, as Senior Operations Manager, has over 200 associates working under his umbrella. The 20 he would address this morning were grateful that he took the time to chat with them over the coffee and donuts he brought. Gerry's team would run through walls for him if asked to do so. He was known as a leader who hired great people and let them do their job. He communicated the 'what' and delegated the 'how' to his lower-level managers and team. Whenever one of his teams started to stray from the overall objective, Gerry would gently nudge them until they were back on track. Praise for his overall teams as well as individuals who comprised them was done in public settings. Correctional and disciplinary conversations were always behind closed doors in total privacy. The difficult, critical conversations, which were sometimes necessary to have with a struggling employee, were always totally open and honest two-way exchanges. Gerry was brutally direct when he felt his point wasn't getting across. The people who worked under his realm loved him for this. Everyone knew exactly where they stood with their leader. Because Gerry worked his way upward through the ranks earlier in his career, he was keenly in tune with what the folks in the entry levels were experiencing. He was not afraid of getting his hands dirty and never asked an associate to do something he wouldn't do himself.

Gerry worked in the retail world his entire adult life. Five years ago, he joined Jimbo's as the Senior Operations Manager for their local, recently opened store. Prior to that, he worked 20-plus years for a large sporting-goods category killer. There, he started out as a store manager and over time, climbed the ladder to the position of Senior Regional Vice President of Sales. The company for whom he spent those 20 years was bought out by a competitor, and Gerry was kicked to the curb along with most of his peers. The merged company was immediately staffed with newly promoted employees from the takeover organization, ready or not. The fact that many of the newly promoted individuals were not ready for their new roles in the organization was not Gerry's problem. However, what was his problem, was the fact that he still needed a job. And with his family settled in to where they were living, he didn't want to relocate again. The other problem staring Gerry squarely in the face was that he was now over 50 years old. In the retail world, managers in their mid-50s are viewed as damaged goods. Jimbo's wasn't Gerry's first choice for employment, but they did offer him a decent salary. They also seemed, at least for now, amenable to his age. They recognized how much his wealth of experience would enhance the profitability of their company. To Gerry, the fact that he would be responsible for a relatively large staff in a 70-million dollar, 200-thousand square-foot megastore made the transition somewhat palatable. Of all the options presented to him, Jimbo's was the best at the time.

Jimbo's Furniture and Firearms was founded in the late 1950s by a lady named Kathy O'Leary and a man named James Johnson. The couple lived in a small town in northern Michigan. Kathy was an avid hunter and made a living managing a small sporting-goods store. She dabbled in all types of sporting goods, but her passion was in shooting sports. James worked at a small, family-owned furniture store directly across the street from Kathy. Both of them were in their late 20s and unattached. They began dating and made plans to travel together to the Upper Peninsula for a week-long hunting trip. One night, in deer camp, Kathy started joking about how she and James should join forces and open their own store. She mused that they could sell firearms and furniture. "While the husband was shopping for another new gun that he really didn't need," they plotted. "The wife could mosey on over to the other side of the store and pick out a new living room." Their concept was borderline evil, but intriguing. "Sure, you can get that new gun as long as I can get the new sofa," they schemed while popping another beer and laughing until their sides hurt.

The following morning, while cooking breakfast in a cast-iron skillet over hot coals, James brought up the subject again. Except this time, he wasn't laughing. One year later, the two were married and sitting in a bank, borrowing money for their new store. Once the place was up and running, their sales exploded. The young couple decided to expand to a larger store which carried not only hunting, but clothing and footwear, fishing, camping, team sports, and exercise equipment along with boats and furniture of course. They named the store after James who was called Jimbo by his close friends. The couple made a tremendous living off the profits and were perfectly content to maintain the two stores. They had the newer, larger, expanded location along with the original, smaller store. One day, as good luck would have it, a Wall Street investor, on his way to a hunting vacation in northern Michigan, stopped at Jimbo's to load up on supplies. He was blown away by the concept and, on his way back from the trip, decided to mix business with pleasure. Six months later, he handed Kathy and James a sizable check for the property and the expansion rights of the concept. Kathy and James have remained on the advisory board for some 30 years as part of the deal. In that time, the chain has grown to its current 150 locations nationwide. Total sales have grown to slightly over seven-billion dollars over the years. Not bad for a couple of young adults who had the courage to follow their dream.

***

Once the half-hour meeting with the overnight crew was over, Gerry headed back to his office and prepared for the morning meeting that was attended by the store's entire opening staff. There would be 50 store associates in the building, getting ready to open to the public at eight o'clock. Gerry ran the same opening meeting every morning that he was in charge. He began with a safety topic of the day. Then, he rolled into a recognition story of an associate giving outstanding customer service. Hopefully that associate was present in the meeting so Gerry could embellish and get a few words from him or her. Next, he would cover sales numbers and give shout outs to those departments who were beating their goals. Finally, he would cover current promotions and communicate anything affecting the general population. Back and forth banter was encouraged but controlled. The opening associates had to be on their toes in a Gerry meeting. They never knew when they would be called on to participate in a subject that Gerry felt the need for them to share their expertise with the general population. Finally, he encouraged a little rah-rah at the end of the session, and the store was ready for business.

Typically, it took him a half hour to prepare for the meeting, and today was no different. He sat down, opened a jumbo jar of antacids which sat hidden in his bottom desk drawer, and popped four of them into his mouth. Gerry's stomach had been bothering him more than usual since he was written up for giving poor customer service to the lady who returned the parka. He knew he had to just let it go, but for some reason, he was having difficulty chasing the episode from his brain. Because the mind stubbornly clung to the situation, Gerry's body was being tortured. With the settling help of the antacids, he managed to complete his meeting preparation. He then paged for all associates to report the store entrance and delivered his message to the team. Gerry's early morning routine was like clockwork. Once complete, the store would now be ready to open for business.

Gerry would typically spend the rest of the morning checking in with the department managers who reported directly to him. Some were present, some were scheduled to work the closing shift, and some had a day off. He made himself available in case any of them needed his support on any operational or customer issue. There were always decisions that needed to be made. Problems that needed to be worked on. Catching up that needed to happen. After making his rounds with the department managers, he would double back to touch bases individually with any hourly associate who wanted his ear. He went out of his way to get to know every employee. He knew their goals and aspirations. Knew if they had something going on at home that they needed to talk about. Most of all, he knew what buttons to push in order to get the best possible performance out of his team.

Gerry wandered over to the customer-service desk. The manager in charge of the cashiers and customer-service associates wouldn't be in until noon, and he wanted to make sure that the staff was okay. Sydney and Clare were the associates on duty. These were the same two who dealt with the customer that got unruly with the outerwear return a couple of weeks ago. The same woman who got Gerry in hot water.

"Good morning to the dynamic duo," Gerry offered cheerily. "Everybody OK?"

"Good morning, Gerry. We are good, thanks for asking," Clare shot back. "Ready to give our customers a world-class shopping experience," she said with a grin.

Sydney looked Gerry in the eye and motioned him over to the far end of the customer-care desk. Although he was usually very comfortable being around Gerry, he was acting a little nervous this morning. "Gerry, do have any time for me today?" he asked.

"I'll make time for you, Syd," Gerry assured him in his calming, approachable demeanor. "Meet me upstairs in the snack bar at one o'clock. Soda is on me." He grinned. "See you then. Okay?"

As Gerry continued to make his rounds, he couldn't get his mind off Sydney. The last time they had a one-on-one sit down together was back in December. Sydney was acting very melancholy, and Gerry couldn't figure out what was the matter. Finally, he arranged a meeting and, after some small talk, Gerry came right out and asked Sydney to tell him what was wrong. Sydney confided in Gerry the fact that he misses his father during the Christmas season. Mike Barrett, Sydney's father, died from soft-tissue sarcoma when Syd was in his early teens. Mike was a highly respected biology professor at the state university. Although his job was demanding and he spent countless hours in the lab, he carved out precious quality time to spend with Syd. Sydney's fondest childhood memories were spent at the pond, hunting frogs. Syd and his dad would pull on their muck boots, stealthily wade into the shallows, and scoop up unsuspecting frogs with their minnow nets. Father and son would spend hours together, collecting frogs and tadpoles which would be placed unharmed in live bait buckets. When they arrived home with their catch, Syd would get to handle the frogs as he placed them in the large-holding aquarium that his father kept in the basement. The aquarium was a natural environment for the frogs. It was complete with rocks, pebbles, vegetation, and a 'pond' crafted from an oversized dog bowl where the tadpoles were placed. Sydney would sometimes name the frogs. The obvious names like Kermit, Hoppy, and Ribbit were always in play. Some would be named Orca or Jaws if they showed a particularly voracious appetite for the small minnows. He would observe their movements and give them small fish and moths to eat. Usually, within a couple of weeks of their capture, his father would gather the frogs in a transport aquarium and take them off to the university. Presumably, they would then be placed back in a large aquarium and live out a long, happy, frog life with his dad and his students. There, in the laboratory, under the guidance of his father, the young scholars would carefully study their amphibian behavior in a safe, natural setting.

One Sunday evening this past December, ten short years after Mike's death, Sydney and his mother, Anna, were decorating their Christmas tree. Sydney drew a hook through his favorite ornament and reached up to place it high on the tree. It was a small red-and-green glass frog given to him by his father. Syd aptly named it Lollihops. Conversation turned to how much they missed having Mike around, especially at Christmas. Each would give anything to have him here, helping them decorate the freshly cut tree. As he admired the ornament he had just placed on the top branch, Sydney reminded his mother about how much he loved collecting frogs with his father. What great memories he had of his youth. He wondered aloud what Dad could possibly want with all the frogs that the two of them captured. Perhaps in the spring, Sydney thought he would pull his old muck boots back on and catch a few frogs in memory of his dad.

"Syd, honey, you do know that your father used the frogs in the lab for experimenting," Anna softly explained. "Daddy was a biology professor. He taught pre-med students. Many of his best students went on to medical school and became fine doctors," she proudly stated. "The frogs that you helped him catch were pithed."

"Pithed?" Sydney was confused. He had never heard the term.

"The students in the lab would each get a live frog and pin it face down on the table," Anna explained. "They then take their sharp probe and quickly insert it through the base of the skull. The probe is then moved side to side in order to destroy the brain and sever the spinal cord which paralyzes the frog. Once paralyzed, the still, very-much-alive frog can be operated on. Theoretically, once it's pithed, the ensuing surgery performed on the frog is painless. Scalpels are used to open the belly of the frogs and the surgery begins. The frog's heart is still vigorously beating. The future surgeons are taught the effect of acetylcholine by applying a few drops directly onto the heart. The heart will slow significantly. Then, the students drip a few drops of adrenaline on the heart and it significantly speeds up. There are other experiments performed, but this one is typically the first one the students will experience. Eventually, the frog has a heart attack and dies. I was pre-med before deciding to go into nursing. Believe me, I didn't like this particular lab. Many accomplished surgeons, however, look back to their college days and remember this lab experiment as being their first surgery on a live subject."

Sydney was ashen faced as he digested the information his mother had just passed along to him. His mind was racing in all directions. He had so many questions. Why didn't his father tell him what was going to happen to the frogs? Why was he allowed to take care of the frogs and get attached to them if they were going to be murdered? Why did his father let him help catch these innocent victims? Syd certainly would have left the poor things alone, had he known their fate. Why couldn't the pre-med students use their experimentally inclined brains to figure out a cure for soft-tissue sarcoma? If they did that, Syd could ask his father these questions directly.

Sydney's recollection of his father's demise was vividly burned into his brain. Mike died a dreadful death right before Syd and his mother's eyes. At times, it seemed like the professor's former students, who were now his doctors, were experimenting on him! *Were they treating his disease or was he just another frog in the lab to these physicians?* Sydney suddenly thought to himself. *Let's see how this drug affects the tumors. Let's see what radiation does to him. How about volunteering for a clinical trial? We're running out of stuff to try. Chemo! Surgery! Radiation! What else can we do to him?* he wondered.

Sydney's father fought the best fight he could, but, in the end, the cancer won. Mike's heart finally simply stopped beating. Sydney needed someone besides his mother to talk to. He wished it could be his father, but that wasn't possible. It had to be someone who he respected. Someone who always checked in to see how he was doing. Someone who he knew genuinely cared about him. He asked Gerry for some time to talk. As always, Gerry found time to sit with Sydney that cold December day.

Gerry recalled how he relayed the conversation he had with Syd to the other managers. Each Monday, at three o'clock, the 18 salaried managers would get together to discuss current and upcoming business. During the meeting held on the Monday before Christmas, the human-resources manager asked about any associate who may be experiencing the Holiday Blues. Many had noticed Sydney's melancholy mood over the past few weeks. Gerry thought it would be appropriate to confidentially share what he had learned. The reaction in the room varied from horror to hysterics. Some were sympathetic. Others were fascinated. Most were pragmatic, and a few were curious to try the pithing procedure themselves. The fishing guys wanted to get Sydney to tell them where he was collecting the frogs so they could catch live bait to fish for largemouth bass. Everyone in the room, however, felt for Sydney in their own way. Some quietly felt the same pain gnawing at their inner core at this time of the year. Syd was not the only one who had difficulty getting through the holiday season. Most of the managers in the room were putting in 65-hour work weeks. And have been doing so for over a month already. Once Christmas has passed them by, the store goes right into inventory season. Four additional solid weeks of pure hell would be tacked on to their current plight for the purpose of counting the store's remaining sellable product. The managers knew what they were in the middle of currently. They also knew what was on the immediate horizon. They were already feeling tired, cranky, and irritable. Many were questioning their own sanity for working in this God-forsaken business at this time of year. Those with families and young children at home were feeling the guilt of spending half of every day working while ignoring the desires and needs of the people closest to them. For the most part, every manager in the conference room on that day had empathy for Syd. They committed to each other to do what they could to try to cheer him up. And with one exception, they did just that.

*\*\**

Gerry walked toward the snack bar and saw that Sydney was already there waiting for him. He bought himself a coffee and purchased a soda for Syd. Gerry couldn't help but notice that Sydney was acting nervously the past week or so. He hoped that Sydney would speak freely to him like he did the last time the two had a deep conversation, way back on that cold December day. The key with Sydney was to get him to relax. Gerry engaged him in small talk. Patiently nudging him into a calm state of mind. Finally, he got to the point.

"So, what did you need to talk to me about today, Syd?" Gerry directly asked.

"Gerry, I need thome advithe about thomething," Sydney nervously managed.

"Syd, it's OK. It's me!" Gerry soothed. "Relax. Speak slowly. I'm on your side, remember?" Gerry pleaded. He knew Sydney's severe lisp worsened when he got nervous or excited, and he was trying his best to get him to calm his nerves. Gerry had worked with him on it many times, and Sydney was getting better and better at controlling his impediment.

"OK...thlowly," Syd began. "Gerry, I have a thituathion going on at cuthtomer thervice, and I need your help and advithe. You thee, I think I'm falling for Clare. I want to athk her out on a date, but becauthe we work thide by thide, I want to make thure it'th OK. How doeth thith work?" he managed.

Gerry listened to what Sydney was saying and felt a wave of relief pass through his body. He didn't know, at first, which direction this conversation was going. As a general rule, Gerry does not like to be surprised. To Gerry, the best surprises are no surprises. He has, in the past, dealt with the situation that Syd was describing a thousand times. Gerry knew he could handle this one in his sleep. Sydney has a crush on Clare. *So does every other guy in the building,* Gerry was thinking. Some of the women do too. Clare has the looks of a lingerie model. She is extremely bright and, at times, displays a mischievous personality that others love to be around. She possesses the ability to soothe the savage beast at the customer-service desk with her witty charm and good looks. Gerry could understand Sydney's feelings toward Clare but couldn't help but think he was attempting to 'outkick his coverage.' In other words, he thought Syd was venturing out of his league by attempting to start a romantic relationship with Clare. However, he couldn't help but to admire Syd's courage.

"Syd, it is not a problem for you to date a coworker." Gerry put on his manager hat and struck a professional tone. "As long as neither one supervises the other, there is no conflict. What I will tell you, in no uncertain terms, is that if you ask her out and she says no, that means she is not interested, and you have to stop asking. No means no! If that happens, don't keep pursuing or you could get yourself in a boatload of trouble. Hopefully, she's going to say yes, and you two can have a nice time together. If you do start dating Clare, come and see me again to disclose the relationship. I'll be required to alert the human-resources folks. They get a little twitchy when we leave them out of the loop on this sort of thing." Gerry smirked at the thought of the H.R. manager getting all twisted over not being informed about the situation.

Sydney listened intently to what Gerry was telling him. He wanted to do the right thing which was the reason he confided in Gerry. Sydney knew he could count on Gerry to provide reasonable advice that would take everyone's best interest into account. Gerry didn't disappoint him.

"Now, something on a personal level, if I may?" Gerry changed hats and took on a softer, fatherly tone. "Syd, Clare has guys hitting on her constantly, as I'm sure you've seen. My advice to you is that I think you need to start out slowly. Ask her to go for a frozen yogurt during your lunch hour. Maybe ask her to have lunch and watch the boats over at the river view on a sunny afternoon. Go easy at first. Not aggressively! I hope everything works out for you. Thank you for coming to me for advice. If there's anything else I can do for you, just ask, and I'll do whatever I can to help. And, Syd, remember. NO means NO! YES means YES."

"Thank you, Gerry!" Syd offered as Gerry stood to shake hands. "If there ith ever anything I can do for you, and I mean anything, I will do it," he committed.

Gerry headed back to his office to prepare for the Monday afternoon manager meeting. Mark, the general manager, was off today, so Gerry would run the meeting as second in command. He felt a feeling of satisfaction knowing that his conversation with Sydney was sincere and productive. On his way, he bumped into Steve, the senior merchandise manager and close friend. The two happened to be riding the escalator together. Both were headed to the office to gather their notes.

"Hey, Gerry, you got the manager meeting under control?" Steve teased. He knew there was plenty of extra legwork required to prepare for these gatherings, and he had too much on his own plate to help. Being third in command, Steve was thankful for Gerry at times like these.

"I got it, Steve. Thanks for your help though!" Gerry shot back sarcastically. "I'm feeling a little bit crappy these days, so you better be careful with me," he warned kiddingly.

"What's the matter with you?" Steve queried. Sometimes, even a close friend couldn't tell when Gerry was serious, kidding, or a combination of the two.

"My stomach has been bugging me lately," Gerry admitted. "Do you have any Rolaids on you, by the way?" he asked while rubbing his stomach. "Plus, my hemorrhoids have been acting up. The last couple of months here have done a number on me. I think I need a vacation," he declared.

Gerry's mind drifted to a white, sandy beach on a sun-drenched tropical island. The thought helped him to settle his inner turmoil. At least, for a few short moments.

# 4

Good manners are one commodity that are free for the asking.

The gentleman wearing a light-gray Givenchy suit hooked the handicap placard onto the rear-view mirror of his Jaguar F-Type and pulled into the front parking spot at Jimbo's. He sat, eyes glued to the store's exit door and patiently waited. It was lunch time. The perfect time of day for the shopping experience he had in mind. Suddenly, he saw what he was looking for and sprung from his seat. His Giuseppe Zanotti loafers barely touched the pavement as he briskly walked to the trash container located on the sidewalk to the right of the store entrance. As he extinguished his cigarette in the sand tray on top with his left hand, he subtly reached into the opening of the trash container below with his right hand. He casually recovered the empty shopping bag which had just been deposited there and placed it into the pocket of his two-thousand-dollar suit. The gentleman waited on the sidewalk for the next group of customers to approach the front door and casually blended in with them as he entered the store. He was careful to have both hands concealed inside his pockets until he reached a secluded section of the store. The front entrance, he knew, was closed-circuit T.V. surveilled. It was important to not have definitive proof as to whether or not he had any items in hand when he walked in. The gentleman didn't know for certain what opportunities may present themselves to him today. What he did know was that he wanted to keep his options open.

*** 

Gerry and Steve were taking an early lunch together in the small conference room located in the senior-manager suite. Mark, the general manager, had just arrived at 11 o'clock and sat in his office next door. He was Gerry and Steve's immediate supervisor, but neither had much use for him. He had a habit of showing up at 10:30 or 11 o'clock in the morning when he was scheduled to open at seven. He would tell any opening manager who noticed that he had decided to work the close shift instead of the open shift. Mark would give the impression that he was actually in an hour or so early for his

34

new shift. The closing managers weren't scheduled to come in until noon. Typically, at five in the afternoon, he would tell the opening managers to take off for the evening. Most of them had been on duty since six o'clock and had already worked an 11-hour day. They would be eager to take him up on his offer. Once the opening managers had left for the day, usually by 5:30, Mark would hightail it out as well. The illusion Mark was attempting to portray to the opening managers was that he was the first closing manager to arrive for his altered shift. The closing managers, not being informed that Mark told the openers that he was now working the late shift, got the false impression that Mark was the last of the opening managers to go home for the day. All they knew was that he was already in the building when they arrived for work. The late managers assumed he was there at six o'clock to open as the manager schedule indicated. In reality, he worked five days a week from 11 o'clock in the morning until 5:30 in the afternoon. Gerry and Steve, both very seasoned managers, were not fooled by Mark's work ethic. Additionally, neither could have cared less. To them, Mark was about as useful as an ashtray on a motorcycle. The less they saw of him, the better.

Gerry was reviewing mid-week payroll numbers with Steve as they shared a sandwich together. The store was already running a thousand dollars over budget for the week, and there were still four days left. There was time to recover, but action had to be swift and severe. As Gerry compared actual payroll dollars used to the budgeted schedule, he noticed every dollar in the overage was coming from the fishing department. Paul, the fishing manager, was somewhat of a loose cannon. He needed constant, close supervision. Paul reported directly to Steve. Steve tolerated having to babysit him due to his immense knowledge of the fishing industry. Nobody on the planet was more informed about the region's fishing specificities than Paul. Customer's drove for many miles to get Paul's recommendations on where the fishing was hot. His expertise was sought by fishermen of all levels. He and his trained staff had a large following which brought a significant amount of business to Jimbo's. Paul was very much aware of his reputation in the industry. This fact made managing him an even bigger challenge for Steve.

If the store ran over payroll by the number it was currently trending, Gerry would be in a lot of hot water. To the corporate accountants in Michigan, the numbers are the numbers. God help those who do not manage expenses appropriately. Gerry's responsibility, as senior operations manager, is to manage expenses. When Gerry realized what was going on with his payroll, his blood pressure went through the roof.

"Steve, what the hell is your guy doing over there?" Gerry was getting more and more apoplectic as he analyzed the numbers. "He has already used

80 man-hours above what we scheduled for him. Did you approve this? I don't know anything about it."

"Gerry, I swear I don't know anything about this either," Steve replied apologetically. Steve knew two things. First, he knew if the store blew payroll, Gerry would be in big trouble. Second, he knew not to mess with his close friend when he was this ticked off.

"What do you want me to do?" Steve asked as he took another bite from his sandwich.

"Let me take a look." Gerry pushed his plate away in disgust. "I'm going to have to cut hours from other departments to cover for this. I'll get with the department managers who are going to lose floor coverage once I play with these numbers."

Gerry was rubbing his forehead and peering at the report, hoping that his eyes were deceiving him. Maybe what he was reading was somehow incorrect. "Meanwhile, the fishing department is going to pay back their share. Cut 20 hours from them right away. Paul is going to learn to stop adding payroll without my approval. Would you like me to have the teaching conversation with him or would you like to?" Gerry barked in frustration.

Steve easily sensed how heated Gerry was right now. On one hand, he would have enjoyed watching Gerry have a chat with his fishing manager. Paul was messing with Gerry's payroll. If it went unnoticed, Gerry would be the one held accountable. Steve knew that Gerry would not make it a very pleasant conversation. On the other hand, Steve really didn't need one of his managers ripped to shreds right now.

"I'll handle it, Gerry. In fact, I'll call him in right now. You have the manager-on-duty shift for the next two hours anyway. I know how much you would hate to give that up," he said jokingly.

Steve realized that it was one of his guys that messed up, and he was willing to fix the problem. He also wanted to let his friend know that he supported him. Steve was a little worried about Gerry lately. He sensed that something was wrong. Gerry wasn't acting like his usual self.

"Thanks, Steve," Gerry replied. He was starting to calm down, but his blood was still boiling. "Make sure he understands, in no uncertain terms, that if he adds a single hour to his schedule without my approval, I will have his ass," Gerry stated for good measure. "Look, I understand. I get it! The store is getting busy this time of year, and he feels he needs more coverage. I don't disagree with him on that. We need more coverage everywhere right now. Check my pockets, Steve. I'm not holding any payroll money back. I'm spending every penny that the boys in Michigan are giving me. The last thing I want to be is a payroll hero. If the fishing manager has a problem, he has to

36

learn how to correctly go about solving it. If he can't, I'll see to it that we find someone who can," he lectured. Finally, Gerry got off his soapbox and reasoned with Steve. "If he had come to me a week ago, I could have helped him. The budgets aren't perfect. I know that. All he had to do was approach me, and I would have listened. Steve, are you sure you don't need me to talk with him on this?" Gerry asked pensively.

"Gerry, I told you; I got it. It was nice having lunch with you. We should do it again sometime," Steve shot back sarcastically.

Gerry tossed what remained of his half-eaten sandwich in the garbage and moved toward the door of the conference room. He was scheduled to be the manager on duty, or M.O.D., for the next two hours. He knew the current M.O.D. would be anxious to turn the duties over to the next person, and it would be rude to keep him waiting. Just before he crossed the threshold leading out of the conference room, he turned and looked back at Steve, grinning.

"You have any Tums on you, Steve?" Gerry asked. "You guys are giving me *odgena,*" he groaned.

***

The gentleman in the Givenchy suit strolled into the crowded fishing area of Jimbo's and stumbled on the sort of opportunity he was hoping for. The salesperson behind the fishing-reel counter was showing a customer a Penn International 70 VIS fishing reel when his supervisor pulled him away and asked him to put line on another customer's reel. Paul, the fishing manager, was preparing to spool the reel himself when he suddenly got called away to meet with Steve, his senior manager. Paul was instructed to finish what he was doing and bring his staffing schedule to the office right away. Figuring it would take too long to finish spooling the line himself, he decided it would be best to turn the task over to the nearest available salesperson. The nearest available salesperson happened to be showing an 800-dollar reel to a customer.

Fishing reels that sell for 100 dollars and up are kept in locked glass showcases, similar to the way diamond rings are displayed in a jewelry store. When a customer wishes to look at a reel from the display case, the salesperson is required to unlock the glass case, remove the reel, and place it on the display mat on top of the case. If the customer decides to purchase it, the salesperson will walk the reel to the nearest cash register with the buyer. If the customer does not buy, the reel is returned to its display location and locked in the glass case. The salesperson is responsible for the exposed reel. The procedure must be strictly adhered to. Every sales associate is thoroughly trained to stay with any exposed, high-end fishing reel. Not only does the policy help sales, but it prevents theft. The sales associate thought he could keep an eye on the pricy reel and take care of the fishing manager's customer at the same time. He thought wrong.

The customer who had been looking at the Penn International 70 VIS reel decided not to purchase it. Therefore, he simply left it sitting on the display mat. Like a smallmouth bass, the same customer spotted another shiny object on the other side of the reel kiosk and wandered over to look at it. The sales associate, responsible for the exposed reel, was now bent over with his head in the cabinet which houses the bulk fishing line. The customer wishing to have line put on his reel requested a specific line that was not frequently used, and the associate was having difficulty locating it. Since nobody was paying attention to the display counter, the gentleman in the Givenchy suit swooped in and palmed the 800-dollar reel. He lowered both of his arms to a natural walking position and quickly blended in with the crowd of customers who were shopping in the adjacent aisle. His heart raced. If he was spotted, he would be offered the assistance of an employee. An associate would ask him if it was his intention to purchase the reel. The last thing he wanted was attention. Several minutes slowly passed and, to his relief, nobody approached him. Perfect.

The fishing associate finished taking care of the customer who had been turned over to him by the fishing manager. He re-approached his original customer who had been previously looking at the 800-dollar reel. The customer explained that he decided not to buy the reel and pointed to where he left it on the display mat, on top of the glass counter. When the fishing associate returned to the display case to secure the reel, he discovered it was not there. Panicked, he looked inside the case to see if, by chance, another associate found the reel and locked it back in the case. It wasn't in there either. He panicked some more. He couldn't find it. There was another Penn International 70 VIS reel under the display case still in its box. Next to it was the empty box from the reel which had been on display. The terror-stricken sales associate was faced with two options. He could take the red pill and call the manager on duty to report the missing 800-dollar reel. He could explain exactly what happened. Tell the truth. The associate made a mistake. He broke policy and, as a result, the store would absorb a significant loss. He could stand up and take responsibility for his actions. In all likelihood, he thought, choosing this option would get him fired for his incompetence. The best he could hope for would be a final written warning for breaking the rules. He could beg for mercy, however, and pray for the best. His fate would be decided by Mark, the general manager. Mark was known as someone who cared only for himself. He would have zero sympathy. Taking strong action against a rule breaker would be what upper management would expect from their general manager.

He would be charged with making an example out of the associate. Letting a crisis like this go to waste would not be in the cards. The other option for the fishing associate would be to take the blue pill and try to cover up the whole incident. He could take the other reel which was still in its box and use that one as the display. The store used a one-to-show and one-to-go system with high-end product. The one to show was missing. He could take the one to go and make it the one to show. Hopefully, the missing reel wouldn't be discovered as being lost right away. If someone wanted to buy the one to go, however, it would be discovered. With luck, nobody would want to purchase a Penn 70 VIS for days or even weeks. Cycle counts will discover it missing, but a cycle count had just taken place a couple of days ago. The next scheduled cycle count would be in two weeks.

So, let's see. Take the red pill and expose what is real? Take the blue pill and mask the truth? Hmmm. The sales associate decided to take the blue pill. He needed his job. Although it only paid him 15 dollars an hour, it was his only source of income. Getting fired for cause was not a good option for him. He took the second reel out of its box, wrapped an E.A.S. security lanyard around the spool of the reel, attached an E.A.S. tag to the lanyard, and placed the reel in the glass-display case. His tracks were covered for the time being. One week from now, when the missing reel is discovered, he will be one of many who could have caused the loss. The entire fishing staff will face undue suspicion and consequences for his carelessness, but none will face termination.

The gentleman who now was in possession of the Penn reel stood next to a round rack of fishing apparel and pushed his body slightly forward so he was partially obscured. Quickly but deliberately, he dropped the reel into an oversized pocket which he had sewn onto the inside of his suit jacket. The gentleman kept his jacket unbuttoned, making it nearly impossible to detect the special pocket and its contents. Now that he had successfully concealed the reel, he made his way to the men's room located in the front of the store. He removed a Leatherman tool from the holder looped onto his belt and sat in the stall furthest from the entrance. There, he would wait for the deafening noise of the hand dryer to mask the loud pop made when he cut the E.A.S. wire lanyard. Now that the security sensor was removed, he put the reel in the empty Jimbo's shopping bag that he had earlier placed in his jacket pocket. Finally, he flushed the cut lanyard along with the E.A.S. sensor tag down the toilet and headed toward the customer-service counter.

The gentleman stood at the front of the line at customer service and waited for the next available service associate to call him over to the counter. He had his arms crossed and was tapping the Giuseppe Zanotti loafer on his right foot impatiently as he waited for his turn. He fancied himself a very busy, very important person, and he needed his transaction processed quickly and efficiently. Clare was cheerily finishing the transaction that she was involved with and was exchanging a few pleasantries with her customer. Sydney was deeply involved in a special order with a young lady. The complex order would take him a few more minutes to process.

"I can help you over here." Clare motioned to the gentleman at the front of the line.

The gentleman approached her and placed the bag containing the Penn International 70 VIS fishing reel on the counter and said, "I would like to return this reel and get a refund. My wife gave it to me as a birthday present, and I don't like it."

Clare took the reel out of the bag and placed it on the counter. She fished around inside the bag and didn't find anything else. "Do you have your receipt with you?" she asked with a smile.

"No. I told you; I got it as a gift," he snapped. "I just want my money so I can get out of here. I have an extremely important meeting in 20 minutes, so I need to get going," the gentleman impatiently snarled.

"I'll get you out as soon as possible," Clare politely replied. "I'll just have to look up the price on this item. We can offer you a credit voucher if you don't have a receipt," she informed. "I'll just have to see your driver's license, or another state-issued picture ID."

"Listen, Honey!" he barked. "I told you I want cash, not a credit voucher. And I'm not showing you any identification. I know my rights!" the gentleman began raising his voice.

"We need an ID on any return without a retheipt," Sydney chimed in. He heard the gentleman starting to get aggressive with Clare and he didn't like it. His special-order customer had finished the transaction and had left. He had researched the Penn reel and had an image on his computer screen already. There were no other customers in line, and he figured he would give Clare a hand in looking up the price of the item.

"I need to see a manager. Now!" the gentleman ordered. "If you two idiots can't figure out how to get me my money, I need you to get me someone who can," he insisted.

Clare pressed the talk button on the microphone of her inner store-radio network and spoke. "M.O.D.?" she asked.

"Hey, Clare, what's going on?" Gerry promptly replied.

Clare was relieved to hear Gerry's voice on the other end. She was savvy enough to read the situation that was unfolding and knew Gerry would have their backs. "Gerry, code nine over here at customer care," she nervously stated.

"Be right there," Gerry replied.

"He's coming right now –" Clare informed the customer. Her voice quivered slightly.

"Thir, in the meantime, pleath come on over here tho I can get the tranthakthon thtarted," Sydney interrupted. He heard the fright in Clare's voice, and he wanted to take the pressure away from her. Unfortunately, he felt the same discomfort that she felt, and his speech impediment kicked in big time. Sydney didn't like being referred to as an idiot. He had mixed emotions, however. For good reason, he was afraid of this extremely arrogant gentleman. He was embarrassed about how he felt he appeared to Clare. Sydney could feel his anxiety level accentuating his speech impediment and couldn't bear the thought of Clare thinking less of him because of it. In the end, however, Sydney was extremely angry at the fact that the gentleman referred to Clare and him as idiots.

The gentleman shuffled to Sydney's computer station. He brought the reel with him and slammed it on the counter just as Gerry rounded the corner to customer care. The gentleman looked at red-faced Syd and, in a muted tone that was still loud enough for Sydney, Clare, and now Gerry to hear, he uttered, "Great, I go from working with Miss America over there to this fucking retard –"

"Whoa, whoa, whoa," Gerry interrupted. "I'm the manager on duty. What can I help with here?"

"Gerry, this man wants to make a return on an item without a receipt," Clare offered. "I informed him of our policy, but he wants cash back and refuses to show us a picture ID. He asked to speak with a manager."

Clare was relieved to turn the situation over to Gerry. She knew he would handle it from here. She also wanted to take the stress away from Sydney. The look on his face was horrible. Clare felt for him. Although Clare felt she could handle herself with the best of them, she appreciated Sydney helping to deal with this guy.

Gerry motioned the customer to come over to the side of the counter so he could get him away from Syd and Clare. The gentleman was six inches shorter than Gerry which required him to tilt his head down when looking the gentleman in the eye. Conversely, the gentleman was forced to tilt his head straight back in order to engage Gerry's stare.

"Did you just call the customer-care associate what I think I heard you call him?" Gerry asked incredulously.

"You heard correctly," the customer arrogantly replied. "He says he won't give me my cash back on the reel my wife purchased. You're going to take care of it, right?"

"Without a receipt, sir," Gerry calmly replied. "I'll authorize a credit voucher for the current selling price of the item. That's providing you present a picture ID at the register," Gerry was typically direct and spoke in a matter-of-fact tone of voice. He was known, at times, to bend policy for pleasant customers with an inexpensive item. However, any time he dealt with someone this abusive, he stuck to his guns. This customer was not nice and had a very expensive item. He had already blown any opportunity for Gerry to bend a rule for his benefit. "I cannot authorize what you are asking us to do," Gerry reiterated.

The gentleman wearing the two-thousand-dollar suit with the thousand-dollar shoes, who was attempting to get cash back on an 800-dollar fishing reel which he had just stolen from the fishing-reel bar, glared at Gerry. He curled the middle, ring, and pinky fingers of his right hand into his palm. The gentleman then stiffened his remaining index finger and drove it directly into the center of Gerry's chest. "Listen, Bud," he stated. "If you can't authorize this, get someone on the phone who can. Now!" And then he pulled his finger from Gerry's sternum.

Gerry had experienced customers laying their hands on him only a few times in his long career. The first time, when he was younger, he needed to be physically restrained. Several years ago, when it happened again, he got so angry that he could barely speak. His hands shook, his face got red, and his jugular vein bulged like it was going to explode. This time, he leaned on his prior experience. Inside, he was seething. He wanted to break this guy's neck. On the outside, however, he remained eerily calm. A sinister smile overtook his face.

"Sir, I need you to come and sit down with me on the bench over there." Gerry pointed to a seating area about 20 feet from the customer-service area. "I want to get this situation straightened out for you. I need to speak with to you privately." He smiled as he spoke. There wasn't as much as a ripple in his voice. "Come on with me." He cheerily waived as he turned to walk on over to the seat.

Gerry arrived at the bench first and chose to sit at the far end facing customer care. The gentleman sat opposite him at the near end with his back toward customer care. The gentleman still felt he would be dictating the terms of this transaction. He wanted to make it clear to this lowly manager that the customer is always right, and he would get what he wanted.

"I've already explained to you what I want," the gentleman began. "Nothing else is going to satisfy me. What's the telephone number to your corporate office? I intend to file a complaint about you if you're not capable of taking care of me. Do you call yourself a manager?" the gentleman sneered. "You aren't even skilled enough to take care of a simple customer request."

Although Gerry physically heard the words and the questions directed toward him, he didn't allow himself to lend credibility to the fake inquiry. Instead, he let the venom being spewed bounce off his recently fingered chest like he was Superman.

"Before I get to your questions, I just have a few things I have to cover with you." Gerry smiled. "What's your first name?" he asked.

"Chris," the gentleman replied.

"Chris, my name is Gerry," Gerry began. "First, Chris, let me explain to you in no uncertain terms that I consider you laying your filthy, stinking hands on me like you did as a physical assault." Gerry smiled as he spoke. "All I have to do is press this little button here on my radio microphone and alert our store detectives to call the cops. They'll be here in a heartbeat and will gladly drag your sorry ass out of the store in handcuffs. I have no problem pressing charges against you. You see, the reason I'm sitting facing this way is because the security camera which earlier recorded you striking my chest is recording my smiling face right now. Do you understand what I'm saying to you, Chris?" Gerry spoke in a monotone matter-of-fact voice.

"Don't do that," Chris stammered back.

"We'll see what happens," Gerry deadpanned. He was still grinning. "I'm going to present you with some options. I'll let you choose how this ends. First option is you can take out your license and hand it to Syd over there. Apologize to him for calling him what you called him. He will process a store credit for you if you do that. The second option is the same as option number one, without the apology. This option will get you a store credit and you get to leave here in handcuffs. Have fun at the police station. I know all the cops. I coached most of their kids in basketball. I'm sure they will be pleasant to you for the remainder of the afternoon. The police station here in town is as posh as a five-star hotel. I think you will fit in quite well. You may even get to take a lesson on proper manners. The third option is you can just leave the reel at the desk and walk out of here. Don't come back. I don't know where you got the reel in the first place. I'm not one-hundred percent certain that I buy your 'got it as a gift' story. I know you said you were in a hurry. I've spent as much time with you as I intend to as well. I'll give you 30 seconds, Chris. Which door are you going to go for, Chris? Door number one, door number two, or door number three?" Gerry's smile resembled a German shepherd that was baring its teeth.

"I'll go with the first option," Chris muttered.

"Good choice!" Gerry offered approvingly. Gerry stood, still facing the security camera and held out his hand with a warm smile. As he shook the gentleman's hand, he looked him straight in the eye and softly said, "You just fucked with the wrong guy, asshole. I want you to know that," he said dismissively.

The gentleman approached Sydney at the service desk and offered an apology for calling him names. Syd entered the gentleman's ID information into his computer. Chris Adamson lived at 256 Blueberry Lane in the town of Chevon. Sydney nervously finished the transaction and handed Mr. Adamson his credit voucher which was worth 850 dollars. 800 for the reel, 50 dollars in tax. Mr. Adamson took the voucher, folded it in two, placed it in his pocket, and exited the building.

Sydney was visibly shaken. His face was still red and his eyes were glassy as if fighting back tears. Clare looked over at Gerry who stood by Sydney's side during the transaction. Gerry not only wanted to offer support to Syd, but he also wanted to make sure everything was properly keyed. Once he was satisfied with the accuracy of the information, he entered his five-digit approval code required for a return that large.

"That guy needs a good whack," Clare informed Gerry.

"Yup," Gerry replied as he started to walk away from the desk. "You two are awesome! Thank you for putting up with idiots like him. No more today. OK?" He flashed a warm, approving smile to both and went back to his rounds.

"You okay, Syd?" Clare looked over at Sydney. He was staring off into the distance in deep thought.

"I'm fine," Sydney lied.

Clare knew that Sydney wasn't fine. In fact, she read him as being totally humiliated. She wasn't blind to the signals Sydney was giving regarding his infatuation toward her. She wasn't sure if she shared his feeling or not. There was one thing she was sure of, however. Sydney stepped in to help her to deal with a very unruly customer. Nobody asked him to. He just did it. Syd's gesture charmed her. None of her previous boyfriends had ever made her feel as special as she felt right now. For the first time in her memory, a guy made her feel appreciated.

"I don't have any night classes tonight," Clare blurted. "Did you know that they just opened an ice-cream parlor across the street?" she asked innocently. "Since we're both getting off at four, well, I was wondering if you'd like to go and get an ice cream with me when we get out of work?"

Sydney raised his eyebrows. It took him a moment to let Clare's unexpected proposition sink in. Suddenly, he no longer felt like the fool that he had just been accused of being. A surge of confidence seeped into the psyche of someone who had always been best described as sensitive and lonely. Maybe his lot in life was beginning to change, he thought. In any event, an unrecognized charge of energy ran through Syd's body as if he had just been struck by lightning.

"Yeah. I'd like that," Sydney replied.

# 5

Sometimes good people are dealt a bad hand.

Gerry pulled into the employee parking lot of Jimbo's at 11:30. Just before lunch. He was scheduled to work the closing shift along with four other managers. There were five managers already in the store working the opening shift. One of them was Jennifer, the manager of customer care. Jennifer has reported directly to Gerry for the past five years. She is responsible for all of the operational functions and staffing at the cash registers, customer care, and cash office. Every purchasing customer would, at some point, interact with one of Jennifer's associates. She was very friendly and outgoing but could be aggressive when she had to be. Jennifer was covering her shift as manager on duty when she saw Gerry walk in. She quickly approached him and waived him over to a spot where they could have some privacy.

"Gerry, I know you just got here," she stated. "Once you get settled, come on over to my office. We have to talk. I give up manager on duty in 20 minutes." The urgency in her tone let Gerry know that she needed to see him about something important.

"I'll get there as soon as I can," Gerry replied. "Let me go and get settled in first. I hope this isn't going to be one of those days," he muttered as he headed to the senior manager suite.

Gerry was feeling tired. Much more than normal fatigue of his hectic schedule. He skipped one of his regular workouts this week and had to drag himself to the gym this morning. Normally, when he worked the closing shift, he would exercise for a couple of hours in the morning before going to work. His other usual gym days were his days off. Gerry looked forward to taking a day off from work tomorrow. He needed to spend some time decompressing. He also needed a stress-free day without any work-related drama. Gerry's stomach was bothering him more and more lately. The more it bothered him, the more stress he felt. The more stress he felt, the more his stomach bothered him. He felt like his body was turning into a pressure cooker. There were pressures feeding into it from all directions. Gerry needed to figure a way to open a release valve before he exploded.

Gerry had to walk past Mark's office on the way to his office. Mark was talking on the phone and offered a wave as he saw Gerry pass by. Gerry got to his desk, turned on his computer, and started getting caught up on the day's activities when his intercom sounded.

"Gerry, I need to see you right away," Mark ordered. "Whatever you have going on can wait. Lynn is on her way as well. See you in a couple of minutes."

This was not what Gerry was hoping for today. Lynn, the human-resources manager, being invited to an unscheduled meeting with the general manager and senior operations manager was not a good sign.

Gerry had a good working relationship with Lynn but the two frequently butted heads. He would often privately opine to her that he felt she was the champion of the useless and the conqueror of the useful. In other words, she always found a good reason to protect someone who needed to be disciplined or terminated. On the other hand, she always had a great reason to meet out the harshest discipline to a high-performing associate who made a simple mistake. Gerry frequently asked her if she felt it was her job to make sure he kept his staff full of inept people and discard the highly motivated.

Gerry's top priority was to keep only the best performers on his staff. He was highly adept at maneuvering throughout the system. He wouldn't let any outside interference pollute his staffing standards. In Gerry's prior job, he called the shots and took the advice of H.R. as just that. Advice that he would take into consideration when making a decision. In this job, however, Mark was in control, and he had a different take on receiving advice from H.R.

For one thing, Mark had the hots for Lynn and felt that agreeing with everything she said would help him get in her pants. For another thing, anyone who ignored the advice offered by human resources would be labeled an ineffective leader. The unfavorable reputation would, thus, be secretly fed to the executives in the corporate office. Mark was all about getting himself promoted. Making waves of any kind would be avoided at all cost. Gerry surmised that he was about to walk into a hornet's nest if Mark wanted to see him with Lynn present. He didn't know if it was about him or one of his reports. He just figured it was going to be trouble. Mark and Lynn, however, knew it was best to not give Gerry the satisfaction of knowing what the meeting was going to be about. The last thing they wanted was to allow him time to gather facts and thoughts when discussing an issue that required human resources to be present. Surprise, in their estimation, always worked in their best interest when dealing with Gerry.

Gerry walked into Mark's office and took a seat at the small conference table opposite Mark and Lynn. Mark had some papers in front of him lying face down on the table. Lynn had a blank, yellow, lined notepad in her lap. She nervously chewed on the blue cap of a ballpoint pen that stuck out from the right side of her mouth. Gerry had seen this act many times before. He didn't know what road they were going down, but he knew he would have to be on his toes for the next half hour. He was in no mood for the ice-breaking small talk that he knew would be first on the agenda. He ignored the question of how his family was doing. Gerry knew neither of them could care less about his family. He could put a gun to their heads and give them each ten tries to get his wife's name right. Neither would survive. He also knew he was feeling a little tired and cranky. He wanted to get this over with.

"What happened?" Gerry asked abruptly.

"Gerry, do you remember a customer named Adamson?" Mark asked. "Chris Adamson is his full name. Does the name ring a bell for you?"

Gerry thought for a moment, but he didn't have any idea to whom Mark was referring. The store deals with hundreds of customers daily. The managers personally work with many of them. Gerry seldom forgets a face, but when it comes to names, his retention is not great. Especially if he only met the individual in question once or twice.

"You know I'm bad with names, Mark. Refresh me," Gerry calmly shot back.

Mark chose one of the sheets of paper from the table in front of him and dramatically pretended to study it. He already knew what was printed on the document, however, he insisted on putting on a show. Especially since Lynn was in the audience.

"He returned a Penn reel the other day," Mark declared. "Clare and Syd were working the customer-care desk," he stated. "The customer wasn't happy with the way he was treated, and he wrote a lengthy letter to corporate. I have a copy of it here. I won't read all of it, but he says you and Sydney were extremely rude to him."

"Really!" Gerry now clearly remembered the customer. "We were rude to him? Did he write down the name he called Sydney? Did he say he stuck his finger in my chest?" Gerry asked, red faced.

"He did mention that he was holding out his arm and you walked into his finger," Mark coldly stated. "Luckily for you, I had the guys in loss prevention show Lynn and me the video. From what we can see, it doesn't look like you walked into his finger. If the video showed that you did, however, you would be in big trouble," Mark warned. "The larger problem with this whole incident is the way Sydney acted. The customer says he was having no issue when dealing with Clare. He referred to her as a lovely young lady. He says Sydney rudely called him over to his terminal. According to the customer, the fact that

Sydney butted in rightfully made him angry. He was in a hurry to attend an important meeting, and Sydney's actions delayed him unnecessarily."

Gerry sat flabbergasted by what he was hearing. He knew enough to not trust Mark with anything involving his well-being. Given the opportunity, Gerry realized that Mark would always twist facts from an occurrence in order to support his warped personal agenda. He reasoned that now, Mark was simply doing what he does best. The incident would soon blow over, Gerry thought, and he could get back to working on what was important. It couldn't get any loonier, he reasoned. And then Lynn spoke.

"Gerry, I think it is very important that you and Jennifer sit down with Sydney," Lynn instructed. "Corrective action is required in this instance, and it has to be a formal written warning," she stated.

Lynn anticipated that Gerry would push back on her direction, but she had already convinced Mark on how to proceed.

"The recommendation from corporate was actually more severe, but we were able to negotiate a lesser response," she added.

Gerry was understandably suspicious of the motives behind the direction being given to him by Lynn and Mark. He knew enough to question their intentions, but in the end, he couldn't refuse to carry out a directive given by his immediate supervisor.

"Just so I understand," Gerry began sarcastically. "Some Bozo calls Sydney a name that I don't even care to mention. In fact, you'd probably write me up for repeating it."

Gerry could feel his blood boiling, and he was doing his best to hide his emotions. He knew they would use his words against him if he shared too much of what he was thinking.

"Look," Gerry began calmly. "Sydney was just following the policies that we, as a company, are asking him to follow. The customer got set off because one of our trained employees was explaining the policy that he learned from us. Then, when I got there, the guy pushed his finger into the middle of my chest. In some universes, that is considered assault. Now, I'm supposed to give Syd a formal written warning? Exactly what am I writing him up for? Doing his job? Helping Clare? Having the bad luck of getting this customer? I'm not smart enough to know what you two want me to do here," he admitted.

"Let me just remind you of our policy here at Jimbo's," Mark chimed in. "Rule number one – The customer is always right! Rule number two – If the customer is ever wrong, reread rule number one!"

"Yeah, I've seen the poster hanging in the break room," Gerry deadpanned. "So, write Sydney up on a written warning because the customer is always right? According to the customer, Sydney is a fucking retard," Gerry blurted.

His blood, once more, was rapidly boiling. "Hey, Lynn," Gerry snarked. "You have young kids. When they get older, if somebody calls them that name at their work, do you think they should write your child up? After all, the customer is always right," Gerry stated as he nodded in her direction, seeking agreement.

Mark could see where this conversation was going, and he was smart enough to end it, and quickly. Gerry was going to defend his people. It was something that Lynn admired, and Mark hated about him. Gerry's staff would run through walls for him if he asked them to. There was a strong two-way loyalty that was impossible for Mark to comprehend. The loyalty of Gerry's staff actually unnerved Mark. Many times, he and Lynn attempted to get a member of Gerry's staff to offer some dirt on Gerry. They needed something on him to later use as leverage. Time and again, they came up empty. Mark's immediate reports, on the other hand, wouldn't even bother to pee on him in the event he accidentally set himself on fire and there was no water available.

"Gerry, Lynn and I have decided that Sydney needs a written warning," Mark instructed. "You have to make sure he doesn't butt in on someone else's transaction ever again. The customer is upset that Sydney took over for Clare. He says that is the only reason he got a little bit testy. The gentleman was fine until Sydney set him off. Syd is at fault here. Not the customer. Correct the problem and move along. We need the warning issued no later than tomorrow. I recommend you take care of this today since you are off tomorrow. I'd hate to see you have to come in on your day off. I know you've been working hard, and you deserve a day for some rest and relaxation. Why don't you play a little golf?" Mark suggested.

Gerry ignored Mark's advice to play a round of golf. He couldn't, however, refuse his direct order. Nothing would make Mark happier than to have the opportunity to deal with an insubordinate manager. Particularly with Lynn as a witness.

"Okay. I've got my marching orders," Gerry replied. "Lynn, you can add to your notes on that yellow pad that I disagree one-hundred percent with what I'm being asked to do here. Put down that I think it's wrong. This is not how you should treat good people. I'm writing up Syd on your behalf. Does Jennifer know about this?" Gerry asked. "She jumped me at the door. Says she needed to see me right away."

"Yeah, we filled her in," Mark replied. "We asked her what she knew about the whole thing. We investigated what we could already and decided to question her. You know how she can get," he stated. "By the way, Gerry. Just so you are properly informed. Corporate sent the customer a 100-dollar gift card and a letter of apology for his inconvenience. I covered for you on this one. As I stated earlier, the customer said you were pretty rude to him."

"Right. Perfect. Thanks for the information," Gerry replied as he stood. "Anything else from you two today?" he pleasantly asked. "Otherwise I have to get going."

"No, that's it," Mark replied. "By the way, I changed my shift to open today instead of closing. Lynn and I are both going to get out of here a little early. The two of us have been working hard lately. We'll be leaving at around 4:30 in case you need us for anything."

Gerry headed over to Jennifer's office which was located behind the customer-service desk. On his way, he amused himself by thinking real hard about what he could possibly need from Mark and Lynn before 4:30. He couldn't come up with anything useful, so he got the thought out of his mind. Jennifer was just finishing her manager-on-duty shift, so he called her to come on back to her office. Jennifer entered and sat at her desk facing Gerry who was sitting with his back to the left side wall, left elbow on the front of her desk. He was already deep in thought, filling out the corrective action form which would be presented to Sydney.

"Gerry, this sucks!" Jennifer scowled. "You couldn't convince them to let this whole incident go?"

"I tried," Gerry replied sternly. "Let's just fill out the warning and have him sign it. They didn't tell me exactly how to word it. We just have to reference the fact that he has to let the other associate complete their own transaction without his interference. I'm going to add the caveat that it is okay to butt in only if the other associate asks for help. Maybe that will help take away the sting for Sydney. And yes, it does suck! I was the one dealing with this Adamson idiot, remember? And where were you?" Gerry asked, trying to insert a hint of levity to the otherwise miserable situation. "How did I get stuck with another customer from Chevon?" he asked incredulously.

"By the way, do you have any Rolaids in this office?" Gerry asked. "My stomach is killing me right now."

"Here you go," Jennifer tossed to Gerry a plastic container filled with antacids that she kept in her top drawer for him. "You should go see someone about that stomach of yours," she advised sternly.

"Yeah, yeah, as soon as we finish this," Gerry replied. "I'll run right to the clinic and visit with the medics. Just for you," he mused.

Jennifer stuck her head out of her office and asked Sydney to join her in the office as soon as the line of customers died down at the customer-care counter. The look on her face revealed to Sydney that something was wrong, but he couldn't imagine what it could be. Several minutes later, he logged off his computer terminal and let the other two associates know that he was heading to a meeting with the boss. He entered Jennifer's office and saw Gerry sitting to the left with his back against the side wall. Jennifer was sitting behind her desk with papers upside down in front of her. Behind her, on the wall at eye level, hangs a motivational poster of four men in a racing shell used in the sport of crew. The inspirational wording on the poster, titled, *TEAMWORK*, states that, "*Coming together is a beginning. Keeping together is progress. Working together is success.*" Sydney sat in the empty chair next to Gerry, directly opposite Jennifer, and reread the words that he has seen many times before.

"Syd, we have to talk about the customer who returned the fishing reel the other day," Jennifer began.

"I'm okay, now," Sydney reported. "We can put it in the rearview mirror for all I care. No need to relive that horrible name that the guy called me. Thank you, though. I'm happy knowing that I can count on you to help me," he said.

"Syd," Jennifer stated. "The customer wrote a complaint letter to our corporate office. He says he would have been able to stay calm if you hadn't butted in on the transaction," she advised. "You have previously been made aware of how seriously the company takes any customer complaints submitted to the corporate office. They sent this customer a 100-dollar gift card as a gesture of apology for his unpleasant shopping experience. We have to give you a written warning about interrupting someone else's customer interaction. Sydney, you just can't interrupt unless the other associate specifically asks you for help. If it happens again, you will be subjected to further disciplinary action up to and including termination. I'll just need you to sign here, acknowledging that we had this conversation," she firmly instructed.

"Do you have any questions for Gerry or me?" Jennifer asked, wishing the meeting would quickly end.

Jennifer's words had a hurtful, stinging effect on Sydney. He felt the blood drain from his face and became a little bit light-headed. His shock, however, turned first to fear and then to anger. How could he be written up for what he did? He thought. A customer can simply write a letter to the corporate office with twisted facts and corporate will discipline the employee? Sydney felt helpless. The thought of telling Jennifer to stick the written warning where the sun doesn't shine was beginning to overwhelm his brain. The more he digested what was going on, the more he thought of walking out and never returning. Suddenly, however, like most males in their early 20s, thoughts of sex figured into the equation.

Sydney had the best ice-cream cone he ever had in his life the other night. He couldn't recall what flavor he ordered, but he could recall every other detail of what it was like sharing his time with Clare. The shifts that he was scheduled to work with her were circled on a large calendar which hung on his bedroom wall. Sydney had a special spring in his step when he was getting ready to go to work a shift at Jimbo's, knowing that Clare would be logged into the computer next to his. If he quit, he wouldn't see her anymore. The ice-cream date was great, but it was only a beginning. It wasn't like they were now a steady couple. He was, however, totally smitten with her. Head over heels. He thought about Clare constantly. He wanted the relationship to grow, and the job at Jimbo's, he rationalized, was the conduit. The job in itself didn't matter very much. Although he was extremely competent in his position at customer service, he realized that the job wouldn't last forever. Sydney was working on a computer-programming certification which was necessary for him to land the fulltime help-desk position he was seeking. His passion, for now, was in the computer world, and he wanted to develop his skills as a programmer.

Sydney didn't intend to stay in retail forever. He did intend to hang on as long as Clare was there. To Sydney, Jimbo's was a temporary stop which would lead to a better position and a high-paying career one day. The job at Jimbo's was strictly viewed as something to have on a resume.

He was totally conflicted with how to best solve the problem that this new development was presenting. The last thing he wanted was to have to explain to a prospective employer why he was let go for cause. He was also savvy enough to know that it is not a good idea to just walk out on a job without giving proper notice. He was angry, but he knew it was in his best interest to gain control of his emotions. He had to calm himself as best he could. Syd, finally, came back down from his seething haze and made his decision.

"I want you to know that I am very unhappy about thith," Sydney managed. "Let me thine the thtupid paper and get back to work," he angrily requested.

"Syd, for whatever it's worth to you," Gerry said apologetically. "Jennifer and I don't like this either. I don't want you to worry about losing your job over this," he reassured. "They'd have to fire me before I'd allow you to be fired over an incident like this one. Jennifer and I both think the world of you," he said.

As soon as Sydney left the office, Gerry reached over and grabbed the signed document from Jennifer and stood up. He would drop it off in human resources on his way to his office. Lynn's team would scan the contents of the form into the electronic employee-tracking system before sending a hard copy of it to the corporate human-resources department.

Gerry told Jennifer before he left her office that he felt like he needed to take a shower. He just felt dirty. And sleazy. Maybe soap and warm water would wash the shame that he felt from his consciousness, he reasoned. He also was boiling mad on the inside. This time, Gerry was having a difficult time keeping his anger in check.

Just as he finished the task at hand and returned to his desk to check on the day's sales results, his phone rang. The call was from an internal line and originated from Jennifer's extension. "Now what?" Gerry said aloud, speaking to himself. "I just left there. This can't be good," he muttered as he depressed the speaker button on his desktop phone.

"This is Gerry," he answered.

"Gerry, I'm hungry," Jennifer announced out of the blue. "Do you want me to bring you a sandwich from the sub shop?" she offered.

"Yeah, bring me a medium tuna fish," Gerry replied, relieved. "Get me the usual. Meet me in my office when you get back," he offered. "We'll have lunch together. Unless you have other plans."

"Sounds good," Jennifer replied. "I'll be back in 15 minutes or so. Unless I decide to take my sweet time," she teased.

Gerry and Jennifer shared a sandwich together and, later, spent time reviewing the upcoming weekend's frontend staffing requirements. Gerry was looking for a scheduling mistake but couldn't find one. Jennifer was very good at her job. She wouldn't allow Gerry the pleasure of pointing out a potential problem that she overlooked. She would never hear the end of it if he did find an error. Jennifer did everything she could to get Gerry's mind away from the incident involving Sydney. She knew how Gerry thought and could almost read his mind. She was fully aware of how much he continued to fume over how the situation was forced to play out. Gerry was a master at masking his feelings from most. He was, however, an open book to Jennifer.

Jennifer sarcastically thanked Gerry for sharing such an enjoyable lunch together and headed back to check on her customer-service desk. Gerry barely acknowledged her exit. He had, moments ago, been emailed the profit-and-loss statement from the month that just ended. His review and written response to the findings of the report would consume him for the next couple of days. Or so he thought.

Although he was fully engrossed in analyzing the controllable expense portion of the critical report, Gerry suddenly changed focus and sprung to his feet. He felt a little peculiar. Did he eat some bad tuna fish? Was he feeling the effect of the inner turmoil he experienced during the Sydney write-up? Was he that angry with the customer? Was he still angry about his meeting with Mark and Lynn? Gerry couldn't determine the cause of his sudden malaise. He also didn't recognize the strange feeling that was overwhelming him. The only thing that he could be certain of was that he felt awful. Gerry sprinted to the men's room, entered the far stall, leaned over the bowl, and vomited.

"M.O.D.?" Gerry gasped into the mic on his radio.

"Gerry, go ahead," came the reply. It was Robbie. The hunting manager.

"Robbie, switch over to channel 11," Gerry instructed. "I have to tell you something." He wanted to speak privately with Robbie but didn't really care if some busy body also switched channels to listen in. Gerry changed to channel 11 and waited for Robby to acknowledge. "Robby, I'm going to head home for the evening. You have the helm for the rest of the night. I'm not feeling well. Something I ate didn't agree with me," he said.

"Okay, Gerry," Robbie acknowledged. Gerry had the reputation of never missing a day of work or cutting out early for any reason. This development was highly unusual. "Feel better," he said. "I'll see you over the weekend."

Gerry took what he needed from his office and hurried from the building. Mary, his wife, had made plans for the evening. Thinking that Gerry was closing and wouldn't be home until it was very late, she and her friends decided to attend a show at the Performing Arts Center. Mary, at this hour, would already be on her way to meet them for an early dinner. Gerry decided not to call to let her know he was leaving work due to his sudden illness. He didn't want to ruin her evening. Gerry knew if he told her he wasn't feeling well, she would worry about him. She may even decide to cancel her plans and come home to be with him. That was the last thing he wanted to have happen. As much as he loved his wife, Gerry wanted to be alone tonight. He had plenty of things to keep himself occupied.

# 6

Are you familiar with Newton's Third Law of Motion?

Chris Adamson steered his Jaguar into the driveway of 256 Blueberry Lane in Chevon and slowly, carefully pulled into the attached three-car garage. The last reddish hues of the day were blending in with the deep blue of the evening sky. Nature's final spectacular color show went unnoticed by the self-absorbed occupant of the beautiful home on Blueberry Lane. He didn't notice the chirping of the insects, the croaking of the frogs, the sweet smell of the lilac bushes, or the tangy smell of the freshly cut lawn. His mind was preoccupied with what has already transpired and what he has planned for the remaining hours of the day.

Chris used the Jimbo's store credit from the fishing-reel return on an 800-dollar purchase. He bought 2500 rounds of handgun ammunition in a combination of 9mm, .38 special, .40 S-and-W, and .380. The drug dealers in the city would have little use for an expensive fishing reel, but they do have use for handgun ammo. Especially since state laws require identification to legally purchase it. The dealer with whom Chris Adamson conducts business on a regular basis was more than happy to exchange eight grams of cocaine for 2500 rounds of non-traceable ammo. Chris Adamson had little use for the ammo. He seldom practiced with the .40 caliber semiautomatic handgun he kept locked in his gun safe. He couldn't wait, however, to ingest the white powder which was carefully hidden under the driver's seat of his F-Type Jaguar.

He sat impatiently with both hands on the steering wheel of his car as the garage door closed behind him, sealing him off from the outside world and into to the dark reality of his drug world. The only thing that matters to him right now is unwrapping the contents from beneath his seat and getting high. He is laser-focused.

The instant the garage door thumped against the concrete floor, Chris located the bag containing his cocaine and sprung to his feet. He became almost giddy with the memory of how he got away with another dangerous transaction in the city streets. The dealer with whom he does business is not someone to be messed with. Chris would not even think about attempting to cheat the drug dealers out of money or merchandise. The way he robs fortunes from the helpless elderly citizens who fall for his Ponzi schemes would be quickly detected by suspicious gang members. Street justice, he knows, is different in many ways than the easily manipulated justice system of the world in which he operates. His arrogance would not be rewarded in the city streets in the same manner as it is in his Chevon community.

Chris walks the length of his car toward the step leading to his empty home. Several months ago, his wife took his three daughters and moved out. She was fed up with his cocaine use and couldn't convince him to seek help. Although his wife was enamored by the lifestyle that a highly successful financial planner could provide, she wanted to shield her children from his illicit drug use. She was also becoming aware of bits and pieces of a rumored Ponzi scheme that Chris was supposedly involved with.

Chris Adamson's wife was not all that savvy about the workings of the financial world. In fact, she didn't really comprehend how a Ponzi scheme worked. All she knew was that the large monthly deposits into Chris's bank account were not happening with the regularity that she was used to.

Chris informed her one day, out of nowhere, that receipts were now being required from him for all Adamson household expenditures. He wouldn't elaborate on who was requesting the receipts or for what reason they were now being required. She incorrectly assumed it was someone from his financial firm tasked with tracking his expenses. When pressed about it, Chris would get extremely angry and tell her it was none of her business. The arguments between them would get heated to the point where Chris was on the verge of becoming violent.

***

Chris Adamson entered his posh home and navigated the narrow hallway leading to the kitchen without turning on any lights. He was feeling slightly paranoid and didn't wish to grant a nosy neighbor or a binocular-toting detective the ability to see what he had in his hands. He figured it would be a good idea to secure the bag of cocaine in a kitchen cabinet before turning on any lights. He pivoted his right leg onto the kitchen tile and, with his right arm, reached up and grabbed the knob of the cabinet that was mounted above the countertop writing desk. That was the moment when everything changed.

Simultaneously, Chris heard a sickening sound as if someone hit a melon with a baseball bat, and felt a searing, aching, intense, mind-numbing pain in his right knee. The force of the blow drove his weight-bearing right leg backward, causing him to fall face first into the desk and finally to the kitchen floor. Dazed, he felt his ankles quickly being tightly bound together. Someone was kneeling on his lower back and, with animal-like strength, grabbed first his left arm and then his right and bound them tightly together at the wrist. All the while, Chris was being served a smorgasbord of pain. The kayak straps around his ankles were stingingly tight. His shattered right knee was throbbing like a bass drum with every beat of his heart. There was a searing pain running throughout his body after being struck in the leg by a short handle, especially designed stake hammer. His wrists, tightly bound, pulled his arms awkwardly to his rear. Struggling was futile. It only threatened to dislocate his arms at his shoulders. Chris's mouth was burning from the exposed nerves in his broken front teeth, having been knocked out when his head struck the granite desktop. He was seeing flashes of light before his eyes. It was as if he was in a virtual reality booth, lying face down at home plate in Yankee Stadium, staring up at the stands on the night Derek Jeter came up for his final at bat. In one, final, involuntary attempt to complement the slimy mixture of blood and saliva puddled beneath his bruised chin, Chris violently vomited.

Chris then felt someone, or something lift his 220-pound frame by his belt and the back of his shirt collar and toss him face down onto the kitchen table like he was a sack of potatoes. One final kayak strap tightly wrapped around the table, secured over his waist, completely immobilized him. He was in too much pain to move, but couldn't, even if he wanted to. Chris's pain turned to fear and then to anger as his head began to clear. He would not allow this to continue in his own home. It was time for him to take control of the situation, he thought.

"What the hell is going on here?" Chris shouted. "Who are you?" he demanded, spitting blood in between questions.

"Quiet, ath-thole. You will thpeak in a thoft tone or I'll thut you up for good," Sydney replied as he flipped the light switch. He moved to the head of the table and lifted Chris's head by his hair so their eyes could meet. "Remember me?" he grinned.

Chris was racking his brain. The voice with the lisp was familiar. He recalled that the pudgy kid at the service desk in Jimbo's spoke like this, but it couldn't be him. That clerk was extremely timid. He almost started crying when Chris got aggressive with him. It can't be. The guy standing in front of him is cut like a bodybuilder. The guy at Jimbo's was wearing a fleece vest over his fat belly. His shoulders even looked fat in the store. Come to think of it, however, it was hard to see them due to the oversized top he was wearing. With the lights now on and his head beginning to clear, Chris was staring at a young man in a long-sleeve, under-armor, skintight top which accented every bulging muscle on his body. There wasn't an ounce of fat on him. His abs were visible through the top he was wearing. It was almost as if he was sporting one of those fake Batman plastic torsos that you see kids wearing at Halloween. Except it was real. This isn't good, he thought.

"I'm the fucking retard. Remember?" Syd sneered.

Chris's angry disposition changed to a condition of trembling horror. His mind raced. He didn't know what to do, but he knew he had better think fast. This hulking monster who was standing over him was obviously angry, cold, and calculating. Maybe he could be calmed and reasoned with, Chris thought.

"Hey, listen, buddy," Chris pleaded. "You got your revenge, OK? No hard feelings on my end. Why don't you just untie me and we can each go our own way. Pretend we never met each other," he reasoned.

"Oh, I'm not through with you yet," Syd barked as he fished around in the backpack he had left on the kitchen counter. "You have gotten me tho pithed off. There ith no way in hell that I'm going to jutht let it go."

"What are you going to do?" Chris asked. His fear was overwhelming him. Adrenaline pumped through his body like a flowing fire hydrant. Speeding his heart rate to a dangerous level. He wasn't sure he wanted an answer to his question, but he felt like he had to ask. Maybe there was a way to negotiate his way out of this.

"I'm going to pith you," Sydney stated.

"You're going to piss me?" Chris repeated. He was confused.

"No! Not pith. Pith!" Sydney exclaimed. "How can I pith you? It doethen't even make any thenthe for you to thay that. Not pith, like take a pith. Pith like what they did to Lollyhopth. You Ath-thole."

Through the pain and the fear, Chris was doing everything he could to clear his head and attempt to communicate with his captor. He could sense this was a life-and-death situation he had gotten himself into, and he had to figure a way out. Chris was confident in his ability to fast talk. He had made millions by misleadingly convincing senior citizens into investing their life savings in his fake investments. Surely, he could fool this dimwitted kid into making a critical mistake. He just had to comprehend what was being said to him so he could formulate an escape plan.

"I'm having a hard time understanding you," Chris conceded. "You say you're going to piss in my asshole?" Chris assumed he correctly paraphrased the last couple of sentences spoken by Sydney.

"Look, if this is some sort of weird sex thing you have planned, maybe we can talk about setting you up with something better than this. I do have a lot of money, and I can buy you whatever you want. You just have to untie me. I swear I won't tell anyone how I got hurt, and I'll set you up with what you are looking for. I can connect you with someone, man or woman, who will let you piss in their asshole. I'll even put up the money for you," he offered.

"Enough!" Sydney growled. "No more making fun of me. No more trying to get me fired from my job. No more picking on Clare," he directed.

"Thay a prayer if you like," Sydney offered. "I have taken all of the bullthit that I intend to take from you!" he stated.

Sydney quickly wrapped a kitchen towel around the shaft of the 20-inch, solid, forged-steel tent stake which he had pulled from his backpack. With his left hand, he gripped the towel and placed the pointed end of the stake, designed to penetrate ice and rock, against the base of Chris's skull just below the natural bump in his head. With his right hand, he raised the hardened-steel stake hammer with the convenient built-in bottle opener above his head. And then, he swung.

The last sound Chris heard was the loud ping of the hammer striking the rounded stake head as the point was driven deep into his brain. He momentarily felt a sharp pain and then endured an intense, dull ache. He tried to scream but nothing came out of his mouth except for a low-pitched moan. His eyes were fixated on a bright light that only he could see. He had a strong metal taste in his mouth as if he were sucking on a nail. The smell of an infant's head just after being given a warm bath permeated his nostrils. His sensed his three baby daughters perched on his lap as was the scene more than ten years ago. And then, everything went black.

Sydney pulled the end of the stake toward him, driving the pointed tip to the right side of Chris's skull. He maneuvered it in an up-and-down motion, scrambling the right side of the contents inside of Chris's head, and then reversed. Sydney pushed the end of the stake forward, driving the tip to the left side of Chris's skull and mashed the grey matter on that side. For good measure, he centered the end of the stake in Chris's head and cranked it in a circular motion, mimicking an organ grinder, he mused.

Sydney made sure the damage he was doing to Chris's brain was thorough. Finally, he pressed the towel firmly against the back of Chris's skull with his left hand and looped the index finger of his right hand through the round hole at the end of the stake and pulled it free. Syd then rinsed the stake with cold water, washed the blood from his leather driving gloves, tossed the bloody towel in the kitchen sink, packed his things, and left.

On his way home, Sydney threw the tent stake far into the middle of the mighty river that separated Chevon from its neighboring town. It settled there into the depth at the muddy bottom. The leather gloves were buried in a random patch of pine straw in the woods a few hundred yards from the river bank. He knew what he had just done was wrong and, yet, he was strangely emotionless about the whole thing. He was in a controlled state of rage during the murder, but now his anger was out of his system. There was no remorse, no guilt, and no glee. It was just something he felt had to be done, and, so, he did it. For Sydney, it was time to move along for now. Sort of like how he felt when moving on to the next level of his favorite videogame.

When Sydney got home, his house was in darkness. His mother was working the overnight shift at the hospital all week and wouldn't be home until at least eight o'clock the following morning. Sydney grabbed a sports drink from the refrigerator and headed downstairs to his quarters in the finished basement of their home. He changed into a pair of running shorts and a tank top and completed two 60-minute sessions of Insanity Workout/Beach-body on Demand. Between sets, he allowed himself a short rehydration break. He then took a quick shower, turned down the covers of his perfectly made bed, climbed in, and slept like a baby. Sydney was at peace with himself. Without a care in the world.

# 7

*Do you have any changes in your health since your last visit?*

Mary got home just before midnight, and she was in a great mood. The show at the Performance Art Theatre was performed to perfection by the local artists. She and her friends already made plans to attend the next show coming two months from now. As she entered the foyer, she glanced over to the family room where Gerry was sitting in his recliner, staring at the glow of his laptop computer. It wasn't unusual to see him looking at his laptop, but it was unusual to see him doing so at this late hour. Mary stepped into the family room, flicked on the ceiling-fan light, and sat on the sofa next to where Gerry was sitting. Gerry didn't look good to her. His color was on the gray side, and his eyes looked heavy and bloodshot. She sensed something was wrong but would let him take the lead. If something happened to one of the boys, she knew he would have let her know already. It had to be something else.

Perhaps something unsettling happened to him again at work, and he was still in a cooling-off mode, she thought. Mary hated seeing the work stress take its toll on her husband. There was the physical stress of working long hours. Sometimes ridiculously long hours. Every time the store took inventory, Gerry would report into work at ten o'clock on Sunday morning. If everything went smoothly, he would wrap it up Monday afternoon at around two o'clock. 28 hours of nonstop work without time for anything other than an occasional bathroom break. Meals were taken on the fly. It was impossible to go more than ten minutes without being interrupted with a situation that needed an immediate decision.

During the holiday season, the store's hours would be extended, requiring extra hours from salaried employees. Since all employees who earn salaries are exempt from overtime, they can and will be required to put in 70 to 75 hours per week when the company deems it necessary. There is no additional pay. In the retail world, this is typical of the one-way street arrangement between the company and the managers. The company gets but doesn't give. The common response to anyone who dares to complain about the heavy workload is simply stated, "This is what you signed up for when you took the job."

Once upon a time, stores were closed on holidays which allowed workers to spend the day with their families. Once the 'remain open on holiday' ice was broken by one retailer, everyone else had to either follow suit or allow the competition to monopolize the day. On Thanksgiving Day, all salaried employees at Jimbo's were required to work a 12-hour shift. However, Gerry's boss, Mark, and his human-resources-manager sidekick showed up for the morning meeting and then conveniently disappeared. Everyone noticed the way they snuck out. Nobody cared.

The mental stresses of the job could be just as bad as the physical stress. Gerry's prior company was taken over by a capital investment firm which combined them with a competitor. Due to logistics plus the fact that Gerry's C.E.O. encouraged the buyout, the new company was set to be operated from the headquarters of the competitor. Gerry immediately had a bull's-eye on his back. From his level on up, everyone would be replaced by employees from the competition. Every day for the next six months, Gerry reported to work with the feeling of having the Sword of Damocles dangling over his head. He had feelers out for jobs of the same level, but at his age, he wasn't going to land a position with the same pay without uprooting his family.

Finally, unmercifully, he was flown six hours to the new company headquarters and fired. In a strange way, finally getting his pink slip relieved him from some of the mental stress he was enduring. Looking for another job in the retail industry while still employed is dangerous. Everyone either knows you or knows someone who does. Confidentiality is a rare and unusual commodity in an industry full of unscrupulous characters. The fact that you are interviewing with another company will inevitably get back to your current company. Once your current employer knows that you are out looking at other options, they will become more ruthless toward you than ever before. You can never let on that you are not 'all in' or '110 percent' committed to your company. In the retail world, nobody understands that there can only be 100 percent. There is the unchallenged opinion that unless you are in excess of 100 percent engaged in your duties, you are worthless.

\*\*\*

Shortly after being fired from his longstanding job, Gerry accepted a position at Jimbo's in late May of that year. His new title there was Senior Operations Manager. The store was still in the process of being built and was slated to open for business in the middle of November. Hiring and orientation of the 400 nonexempt or hourly employees would take almost three months. Store setup began the first week of October. This was the time when the team took occupancy of the empty store and began to receive massive quantities of inventory. The product had to be checked for accuracy, ticketed or tagged, and displayed on the shelves for customers to purchase. Gerry and the rest of the managers worked 14 hour shifts for 32 straight days. There were no days off from work granted to the salaried employees during that timeframe. The executives from corporate made it quite clear that it was highly inappropriate to even ask for a day away from work. Since they were salaried employees and, therefore, exempt from overtime, managers could and would be required to work nonstop until the store was ready to open. The 400-plus nonexempt hourly associates would be required to work no more than 40 hours per week. Because they were not exempt from overtime pay, any hours that they worked in excess of 40 would be paid at a rate of time and one-half of their regular hourly rate. Since overtime pay was strictly forbidden, their cumulative hours in any given week required strict monitoring. Once the store setup was complete, each manager would be allowed one day off per week until the end of January.

The newly opened store had to get through the holiday season and then execute the crucial January inventory process before the managers could expect to take two days off in any given week. When February finally came that year, the managers were physically exhausted. Mentally, Gerry questioned his own sanity. How in the world did he get duped like this? Obviously, when he was being hired, the corporate-hiring team had to distort and conceal the dirty details of the position. Otherwise nobody in their right mind would take this job.

Gerry internalized the strong feeling that he thought of himself as being a complete idiot for getting himself into this predicament. He beat himself up constantly over his incredibly poor decision to join this organization. Gerry knew he was way better than this. Still, he tried to reason; it was his best option at the time. He was making a decent pay. Gerry figured if he could just hang in there for another eight years, he could get out of retail for good. The culture of this company had him convinced that there was a better life to be had away from the lifestyle offered at Jimbo's.

He had visions of retiring once he hit his early 60s. The thought of family time, playing golf, and working out at the gym kept him going. Just hang on. Be mentally tough for a little while longer. There were two more lousy miles for him to run in a 26-mile marathon. "You've come this far," he said to himself. "Don't give up now!" Gerry joined Jimbo's four long years ago. He was getting closer to the finish line. There was a distinct light glowing at the end of the tunnel for him to focus on. Just as the pale light that glowed from the laptop computer perched on his lap illuminated his pale, gray face at this late hour.

*** 

"Hi, Honey," Mary offered cheerily as she sat down adjacent to him on the sofa. "You're up late. I expected you to be in bed when I got home," she said. "The show was great. The ladies all said hello," she encouraged.

Gerry looked up but reacted as if he was caught off guard by the question. He had been deep in thought and barely noticed Mary as she entered the room.

"How was work?" Mary finally asked, hesitatingly.

"Work was fine," Gerry deadpanned. "I left sick though. I'm not feeling so hot," he stated.

"Why? What's the matter?" Mary asked.

"I have cancer," Gerry replied.

"What!" Mary shrieked. "You have cancer? When did you go to the doctor? Why didn't you tell me you had an appointment?" she cried.

"I went into the Web M.D. site on the internet and put in my symptoms. It came back that I have cancer," Gerry declared. "This isn't good," he stated.

"Oh, Jesus H. Christ," Mary cursed. "Don't scare me like that!" she snarled. "I've told you a thousand times. Stay off those internet self-diagnosis websites. God, you make me crazy!" she lectured.

Mary retreated to the kitchen to get herself a glass of cold water and to get away from Gerry for a moment. She returned to the family room and sat back down on the sofa next to her husband. Mary brought a glass of water for Gerry without asking him if he wanted one. Her act was more a gesture of kindness than it was to provide Gerry with something to drink.

"You left work sick?" Mary asked, her blood pressure returning to normal. "Your color doesn't look so good," she observed. "Seriously, what's the matter?"

"I don't know," Gerry replied. "I had a tuna sandwich for lunch and, all of a sudden, I had this weird feeling and threw up. I can't remember the last time I got sick like that. To boot, I've been constipated the past few days. Plus, I'm feeling really tired," he admitted.

"You're feeling really tired, and you're sitting here at midnight, reading crazy internet stuff," Mary shot back. "How about getting some sleep and if you're not feeling better in the morning, we can call and get a real doctor to take a look at you?" she suggested. "Meanwhile, turn that computer off and go get some sleep," Mary ordered.

"You are probably right," Gerry admitted. "I'm going to turn in. I do feel like I need some sleep," he said. "I'm happy to hear the show was good. How about if you tell me all about it in the morning?" He yawned. "Goodnight, Dear," Gerry said as he kissed Mary's forehead and hugged her for dear life.

Gerry slept that night like he had been drugged. The next morning, he woke at around 7:30 and went downstairs to the kitchen to get breakfast. He was starving. His dilemma was deciding on whether to have a big bowl of mini wheats and banana or a stack of blueberry pancakes. Instead of wasting precious time to mix the pancake batter, Gerry decided it would be much quicker to devour his first bowl of mini wheats and a banana. He washed it down with a healthy cup of strong coffee. He figured the coffee would get his system going as he was feeling bloated and constipated. The last thing he ate was the tuna sandwich at lunch yesterday and that didn't last long in his stomach. Probably something in the mayonnaise didn't agree with him, he thought. The bowl of cereal, this morning, went down much better, and the coffee gave him a nice jolt of energy which he sorely needed.

Mary joined him at the breakfast bar and the two were able to catch up on the events of the previous evening. Gerry did a great job of pretending to be interested in every detail of the show at the Performance Arts Center. He even asked some follow-up questions so Mary could further elaborate on the full experience of the evening. Mary knew that Gerry wasn't exactly on the level of a Broadway critic, but she still appreciated the fact that he was letting her talk about the show that she and her friends attended the night before. Even if Gerry's mind was elsewhere, he was putting on a good show for her benefit at this point.

Suddenly, abruptly, Gerry got up from his chair and, without saying a word, quickly headed to the bathroom. Not only did he throw up the breakfast he had just eaten, but on top of that came some brownish contents from his stomach that he couldn't identify. At this point, he couldn't stop heaving. He stayed in the bathroom a full 15 minutes, throwing up the brownish, blackish contents of his stomach. His head felt like it was going to pop. His intestines, however, gave his brain the strong, unmistakable signal that he needed to have a bowel movement. When he was able to stop vomiting, he tried with all his might to empty his bowel, but nothing would pass. Finally, Gerry surrendered. He stood over the sink, washed up, and threw cold water in his face until he couldn't stand it anymore. It was more a delay tactic than anything else, because, in his heart, he knew what was coming next. He opened the bathroom door and took two steps into the kitchen. Looking like he had just finished a ten-mile run, Gerry focused his severely bloodshot, watery eyes in the direction of his wife. Mary stood only a few feet away from Gerry and, from there, she returned his stare. The look on her husband's face horrified her.

"Honey, something's wrong with me," Gerry announced. "Take me to the emergency room," he pleaded.

Mary didn't hesitate or ask any questions. She knew there would be plenty of time for that later. Other than being treated for sprained ankles and broken toes, Gerry hasn't been to a hospital since he got his tonsils out when he was three years old. Back in those days, for the anesthesia, the doctor would spill some ether on a rag and hold it over your nose and mouth until you passed out. That could be one of the reasons why Gerry wasn't big on going to the hospital. For him to ask to be taken to see a doctor was something Mary took very seriously.

Mary quickly got herself organized and jumped into the driver's seat of Gerry's car. Gerry opened the door to the passenger seat and gingerly got in. On the way to the hospital, he let Mary know that he was not feeling right. He had been taking laxatives the past couple of days and they didn't help at all. Gerry just had the feeling that something was not right and, finally, he was listening to what his body was trying to tell him. He called Jimbo's while Mary drove to the hospital and informed the manager on duty that he would not be available for work today either in person or via telephone. Problems, he directed, would have to either be solved by the department managers or put on hold until he returned to work. If it were an emergency, they could give Mark, the general manager, a shot at helping them. But don't expect much there, he thought to himself. Mark was unlikely to make any decision that could directly be traced back to him should it be the wrong one.

Mary dropped Gerry off at the entrance to the emergency room and drove to the patient-parking lot. She was having a dreaded, strange feeling that pulling into this lot would become a familiar routine. After finding a suitable parking spot, she hurriedly made it into the waiting-room area and joined her husband who was busy filling out forms. Luckily, it was a slow day at the hospital, so they only waited an hour to be called. Gerry answered a slew of interview questions that the nurse mustered and then was ushered into a small examination room. There, he was told, a doctor would be in to visit with him shortly.

The room smelled of antiseptic cleaners. Gerry took a seat on the examination table which was covered in a noisy, white, crinkly wax-paper sheet. There was no way to get comfortable on the table. His feet didn't reach the floor, so he tried resting them on a low step stool that was also just barely out of reach. The angle of the back of the examination table reminded him of the abdominal workout bench at the gym. The white crinkly paper-covered cushion that he sat on was hard as a rock. The only thing Gerry could do while he waited for the doctor was to nervously fidget and look at the colorful posters on the wall which showed all sorts of human anatomy diagrams. Gerry was hoping the doctor he got didn't have to use the anatomy posters. With any luck, the doctor already had the information displayed on them memorized. God help me, he thought, if he told the physician he was having stomach problems and the guy had to go to the posters on the wall to see what sort of problems he should be looking for. All the while, Gerry was doing his best to not tear the crinkly paper under him. He didn't know if ripping it would be considered a faux pas and didn't want to find out the hard way. Gerry's goal was to be a model patient. Get a quick diagnosis, a prescription to fix it, and I'm out of here like my pants are on fire, he was thinking.

When the doctor finally came into the room, Gerry was slightly surprised. She appeared to be young. Gerry estimated that her age was somewhere in her late 20s. She also looked like she hadn't slept in a week. After confirming the answers to the same questions that the desk nurse asked him about an hour ago, she informed Gerry that he would be taken to radiology to have an ultrasound done. She wanted a radiologist to have a look to see if there was a blockage detected in his digestive tract. Based on what Gerry was describing, she felt it was a good idea to have a better look at what was going on inside his belly. *Great!* Gerry was thinking. *This is going to be a while*, he thought.

Gerry remembered the times when Mary had ultrasound procedures performed when she was pregnant with the boys. She seemed to be none the worse for wear after the procedure was over, so he figured he could handle it as well. The thought of him having an ultrasound procedure, however, did seem to be a little odd to him. But, then again, he was brand new to the wonders of the medical world. Gerry chatted with Mary while waiting for his turn and was wheeled into radiation an hour later.

Several hours after Gerry's arrival at the hospital, the same sleep-deprived doctor who Gerry had dealt with earlier returned to his examination room. She toted a large white clipboard full of papers and announced that she was ready to review the results of the ultrasound test with him.

The test procedure uses instruments to send high-frequency sound waves through the body tissues. The waves echo back and are picked up by a transducer and displayed on a computer screen. Once the procedure was explained to Gerry, he was able to relate it to the fish finder that he and his buddies use when lake fishing. The same high-frequency waves aimed at the bottom of the lake bounce off swimming fish, and the transducer sends the image of them to a computer screen on the boat's console. Unfortunately, for Gerry, the transducer in the hospital was fishing for something else.

The bleary-eyed doctor explained to Gerry that the ultrasound results examined by the radiologist reveal a blockage in his large intestine. The doctor was not positive as to exactly what type of blockage he has. More testing will be performed beginning tomorrow morning to help figure it out.

The news of Gerry having a blockage certainly helped to account for his complaint that he hasn't had a bowel movement in days. It also gives good cause to explain his throwing up after eating. Hopefully, the blockage is something simple that can be broken up and cleared from his system. At least, that was what the emergency-room physician was going with at this point. She explained to Gerry that he would have to stay overnight and prepare for the further testing in the morning. She suggested to Mary that it might be a good idea for her to go home and bring an overnight bag back to the hospital for her husband.

"Take your time," the doctor suggested.

Mary understood the subtle hint that the doctor was offering. She gave Gerry a kiss on the forehead and told him she'd be back in a couple of hours. A nurse was then called into Gerry's room to assist the emergency-room doctor with what was coming next.

"Gerry?" the doctor began with a questioning tone in her voice. "When you came in, you said you were having some pain, if I recall. On a scale of one to ten, with ten being the most severe, how would you rate your pain right now?" she asked.

Gerry thought for a moment. He was a little bit uncomfortable but didn't feel like he was in severe pain. His pain tolerance was very high, and he was actually getting used to the discomfort he was feeling.

"I don't know," he began timidly. "Maybe a two or a three?" he suggested.

The doctor, tired as she was, was turning on a bedside charm that Gerry didn't see coming.

"Gerry, I need you to work with me here," she instructed. "You said you were having some pain issues. Right?"

The nurse who had been called in to the room to help the doctor took a position directly behind her. Gerry would discover in the coming days, weeks, and months, that nurses are the angels of the medical industry. Most are there because of their concern about the wellbeing of the patients under their care. The assisting nurse assigned to Gerry was standing at an angle so that Gerry could see her, but the doctor would have to turn around if she too wanted to see. The doctor, being fully aware of what was transpiring behind her, didn't care to turn and look. The nurse standing in her rear was animated. She was staring at Gerry, aggressively gesturing upward with her thumb and mouthing the words, "UP! HIGHER!"

At this point, Gerry was unable to comprehend what the two of them were up to, so, he figured he'd just play along and be a good sport. He didn't want to go with a rating of ten as he figured that would be overkill. The nurse was trying to get him to bump it up though, so he figured he'd give it a good boost.

"Eight!" he declared confidently. "My pain level is eight."

Suddenly, the mood in the examination room changed from a get-to-know-you-with-silly-questions atmosphere to a dead seriousness that caught Gerry off guard. The doctor had a stern look on her face and obscured all memories of a few moments ago. Apparently, the pain level reported by Gerry resulted in a total reversal from the lighthearted interaction that he was previously enjoying.

"Nurse, I have a patient who is reporting severe pain," the doctor ordered. "I need an I.V. started. S.T.A.T. Let's get him hydrated, and I need you to get a morphine drip started. I'll be back in a half hour to get his tube inserted."

The nurse who Gerry previously found to be on the playful side was now extremely businesslike and serious. She hurriedly shuffled the papers given to her by the doctor and arranged supplies on the side counter. Before leaving Gerry's room to get the cart and medications ordered by the doctor, she put her hand on his forearm and leaned over his bed.

"Gerry, you did the right thing coming here today," she stated. "It's a blessing you didn't wait until tomorrow. Don't worry. We are going to take good care of you."

Gerry's head was spinning. They were going to get him some strong pain medication, and he didn't realize that he was in that much pain. What did the doctor mean when she said she'd be back to get his tube inserted? He wondered. This is getting a little bit crazy, he thought.

The nurse returned with the prescribed medications and asked Gerry to turn his arm over so she could get at the back of his left hand. Quickly and efficiently, she inserted the I.V. needle and taped it down so it would stay put. She brought over a tree and hung a couple of plastic bags holding clear fluids on it and started the drip. The first bag was to hydrate him. The second bag was the pain medication. The pain medication had an instantaneous effect on Gerry. He literally felt no pain as the medication circulated throughout his body. Consequently, he was beginning to lose the anxiety he felt about being worked on in an emergency room.

When the doctor returned, she told Gerry that it was necessary to have a tube inserted so that his stomach could be voided of its contents.

"The tube would be passed through your nose," she said. "You may find the process to be a little uncomfortable," the doctor advised.

The nurse swabbed a goopy, snotty substance up into his right nostril and instructed Gerry to just let it sit there for a minute. He was then handed a tall glass of water which the nurse said he would need in a few moments. The doctor, who was extending the length of the curled rubber tube, came over to his bed and told Gerry to drink the entire glass of water when she said go.

"Are you ready?" the doctor asked.

Gerry wasn't quite sure what he was getting ready for and, therefore, he didn't feel qualified to give a definitive answer to the question being posed to him. He did figure, however, that the answer they were looking for was in the affirmative, so he replied.

"Yes. I'm ready!" he said in nasally voice.

"Okay, start drinking the water," the doctor ordered as she slipped the tip of the rubber tube in his nostril and began aggressively pushing.

"Swallow! Swallow! Swallow!" the nurse coached. "You're doing great."

As Gerry gulped the water, it washed the rubber tube that the doctor was shoving down his throat, via his nasal passage, all the way to his stomach. Once it was all the way where it needed to be, the contents of Gerry's stomach would be pumped. Even though he was in a morphine-induced, pain-free state of mind, Gerry felt a terrible discomfort in the back of his throat. It felt like he had somehow managed to swallow a plastic straw and it got stuck in his throat. He was also having a difficult time breathing normally. Half of his nose was now out of commission and breathing through his mouth caused even more discomfort. The air he inhaled irritated the nerve endings all along the tube that ran the length of his throat. His gag reflex involuntarily caused him to continue trying to swallow the implanted foreign object.

As numb as he was, Gerry now understood why the doctor was coaching him to report his pain level as being high. Gerry made a living out of reading people's words, thoughts, and motives. A less-caring doctor and nurse wouldn't have gone through the trouble of bending a couple of rules in order to make a very unpleasant procedure a little less stressful. In that moment, as uncomfortable as he was, Gerry felt that he was in good hands. His perception would serve him well in the months to come.

"You did great," the doctor informed him. "Everything is working fine."

"How long do I have to keep this thing in my nose?" Gerry asked.

"I don't have an answer for that one," the doctor replied. "It could be a day or two, or it could be a lot longer. We have you scheduled for a C.T. scan first thing in the morning. Once those results come back, we'll have a better idea of treatment for you. Right now, the best thing for you is to get some rest. I'm having you brought upstairs, away from the emergency room, to a room where you will be more comfortable. Your wife is already up there waiting for you," she pleasantly informed him. "Gerry, I won't be treating you any further," she said as she squeezed his right hand. "I want to wish you the best of luck."

With that, the young, tired doctor turned and exited from the examination room. She was like a ghost to Gerry. He couldn't remember her name. He forgot what she looked like. He didn't even get a chance to thank her for her help. He wasn't sure he wanted to thank her at this point, but his senses told him that she did what she had to do. All he knew was that he had an uneasy feeling that he was recklessly headed down a rabbit hole. One that he didn't care to explore.

Gerry was ushered upstairs to his room by the orderlies on duty. Mary was sitting nervously, waiting for his arrival. She had a difficult time trying to conceal her shock of seeing her husband with a tube taped to his nose and an I.V. in his hand being wheeled into the semi-private hospital room. Gerry had always been so healthy. He suddenly looked beaten and tired. Mary stayed with him, only leaving his side to get a bite to eat or use the bathroom. Finally, the voice on the intercom announced that visiting hours were over. Time for her to leave.

"Honey, why don't you get some sleep?" she said softly as she kissed his forehead. "You've had a long day. I'll see you in the morning."

"Good night, sweetheart," Gerry managed. "See you tomorrow. I have to get myself out of here," he moaned as he closed his eyes.

The next morning, Gerry was informed that he would be taken to radiology for a C.T. scan. He wasn't quite sure about what a C.T. scan was or what it was used for. What he did know was that everyone wanted to know if he was allergic to eggs. Four different people asked him the same question.

"Do you have an egg allergy?" each would ask when it became their turn.

He was hoping they were having over easy eggs with toast and bacon for breakfast. Surely that has to be the reason for everyone's egg-allergy concern. Maybe he was doing so well that it was time to take the tube out of his nose and serve up a big, hearty breakfast as a going-away treat.

Instead, he was wheeled into a room with a large donut-shaped object occupying the floor space in the middle and all sorts of beach-vacation scenes painted on the ceiling. The walls were blank with white paint. The technician helped Gerry slide over to a long table and positioned him in a prone position face up. The table would slide him into the middle of the donut-like object once the procedure began. Gerry was asked again if he was ready. He once again figured the correct answer was in the affirmative.

The C.T. scan was basically a series of x-rays taken from all angles that the computer would piece together for a three-dimensional look. It is an extremely useful tool when looking at soft tissue inside the body. Doctors get a good visual understanding of what is going on internally without having to go in and look surgically. Before the development of the C.T. scan, the only sure way to see what was causing internal problems would be to surgically open the patient up and look around. The egg-based contrast dye that Gerry would have delivered to his system would make the imagery even more resolute. It is an extremely important part of the procedure.

"Okay, Gerry, I am going to start the flow of the contrast dye," The technician said. "I will connect it directly to your I.V., so you do not have to do anything special for me."

The technician used a handheld controller to slide the table, so that Gerry's body could move halfway into the donut. Once the dye had a chance to circulate throughout his body, she would leave the room and enter the secure, insulated control room toward the rear of the x-ray room. From there, she would have total control of the C.T. scanner and the table Gerry was laying on. For now, however, she stayed with him to offer some final instructions and check on his wellbeing.

"Place your hands on the top of the entrance into the machine and leave them there for the entire procedure," she instructed. "Some people feel a little peculiar when we start the flow of the dye, so just let me know if you have any difficulties. You did say you have no allergies to eggs. Right?" she asked.

"No allergies to eggs," Gerry confirmed.

The dye began to flow. Gerry's blood stream carried it throughout his body in no time.

"Is everything okay?" the technician asked.

"As far as I can tell," Gerry reported. "My ass is hot, though," he said. "It feels like I ate a dozen jalapeno peppers last night and they're getting their revenge."

"That happens sometimes," the technician informed with a smirk. "As long as you're not having any breathing issues, I'm going to start the scans. I'll be in the next room. If you need anything, just speak. I'll hear you. Otherwise, just do what the computer voice tells you to do. Try to relax. This won't take too long."

Once the tech left the room, the table Gerry was laying on was fully inserted into the donut. Gerry's hands were behind his head and raised up so he could keep them in the desired position on the outside top of the donut hole. The machine was turned on and the procedure began.

Gerry was, on occasion, instructed by a creepy computer voice to, "Hold your breath." Shortly thereafter, the same macabre voice would tell him to, "Breathe." All the while, the donut he was inserted in sounded like a clothes dryer with a bunch of loose change being tossed around in it. It was loud.

Finally, the procedure ended, and Gerry was wheeled back to his room where Mary was waiting for him. She was sitting there, having a cup of coffee and watching the news on T.V.

"Where'd you go?" she asked.

"I had to have some x-rays done," Gerry told her. "They told me the doctor would be here to go over the results with me in a little while. You don't have to wait around if you don't want. I get the feeling this may take a while," he offered.

"It was so noisy in here last night," Gerry complained. "I don't think I slept more than an hour total. If you don't mind, I think I'll try to take a short nap."

"I'll wait here," Mary informed him. "Try to get some rest. Maybe I can help control some of the noise."

Gerry closed his eyes and fell into a deep sleep. He discovered that hospitals are not the best places to be if sleeping was on the agenda. Patients in the middle of the night were complaining of whatever pain they were having. Nurses were scrambling to help. Every so often, Gerry had to have his oxygen, blood pressure, and pulse measured which required his full cooperation. If he had fallen asleep, he would have to be awakened. Gerry's roommate had the T.V. on all night. He either really enjoyed watching T.V. or didn't even know it was on. Either way, it was just another thing keeping Gerry from getting much-needed sleep. The morning sleep he was about to get was a total relief. Power napping was a required skill for surviving a hospital stay. It is something that should be covered in detail during orientation.

Two full hours later, a woman in a white coat with a stethoscope dangling from the back of her neck and a clipboard in her left hand walked into Gerry's room. She was an attractive woman in her late 30s of medium height, slight build, shoulder-length brown hair, and green eyes. Mary nodded to her as their eyes met and made a gesture to her, indicating that Gerry was sleeping.

"Are you Mrs. O'Driscoll?" the woman in the white coat softly asked.

"Yes," Mary replied. "And you are?"

"My name is Doctor Backus," she replied. "Doctor Christine Backus. I am a surgeon who specializes in colon and rectal surgery. I'm here to help."

"Nice to meet you," Mary said. "Gerry has been out like a light. I don't think he slept much last night."

Without hesitation, Doctor Backus moved to the foot of Gerry's bed and put her hand on his shin.

"Mr. O'Driscoll?" she asked as she put soft pressure on Gerry's lower leg and gently shook it.

Gerry opened his eyes and focused them on the strange woman who was holding onto his leg. His dreams had taken him to the country club where he was enjoying a perfect round of golf with his boys. The dream was so real, so vivid that he could still smell the freshly cut fertilized fairways. His hands still had the feeling that one gets after striking a perfect five iron directly on the sweet spot of the clubface.

*Who is this person, and why am I in bed?* He thought. *Where am I?* he wondered. *What are these tubes doing running from my hand, and why does my throat hurt like I have something stuck in it?*

As the moment passed, Gerry regained full consciousness and remembered his adventures in the radiation room of the hospital. He remembered the tubes and medications being injected into his once-healthy body. Gerry's head cleared, and he snapped back to his reality from the blissful sleep that he was enjoying.

"Yes. I'm Gerry O'Driscoll," he replied. "You can call me Gerry. Who are you?"

"My name is Christine Backus, and I am a surgeon who specializes in colon and rectal surgery," she said.

Gerry and Doctor Backus engaged in ice breaking, get-to-know-you-type questions for the next 15 minutes. They each spoke briefly about their family and hobbies. Doctor Backus did most of the questioning, and Gerry did most of the talking. Gerry felt that Doctor Backus was a good listener. Doctor Backus felt that Gerry was a good talker. Christine seemed to take a genuine interest in Gerry. She not only questioned him about his health but wanted to know about the boys and brought Mary into the conversation whenever possible. Gerry and Mary both found her to be very personable and quite charming. She and her husband would be a nice invite to the club for dinner sometime, he was thinking. Suddenly, however, and without warning, Doctor Backus broke into the presentation that she had prepared for him.

"Gerry, I have reviewed the results of your C.T. scan with the radiologist," she began. "You have a total blockage of your descending colon. The reason you can't have a bowel movement is because you are totally blocked. You need surgery right away. I've scheduled you for ten o'clock tomorrow morning. I need you to sign this consent form," she instructed as she handed Gerry the clipboard that she brought into the room. "Whether or not you sign it, however, I'm going to perform the surgery. You will die if we wait any longer," she stated.

Gerry absorbed the information like he had been hit over the head with a baseball bat. He was stunned. At the same time, he felt like he was in an interview, and the candidate just gave a response to a question he hadn't asked yet but was about to. Doctor Backus, he concluded, was a very direct individual. She just unloaded a bunch of thought-provoking tidbits on Gerry's plate using very few words. He was beginning to think that she was a lot like him.

"What kind of blockage do I have?" Gerry managed. "How experienced are you in performing this procedure?" he asked.

"Don't let my youth and good looks fool you," Christine answered with a smile. "I am a highly seasoned surgeon. Frequently, I am assigned difficult surgeries that other doctors are reluctant to perform. You won't find a better or more qualified surgeon. There may be others who are as qualified in these parts, but you do not have the luxury of time to see if you can find them. As far as the type of blockage that you have, I won't know for sure until I get in there and look," she stated. "The surgery shouldn't take more than three hours. We'll get you in at ten and back to your room sometime in the afternoon."

Gerry liked the fact that this doctor had fighter-pilot cockiness. She convinced him that she felt she knew what she was doing. As confident as she came off, he also felt a sense that she genuinely cared about treating him. He felt the need to confirm what his senses were telling him, however, so he strategized and formulated a few questions to ask her.

In Gerry's business world, interviewing and hiring the right candidate was the key to survival. This, he felt, was no different. Gerry always force-ranked the managers who reported to him. If there were 20 managers on his team, someone had to be ranked number one and someone had to be ranked number 20. His success in the business world revolved around him taking real good care of those who ranked on the top and replacing those who were on the bottom. Similarly, he thought, if there are 100 surgeons in this hospital, someone was the best and someone was the worst. Gerry was thinking he would be dipped in shit before he let any doctor who was ranked on the bottom cut him open. Doctor Backus seemed confident enough in her technical abilities. What if she gets in there and runs into trouble? Technical is one thing, but he felt he had to know whether or not he could trust her in a pinch.

"Doctor Backus," Gerry began. "You say you are the best. I won't find a more qualified or more experienced surgeon in these parts," he paraphrased.

"That's right, Gerry. There really is nobody better," she confirmed. "I am the one who you need to perform this surgery," she replied. "I can help you."

"I bet you have seen thousands of C.T. scans in your career," he stated.

"Thousands," Christine confidently confirmed. "This is what I do every day."

"If you have all this experience and expertise like you claim," Gerry said. "I only have two further questions for you. First, what kind of blockage do I have? Second, what's wrong with me?" he pleaded.

And there it was. Just like that, a pivotal moment of truth occurred between Gerry and his new doctor friend. Every interviewer worth his salt has the ability to come up with a money question toward the end of the meeting. It makes or breaks the new relationship, depending on how the question is answered. As much as Gerry was trying to absorb the blow tied into getting the unsettling news that he needed surgery, he focused himself. He knew this hiring decision would be the most important one of his life. Like any other interview, Gerry had mentally prepared for this one. He knew something was wrong with him. He didn't know he needed surgery, but he felt there was a real good chance he would have to rely on a doctor to help him. A doctor whom, until now, he has never met. Blind off the street.

*What are the qualities and qualifications I am looking for?* He thought. What matters the most? He wanted to know.

Just like interview preparatory notes on a yellow pad, Gerry had mental notes chiseled into his brain for this interview. He needed the questions answered to perfection before a deal, or before a hire would be made. He wanted experience, and Doctor Backus claims to have that covered. He can easily check to confirm that one after the interview. Just like he checked references before hiring a store manager, he could easily confirm the good doctor's qualifications. He required a surgeon who possesses a lot of self-confidence. Gerry used to fly twice a week, and the one quality he demanded in an airline pilot was extreme confidence. 'I hope I can land this plane safely' was not a pilot strategy he wanted to hear when he was boarding an airplane.

Doctor Backus had a supreme confidence in herself that bordered on arrogance. Maybe cockiness was a better description. Regardless, Gerry was enamored by her attitude. He was enjoying the interview much more than Doctor Backus was. He wanted the pressure to be on her.

*Convince me that I should hire you for this job,* He thought. *This is the most critical hire of my life and it's up to you to win the job. Everything is on you,* Gerry said to himself.

Finally, Gerry needed to know if she wanted to do the surgery because she needed the business or because she was a doctor who truly cared about the health of her patients. Both categories of doctors exist in the world, and he needed to know for sure which one she fell into. Experienced, confident doctors are everywhere. Doctors with good bedside manners, not so much. If Christine flunks this part of the interview, she will not be hired. Gerry was not looking for bullshit on his final question. He isn't a doctor, but he felt that Doctor Backus should have a real good idea about the correct answer to his final questions. And he wanted the answer right now.

Gerry's eyes locked in on Christine's as he asked his money questions. She didn't look away for even an instant. Christine was not only a highly skilled surgeon but was also smart enough to know how patients think. She was fully aware that Gerry was interviewing her. She welcomed it like a world-class chess player welcomes a highly skilled challenger. She read his thoughts like he was an open book. *Gerry wants to know if he can trust her to take good care of him,* she concluded. However, he just asked her a very direct question that she didn't care to answer. The way he put her on the spot both irritated her and amused her at the same time. It was irritating knowing that she would have to give him a direct answer to his question. It amused her to think that he had the guts to ask it in the first place.

The patient really doesn't require too much information the day before surgery. The less stress the patient is under, the better off he is. Christine already told Gerry as much as she felt he needed to know. She was already looking out for his best interest. She was amused at the way he drew her into a trap, however. Doctor Backus would not underestimate him again. Christine was at the top of the food chain when it came to the ability to study and learn. She gained volumes about how Gerry thinks by listening to his questions.

Gerry suckered the best doctor in the world into showing him how great she was. Clearly, the best surgeon, with all that experience and expertise, would have the answers to his basic questions.

*I guess I had better pull my foot out of my mouth and give him a straight answer,* she was thinking. *If I give him bullshit, he won't allow me to help him,* she correctly assumed.

It's a difficult undertaking to convince someone whom you have just met that the reason you have chosen the healing profession is because you genuinely care about the people whom you are assigned to treat. Some doctors are in it for the money. They treat the profession totally as a business. Some are in it because they like to experiment. Their passion is toiling in a laboratory. At times, their patients may feel like they are nothing more than the subject of their research. Others are in it strictly to save people's lives. Doctor Christine Backus chose this profession because she has a passion to save lives and battle disease. No doctor on this planet cares about their patients as much as she cares about hers. Nobody is as tenacious when fighting disease. She was fully aware of how she had to answer Gerry's annoying questions in order to convince him of her mettle. It would only take a few words.

"Gerry, you have cancer," she replied.

# 8

His chosen lifestyle was a great one to keep from growing old.

David roared into the driveway on Blueberry Lane in Chevon and killed the engine of his high-performance sport sedan. The home was surrounded by yellow, caution, crime-scene tape. He approached the home with a slow, purposeful stride while absorbing the signals being sent to his brain by his highly alerted senses. David couldn't put his finger on it, but he was getting an odd feeling about what he was about to walk into. The chief called David directly to tell him to meet him at Blueberry Lane right away. There was another murder, and he was to drop whatever he was doing and get to the crime scene. His brother, Rick, greeted him at the door of the sprawling home with a look of panic in his bloodshot eyes. David had been working tirelessly on the Grayson murder which happened less than a mile away from Blueberry Lane. Rick had been scouring Grayson's emails and social-media accounts for clues as to who might have wanted her dead, but, so far, no definitive leads had surfaced. As the brothers embraced, David's older brother disclosed the source of his panic.

"Have you spoken with Mom?" Rick asked.

"A couple of days ago," David replied. "I've been working some whacky hours the last couple of days and haven't had time to call her. You look stressed," he observed dismissively. "What's going on here?" David wondered. "Chief called me and told me to get my butt over here right away –
"

"Dave," Rick interrupted. "Dad's going in for surgery this morning. Mom says he has some sort of blockage in his intestines. She's freaking out about it. When I pressed her for more information, she started crying and told me she'd call later on when the procedure is over with. I couldn't get anything else out of her. She was headed to the hospital when I spoke with her. Said she was going to keep him company until they wheeled him into the operating room. She says the doctor told her that it would be best if she went home once the surgery started. It would take several hours, and Mom would be more comfortable waiting at home. The surgeon will call her to let her know how everything went and then Mom can head back to see Dad when he wakes up."

David felt the blood draining from his face as he tried to process the information his brother just gave him. When he arrived at the crime scene, he was in full investigation mode. His brain was fully focused to gather as much pertinent information as possible about what happened there. With the bomb Rick just dropped on him, his brain was now a convoluted mess. He sensed the worry oozing from his brother's pores but couldn't fathom the extent to which the concern should be shared.

Surgeries were all serious business, he rationalized, but there were certainly degrees of seriousness. At this point, David felt pulled in many different directions. He didn't like the feeling of not knowing what his father was about to go through, but he did know there was nobody tougher. David convinced himself that Dad would be okay. *There's not much we can do for him right now,* David thought to himself. He had to get his brain refocused on the task at hand. There's a dead body in the next room, and the cause of death was not old age.

"Thanks for the news, Bro," David said sarcastically. "Let's finish up here as quick as we can. As soon as we're done, I'll meet you back at the house. Mom is going to need some company. Maybe she'll fill us in a little more about what's going on with Dad. It might not be as bad as it sounds," he said reassuringly. "Meanwhile, I have to get my head back in the game here."

The home on Blueberry Hill Lane was suddenly buzzing with activity. The area was sealed off so the detectives could gather evidence and pictures could be taken. The body needed to be examined and prepared to be sent to the morgue for autopsy. News of the murder had been leaked to the press, and they were swarming the perimeter of the scene. Pushing to get interviews from anyone who came from the house. The chief snuck in through the garage via his dark sedan in order to avoid the throng of reporters in the way. There hadn't been a murder in Chevon in several years and, suddenly, the town was faced with two of them within a couple of weeks. Further, the killing technique in the two crimes was eerily similar. The chief approached David, looking for answers.

"What are you thinking, Dave?" the chief asked.

"Looks like we have a serial killer," David replied. "There are all sorts of valuables that could have been taken but were left behind. This doesn't appear to be a robbery unless something specific is missing that we don't know about yet. We had a canine officer in, and he sat down in front of that cabinet over there. It appears that the victim was in possession of some white powder. Unless it's a plant, the victim was messing around with drug dealers. The question is, what does this victim have in common with Melinda Grayson? I've never seen or heard of this murder method before. Same hole in the back of the head. Same town. It must be the same murderer. Unfortunately, we don't have much to go on in the Grayson killing. All we know is that something solid was stuck into the back of her head and her brains were scrambled. This guy has the same hole. Same scrambled brains," he summarized.

"There's something else about this victim that you probably aren't aware of," the chief declared. "We have been onto him for several months now. The F.B.I. is investigating him as well. His assets have been frozen which could explain the drugs. It's possible he started dealing which might help to explain where he could get the money to buy the stash in the kitchen cabinet. Messing with drug dealers can be dangerous business. Usually, though, they just put a bullet in one's head when they get mad at them. This doesn't line up with their normal method of execution," he reasoned.

"The feds have been all over him for a Ponzi-scheme operation," the chief revealed. "Adamson, over there, is a financial advisor by trade. Before he was dead, he supposedly had quite the convincing charm with senior citizens. In several instances, he visited his marks in the nursing homes where they were being cared for. According to the daughter of one of his targets, when the daughter stepped out to use the restroom on the day of Adamson's visit, he convinced her mother to sign a blank check so her money could be 'better invested.' Instead of investing the old lady's money in conventional accounts, he transferred her life savings into one of his personal bank accounts. He used some of the funds to pay a 'dividend' to other victims who thought they too were investing in brokerage accounts that he represented. All of the money that he convinced his victims to put into these supposed investment opportunities went to Adamson's accounts. He paid out some small interest dividends once in a while to his targets in order to keep them in the dark. He kept them thinking their money was safe and earning yearly dividends when, in fact, their life savings were gone. Because of the age and mental capacity of many of the victims, the scheme was going great for him. Adamson had stolen over four-million dollars over the past three years that we know of. There's a good chance we don't know about all of his victims yet. Mainly because there's a good chance some of his victims don't yet realize their hard-earned savings have been stolen."

David stared at the chief in horror. He vaguely knew about Ponzi schemes and had jokingly spoken to his parents about vetting any financial advisors that they might be tempted to use. Although David would work tirelessly to find the perpetrator of this crime, he was feeling less sympathetic toward the victim with each morsel of information he gained about him.

"How did the feds get tipped off?" David asked.

"Adamson finally ran into a 90-year-old woman who seemed mentally out of it but, in reality, was sharp as a tack." The chief grinned. "She signed over to him access to her remaining one half of a million dollars in savings. Adamson claimed that the money would be moved into a low-risk investment account. It was all the money that the elderly woman had in the world. He took the money and, naturally, spent it on himself. Maybe he used it to help pay for this home we're standing in. Who knows? Anyway, she handed the phony investment document to her lawyer while updating her will. The lawyer did a little digging and immediately called the feds."

The chief sipped coffee from his thermos and observed the activities surrounding the body. His expression changed to one of disgust as he turned to face David.

"The families of this guy's victims are devastated and, to put it mildly, pissed-off," the chief continued. "So, let's review. Adamson's wife left him for only God knows what reason. Usually when a wife moves out with the kids, it means she's not too happy with the husband. I'm giving you that little tidbit in case you need it for future reference," he snidely advised. "Next, he was messing around with drug dealers. Probably gang members. Sometimes, gang members can't be relied upon to look after your good health," the chief reported sarcastically. "Finally, your victim over there stole millions of dollars from elderly people who were eventually going to leave said money to various family members. I'm going out on a limb by providing my expert opinion that there is at least one person in the afore-mentioned groups who wouldn't mind seeing Adamson dead. The question is, who actually followed through with their plan and croaked the guy? What does this murder have to do with the Grayson murder, though?" the chief wondered aloud. "David, it is possible that someone is just randomly selecting victims in this town, and Adamson and Grayson were just unlucky enough to be picked," he stated. "This victim, however, had a variety of people who certainly might have wished to see him harmed. Melinda Grayson didn't have many friends, but we haven't come across anyone who stands out as wanting her dead. Her husband, maybe. But he has a solid alibi. David, you have a lot of work to do," he realized. "See if you can tie the two victims together somehow. That's going to be the key to figuring this out. Don't dilly dally either. We've got to get these cases solved. And I mean, solve them yesterday. Meanwhile, I'm going to go and deal with the reporters outside," he said. "I'm going to tell them we have a murder with some similarities to the Grayson crime. That's all they need to know right now. If they stick a microphone in your face when you leave here, give them nothing but bullshit. Pretend you just came off the basketball court. You know what to do. Thank your teammates. Tell them we'll figure it out as a team. Enlighten them on how the coach gave us a great game plan. Make sure they know that what we are committed to do now is execute. Blah, blah, blah. You know how to handle them. They're not the sharpest tools in the shed, and they're not going to print what you tell them anyway. Either they will twist your words or just plain get it wrong. Just be careful to not get caught saying anything specific," he ordered.

David let the information from the chief sink in. He had read about investment firms who had problems with rogue financial advisors. Today was the first time he had the pleasure of meeting one. Dead or alive. One thing was for sure. David didn't feel any sense that he had to solve the murder in order to vindicate Adamson's good name. If the victim got caught up in using drugs and was killed over a deal gone bad, he could empathize. People do make mistakes and do things they regret. Lots of people David has been exposed to once used illegal drugs and were able to straighten out their lives. However, taking advantage of elderly people, who were dealing with mental disabilities like Alzheimer's, was despicable in David's view.

He tried to mentally put himself in the shoes of the victims of a Ponzi-scheme artist. An elderly person, living out their last few years, would be crushed, knowing they were robbed of their life savings. How would I feel if my elderly parents were taken advantage of by someone like Adamson? What degree of hatred and outrage would I have, knowing that the fruits of my parent's lifelong efforts were stolen by someone of his ilk? He felt no sympathy for the victim. His mind would not be clouded with a feeling of sorrow for Mr. Adamson.

David felt he could rule out this crime having anything to do with whatever drug scene the victim was getting into. His involvement in drugs was just a coincidence, he thought to himself. However, the possibility of a family member of a Ponzi-scheme victim carrying out the crime intrigued David. It was guaranteed that someone in this group wanted Adamson dead. *Let's see who shows up to the funeral with lime-green party hats, red balloons, and purple noise makers,* he thought to himself. Someone is going to tip their hand in this card game. He would have his brother, Rick, research those who were ruined financially and get a list of candidates upfront. Maybe somewhere in that group, he will find a link between the Grayson family and the Adamson family.

David didn't know at the time that he was barking up the wrong tree. He and his brother, Rick, had spent hours at the crime scene, playing out possible scenarios. They looked for any detail that could have been previously missed which may confirm their suspicions and send them down the right path. David,

83

however, felt a euphoric sense of relief, knowing his father had an alibi for this crime. Up until today, he was having difficulty keeping horrific thoughts from surfacing in his consciousness. In fact, he was finding himself staring at the ceiling at two in the morning most nights, thinking about the Grayson crime scene. If he didn't personally know Gerry O'Driscoll, he would have considered him a strong candidate as a suspect in the Grayson murder. David couldn't get the thought out of his head the way his dad reacted to the news of Melinda Grayson's demise. Not only did his father have an interaction with the victim, but it was an unpleasant one. She made some awful things up and had no problem jeopardizing Gerry's source of income for her petty purposes.

David realized that in the real world, the action of trying to take someone's livelihood away could cause a major offsetting reaction. David and Rick never knew their father to be a violent person, however, they had observed him forcefully standing up for his family when cornered. David felt a strong sense of relief knowing that the whacky letter that Grayson sent to Jimbo's corporate had nothing to do with Melinda Grayson's demise. He was positive the killer in the Grayson murder and now the Adamson murder was one in the same. Was it just random, though? Both victims lived in Chevon, not too far from each other. Did the victims know one another? Were they in the same social circles? Was Melinda Grayson somehow involved in Adamson's Ponzi scheme? David knew the answers to these questions would link the murders and lead him to the killer. *Thank God,* he thought, *Dad has nothing to do with this.* He was having an overwhelmingly guilty feeling about even thinking about having to include his own father in a murder investigation.

As David finally began winding down from the crime scene, he started thinking about his father's alibi. He felt terrible knowing how consumed he has been in his work and how it had kept him from being in better communication with his dad. David wasn't very savvy when it came to medical issues, so when his brother told him about his father needing surgery, it did send waves of concern throughout his entire body. It also sent waves of questions throughout his brain.

Suddenly, and right on cue, David felt his phone buzzing in his right pocket. He fumbled around, trying to dig it out so he could see who was looking for him. By the time he was able to retrieve it from his pants, it had stopped buzzing. *Great*, he thought. *This is why I carry a hammerless revolver when I'm not on duty.* Calling a timeout when being assaulted by a gang member in order to be able to draw a defensive weapon from your pocket usually doesn't work. Getting the hammer of a gun caught in pants or a jacket pocket can be a fatal error. Most violent criminals won't wait for you to get it unstuck. He looked at the screen on his phone and saw that the missed call was from 'Mom.' David immediately touched the redial button and nervously waited.

"David?" his mom answered. "David, I just got home from the hospital. Do you know where your brother is? He's not answering either," Mary said frantically.

"He's with me, Mom," David replied. What's going on with Dad? I'm sorry I couldn't get to the phone in time."

"Your father is still in surgery," she stammered. "He's been in there going on seven hours now. Are you two in the neighborhood?" Mary's voice began to rise in tone. "I could use some company, and I want to talk," she managed.

"We'll be there shortly," David said reassuringly. "I'll grab Rick. He's in the next room. No need for you to call him," he said. "I love you, Mom."

"I love you too, honey," Mary managed to reply through her emotional voice. Tears were welling in her already-bloodshot eyes. "Bye," she said as she disconnected.

David and his older brother, Rick, each jumped into their cars and raced to their parents' house on Mason Road in the town of Medbury. David was first to pull into the driveway of the modest home where he and his brother spent their childhood. Just pulling in brought back many fond memories. At this time of year, and this time of day, there would be a serious Whiffle Ball game being played in his backyard. The kids in the neighborhood would gather for some fierce competition after dinner and play until the sun went down. Looking back, Dave and his brother cherished the unsupervised backyard play. There were no umpires. No helicopter parents making sure their kid got to pitch. When problems arose, the kids learned how to work them out. They learned to compromise and to empathize. They learned how to stick up for themselves, their brothers and their sisters, and their teammates. There would be ten to 12 kids choosing teams on their own. It was nothing more than kids being kids. Right now, David wished he had a time machine. He wished that his biggest problem was dealing with a man on second base with two out in a tied game.

David burst into the kitchen like he was Kramer, about to make an Earth-shattering announcement to Elaine and Jerry. His mother, who was sitting at the kitchen table, didn't even flinch. She had her phone pressed to her ear and was taking notes from the deep conversation she was having. In a strong, clear voice, she told whomever she was speaking with that she would get there in an hour. She then disconnected, stood up, walked over to her son, and wept in his arms.

"Mom, what's going on?" David asked softly as he held on to his mother for dear life. "What's happening with Dad?"

As David was asking for information, his brother, Rick, joined them in the kitchen. His face went ashen as he began to process the scene he just walked into. Rick embraced his mother for a moment and then stood back so he could hear the answer to his brother's questions.

"I just got off the phone with Doctor Backus," Mary steadily began. "She is the doctor who performed the surgery on your father. The procedure was originally expected to last up to three hours, but it ended up taking almost eight. She says the fact that Dad is in such good shape allowed his vitals to remain steady enough to keep him under as long as necessary. Your father had a tumor in his rectum which she removed. He also had a larger tumor that was blocking his descending large intestine. This one had actually broken through the wall of his colon and was starting to spread. She removed the portion of his colon along with 30 nearby lymph nodes. The reason she took so long was because she kept sending samples of his colon to the lab. The tissue samples were from what she removed around the margins of the tumor. She wanted to see if cancer could be detected. As soon as she was able to send his samples to the lab with no cancer detected, she could stop the process. Doctor Backus feels she got everything that was cancerous. Five out of the 30 lymph nodes that she removed were cancerous. The doctor feels confident that she got the infected ones, but cautioned that the lymph-node system of the body is complicated and somewhat mysterious. She examined your father's liver and didn't feel or see anything that concerned her. She also had time to examine his entire digestive tract and feels she got all the visible cancer. Your father is in the recovery room now. I'm going to head to the hospital in a half hour to be with him. Doctor Backus said she will meet with your father and me in the morning to better fill us in. She said he did great and feels the operation was a success. You boys should probably wait until tomorrow before you go to visit," Mary cautioned.

Rick and David listened intently to what their mother was telling them. Each tried to comprehend what they just heard. David drifted into a dreamlike state of mind. *This can't be happening,* he thought. *None of this is part of the plan. We are way off target here. Dad is supposed to work a few more years and then enjoy his retirement on the golf course, travelling, visiting friends, and sitting around the pool.* David was in total denial of the facts that were just presented to him and was unable to speak. Rick passed through that stage quickly and felt the need to fight back against someone or something. He wasn't sure of what to do, but he needed answers.

"Mom, did you just say Dad has cancer?" Rick asked. "What kind? Is he going to die?" he pleaded.

"He has colorectal cancer," Mary replied. "The fact that the tumor has broken through the wall of the organ and has spread to some of his lymph nodes makes it 'stage three.' The doctor removed his rectum along with the tumor that was there. She also removed a sizable chunk of his colon along with that tumor. He had two large tumors. Thank God the cancer hadn't spread to the liver. Once it spreads to another organ, it is considered 'stage four.' Not too many people survive 'stage-four' cancer. Your father is a fighter. He has a chance."

"Mom, I want to go with you to the hospital," David insisted as his mind came back to reality. "You shouldn't drive. Your mind is too distracted."

"No," Mary managed. "My friend, Jan, is picking me up in 20 minutes. I don't want too much commotion around your father when he wakes up. He's not going to be a pretty sight, and I know he wouldn't want you boys to see him like that. Come to see him tomorrow afternoon. I didn't want to tell you boys about this over the phone. Thank you for coming here to be with me," she sobbed.

With that last bit of information delivered, Mary flopped into a kitchen chair and wept uncontrollably. Until now, she had been remarkably strong all day. Suddenly, however, the magnitude of the situation her family was thrust into totally overwhelmed her. Her boys sat teary eyed next to her, each with their hands on her shoulders, attempting to console her as best as they could. The three of them hugged and comforted one another.

There was much to come to grips with, and the three of them knew they would have to be strong in support of their patriarch. Their tightly knitted family had just been intruded upon by an interloper. An uncaring, unforgiving, viciously cruel, and tenaciously evil interloper. The O'Driscoll family was about to collectively discover just how much cancer sucks.

# 9

Who is in charge of the "to do" list?

Gerry thought he heard his name spoken in a loud but friendly tone of voice. He also imagined that he felt someone's hand softly rubbing the front of his left shoulder.

*It must be Mary,* he thought. *She must be cleaning,* he reasoned to himself.

Gerry could have sworn he could smell the fumes of an antiseptic cleaner in the air. Anyway, it was time to get up and get ready to go to work. As he awakened, he felt a sense of relief with the knowledge that he could clear his head and make the whacky dream he was having fade away for good. He couldn't remember every detail of his restless night, but he was still feeling horrified at how his brain could conjure up such a nightmare.

Gerry opened his sleepy eyes and focused them on the clock mounted to the white wall directly across from his warm, comfortable bed. The big hand was on the 11, and the little hand was pointed directly toward the number eight. Five minutes before eight, he thought. He assumed that he must have been in a deep, comatose sleep. No wonder Mary was waking him up. He hasn't slept until eight o'clock in years. Plenty of time to get a hot shower, shave, and get to work in time for the closing shift.

*I wonder when I mounted a clock on the wall in our bedroom,* Gerry pensively asked himself.

He neither remembered hanging it there, nor did he recognize it. The large face and hands did, however, remind him of the clock that hung behind Mrs. Mac Guillicutty's desk. The one that was mounted just above the blackboard in his second-grade classroom.

Suddenly, Gerry gained full consciousness. It was as if he just realized the severed head of his favorite horse was in bed with him, spilling blood all over his satin sheets and staring at him with cold, dead eyes. This was no dream he was waking up from.

The last thing he remembered was being wheeled into the operating room. Mary was holding his hand as she kissed his forehead and told him how much she loved him. The lights in the operating room were extremely bright, he recalled. The air felt so clean and easy to breathe but was also freezing cold. The last person Gerry spoke to was the anesthesiologist. He was of Asian descent and had a warm, friendly bedside manner. He took his time with Gerry in the surgery-preparation area, making sure every detail was carefully covered. He leaned over to speak to Gerry as the gurney carrying him was wheeled over to the middle of the operating room.

"Gerry, you okay?" the anesthesiologist asked.

The look in Gerry's eyes and the nod of his head indicated that he was as ready as he was going to be.

"You go sleep now," he assured.

These were the last words Gerry heard before everything went black. Now, like the Phoenix, he was coming back to life.

"Nurse," Gerry shouted.

"Hi there," Nurse Leslie responded as she came into the recovery room where Gerry was laying. "My name is Leslie. Glad you're back with us." She smiled.

"Leslie, what time is it?" Gerry panicked. "Is it eight at night or is it eight in the morning? The last time I remember looking at a clock, it was late morning just before I went into surgery," he said.

"It's eight o'clock in the evening," Leslie replied. "Your surgery took a little longer than expected," she informed. "There's someone special upstairs waiting to see you. I'll be right back. I need some help to get you out of recovery and up to your room. Give me five to ten minutes, and we'll get you out of here," Leslie promised.

Gerry continued to stare at the clock on the wall. He figured he was in surgery at least eight hours. This can't be good, he thought. *Doctor Backus must have opened me up and found cancer everywhere,* he reasoned. The surgery was supposed to take two to three hours, and, here, it is eight o'clock in the evening. *I'm screwed,* he was thinking.

Gerry felt an itch on his nose, but when he went to scratch it, he discovered both arms had rubber tubes attached, running clear fluid into them. Moving either arm was possible but uncomfortable. He still had that raspy feeling in the back of his throat and felt the presence of the tube still running through his nose and down to his stomach. His abdomen felt a little peculiar, but the pain meds were helping to mask the reason for it. Gerry's incision ran from two inches above his navel straight to the base of the top of his penis, a few inches from where the Foley catheter was inserted. He would endure living with the Foley for the next seven days. His right hand unintentionally rested on the squishy colostomy bag attached to his lower right abdomen. Gerry had no idea what it was. He was too numb to ask and, at this point, didn't really care. All he wanted to do right now was to see his wife.

The journey from the recovery room to his semiprivate residence for the next seven days seemed to take forever. It was all Gerry could do to keep his eyes open, however. The jolt of adrenaline he got from his rude awakening a few moments ago had subsided. The anesthesia from the surgery hadn't worn off completely, and Gerry felt like he had pulled an overnight shift at work. The nurse was continually asking him questions about "nothing in particular", and Gerry was able to provide the obligatory, drug-induced, nonsensical answers to the best of his ability. Finally, the orderly exited the elevator to the sixth floor and steered Gerry's bed toward the hallway where Mary stood, waiting to see her husband. Gerry didn't see her at first, but he felt a familiar hand take his. Mary leaned over the rails of Gerry's hospital bed and greeted him like he had just come home from a day at the country club.

"Hi, honey," Mary said softly. "How are you feeling?" she wondered.

Gerry looked up into Mary's eyes with the same feelings as he did on the day they were married. Hours ago, when he was wheeled into the operating room, he understandably wondered about whether he would ever see her again. He heard but ignored the question she was asking. Gerry had a question of his own.

"Mary, am I going to live?" he managed.

"Yes, honey. You are going to live," Mary replied wishfully.

"I should have bought that boat," Gerry mumbled. "I can't believe I didn't buy that boat," he cursed.

"We'll talk about the boat in the morning, Gerry," Mary said wearily. "How about if you get some sleep? It's been a long day for you," she suggested.

"All I did was sleep today," Gerry replied. "You're the one who looks like you could use some rest. Why don't you go home and get some sleep?" he asked.

The two argued back and forth for the next 30 minutes about who needed sleep the most. Both were thrilled with the banter and each was convinced they got the better of it. Gerry's night nurse, Anna, came and introduced herself while taking his vitals for the first time of the evening. Anna was so reassuring to Mary that her husband was in good hands and would be well-cared for, that Mary felt it would be okay to leave for the night. Mary kissed Gerry on the forehead and tucked his hospital blanket up to his chin. She told him that she would be back first thing in the morning.

Mary didn't want to leave Gerry's side but knew some rest would do both a lot of good. The day had been long and stressful. To this point, Mary had been solid as a rock, but as she strolled into the waiting room where her close friend was waiting to drive her home, her emotions came crashing down on her. As the two friends tightly hugged one another, Mary burst into tears from her panic, from her fear, from her anger, and from her compassion. On the ride home, she had cried herself out. *Time to stop feeling sorry for ourselves,* she concluded. *We have a major brawl on our hands.* Mary convinced herself that no matter what, she would stay strong, especially when she was in Gerry's presence. If she had to have moments of weakness, it would be when she was alone. In the coming months, Mary would discover that her plan was easier said than done.

***

Early the next morning, Gerry said goodbye to Anna, the night nurse, and began his rehabilitation routine. He felt like he had just completed a marathon. His body was sore and tired from head to toe. He had never felt fatigue like this in his life. Anna taught Gerry how to stay ahead of his pain levels by pushing the red button leading to the dispenser whenever he felt his pain levels rising. There were times when he needed pain relief, but when he pushed the button, he discovered he had already exceeded the allotted dosage. He would later find out that each time he pushed the button, the staff had a record of it. When Gerry suggested he would like to switch to a pain pill instead of the drip, he was shown the frequency of his button pushing. Best leave the pain management to the nurses, he concluded.

The daytime nurse introduced herself as Monica. Monica was a no-nonsense, middle-aged woman who had 20 years of nursing experience under her belt. She had seen thousands of patients, just like Gerry, in her career and treated each accordingly. She quietly and quickly took Gerry's pulse, blood pressure, and blood-oxygen level just as Anna had done every couple of hours throughout the night. She then gave an instruction to Gerry which took him by surprise.

"OK. Time to get up and go for your walk," Monica ordered. "I need you to take it slow at first. Swing your legs over the edge of the bed, and I'll get your tree set up. Come on! Let's go! You're not going to get any better just laying around," she pushed.

Gerry didn't think he could move, never mind get up out of bed and walk.

"Do you realize I just had a major surgery?" he asked incredulously.

"Yes! Let's go! Get up!" Monica demanded. "If you want to get your butt out of this hospital, you have to get your system going. The only way to get your system going is to move. Come on. One leg at a time," she instructed.

Gerry managed to get both legs on the floor, and, for the first time since his surgery, he stood up straight. He reached both arms up as high as he could and breathed like it was his first breath. As he exited his room and entered the bustling hallway of the sixth floor, he instinctively grabbed the side rail running along the walls. He didn't know if he could make it the 50 feet to the nurse's station and back, but set it as his goal. To Gerry, completing the short walk felt like he was attempting to climb Mount Everest. He reached the nurse's station, exhausted, and felt that perhaps he had attempted to take on more than he could handle. The thought of a 100-foot walk beating him up the way it was doing both frightened and enraged Gerry. He used his anger for the first time to spark the fight he would need. One foot in front of the other. One step at a time. He thought.

"Need some help, Gerry?" Nurse Monica offered. "Don't try to do too much on your first outing," she instructed.

"Leave me alone," Gerry snarled. "If I need your help, I'll ask for it," He said breathlessly.

Suddenly, Gerry took to the offensive. *I'm not taking this crap laying down*, he thought to himself. *If this disease kills me, it's not going to be due to lack of effort,* he reasoned.

Gerry shuffled his feet and clung to the handrail for dear life as he navigated the final 20 feet of hallway leading back to his room. Once there, he collapsed in silence into the padded bedside chair conveniently placed for just such a purpose. The journey fatigued him but strengthened his resolve to get better. He felt a sense of shame in the way he snapped at the nurse. Gerry was used to taking care of himself. He motivated himself. Coached himself. However, he realized if it wasn't for Nurse Monica, he would still be laying prone in that hospital bed. His recovery was in his own hands, but he needed the expertise of the nursing staff to guide him.

Gerry decided, at that moment, to be as ideal a patient as he could be. He wanted to get himself out of this mess he was in and had no idea of the steps needed to be successful. Gerry needed the nurses much more than they needed him.

"Monica, I'm sorry for snapping at you back there," Gerry said sheepishly. "I know you are being helpful to me, and I appreciate it. Just smack me around if you find me getting out of line in the next few days. Okay?" he asked.

"Gerry, that was nothing," Monica chuckled. "You wouldn't believe some of the stuff we get to deal with in this place. Just follow instructions and do your best. We'll have you out of here as soon as possible," she promised. "And I don't need an invitation to smack you around, either. I'll be back a little later. Doctor Backus is making her rounds and should be here in an hour. Hit the alert buzzer if you need anything from us," she instructed as she exited his room.

Mary passed Monica in the hallway as the latter was leaving Gerry's room and heading back to the nurse's station. She took a deep breath, not knowing what she would find, and entered Gerry's room.

"Hi, honey," Mary beamed. "I wasn't expecting to see you sitting up already. You look good," she lied.

Gerry sat slouched in the bedside chair, sporting his hospital-issued, no-skid, blue-and-white socks with rubber strips glued to the bottom of each. His green-and-white checkered gown with one spaghetti tie behind his neck and the other secured in middle of his back left his sorry-looking bare ass exposed as he walked the hallways. Gerry had one tube inserted through his nose, leading all the way to his stomach. Another tube, less visible at the entry point, was inserted through his penis, extending to his bladder. The other end of that thick tube attached to a clear bag that hung from the side of his bed, containing his urine. Intravenous tubes inserted via the needle that was stuck into the back of his left black-and-blue hand fed him fluid, pain killer, and various antibiotics to ward off infection. The opposite end of those tubes led to the wheeled tree-like apparatus where transparent pouches holding medicine fed into his system and bodily fluids drained out. Under his gown, glued to his abdomen was a colostomy bag collecting intestinal waste product. Gerry hadn't shaved or showered in three days. His hair was a cow-licked matted mess, and he smelled like a dead goat. His three-day-old salt-and-pepper beard was scratchy and scraggly.

"Sweetheart, you have low standards," Gerry declared. "I need a hug, though. Just be careful you don't knock a hose out of me. It can't be pleasant putting them back in," he reasoned.

Mary helped Gerry to rise from the chair and climb back into bed. She took his place by sitting in the padded chair and leafed through a magazine she had purchased in the lobby gift-shop. The morning exercise had worn Gerry out, and he felt a power nap would do him some good to get ready for his next hike. Sleep and hospitals mix about as well as oil mixes with water, Gerry was discovering. Predictably, just as he started to nod off, there was a knock on the door. Doctor Backus floated into the room as if she was riding a hover board. "Good morning, sunshine," she declared. "How are you doing?"

"You tell me," Gerry managed as he opened his eyes and looked up. "How am I doing?" he asked.

"Gerry, you had a big surgery," Doctor Backus began. "I removed a large tumor which was blocking your descending colon." Doctor Backus drew a diagram on the white board mounted to the wall opposite Gerry's bed and pointed to the area where the tennis-ball-sized tumor had taken root. "You also had a fairly significant tumor in your rectum. I felt it was necessary to remove your whole rectum. I use a little trick I learned to sew a piece of your colon to make the shape of a sack. A fake rectum if you will. It won't work as well as the one God gave you. However, the one I made for you doesn't have any cancer in it. I removed 30 surrounding lymph nodes and found cancer in about one-third. The good news is, as I moved further away from where the main tumor had busted through the wall of your colon, no cancer was detected. We were able to keep you under long enough for me to continuously send samples of your colon to the lab until we found clean margins. That's what took so long. Because you are in good-enough shape to tolerate being under anesthesia, I could be more thorough. I didn't see any cancer in your liver or in your intestines," she assured him. "I had to pull a piece of your colon through your abdomen, and I stitched it into place. You'll see it sticking up out of your belly when you have to change your bag. We call it a stoma. You'll have a colostomy bag fitting over it which essentially collects your waste. The good news is, I can reverse the process and hook your system back together once everything has properly healed in there."

Doctor Backus drew a circle on her diagram around the area where the cancer was removed and turned back to further explain her handiwork. She detected a concern from the look on Gerry's face.

"The colostomy is not permanent," she said, sensing Gerry's distress about the subject. "We'll talk about a timeline after you visit with your oncologist. Gerry, I got everything I could see. The surgery was successful," she confirmed. "Now, pull up your gown and let me look at your incisions. Then, I'll be happy to leave you to get some rest."

"Are you sure you got all of the cancer?" Mary asked.

"I got everything I could see," Doctor Backus replied as she inspected her handiwork. "Your incision looks great. You won't be showing off your abs at the beach this summer, but, to me, it looks perfect."

"What's next?" Gerry wanted to know. "You said something about an oncologist. That's a cancer doctor, right? If the cancer is gone, why do I need a cancer doctor?"

"I'm going to recommend you go to see Doctor Hearms," Doctor Backus began. "He's very good at what he does. His office is in the building opposite to where I'm located. It will make things convenient for you on days that you have to visit with both of us. The regimen he will prescribe is fairly standard in this type of cancer. There's no need for you to be traveling all over the place to get your treatments," she advised. "Gerry, as it stands right now, I think I got all of the cancer. It only takes a couple of rogue cells to grow and cause more trouble in another location of your body. Doctor Hearms is going to recommend chemotherapy to try to kill any cancer cells that I couldn't see. It's impossible, with the naked eye, to see minute, individual cells that may be cancerous. The kind of cancer you have would typically spread to the liver or lungs if it did spread. You'll increase your chances of survival if you see an oncologist," Doctor Backus stated. "Right now, it is important for you to recover from your surgery and get some of your strength back. You are going to need all the strength you can muster to fight the battle ahead of you. Gerry, to put it mildly, you are going to have a shitty year!" she flatly stated.

Gerry thanked Doctor Backus for what she had done for him, both in the operating room and at his bedside. She was not only his surgeon, but, now, he relied on her to be his teacher, coach, and mentor. Doctor Backus read her patients like no other. She knew Gerry wanted the unvarnished truth and had no problem delivering it to him.

"One more thing, Gerry," Doctor Backus offered as she walked toward the door. "You can beat this. It's not going to be easy, but you can survive. Be strong. I'll see you sometime tomorrow," she said.

Later in the day, after another grueling stroll through the hallways of the sixth floor, Gerry decided he had better call out sick to Jimbo's. Mary had called to inform Lynn in human resources a couple of days prior about everything that was going on with Gerry. She told Lynn to feel free to share the information with the team. Steve, the merchandising manager, had sent Gerry a good-luck text the night before surgery, but Gerry didn't have a chance to respond. Gerry touched the autodial on his phone and patiently listened as the automated operator listed the numerical options available. Press one for store hours, two for directions, three to speak with an operator, etc. etc. Gerry grinned at Mary as he chose option three and then moaned as if being tortured while he listened to the on-hold music of Abba's rendition of *Mamma Mia*. Finally, the operator picked up.

"Thank you for choosing Jimbo's Furniture and Firearms. My name is Georgina. How may I direct your call?" came the cheerful voice on the other end of the line.

"Georgi. It's Gerry," he announced. "How are you?"

"Oh my God. Gerry? It's so good to hear your voice," Georgina screeched. "Gerry, are you okay? We are worried sick about you around here."

"I'm doing fine, Georgi," Gerry assured her. "Just hearing your smiling voice brightened my day. Everything is going as well as can be expected. I'll be back to work in no time," he stated. "What manager is on duty? Is Mark around?" he asked.

"Mark was here, but he stepped out with Lynn a few hours ago," Georgina informed him. "I haven't seen them come back yet. Steve is around. I'll patch you through to his line. Gerry, you take care of yourself and get better, okay? We'll be fine here. We all want you back here in one piece," she said.

"Thanks, Georgi," Gerry replied. "You're the best. I'll talk to you soon. Okay?"

For a split second, Gerry felt like he was back in the pressure cooker of his job at Jimbo's. His sleepless nights gave him time to reflect on the recent turn of events he was experiencing. Just a few short days ago, cancer was not any part of the equation for Gerry. Now that it had suddenly reared its ugly head, his perspective on life had drastically changed. Faced with the fact that his life could be coming to an abrupt end, Gerry thought of things he wished he could do. Being wheeled into the operating room for a major surgery was a humbling experience for Gerry. While lying face up on the gurney, surrounded by medical personnel, he didn't know if he would ever again regain consciousness. There was one thing he was certain of when he did finally open his eyes and clear his head after his surgery. He never once regretted not spending more time at work. He never thought to himself, if only I had put more emphasis on my job. If only I had disrupted my family by moving them from state to state for some company or for some job. If only I skipped more family events to be at work. If only I had worked more than I did, how much happier I would be as I'm lying here on my potential death bed. If I get a second chance at life, Gerry thought, things are going to be different.

"This is Steve, how may I help you?" Steve answered the external call showing on his handheld.

"You can give more to the American Cancer Society for one thing," Gerry instructed. "I blame you, Steve. How could you let this happen?" he asked.

"How could I let this happen?" Steve replied. "How could you let this happen?" he exclaimed. "Gerry, it's great hearing your voice. Are you okay? You have to get back, brother. I have no freaking clue about operations, and they want me to cover for you while you're out," he halfheartedly pleaded. "Gerry, seriously, you have us scared shitless. How did it go?" Steve asked his friend.

Gerry filled Steve in on every detail. The two of them are close-enough friends that Gerry felt he could trust Steve with his life. It did both of them good to be able to talk. Steve let Gerry know that he would handle the necessary communications. He assured Gerry that he would have Lynn from human resources give him a call to arrange the leave of absence that Gerry would be required to take for the next six weeks.

"Steve, I left my briefcase in the bottom drawer of my desk," Gerry said. "I'll have someone come by to pick it up in the next couple of days. There are things in there I could use to keep my mind occupied. I'll probably send Mary or one of the boys over. Just leave it at customer care in the locked cabinet if you would."

"Will do, my friend," Steve reassured. "You take care of yourself. I'll call you in a day or two," he promised.

Gerry spent the remainder of the day walking the halls of the hospital ward with Mary and power napping. He wasn't allowed anything to eat or drink yet, but, as a treat, the nurses would bring him small cups of ice chips which were soothing on Gerry's dry tongue and cracked lips. Luckily, for Gerry, he had Mary to help manage the flow of incoming calls, text messages, and visitors. All the contacts were well-intentioned and greatly appreciated, but Gerry didn't have the energy or stamina to take each one and respond in turn. Mary would screen his calls and schedule his visitors for the next seven, long, grueling days of recovery. The only people allowed free access to Gerry were Mary and the two boys. Otherwise, Gerry would welcome and appreciate visitors provided the visits were short. He had a new job to do, and it was labor intensive. Getting healthy would take all of Gerry's time and effort. He was fighting against a formidable opponent that would be relentless in its bid to take over his body. It was okay for Gerry to become selfish.

The boys came for a visit on the evening following Gerry's surgery. Mary gave them a heads up as to what they were walking into. Dave and Rick were used to their father's role as the rock of the family. They viewed him as being bulletproof. Tough as nails. Despite the warning, neither was mentally prepared for the sight they would see as they rounded the corner and entered Gerry's room.

Luckily, Gerry was deeply immersed in a much-needed power nap when the boys first laid eyes on him. He looked like he was dead. Both tried to comprehend what they were seeing, but neither was successful in hiding their emotions. Mary stood to greet them, and, with her index finger, she vertically covered the middle of her lips, pointing straight up to her nose, signaling them to be quiet. Then, she moved toward them and gave each a hug. Mary read the shock on their faces and knew Gerry wouldn't want to upset them the way he was unconsciously doing. She let them take a good look and then escorted them to the waiting area next to the nurses' station for some coaching.

"Listen, you two," Mary began. "Your father does not want to see you guys all freaked out by the way he looks. Get over it!" she demanded. "This is how it is right now. He needs you to be strong and be yourselves with him. Take a deep breath, get your act together, and try again. This time, act like you're happy to see him. I know he'll be ecstatic to see you! You are all he's been asking for," she stated. "How are the boys? When are they coming to visit? He asks constantly. Don't let him down. I'll go and wake him up and then you can come back and cheer him up," she instructed.

Dave and Rick took their mother's advice to heart. This time, they entered Gerry's room, noisily arguing about who would win the playoff N.B.A. game tonight.

"What's up, Dad?" Rick casually interrupted the conversation that he was having with his brother. "What's your opinion about tonight's game?" he asked.

"I think if the Celtics are able to win the championship," Gerry began. "I'll get a shamrock tattoo on my ass."

Gerry's comment struck the boys as comical. Their father never mentioned getting a tattoo and always frowned on the idea to the family. "You can't just erase those things if you get sick of them, you know," he would always comment. The thought of Gerry getting one was hilarious to everyone in the room.

"Dad," Rick managed through his laughter. "If you get one, I'm getting one too."

"Oh no, you're not!" Mary chimed in.

"Oh yes, we are," David concurred.

The boys kept Gerry company until the announcement of the end of visiting hours at eight o'clock. Gerry's spirits soared. He thanked the boys for coming and asked a favor before they left.

"Can either of you stop by at Jimbo's in the next day or two?" he asked. "My briefcase is being held at the customer-care desk, and I want to have it here," he stated.

"I'll be in the neighborhood in a couple of days," David volunteered. "Who do I ask for?"

"My friend, Steve, is the manager. You can ask for him," Gerry instructed. "If you just go over to the customer-care desk, though, you'll probably run into Clare or Sydney. They work most afternoons together. Both are great people. Clare is a sweetheart. Young college kid. Syd is slightly older. He's a great guy. You may find him a little timid at first, but once you break through his façade, he can be pretty funny. Where I grew up in the Boston area, we'd refer to him a being a real pissah," he described.

"Good God, Dad," David smirked. "Enough with the Boston accent. You people leave out r's when they belong and add them in when they don't. Paak the cah in Atlanter lately?" he asked. "Anyway, we have to go. The nurses are going to kick us out. I'll see you tomorrow. Don't forget, the game starts in an hour," he reminded.

Dave and Rick patted Gerry on the leg, and Mary kissed his forehead before departing for the evening. For the next couple of hours, Gerry felt more alone than he had ever felt in his life. The basketball game on the television provided some meaningful distraction for him, but it wasn't enough. He had to keep his mind in a positive state. Negative thoughts would be embraced as cold comfort for the enemy.

Anna, the night nurse, came to take Gerry's vitals for the second time since she arrived for her shift. She sensed he was struggling. Maybe he just needs someone to talk to, she thought.

"How is your pain level?" Anna asked.

"Probably a six or a seven," Gerry replied. He was getting pretty good at gauging his pain and keeping it under control. "I just pushed the magic pain-relief button so it should be okay in a couple of minutes," he reported.

"Okay, good," Anna replied. "What do you do for a living, Gerry?" she asked. Anna was hoping to distract Gerry from his perceived state of mind.

"I'm in retail," Gerry replied. "I've been in it my whole working life. Right now, I work as the operations manager at Jimbo's Furniture and Firearms. Have you ever heard of it?" he asked.

"My son works at Jimbo's," Anna replied. "Do you know Sydney Barrett?"

"Your son is Syd?" Gerry exclaimed. "Of course I know him. He works under my supervisory umbrella," he said. "What a fine young man your son is. And what a coincidence this is," he complimented.

"I can't believe I didn't put two and two together," Anna said. "Syd told me this morning about how his favorite manager got sick and was in the hospital. He was extremely upset about it. Gerry, I don't know if you realize it, but my son looks up to you. He lost his father to cancer several years ago, and it devastated him. He says you are a fatherly figure to him. Someone from whom he seeks advice. I want to thank you for being there for Syd when he needs someone other than his mother to talk to," she said.

"It's been my pleasure," Gerry replied. "I love doing anything that I can do to help fine young people like Sydney. I find it extremely rewarding. You should be very proud of him," he stated.

"I am," Anna admitted. "What about you, Gerry?" she asked. "Do you have kids?"

"Two boys," Gerry replied. "They both work in law enforcement. My oldest is a computer genius. They use him to help find evidence buried deep in hard drives of the criminals they are after. My youngest is a hotshot detective. He chases all sorts of bad guys. Most of his time is spent on murder investigations. He has a God-given gift of being able to figure out who dunnit," He laughed.

"Well, I guess I won't have to worry about dealing with either of them," Anna smiled. "I can't believe I never put two and two together before now with you under my care. It's a small world, don't you think?" she asked. "I'm going to help you to get better, Gerry. Don't worry, you are in good hands," she assured him.

"When do all of these tubes come out?" Gerry asked. "I know it's only been a couple of days, but I really want to go home. No offense, but this place sucks," he stated.

"Gerry, we have to get your system regulated," Anna replied. "Infection is what we most worry about after a major surgery like the one you had. You're doing great, but we have to make sure your body is healing. You can't eat or drink anything yet, so we can't remove those tubes. We have to wake up your digestive system and get you used to your colostomy. It's going to be several more days, Gerry. Just keep exercising. You'll never get out of here if you don't go for your walks. We want to see you up and about four times a day. Your nurses will take care of the rest. See if you can get some sleep, Gerry. I'll be back in a couple of hours to check up on you. We'll chat then."

For the rest of the night and throughout the next morning, Gerry dealt with the noise and the boredom of hospital living. He would sleep a couple of hours at a time and be awakened by either noise, pain, or someone on staff coming to take his temperature, blood pressure, pulse, and oxygen levels. All were temporary interruptions but effective means of sleep-depravation. Gerry found a rhythm of napping, reading, watching television, and short walks broken up by the occasional visitor or phone call that Mary allowed. He was tired, and, to Mary, he looked it. She and the nurses would tend to his wellbeing more than anyone else for the duration of his stay.

***

Dave and Rick separately wandered in to visit with their father the following evening as promised. Gerry reminded Dave about picking up his briefcase at Jimbo's. He needed mind occupying material, and he figured he could spend some of his time analyzing profits, payroll-staffing levels, and sales-verses-inventory reports. He wanted to get his mind back to normal in the worst way. Even if it included working.

"How's work going for you guys?" Gerry asked. "I know I'm not supposed to ask about investigations, but did you catch the killer of that woman over in Chevon yet?"

"Dad, there was actually another murder in Chevon last week," David replied. "Not to get into details, but we think it's the same killer."

"Chevon again?" Gerry asked. "You know, we always say at work that you have to take a special test to live in Chevon. Nine out of ten of our problem customers live in that town. Birds of a feather flock together," he mused.

"Test?" Rick laughed. "Dad, what test? You always say there's a Chevon test. What is it, like a driving exam?" he wondered.

"No." Gerry smiled.

Gerry was totally amusing himself right now. Laughter can be a powerful medicine. He figured he might as well take the opportunity to enlighten a couple of cops about the customer-service industry and give himself a good dose of humor while he was at it.

"Town representatives of Chevon ask you a series of yes or no questions before they allow you to buy a house and move into town," Gerry deadpanned sarcastically. "Here's a quick sample of the questions you'll be asked if you want to purchase a home there:

1. Have you ever made a high-school-age, grocery-store cashier cry while berating her for ringing the customer in front of you too slowly?
2. Have you ever sent a three-quarters-eaten steak back to the kitchen because it isn't cooked to your liking and then blame the waitress to justify not tipping her?
3. Do you refuse to put your shopping cart in the parking-lot cart corral even if the corral is only 20 feet away, and the wind is howling?
4. Do you write complaint letters to corporate offices of every retail store you patronize, threatening to never shop there again unless you get some sort of compensation due to the rudeness of the staff? Plus, demand additional compensation for the inconvenience of having to write the letter?
5. Do you return nonreturnable items like used underwear, swimwear, and socks to your favorite store in exchange for the exact same, unused items?
6. Do you swear at and threaten the employees involved with number five above when they point to the sign that says the items you are trying to return are not returnable?
7. Do you demand free delivery as well as pain and suffering compensation when your furniture or appliance-delivery truck arrives five minutes after the scheduled timeframe?

8. Do you inform your hairdresser when you are paying that the reason you are not going to tip them is because they took too long with the customer before you?
9. Do you make guests to your home park around the corner if they are not driving at least a 40-thousand-dollar car?
10. Do you consider yourself a thoughtful, caring individual who would be an asset to our loving community?

"If the answer to any of the above questions is 'no,' you won't fit in to the Chevon community and should look elsewhere for your residence," Gerry advised. "We'll ask a secondary set of questions only if we get the desired answers to this preliminary set."

"Dad, I think you are taking too much pain medicine," David advised. "You are definitely close to losing your mind if you haven't already lost it." He laughed.

"Maybe," Gerry conceded.

"Thanks for brightening my evening, guys," Gerry beamed. "I really appreciate you stopping by to keep me company. You're going to get kicked out of here in five minutes," he said. "Visiting hours have expired. By the way, part of the next set of questions for Chevon residents involves your conviction about how rules apply to everyone else. People who stay after visiting hours only inconvenience patients that they don't know. It's not their problem that some sick person is trying to get some needed rest. Chevon residents are entitled to stay for as long as they want. Plus, they can make all the noise that they want to make. You have to get with the program if you truly want to live in Chevon," Gerry joked.

Both boys stared and shook their heads in perplexity.

"Good night, boys! See you tomorrow? And don't forget my briefcase, Dave," he demanded.

David and Rick left Mary and Gerry alone. They knew their mother wanted to spend a final few moments alone with Gerry before she went home for the evening. As they rode the elevator to the garage level, Dave looked at his brother who seemed deep in thought.

"You okay, Rick?" David asked. "Dad seemed in pretty good spirits tonight. He looks terrible, I know, but he's got a good positive attitude. I feel better about him than I did yesterday. That's for sure."

"I feel better about him too," Rick replied. "He said something that struck me a little strange though."

"What did I miss?" David asked.

"Think about that list of questions that Dad was kidding us about," Rick replied. "There is truth in comedy. Both of our dirt-napping friends have evidence on their hard drives which would lead me to assume that they answered yes to every Chevon-admittance test question. Coincidence? Maybe. Dad says everyone in that town has the same mannerisms. You know how he exaggerates though. I'm starting to think there might be a link in all of this to the killer's motivation. Maybe it's helpful, and maybe it isn't, but God only knows we haven't been given a lot to go on," he reminded his brother. "Anyway, I'll see you tomorrow, bro. My car is on this level. It's time for me to get back to reality," Rick noted as he stepped out of the elevator and into the concrete garage.

"See you tomorrow, Rick," David replied. "Keep thinking! You never know what we might stumble upon," he encouraged. "One of us could run into the killer tomorrow and not even realize it. Remember, given the option between the two, I'd much rather be lucky than good," David shouted to his brother as the elevator doors slid closed, sealing him off to be alone with his thoughts.

# 10

There must have been a full moon.

Sydney was awakened by an annoying, recurring dream.
He was back in high school, wandering the corridors, searching for his classroom. Aimlessly, he strolled the empty halls that were abandoned at the bell by all the other students who were successful in finding their rooms. He begins to get frantic, trying to find the location where the crucial final exam that he didn't study for will be administered. Surely, the test was already being handed out to his student competitors, but where was he supposed to be? What was the subject? Better move faster to find out where the room is and what the topic of the exam is. Maybe there's still time to study, but, first, it is crucial for him to find out where he is supposed to be. How could he be so irresponsible? Move faster! Think! The harder he tried to run to his classroom, the heavier his legs felt. Sydney's legs were encased in lead as he tried running up the steep hill to the room where he thought he belonged. Why is there such a long, steep hill in school? Trying to scale it is brutal, exhausting. Then, suddenly, thankfully, consciousness. It was six o'clock in the morning.

Sydney removed his sweat-drenched Bugs Bunny t-shirt, tossed it in his clothes hamper and made his way upstairs to the kitchen. He was hungry, but he decided to put off eating breakfast until after his morning workout. Instead, he hydrated himself for the next 15 minutes and stretched his knotted muscles. He then headed back down the staircase to the finished basement of his mother's home where he resided. Sydney exercised for a full hour-and-a-half by following along to his 'Insanity Workout' recording. He still had plenty of time to kill once he finished, as he didn't have to be at work until noon. Clare would join him for the afternoon shift which always put a little extra spring in his step. First, though, he had to eat something.

Sydney's breakfast was fairly simple. He made himself a protein shake with three scoops of whey, frozen fruit, and almond milk, blended to a creamy, milkshake-like consistency. In a large mixing-bowl, he dumped half of a box of Cocoa Puffs, two sliced bananas, and a quart of coconut milk. While he plowed through his breakfast, he checked his phone for any social-media messages that may have been sent his way.

Sydney was friendly to many but had no close friends. Clare had sent him a smiley-face emoji text an hour ago which made his breakfast that much more enjoyable. He looked at the news reports of the recent killings that had occurred in Chevon with total indifference. The media had jumped to their usual unconfirmed conclusions, attempting to be the first to get the story right, but their unnamed sources were laughably inaccurate. Sydney was starting to enjoy the power he felt after a kill.

The first time he killed someone, he became frightened by the realization of the power of his own strength. A year ago, Sydney was returning to his car which was parked in a remote commuter-parking lot. He had just completed a five-mile run on the rails to trail bike path. The local gang member, who was about to steal his car, ducked down low behind the rear bumper when he saw Sydney approaching. *It would be much easier to hijack the thing than it would be to break into it and have to hot wire the starter,* the thief was thinking. As Syd opened the driver's side door, the misguided youth sprung toward him, wielding a six-inch switch blade in his right hand. Sydney, without thinking, quickly curled the fingers on his right hand, planted his right leg behind his left and, with all his might, pushed off with his right foot, effectively shifting his body mass to his lead, left leg. The heel of Sydney's right hand, backed with every ounce of force he could muster, landed squarely on the jaw of the headfirst leaning gangster. The force of the blow dropped him unconscious to the pavement in a flaccid heap immediately after contact. Sydney heard a loud crack as the heavy young thug collapsed onto his ankle with his full weight, shattering his lower leg in three places. Jaw broken, fractured bone protruding through his lower calf, the would-be thief settled on his back, gurgling his own blood and gasping for air. For whatever reason, Sydney, in his adrenaline-induced angry state of mind, dealt a fatal blow to the young criminal's temple with the heel of his right foot. He then looked around, saw nobody, and calmly got in his car for the drive home.

Sydney had always been taught that taking a life was wrong, but he was having difficulty feeling any sense of remorse. To the contrary, he was feeling pleased with himself. The sudden realization of how powerful he had become both frightened and exhilarated him at the same time.

His first kill was unexpected. The second two killings were premeditated. His recent murders kind of reminded him of the experimentation on his pet frogs. Certainly, killing the frogs was planned out in advance. In fact, Sydney was an unwitting participant in those killings too. After all, he was the one who captured the frogs and put them on death row. For the frogs, he felt terrible.

For the people, not so much. Sydney thought that, one day, maybe he could allow someone to unwittingly choose one of his victims. It should be someone close to him who would have no idea about their participation in sentencing the offender with capital punishment. *If only I could find someone willing to be friends,* he dreamed. *This killing hobby could turn out to be a lot of fun,* he thought. He knew there would be more killings to come. Picking out victims was simple for him with his warped mind. Find someone who treats you badly, there will be plenty of them to choose from, and pith them.

Sydney fastened his waist-trimmer abs-developer belt around his waist. He had purchased it online a year ago. The wrap was guaranteed to reduce fat and develop six-pack abs in weeks. Sydney did like to exercise his rock-hard abs while he worked at Jimbo's. He also liked the chubby look he achieved from wearing his long-sleeve uniform shirt over the thick abs-sculpting wrap. Everyone at Jimbo's thought Sydney was on the pudgy side of the spectrum. His belly looked fat underneath the oversized top, and his round shoulders and thick arms were assumed to be chubby as well. Sydney wore his jeans pulled up to his bellybutton where his belt would strain to keep his pants in place. The look was all a part of Sydney's warped sense of humor. He loved fooling people into thinking things that just weren't true. Sydney loved surprising people.

***

Jimbo's was buzzing when Sydney arrived for his shift. The customer-care staff was happy to see him, as they were wrestling with a difficult special-order situation. The customer at the counter was pleasant enough but growing impatient with the staff's inability to locate the product she was looking for. Sydney took over the order and was able to get the transaction processed in no time. He had placed a similar order through the same vendor last week and knew how to navigate their extremely confusing ordering process. Some manufacturers make their special-order process easy and some make it as complicated as possible. The difficult ones put the store associates in a tough spot. Customers are rarely understanding when they wait for the employee to figure out the nuances. In this case, the customer was thrilled with the fact that Sydney was able to figure it out and place her order for her.

While Sydney was working on the special order, Clare reported for duty. She playfully pinched the tip of Sydney's left ear as she passed behind his station and took her place in the workstation next to him. Sydney was instantly intoxicated by the strawberry fragrance emanating from her shampoo. He savored the tingling feel from her touch, wishing it would remain forever. *This is going to be a wonderful afternoon of customer service at Jimbo's,* he thought to himself.

The line was predictably long, leading to the service desk, as will frequently happen during the lunch-hour rush. Two things can always be counted on during lunch hour. First, customers are always in a rush to get their transaction completed and get back to work. Secondly, customers are shocked to find out that there are other customers who are on their lunch hour with the same idea. The special-order fiasco that Sydney had to resolve caused the line to further back up. Two of the customers in line had their arms crossed while they aggressively tapped their right foot on the polished concrete floor. They glared at the four customer-service associates working the desk. Clare, looking as cute as ever, signed on to her computer terminal and signaled the next customer to come to her station.

"Hi, how can I help?" she pleasantly asked.

"I just need a refund on these shoes," the woman replied. "They don't fit right," she said. "I'm on my lunch, so I'm in a hurry to get back to work," she advised.

"No problem," Clare replied. "I'll just need to see your receipt," she smiled.

"Here you go," the woman offered. "I ripped it by accident, so I only brought the top part with me. It's the part with the shoes on it though," the customer added helpfully.

Clare took the half of the receipt the customer handed to her and looked up the purchase on her terminal by using the transaction number. It was necessary for Clare to determine the payment method so she could render the correct refund. If the customer paid using a check or cash, she would give a cash refund. If the customer used a credit card, she would put a credit on the same card used for the purchase. If the customer used a credit voucher or a gift card, she would be issued another credit voucher. In this case, the customer purchased the items two weeks ago using a credit card issued to Emily Greene.

"Emily Greene?" Clare asked.

"Yes. I'm Emily Greene," she replied.

"I'll just need the credit card ending in 4223," Clare instructed. "I'll put the credit back on that card."

"I can't get cash back?" Emily Greene asked.

"No, I'm sorry," Clare replied. "We can credit back your card though."

"That sucks," Emily Greene declared loud enough for everyone nearby to hear. "Let me get the card out for you. I can't believe this."

As Emily Greene looked for her credit card ending in 4223, Clare took the shoes out of the box that had been set down on the counter for her inspection.

The shoes were in new condition which was a requisite for a footwear return at Jimbo's. There was, however, another glaring problem with the pair of shoes that Clare was trained to look for. The pair of shoes that Emily Greene was trying to return consisted of a size-seven left shoe and a size-eight right shoe.

The customer had brought back the top part of the receipt which had the size-seven pair. The bottom part of the receipt which the customer did not bring with her, due to her claim of it being torn by mistake, would have shown that she purchased the exact same pair of shoes in a size eight as well. Clare had the whole transaction on the computer screen in front of her. As she looked at the computer and examined the mis-mated pair of shoes she had just been handed for a refund, she could feel the blood draining from her face. Clare has extremely cute looks and an extremely high I.Q. to match. It took a nanosecond for her to figure out what the customer was trying to pull off. Many people have two different size feet. The honest ones simply declare their problem to the footwear associates and a special order is generated to accommodate their needs. Most brands do not charge any additional fee, providing the customer is willing to pay in full for the order and wait for it to ship. The dishonest ones use a common trick which they believe they are the only ones clever enough to devise. The customer simply purchases the same pair of shoes in two different sizes and keeps the two shoes that fit their mismatched feet. Next, they return the other two shoes to the store with their mutilated receipt, attempting to stick the store with a non-sellable pair of mis-mates. Just a victimless crime, they justify to themselves as they fraud the business out of the cost of a pair of shoes. Store employees can face disciplinary action for not catching the fraud. They are trained to check for mis-mates on every sale and every return of footwear.

Other dishonest customers will simply place the size-seven right shoe in the same box as the size-eight left shoe and take the mis-mated pair to the cashier in hopes it won't be caught at the point of sale. Either way, mis-mates cause retailers a tremendous loss to their profits every year. These losses are passed along to honest customers through higher prices at the cash registers. The losses are also absorbed by cutting back on other expenses such as payroll. Cutting back on payroll means cutting back on staffing. Customers who steal from retailers directly affect prices charged to honest customers. Thieves also affect the number of associates a retailer can afford to hire. Fraud is, by no means, a victimless crime.

Clare would be required to deliver some unpleasant news to Emily Greene in the most pleasant way possible. Her experience gave her the feeling that this would not go well.

"M.O.D.?" Clare spoke into her store-radio headset.

"Hey, Clare. Welcome to the jungle. What's up?" Steve replied.

"Oh, Steve. Happy to hear your voice," Clare replied. "I have a code nine," she quietly stated.

"Be right over," Steve reassured.

Clare knew what she had to do and had no problem delivering the news to this customer. Sometimes the customer would concede and other times they would act up. She wasn't positive on how this would go, but she had an inkling it was going to blow up. That's why she called the manager on duty for a backup. Clare took a deep breath and took charge in her pleasant, charming way.

"Emily, these shoes are two different sizes," Clare began. "Do you want to return the size seven or the size eight?"

"I want to return the shoes in the box," Emily replied. "I purchased them just like they are in front of you, and I want my money back. Now!" she demanded.

Emily's voice began to rise, right on cue. It is a typical reaction from someone who is subtly called out for trying to steal or get away with something unethical. The first thing they do is to raise their voice and begin to fuss. Clare had seen the act too many times before, performed by people just like Emily. Her behavior wasn't unexpected. Clare was learning to become less offended by it all. She took her first few experiences personally. Later, she learned to consider the source of the vitriol, and she was better able to maintain her calm, pleasant demeanor. Usually, however, the fraudulent customer's elevated voice is followed up by some sort of name calling. This one would be no different.

"Actually," Clare calmly began. "If you look at the entire purchase, you paid for the same shoes in two different sizes. Maybe if you bring the other two shoes back, we can sort out which pair you would like to return. Do you have the other shoes with you?" she asked.

"No. They are home. I mean, I don't have any other shoes," Emily stumbled. "These are the only ones I have," she shouted. "Who's your manager? You bitch! I want to see your boss right away. You are accusing me of lying, you piece of shit. I'm going to have your job!" she screamed.

"My manager's name is Steve," Clare softly replied. "He's been standing right behind you." Clare pointed to Steve who was standing ten feet behind Emily. "Steve, this is Emily Greene. Emily, this is Steve. Emily would like to return these shoes, but they are mis-mates. Here is a copy of the entire purchase, and here are the shoes that she wants to return. I'll let you two sort this out while I take the next person in line," she explained.

"Can I help the next person please?" Clare asked. She directed her attention to the line of customers and greeted the first in line with a warm smile.

Steve had been listening to the entire conversation between Clare and Emily, and it took him seconds to figure out what the customer was trying to pull off. Unfortunately, he had the dubious pleasure of dealing with thousands of people just like Emily Greene in his long retail career. This one, he knew, would be simple for him to deal with. The first thing he would explain to the customer was the process for getting a special order. The method this customer chose was inconvenient for the customer and costly for the store. He was skilled at not telling a customer what he couldn't do but, instead, what he could do. In this case, he would make her a reasonable offer and let the customer choose.

"Emily, come over to the end of the desk with me so we can figure this out," Steve instructed. "I heard the conversation between you and Clare, so it's not necessary to rehash. If you bring in two unworn shoes in the same size, I'll make sure you get a full credit to your card. No questions asked. If you insist on returning the two shoes I have in front of me, I'll issue you a store credit for half the price you paid. The best we'll be able to sell those two, odd-size shoes for will be on the half-off-price rack. The most likely scenario, however, is we'll throw them away and take the full loss in a couple of months. We don't have a good chance of selling them like this. Your third option is to keep them. Which option would you like today?" he asked.

Emily, red faced, reluctantly chose to get the store credit for half of what she paid for the shoes. She figured it was better than nothing, and she would get the difference back by switching tickets on her next purchase. There was an exercise outfit she had her eye on which retailed for 120 dollars. Emily figured she could take price tickets from a 30-dollar outfit and change the tags while in the privacy of the fitting room. She would, however, make sure that Clare felt her wrath before leaving the store.

"I'll take the store credit," Emily snarled. "But I want that bitch disciplined for accusing me of being a liar. What are you going to do to her? I want an answer," she demanded.

"We'll take care of everything internally," Steve replied. He had heard this demand before and always handled it with the same response.

"We do not disclose personnel decisions publicly for privacy reasons," Steve informed her. "Sydney, over there, just finished his transaction, and he is available. Come on over with me, and I'll have him process your store credit," he directed. "You'll have to show him your driver's license, so you may want to get it ready. He can't process the transaction without it."

Steve escorted Emily Greene over to Sydney's work station at customer service. Neither of them knew it at the time, but Steve was introducing a cobra to a mongoose. Sydney observed the venom being directed toward the love of his life by this elitist snob, and he did not appreciate her actions. Inside, he was seething. On the outside, for now, he would show his timid mannerisms. His speech impediment was on full display. Suddenly, Emily was exposed to the pudgy wimp behind the counter who spoke with a lisp. Emily incorrectly detected fear and, like a mad dog, went on the attack. Her arrogance bloomed as she condescendingly cooperated with her soon-to-be killer.

"Ma'am, I'll need to thee your ID tho I can get you your thtore credit," Sydney managed.

"Here!" Emily snapped as she tossed her license like a Frisbee into Sydney's chest. "I want my credit, and I want to get out of here. I also want that ugly bitch fired. Do you hear me?" she screeched.

"Yeth, ma'am," Sydney replied as he quickly processed the return.

Sydney had all the information he needed from her license. The ID numbers from the top were keyed into the return tracker for the purpose of identifying chronic returners. The address on the license was memorized for the purpose of the unannounced house call that Sydney would make in the coming week.

"Here you go. Thank you and have a nithe day," Sydney annunciated to the best of his ability as he handed her the store credit and returned her license.

He briefly looked Emily directly in the eye with a laser-like stare. For an instant, the look on his face went from fear to cold-blooded killer and then back to fear again. Emily detected the split-second of hate directed her way, but then saw the look of fear come back to Sydney's face. She flashed a final look of disgust toward Sydney before looking away from his frightened face. She laughed out loud at the gall of this inferior wimp displaying his paltry moment of anger toward her.

"Have a nice day yourself, asshole," Emily chuckled as she took her credit and walked off.

"Thanks, Sydney," Steve said as he started to walk away. "She was a tough one. You guys did great as always," he complimented.

"No problem," Sydney replied. "No problem at all," Sydney's voice trailed off as he let his mind envision a perfectly placed tent stake sticking out of the back of Emily Greene's head.

Give it a week, he was thinking. See what her habits are as far as coming and going from her home in Chevon. Maybe bring her something special like a nice cupcake for her pithing party. *Sweets for the sweet,* he silently mused.

"Next in line. Can I help you?" Sydney asked as he snapped back into focus.

"Yes, you can. My name is Dave O'Driscoll. I'm Gerry's son," David replied as he approached Sydney's station. "He sent me here to pick up his briefcase and said to ask for Sydney or Clare at customer care," David said. "Are all of your customers as nice as she was?" he asked. "I saw the whole thing. I don't know how you can deal with people like that. In my line of work, we insist on our customers giving us a little more respect than what she just gave you," he stated.

Sydney looked directly into David's eyes and he froze. He was told someone would be stopping by to pick up Gerry's briefcase but didn't know it would be his son, the detective. Sydney and Gerry had often spoken of the chosen professions of Gerry's boys. Gerry had even asked Sydney if he would like to put his computer skills to work in a more meaningful way in law enforcement. Gerry could have Rick, his older son, put in a good word if it were something Sydney wanted as a better career for himself.

Lately, Sydney amused himself with thoughts of working in law enforcement and being assigned to catch the pithing killer. As he stuck his hand forward to shake David's hand, he felt like a boxer touching gloves in the center of the ring before the bell signals the start of the bout. Sydney did everything he could to conceal his excitement and his terror. He knew his lisp would kick in big time, but his nervousness could be attributed to the last customer he dealt with.

*This is going to be a little awkward,* he was thinking. *May as well have some fun with it,* he said to himself.

"Hi! Great to meet you," Sydney said as he gently shook David's hand. "I'll get it for you. We have it locked up over there in the cabinet. We need an update on Gerry. Everyone here ith tho worried about him," he revealed.

Dave observed the strange look of horror in Sydney's eyes but couldn't place its source. However, he couldn't help thinking about how much his father's employees adored him. Gerry briefed David on some of the staff at Jimbo's and elaborated on his relationship with Sydney. Dave was proud of the fact that his father took the time and interest to be a mentor to some of his staff. He knew Sydney had lost his father earlier in life and realized that Gerry had, many times, given him some fatherly advice. The concern displayed on Sydney's face actually had David feeling sorry for the young man.

"Gerry is doing just fine," David replied as he reached over with his left hand and held Sydney's right hand with both hands. "I'll be sure to tell him that you were asking for him," he promised.

112

"I only know one doctor joke," Sydney offered. "Will you tell it to him for me?" he asked.

"Sure," David tried to humor the awkward young man.

"A very old man went to the doctor and brought hith wife along," Sydney began. "The doctor thaid to him, 'I need a thtool thample, a thperm thample, and a urine thample.' The old boy, who couldn't hear very well, looked over at hith wife and athked, 'What did he thay?' The wife loudly replied, 'He thaid he would like to thee your underwear.'"

David was horrified. He refused to let on, however.

"Too funny," David pretended. "I'll be sure to pass it along to my dad from you. You know, Sydney, my father says you can be a real pisser at times, and now I know why he thinks that," David stated.

"Gerry thaid I'm a pither?" Sydney asked.

"Not quite that same way," David replied. "With my dad's Boston accent, it comes out pissah. You pronounce it pither. I'll go with pither if it makes you happy. Sydney, you are a pither," he confirmed.

"Pither ith thpot on." Sydney laughed awkwardly. "I'll go get the bag for Gerry. I know you have better thingth to do than talk to me," he said.

"Thank you, Sydney," David replied. "I appreciate your help. If there's ever anything I can do for you, don't be afraid to ask," he offered.

David took the briefcase from Sydney and thanked him for his help. It warmed his heart thinking about what a great group of people his father worked with. He would pass along all of their well wishes and Sydney's joke this evening when he had the chance to visit his dad.

Meanwhile, he had to get back to work. The police chief was up his ass about the Chevon murders. So far, there was almost nothing to go on, and the community was getting more and more antsy with every passing day. Pressure was intensifying. The residents were getting boisterous and obnoxious. Patience was a thing of the past. Hysterical name-calling was in full swing. If only David could figure out the motive behind the killings, he could narrow his investigation.

As he walked through Jimbo's parking lot toward his car, he couldn't suppress the feeling that he couldn't see the forest for the trees.

*I'm missing the obvious,* he thought. *The killer is probably right here in front of me, and I'm too distracted to notice.*

He was scared to death for his father. Every spare moment was spent on the internet, looking up colon-cancer treatment. He, like the rest of his family, felt helpless, but not hopeless.

David approached his car and carefully moved the shopping cart which had blown into his front-left fender. He grimaced as he inspected the three-inch gash it created. David blindly cursed at the inconsiderate asshole who left it, pushed it the ten steps over to the cart corral, hopped into his car, and sped off.

# 11

*The face on this side is "heads." The building on the back is "tails." Call it in the air.*

Gerry learned an interesting and helpful trick from an article that he found on the internet. The webpage shared accounts from many different cancer patients and how they were able to cope with their specific treatments. This one, specific patient learned how to train his mind to leave his body and occupy a position in the upper far corner of the room. From there, he could observe the treatment being performed on his body as if someone else was being worked on. Gerry related it to his days of playing basketball. It was always kind of funny watching another player sprain his ankle. At the very least, the other players were curious to examine the extent of the injury. It was never funny, however, when the injured player was you. Training one's mind to observe the medical team as they performed some ridiculous procedure on someone else could be somewhat entertaining. The typical reaction from the gallery would be on the line of, "Ouch, look at what they're doing to that poor bastard! That's got to hurt!"

The experience of having the medics perform the same procedure on one's self could be terrifying. With the body and mind intact, the pain is naturally intensified exponentially in a direct relationship to the terror from it all. Simply pretend that they're doing the dastardly deed to someone else, and fool yourself into thinking you are being allowed to watch the goings-on from the distance. That's the mind game that one must learn how to play. If you do learn to play it, you'll physically get through the whole ordeal with the added bonus of having your mental faculties intact.

Gerry quickly learned to prepare his mind to abandon ship when a doctor or a nurse entered his hospital room, pulled the curtain completely around his bed in order to shield it from view, and uttered the following six dreaded words, "This might be a little uncomfortable."

Gerry was starting to get his strength back and hoped to be discharged within the next few days. He had been in the hospital a total of six full days already and couldn't wait to get home. He tried not to think about being discharged, as it would depress him emotionally.

When the physician's assistant pulled the curtain around his bed and told him it was time to remove the Foley catheter, he was ecstatic. Gerry knew he could not be liberated from these confines until every one of his tethers to this miserable place were severed. Per instruction, he pressed the magic button and gave himself a dose of painkiller. He then freed his mind and allowed it to drift out of his body to a location where it could observe the show.

The physician's assistant, without further warning, opened Gerry's gown and gripped his penis with her left hand like it was a hot dog about to be tossed onto a hot charcoal grill.

"Take a deep breath," she instructed. "As I start to pull on the tube, slowly exhale."

"Got it," Gerry confirmed. "Deep breath, exhale slowly. Ready when you are."

The P.A. slowly and steadily pulled on the catheter, re-gripped it toward the end of Gerry's penis, and steadily pulled some more.

"Jesus!" Gerry gasped. "How long is that thing?"

"You're supposed to be breathing, not asking questions," she replied. "But here it is," she displayed. "Finished! Now you're going to have to prove to us that you can urinate, or we'll have to put it back in," she warned.

"I'll be dipped in shit before I let you stick that thing back in that little hole," Gerry promised. "Thanks for taking it out," he said. "By the way, how much longer do you think they're going to keep me in this place? I'm dying to get out of here."

"We're hoping for not more than another couple of days," she replied. "You're doing fine, Gerry. Control what you can control. Just keep exercising your body as much as you feel you can. You're going to need your strength."

***

Doctor Backus interrupted Gerry's breakfast of scrambled eggs and toast on the morning of his eighth day. He was sitting in the bedside chair with a tray in his lap while watching the morning-sports news network. Mary had just arrived with her morning coffee and magazine, prepared for another long day.

"Good morning, sunshine," Doctor Backus beamed. "How are you feeling, Gerry?"

"Feeling fine," Gerry replied. "I want to get out of here, though. I've had enough."

"Who's stopping you?" Doctor Backus teased.

116

"I don't know. You tell me," Gerry shot back.

"You should pack your things, then," Doctor Backus advised. "I'm signing your release right now," she said. "It's going to take the staff an hour or so to get you out of here, but plan on having your lunch at home."

Doctor Backus leafed through some of the papers that were clipped to her clipboard. She stopped at one of the documents and briefly studied the information contained within.

"Gerry, Doctor Hearms will see you at the end of this week," Doctor Backus informed him. "I've already spoken to him. I recommend you give him a call later today to confirm the appointment. You shouldn't wait too long. He is an excellent oncologist and will take good care of you," she promised. "Meanwhile, I want to see you in my office next week. I have you down for one week from today at nine o'clock in the morning. I'm going to remove the staples in your belly and leave you with a big, beautiful scar that you can show to your friends. Don't worry, Gerry, I'm going to keep an eye on you." She smiled.

The good doctor handed homecare information to Mary along with a card which contained contact information for Doctor Hearms. She made sure that Mary secured the information in her handbag before finally turning to Gerry for one last time.

"Congratulations, Gerry!" Doctor Backus beamed. "You just got over a big hurdle. Get out of here, now. Go home!" she ordered.

Two hours later, Gerry was wrapped in a blanket and helped into the passenger seat of Mary's car by the hospital's volunteer orderlies. The short drive seemed to take forever, but as Mary rounded the last turn leading to their street, Gerry felt like he was seeing his surroundings for the first time. He had driven past his neighbor's rose bushes thousands of times but never took notice of how beautiful the flowers were. The naturally growing flowers in the unkempt, vacant corner lot were vibrantly blooming. Everyone's grass looked carpet-like and brilliantly green.

As they approached the driveway, Gerry experienced the same exuberant feeling he invariably got as he made his way up through the dark, dank tunnel to his seats at Fenway Park and laid eyes on the outfield grass.

Many times over the last eight days, Gerry wondered if he would ever see his home again. Emotion began to overwhelm him, sapping him of what little strength he could muster. Gerry gingerly stepped from the car and was enchanted by the sounds of birds chirping and calling to one another. He never appreciated the cheerful whistles from his feathered friends in the past, but, now, Gerry felt as if he was being reborn.

As Gerry tested his wobbly legs and inhaled the sweet, clean air, he stood for a moment, rubbed his red swollen eyes, and listened to the sounds of the whistling choir. Mary took his hand and helped guide him along the short concrete walkway leading to the entrance of their home. Gerry navigated the threshold, passed through the kitchen, and stumbled into the family room. There, he collapsed into his favorite recliner, put his feet up, and passed out from exhaustion.

Gerry hadn't slept for more than a couple of hours at a time in well over a week. He was still so weak from the surgery that walking to the mailbox at the end of the driveway and back turned into a major undertaking in the days to come. For now, however, he needed a nap. At home, there were no nurses prodding and poking him in order to get his vitals. There weren't any noisy, bustling hallways. He didn't have to deal with noisy roommates and their boisterous visitors. At home, there was nothing but peace and quiet. The remainder of Gerry's next several days would be spent resting, eating, short walks, and then repeat. Finally, mercifully for Gerry, the hospital nightmare was over. At least for now. Thankfully, Gerry made it home.

*** 

For the next few days, Gerry focused on rest and exercise. He would go for short walks four times a day, gradually increasing his distances. At first, he couldn't make it 200 yards to the bend in the street and back without stopping to rest. He was flabbergasted at how weak he had become. Two weeks ago, he walked 18 holes of golf on a warm day. Today, he couldn't walk a short par three without resting. Hitting a golf ball was out of the question. For one thing, he didn't have the strength. For another thing, he didn't know how he could possibly swing a golf club with the colostomy bag hanging from his abdomen.

Gerry's recovering digestive system was working well, and his eating was getting better every day. However, he had no control over the frequency of his colostomy bag filling with digestive waste product. Sometimes, it filled quickly and had to be emptied often. Other times, it filled slowly, and he could go a couple of hours without having to deal with the process. One thing was for certain. Emptying the bag was always a smelly process and, sometimes, no matter how careful he tried to be, it could be very messy. Of everything he had to endure up to this point, Gerry despised having to deal with a colostomy bag the most. In the weeks to come, however, it would prove to be helpful to him in dealing with the side effects from the powerful medicine he would take.

Every day, Gerry's strength was building, almost doubling. Four days of being at home, resting, and exercising were doing wonders for him physically.

Mentally, he was still a little fuzzy from the pain meds, but his attitude was positive. He felt that he was ready for the big fight ahead. It was time for him to put on the padded gloves, take off the robe, and step into the ring.

Mary loaded him into the passenger seat of the family car and drove the ten miles to Doctor Brian Hearms' office. Doctor Backus recommended him highly, and Gerry knew she wouldn't send him to anyone who wasn't topnotch.

Gerry opened the glass door to the unassuming brick building with large white numbers affixed to the side and followed Mary into the modest lobby. Across the hall from where they stood, there was a directory hung in a glass case, next to the elevator. Gerry had an out-of-body experience as he read Doctor Hearms – Oncology, room 110. Like most men, Gerry avoided doctor visits like the plague and, yet, here he was, scheduled for an appointment with a cancer doctor.

He and Mary stepped into the elevator and pressed the button headed down. Gerry hoped the elevator doors would never open, but, in a short time, they did, and the two of them stepped out into the corridor. Mary opened the glass door leading to the receptionist of suite 110, and Gerry passed over the threshold and into the valley of death. There were other patients in the waiting area, sitting in stiff, unpadded chairs lined against the wall with grim looks and sunken eyes. Some nonchalantly glanced away from their magazines in order to size up the newcomer. Others didn't even budge.

Gerry checked in with the receptionist, took a seat, and waited for his name to be called. Patients came and went after visiting with one of the other six oncologists who were part of the same practice. Finally, a clipboard-toting nurse with a friendly smile called Gerry's name, and, with Mary in tow, he dutifully followed her to the far end of the hallway. First, she determined his weight, blood pressure, and his pulse. She then dutifully recorded her findings in the database. Next, she jabbed his left arm with a needle and filled three test tubes with his blood. Finally, she escorted Gerry and Mary to a small examining room a few feet away and closed the door behind her as she exited.

The room was very unassuming. There was the obligatory examination table covered with crinkly white paper, a counter and sink with cabinets above, two armchairs with a small wood table in between, and a short, round, swivel stool on wheels. The walls were barren. On the counter, there were two boxes of tissues, one on each end. A third box was conveniently positioned on the wooden table which separated the two chairs that Mary and Gerry occupied.

*There are lots of tissue boxes in here,* Gerry noted. *Must be because a lot of patients come here who have a cold,* he reasoned.

Soon, there was a soft knock on the door and Doctor Hearms quietly entered the examination room. He looked a lot younger than Gerry imagined he would be. Gerry placed him in his late 30s or early 40s at most. His hair was light brown and medium in length. It was full on his temples but thinning on top. Doctor Hearms clearly wasn't one to spend a significant amount of time worrying about what his hair looked like. At first glance, it appeared that he combed it with his fingers. He stood at around six-feet tall, with a medium build. He was soft in the middle as if, at one time, he was in great shape, but, now, he couldn't find time for exercise. His white shirt, purple tie, and dark pants could have been purchased at a bargain basement. Doctor Hearms gave the impression that he was not one to obsess over clothes shopping. He did, however, maintain a neat, clean-shaven appearance. Instead of a white coat, he wore a stethoscope around his neck, identifying his status as a medical doctor. He spoke in a gentle, monotone, matter-of-fact-tone of voice.

"Mr. and Mrs. O'Driscoll, my name is Doctor Hearms. Brian Hearms," he announced. "I'm pleased to meet you."

"Hi, my name is Gerry, and this is Mary," Gerry said as he held out his hand. "Feel free to call us by our first names."

"Likewise," Doctor Hearms replied. "Brian works just fine for me."

Brian, Gerry, and Mary spent the next 15 minutes getting to know one another. Gerry asked most of the questions and did most of the listening. Brian and Mary did most of the talking based on the topics Gerry threw out there. As the conversation went on, it became more and more apparent that Brian had two major passions in life. First and foremost, he cared for his family. Nothing seemed to be more important to him than his described lovely wife and his two, beautiful, young daughters. Second, and right behind his first passion, he hated cancer.

Doctor Hearms, after a short, silent break in the conversation, lifted his clipboard and leafed through the pile of papers he had attached. He was double checking to make sure that he had everything he needed. He settled back to the top page, studied it for a moment, and then lifted his head so he could look Gerry directly in the eye.

"Gerry, we've examined your tumors in the lab, and I have spoken at length with Doctor Backus in regards to what she discovered during surgery," he began. "We have a very good handle on the type of cancer you have and its progression thus far. Your chance of survival right now, as we speak, is 50-percent. Successfully completing 12 rounds of chemotherapy will improve your chances into the 75-percent range. Survival means you'll live another five years. Are you with me so far?" he asked, concerned that Gerry wasn't understanding.

Gerry's mind left his body and hovered in the top corner on the opposite side of the room. This time, it wasn't a game Gerry was playing with himself.

His mind abandoned ship on its own. *Look at that poor bastard,* his mind gasped as it looked at the scene unfolding across the room.

Gerry returned the doctor's gaze with a blank stare as he attempted to process the information which had just been provided to him. Mary pulled one tissue from the box on the table beside her and another from the box offered to her from Doctor Hearms. The end of her nose suddenly turned a bright red and her eyes watered uncontrollably. She reached over and grabbed Gerry's hand in a vicelike grip as if he had just slipped off a ledge and she would not let him fall to his death. Doctor Hearms sat stoically, patiently waiting for the response to his question.

"So, what you're telling me is if I'm in a room with 100 people with the same cancer, 50 of us will live, and 50 will die?" Gerry paraphrased. "That means I only have to beat out 50 people in the room," he reasoned. "I can do that easily."

"Gerry, it doesn't work like that, unfortunately," the doctor deadpanned. "If there are a 100 of you in a room, each of you has a 50-percent chance of survival. Think of it like each of you gets to toss a coin. Heads, you win. Tails, you lose," he clarified.

Doctor Hearms correctly read the panicked look on Gerry's face and realized that he needed to promptly provide him with some positive news. Unfortunately, the only positive information that he could share with Gerry was to verbalize the plan of attack that could help him to increase his odds.

"What I'm recommending is that you can better your odds with a chemotherapy treatment," Doctor Hearms explained. "You'll get three drugs. 5-FU, leucovorin, and oxaliplatin. We call it the FOLFOX regimen. I printed these handouts on each of the drugs for you to look over," he said as he handed the sheets of paper to Gerry. "There is a page on each, describing possible side effects. They are the most common side effects. There may be others that are not listed because they are not so common. Take a few moments to read what I have handed to you. Let me know what questions you have."

Gerry and Mary took a few minutes to read the handouts that Doctor Hearms provided regarding the drugs that Gerry would take. Neither could decipher the medical jargon on the front page other than they were cancer-fighting agents. The back pages listed approximately 50 side effects per drug. Everything from mild nausea to death was possible.

"Doc," Gerry began. "There are a lot of side effects here. Am I going to get all of these?"

"No," The doctor replied. "Nobody gets all of them."

"Do I get to pick and choose which ones I have to have?" Gerry asked. "You know. Is it like taking items from a buffet line? Some of these I think I can deal with. Others, I'd rather avoid if possible."

"You can circle the ones you like, Gerry." The doctor smirked. "Just like you do when going to a Chinese restaurant, I guess. No promises though. You're going to get what you get. Not necessarily what you order. There are some things, however, that pretty much come with every meal. We are going to have to stay on top of those," he warned. "You're going to have nausea. We'll treat it with anti-nausea medication. I know it's still summer, but you'll need winter gloves next to the refrigerator. Don't touch anything cold. If you do, you'll lose feeling in your fingers. Don't drink anything cold. Everything you drink must be at room temperature. Your throat will feel like it has swollen closed if you have cold drinks. Also, stay out of the sun. You will experience skin damage if you expose it to the sun. Plus, you will turn purple. And I do mean purple. Just like Barney the Dinosaur. These drugs will also give you a severe case of diarrhea. I'm sure you're not thrilled with having your colostomy bag, but it actually will come in handy in dealing with the digestive problems you'll experience," he said.

"Okay," Gerry acknowledged. "It sounds like I really don't have much of a choice in the matter. I'm not the luckiest person you've ever met. I can get cancer, but I can't win the lottery, if you know what I mean," he digressed. "The thought of tossing a coin and if it comes up heads, I live, and if it comes up tails, I don't get to live long enough to see Christmas, doesn't thrill me. However, I can't just sit back and hope for the best," Gerry reasoned. "That said, what's next? When do we get started?"

"First, I need you to sign the authorization for treatment," the doctor began. "Gerry, these are very powerful drugs. They can help you, or they can kill you. Some people do very well on this regimen. Others do very poorly. Most patients land somewhere in the middle. Second, if you choose to sign the authorization, I'd like you to have a port surgically implanted. I can recommend a surgeon who is very good at the procedure. The port sits just under your skin, a few inches below your right collarbone. The nurses will be able to administer your drugs and draw your blood through the port by inserting a specialized needle into it. It keeps them from trying to find a vein in your arm each time you need treatment. Once you have the port in place, we'll begin. Let's figure on three weeks from today. Wait two more weeks before having the port surgery. You will be put under, so it's best we give it a week after that for recovery," he plotted.

The thought of Gerry having another surgery so soon, even if it was comparatively minor, was too much for Mary to take. Mentally, she was doing relatively well up until now. She broke down for a moment at the thought of Gerry having another surgery. But then she rebounded when she realized how much her support would matter in this battle. Mary had to stay positive and strong for Gerry. He can't feel like he is fighting this war alone, and she knew her support would be crucial in the coming months. She may have her sad moments, but she vowed that they would be in private. As she dried her tears and gathered herself, she thanked the doctor for his candor. She only had one more question for the doctor before scheduling the next appointment. It was a bottom-line-type question.

"So, if we get through the 12 sessions of chemo," Mary began. "Do you think he's going to survive this?"

Doctor Hearms had heard the question before, but he never liked answering it. He had experienced cancer in his own family and could empathize with the many conflicting emotions being experienced by the patient and the caregiver. One thing was for certain. Difficult questions would be asked and immediate answers would be expected. Patients that he treated were scared to death and begged for reassurance that everything was going to be okay. Cancer treatment, however, doesn't always cooperate with the needs and wants of those affected.

"I honesty, don't know," Doctor Hearms replied as his voice trailed. "I hope so, though. I truly hope so."

# 12

Well then. That was an unexpected pleasure.

Gerry was ushered to a semi-conscious state from a deep, satisfyingly restful sleep by the buzzing of his cellphone which sat on the end table next to his recliner. It had stopped buzzing, and, as Gerry focused his eyes on it, he had the strange feeling that it was staring right back at him like a dog that was trying to awaken its human to go outside and pee. Persistently, right on cue, it started buzzing again, attempting to garner Gerry's attention. The illuminated screen flashed 'Steve.' Gerry thought for a moment about pressing the red ignore button, but then thought better of it and chose the green answer option.

"Steve! How are you doing, brother?" Gerry did his best to disguise the weakness in his voice.

"Hey, Gerry!" Steve replied, taking the bait. "You sound terrific," he pretended. "I hear you are thinking of coming back to work soon. As much as we'd love to have you, I hope you take your time. Don't try to be a hero. The assholes above our grade level aren't going to appreciate you any more than they do now," he stated.

"I'm not doing it for them," Gerry replied. "I got a letter from Jimbo's corporate human-resources department a few days ago. They're telling me that once my medical leave of absence reaches six weeks, they will proceed with termination if I'm not immediately back on the job. I get my first dose of chemotherapy next week which will be the sixth week of my leave. I already informed them of my intentions to be back to work on the following Monday. Do I feel physically strong enough to return? Not even close," Gerry answered his own question. "The problem is, at this point in time, the company has me right where they want me. For many reasons that I don't want to go into, I can't quit my job right now. So, I'm going to have to surrender to them in this battle and drag myself into work. Plus, more than anything else, I want to offer them the opportunity to kiss my Irish ass in person. If you know what I mean."

"I want you in my foxhole, right next to me," Steve said, laughing. "Gerry, I overheard a conversation via a conference call that Mark, Lynn, and the boys in the regional office were having about you. Mark was in Lynn's office over in the human-resources wing, and they didn't realize that I was in earshot. Mark was complaining to the regional staff about having a cancer patient working as an operations manager. He said it would be very inconvenient for him to be expected to pick up any of your slack. Mark then explained how he had some ideas on a Plan B. That was right after he came right out and said he hoped you wouldn't be able to return to work. Lynn closed the door to her office at that point, so I didn't get any more specifics about what this 'Plan B' was all about. I did hear muffled voices for another 15 minutes, but I couldn't catch what they were saying. They are up to something, Gerry. You're walking into a trap here. Don't trust them."

"I've had that same feeling," Gerry confirmed. "Mark only called me once since I've been out of work, and I could tell he was on a fishing expedition. Someone must've asked him how I was doing, and, since he never called me to find out, he couldn't answer their question. You know how he always fancies himself as a people person. Especially when all the big shots come for a visit. Too funny, don't you think? Anyway, I have spoken to Lynn at least a dozen times since I went out on leave. We have had some long conversations. Even with our differences of opinions, I think we have a lot of respect for one another. The last couple of conversations we have had, I began detecting a conflicted H.R. manager on the other end of the line. I have made a pretty good living by reading people, and I sense Lynn is involved with something having to do with me that she vehemently disagrees with."

"I agree with you on that one," Steve confirmed. "Lynn has been acting somewhat differently to me since you got sick. She has been trying to be more friendly. It seems forced to me, though. Maybe I'm being too cynical, but it doesn't strike me as being natural. I still don't trust her," he admitted

"Lynn is in a tight spot," Gerry observed. "She has to either tow Mark's line or find another job. It's all making more sense to me now. I already knew that Mark was a sleaze, but I didn't know how low he could go. I'll be careful and will be more than prepared for whatever bullshit he tries to throw at me," he reassured. "Thanks for the heads up, my friend. Now, get off the phone and go find an angry customer to deal with, will you?" Gerry teased. "If there's one thing I don't look forward to, it's dealing with some whacky customer-care issue on my first day back." He laughed.

"Will do, my brother," Steve replied. "Call me after your chemotherapy treatment. I want to know how you make out. I won't call you. You can call me whenever you feel up to it," he said.

"Will do, my friend," Gerry assured as he disconnected and closed his eyes. Within minutes, he had already drifted back to his sweet dreams.

***

Steve was in the middle of a firearms-paperwork audit when he decided he needed a break. For a moment, he lost sight of the unsettling predicament involving Gerry and instinctively considered calling him. Steve then wisely thought better of it and, instead, strolled on over to the restaurant for a cup of coffee. The jolt of caffeine helped to stimulate his brain and brought him back into focus.

Now that his head was clear, he felt ready to get back to the task at hand. The vault where the federal and state firearms' forms are stored was in a tightly secured location of the store. It had limited access for authorized personnel, and cameras were mounted everywhere for observing and recording any and all movement in and out.

Each firearm transaction had a folder full of documents which needed one more final review before being filed by date and retained for 20 years. For this reason, the vault room was a 40-foot-by-40-foot, brightly lighted area with concrete floors and storage shelves lining three walls. On the fourth wall was a small desk next to the thick metal door which exited into the narrow hallway. Rolling storage shelves occupied every possible square inch of the floor space. They would be pushed together, accordion-like, for storage and could be rolled away from one another to create an aisle if a document search became necessary. If a firearm that was previously sold at Jimbo's was used in a crime, an A.T.F. agent would appear unannounced to inspect the documents related to that specific gun sale. It would be considered bad form to keep the agent waiting while the paperwork search was being conducted. The longer the agent had to wait, the more time they would have to poke around, inspecting other transactions. If the forms couldn't be located, or if they were not in perfect order, it could result in fines or, in extreme cases, the removal of the store's Federal Firearms License to sell. Essentially, such an infraction could put the store out of business. For this reason, the storage vault as well as the completed forms being stored in it had to be perfect. Normally, it was Gerry's job to conduct the final audit before filing the forms. However, since Steve was helping to cover for Gerry's absence, he would be the final inspector of the documents.

Steve's eyes were beginning to glaze over as he peered at transaction after transaction. Since so much care, and so many checks and balances were in place to make sure of every transaction being properly conducted, the job of auditing paperwork could get painfully boring.

Steve pulled the next folder from the large pile and as he started reviewing the federal form 4473, it was painfully obvious to him that something was very

126

wrong. The answers on the form, beginning with question 11a, should be 'yes,' followed by the remaining questions which were required to be answered 'no.' In a quick glance, Steve noticed that the answer to question 11a on this form was clearly marked 'no.' Steve looked away, rubbed his eyes in the hope that the act would somehow change the answer, and looked back at the form. Unfortunately, the checkmark was still in the box which indicated that the purchaser's answer was still 'no.' Question 11a on the federal form 4473 basically asks the customer if they are buying the gun for themselves. Buying a gun for someone else, especially for someone who is not eligible to own a gun, is illegal. Selling a gun to someone who says they are buying it for someone else is also illegal. Changing an answer for someone on the federal form 4473 is not only illegal, but it is unethical and could be argued immoral.

Steve wiped the sweat that had formed on his forehead before it could drip into his eyes and pondered his predicament. He, once again, considered calling Gerry for advice, but then he thought better of it. Instead, he channeled his good friend and did what he knew Gerry would advise him to do. "Just play it straight. Do the right thing," he said to himself.

Mark's phone buzzed on his hip, startling him. It annoyed him to no end, having to interrupt his mindless chat with Lynn in the H.R. office.

"Why can't Steve just do his job and leave me alone?" Mark whined in Lynn's direction as he stared at his phone screen and pressed the speaker button.

The only thing Mark liked more than chatting with Lynn was showing off in front of her. He took advantage of every opportunity that presented itself in order to show Lynn how much of a big shot he was. With a little luck, Steve would make a total fool of himself with his voice being blasted over the speaker phone in order to add a little levity to the situation.

"Yeah! What can I do for you, Steve?" Mark answered sarcastically. Lynn slouched uncomfortably in her chair, pretending to not listen.

"Mark, I'm auditing the gun paperwork," Steve offered. "A customer answered 'no' on 11a and we transferred the gun to him. How do you want to proceed?" he asked.

Suddenly, the smirk on Mark's face disappeared. The blood noticeably drained from his face, taking with it the sarcastic look from his now ashen, raised brow. He thought for a moment, and then delivered what he considered to be obvious instructions to Steve.

"I want you to change his answer to 'yes' and file the paperwork," Mark nervously replied as he scrambled to take the phone off speaker mode and pressed the handset to his ear.

Mark was reasonably confident that Lynn would have no idea what Steve was talking about. Still, he regretted allowing her to hear that part of the conversation. He could easily make up a story if she pressed him later on it, but, for now, the less she heard, the better.

Store managers who flunk A.T.F. audits do not remain store managers for long. The best way to avoid flunking an audit is to not have one in the first place. Hopefully, Steve will help bury the problem in the mountain of paperwork sitting in the storage vault, and everyone can live happily ever after. At least, that was what he planned.

"No can do, Mark," Steve replied in his no-nonsense, military tone of voice. "Are you asking me to do something illegal?" he pressed. "You do realize that there's a law on the books which requires that anyone involved in a straw purchase gets put in prison for ten years. That would include the seller if he is complicit," Steve stated.

"Come on, Steve," Mark lectured. "You know as well as I do that we have more gun laws in this state than Carter has Little Liver Pills, and none of them are enforced," he scoffed. "Nothing is going to happen to you."

"I'm still not willing to risk it," Steve replied. "Gerry told me he has had to deal with this situation in the past. He calls the customer and has the person return the gun to the store at once. Then, he notifies the local A.T.F. agent and tells him about the error," he advised. "I think the best plan is for us to get Jennifer from customer care involved. Let someone from customer care act as the nice guy in dealing with the customer," he reasoned. "You may want to let your bosses know about this unless you feel you want to take over for me. I have no emotional attachment to this fiasco. I'll be happy to turn it over to you," Steve offered.

"Um, no. I, uh, think your solution is appropriate," Mark stammered. He glanced over at Lynn who continued to pretend that she wasn't paying attention to what was being said. "Please get with Jennifer at customer service and ask her to contact the customer per my direction," he bloviated. "Thanks for the information, Steve. If I can be of further help, you know that I'm here for you. I am always happy to help my team solve issues that may arise," he gassed.

Steve hung up and muttered, "Asshole," under his breath as he started making his way over to customer care. He knew if he changed the answer on the federal form, Mark would claim ignorance and push him under the bus with both hands if this thing ever got exposed. Steve had seen Mark in action plenty of times and knew what a serpent looked like when he saw one. Steve was savvy enough to always remember to put on his snake boots when dealing with snakes.

As Steve rounded the corner and eyed customer care, his heart sunk. Jennifer, the customer-care manager, was standing next to Clare who stared red-faced at a customer who was frantically waiving her arms and pointing her index finger in her direction.

*Great!* Steve thought to himself. *Just what I was hoping for right now,* he sarcastically mused.

"You called me a thief, and I want an apology. Right now!" the customer demanded. "Who is your boss?" she shouted while pointing at Jennifer.

"Ma'am, nobody is calling you a thief," Jennifer calmly replied. "I'm going to restate again. If you want to use the credit card in your hand, it must have your name on it. You can't use your husband's card, your friend's card, or any other card from this credit-card company unless it is issued to you. My boss happens to be walking toward us right now. His name is Steve, and that's him right there," she said.

"Are you the manager?" the customer loudly shrieked at Steve as she turned away from the counter. "These two are treating me like a common criminal. They just called me a thief," she pleaded while turning to point at Clare and Jennifer. "I demand an apology. Over the loud speaker. I want you to apologize for calling me a thief."

The customer's voice raised and lowered as she reached and retreated from differing levels of anxiety. Presently, her voice and anxiety levels were elevated. Her blood pressure was assumed to be dangerously high.

"I'm the manager," Steve calmly replied softly as he held out his hand. "My name is Steve, and you are?"

"I'm Mrs. Waters. Elizabeth Waters, and my husband is Robert Waters," she barked. "You may have heard of my husband. He is a well-known lawyer. We live at 200 Wells Street in Chevon. Perhaps you know the neighborhood?" she bragged.

"I'm not familiar with your neighborhood," Steve deadpanned. "I will tell you, however, that, unfortunately, you can't use someone else's credit card. The ladies are correct. I might suggest that you have your husband call the credit-card company and ask them to issue a card in your name under his account. It will head off any future confusion and make your shopping much easier," he advised.

"It's none of your business what my husband does with his time," Mrs. Waters shrieked.

Suddenly, unexpectedly, her voice and anxiety level seemed to return to a somewhat normal tone.

"He isn't going to get me my own credit card, just so you know," Mrs. Waters eerily lectured. "He says I spend too much."

"I'm sorry for your inconvenience," Steve offered.

He was caught off guard by the sudden but strange civility of the customer. Steve wasn't sure how long it would last but hoped for the best. He had the same feeling one gets while experiencing the calmness of being in the eye of a hurricane.

"Is there anything else I can help you with today?" Steve nervously wondered.

"I want both of these whores fired," Mrs. Waters screamed as she pointed at Clare and Jennifer.

Her calm demeanor abruptly ended. Steve was about to face the back wall of the storm, he thought.

"And what are you looking at?" Mrs. Waters barked. "You should mind your own business. You, fat twerp," she screeched. Mrs. Waters was pointing her right index finger directly at Sydney.

"Mithtake," Syd muttered under his breath as he turned to look away from the embarrassing scene taking place a few feet away from him.

"Okay then," Steve interrupted. "Since there doesn't seem to be anything else I can help you with today, I hope you have a great rest of the day. It was very nice meeting you," he pretended.

"You haven't heard the end of this," Mrs. Waters continued as she turned to walk toward the exit. "My husband is a lawyer. You will be hearing from him!" she promised.

Mrs. Waters could be heard shouting at everyone and everything in her path on the way to the exit. She was thorough in her effort to enlighten one and all to the fact that her husband was a very powerful lawyer.

"Lawsuits are imminent," she warned the fake-potted plant which decorated the store entrance. For a moment, she paused, waiting for the plant's acknowledgement.

Finally, Mrs. Waters exited the building and climbed into her car. Undoubtedly headed to another hysterical adventure.

Steve stared in wonder before focusing his attention toward Jennifer.

"Jennifer, I need to go over the contents of this folder with you," Steve continued as he switched gears. "Let's go back to your office. This is a long story. I swear I didn't come over here to deal with some wing-nut. I actually have something important that I hope you can help me with."

"Uh oh," Jennifer responded. "I don't like how you said that. But since you helped me to chase the Wicked Witch of the West out of here on her broomstick, I guess I can help you out. Besides, I could use a chocolate fix. There is a Snickers bar in the top drawer of my file cabinet, and I think I can hear it calling out to us," she said as she opened the door leading to the back hallway where her office was located. "After you," she said invitingly.

As soon as Steve and Jennifer were out of sight, Clare turned to her right to look at Sydney. She teasingly shot him a cute smile and an exaggerated wink. Tonight was the night she would meet Sydney's mother, and, right now, she was as nervous as a long-tailed cat in a room full of rocking chairs. So far, their after-work dating has been limited to lunch, dinner, and movies. She was enamored by Sydney's reserved mannerisms and how he treated her like she was someone special.

Clare's previous boyfriends all seemed to have only one selfish thing on their minds from day one. Sometimes, she accommodated them, other times, she broke off the relationship before it had a chance to get started. Syd had promised to fix Clare's laptop, as she complained to him that it has been running very slowly. He figured it was probably just a matter of him cleaning up a virus or two, but it may take some time to run the necessary programs.

Once Sydney's mother caught wind of their plans, she insisted on meeting Clare over a home-cooked meal. Anna had become more and more protective of Sydney since the passing of his father. Lately, she detected a slight change in her son. He was acting a little more aloof than normal. She didn't know if it had anything to do with him dating the young lady whom he has been frequently alluding to or not. One thing Anna did know. She would figure out a way to meet this girl. From there, she would size up the situation and find out for herself. The last thing Anna would allow would be to have some siren come along and break her 23-year-old, baby boy's heart. Dinner, she decided, would be served promptly at seven o'clock at her kitchen table. This will give her plenty of time to evaluate Sydney's new friend before heading to the hospital for her overnight shift.

\*\*\*

Clare parked in front of Sydney's home at exactly six o'clock and walked the short distance to his front door. She was conservatively dressed in a long sleeve, buttoned-down plaid top. The shirt sleeves were carefully rolled up to her forearms. Her jeans were fashionably worn but neat and clean. They had no skin-revealing tears and were not overly tight fitting. She wore simple flip-flop-like sandals, and her hair was pulled back in a ponytail. She couldn't obscure her attractiveness, but for the first-time meeting Syd's mother, she figured it was best to not look 'hot.'

In her left hand, she carried a small zippered case which contained her laptop and some of her schoolwork. In her right hand was a bag containing a baguette and a wedge of brie cheese that she thought would go nicely with the lasagna being served for dinner. Although she was still a little nervous about meeting Sydney's mother, she had calmed herself down and looked forward to what she hoped would be a pleasant evening. Whichever direction the night took, she felt prepared to embrace it and just go with the flow. Clare figured she would take her cues, and let the evening come to her.

Sydney opened the front door and greeted Clare with a gentle hug as he took the packages from her hands. He was casually dressed in a long-sleeve branded, polyester, heat-gear top, jeans, and sneakers. To Clare, Sydney looked different somehow. She was having difficulty putting her finger on why at first, but as he invited her in to meet his mother, she realized why.

"Syd, did you lose some weight?" she asked.

The fitness shirt he was wearing was a snug fit and accented his muscular build and tight midsection.

"Oh," Sydney replied. "I don't have my fat-burning belt on. That thing can make me look a little heavy," he said. "Why? Do you want me to put it on?" Sydney asked.

"No!" Clare shot back, laughing. "I like you better this way. You look like, um, nice," she said, blushing.

"You do too," Sydney replied. "Come and meet Mom," he invited.

The kitchen smelled wonderful with the aroma of the lasagna baking in the oven. The fragrance emanating from the freshly cut flowers standing upright in the clear glass vase on the kitchen table competed for attention.

Anna and Clare, after Sydney's introduction, sized each other up like Sumo wrestlers squatting at opposite ends of the ring while tossing salt into the air. Meanwhile, Sydney performed some diagnostics on the slowly working laptop while Clare helped to set the table and prepare the salad for tonight's dinner. At first, Anna focused on questioning Clare's background and ambitions. Shortly thereafter, she couldn't help but draw the conclusion that Clare was a sweet, wonderful, young lady. She could see why Sydney was enamored with her.

Clare, on her end, shifted the conversation to Anna's job. She probed Anna for the good, the bad, and the ugly realities of being an overnight nurse at a major hospital. Clare also asked lots of questions about Sydney when he was a child. The two laughed and pointed at old photos kept in a dusty family album that Clare insisted on being shown.

After being allowed a sneak taste test on the tomato sauce used to make the lasagna, Clare pressed Anna for the recipe. Flatteringly, she asked Anna for cooking instructions, so she could give it a try herself one day. When Sydney rejoined the ladies in the kitchen, at first, he felt like a third wheel.

Clare and his mother were so engrossed in conversation that he had to butt in to let Clare know the status of her computer.

Once dinner was finished, Clare insisted on doing the cleanup with Sydney. Anna, having been distracted by the evening, was running a little late. Clare offered her help in order to make sure Anna didn't get in any trouble at work. Anna laughed the whole thing off but was very appreciative of the gesture. She scurried upstairs and quickly got herself ready to go.

One last inspection of the progress being made in the cleanup effort reassured Anna that everything was under control. She grabbed her handbag and her keys and returned one last time to her kitchen. She approached Clare, put her free arm around her shoulder, and gave her a warm hug.

"It was so nice meeting you, Clare," Anna said. "I hope you'll come by again."

"Nice meeting you as well," Clare replied as she covered the leftovers and put them in the fridge. "I'd love to come again sometime." She smiled.

"And, Sydney," Anna warned. "Make sure you get that laptop running like new. I don't want Clare at a disadvantage in her classes," she ordered.

"Yeth, Mom," Sydney replied. "It'th nothing I can't handle," he reassured. "Good night. Thee you tomorrow."

"Good night you two," Anna responded as she headed out. "Don't stay up too late," she advised.

Sydney estimated that the time remaining on the cleanup program he was running on Clare's computer would take at least another hour. Potentially, it would take longer if some other bugs were detected. The two decided to get a cold drink, stream an old movie on T.V., and relax on the family-room sofa to kill some time. Sydney cued the flick and dimmed the lights while Clare got up to use the bathroom and freshen up.

Sydney had his head tilted down at his phone screen, checking his social-media feed when the scent of Clare reentering the room caught his attention. He glanced over to see she still had on her flip-flop sandals, but the plaid top and conservative, loose-fitting jeans were nowhere in sight. Clare's shoulder-length hair was no longer in a ponytail. It hung freely slightly above her exposed black, satin bra which barely covered the erect nipples of her firm, pear-shaped breasts. On her right breast, just above her areola, was a small, brightly colored butterfly tattoo. Her midsection was tanned, tight, and muscular. Just below her pierced navel, he fixated on the band of her red, lace thong connected to the thin patch of fabric which barely covered her cleanly shaven erogenous zone. The back of the thong disappeared between the cheeks of her firm, perfectly shaped butt. Sydney was having an out-of-body experience. He was processing the situation he suddenly found himself in, but, clearly, he didn't know what to do as he stared in wide wonder.

"Syd, I've had a long day," Clare began as she lounged on the opposite end of the sofa from Sydney. "I could really use a nice foot massage," she purred as she kicked off her sandals and lifted her right foot onto his left shoulder. She brought her left leg up onto the sofa and nestled her left foot into his lap. "Don't worry. You can't mess it up," she said as she rubbed the back of his head with the arch of her right foot. "Here, start with my right foot," she instructed as she brought her right shin under his left arm and raised her foot into his chest. As Sydney gently massaged Clare's right foot, she traced the outline of his growing erection with her left big toe.

"Syd, I think you are enjoying this as much as I am," Clare softly moaned. "Something is getting really hard over there. I think I need to investigate," she said as she spun around 180 degrees on the sofa.

Clare moved her right hand to the back of Sydney's head and nibbled his left ear before moving his face toward her for a deep, sensuous kiss. Her left hand moved from his chest to his waistband where she reached beneath his boxer shorts and gently stroked his blood-gorged penis. She then quickly brought her right hand to his waist, unbuttoned his jeans and unzipped his zipper. Before Sydney knew it, Clare had him naked from the waist down and was kneeling between his legs, staring up at his wide eyes. Clare then grabbed the bottom of Sydney's shirt with both hands, lifted it upward, and squealed with delight.

"Syd, I didn't know you have a tattoo!" Clare exclaimed as she examined the sizable tattoo of a bullfrog which she unexpectedly uncovered.

The frog, which straddled Sydney's bellybutton, stood in a defiant pose with a spear in its right hand, pointing upward toward Sydney's right collarbone. The frog's left hand was on its left hip. Its feet were in a wide, combat-like stance. Clare grabbed Sydney's penis and pointed it straight up toward his navel.

"Syd, did you know if I move your dick up like this, it looks like your froggy is taking it up the ass?" Clare teased. "Is it bi?" she asked, sensuously.

"Dunno," Sydney managed breathlessly. "I didn't have a hard-on when I got the tattoo," he stated. "Your quethtion ith kind of a thurprithe to me! Right now, though, I really don't care what it ith," he admitted.

"Let's see if your froggy likes my butterfly," Clare said as she maneuvered upward and lightly tongued the swollen head of Sydney's penis.

She sucked on his throbbing member with her soft lips and gently stroked him with her right hand. Her left hand lightly tickled his balls until he was on the edge of having an orgasm.

Quickly, Clare moved her thong to the side, straddled Sydney, and took his manhood deep inside her. She grabbed his right hand and moved it to her swollen clitoris.

"Just rub me gently. Right there," Clare instructed a willing Sydney.

She rode him with deep, long, strokes until she felt a massive orgasm building.

"Oh God! Syd, I'm cumming," Clare screamed as she tightened her bear hug around his neck.

Clare's orgasm sent shivers from her pink-colored curled toes to the velvety tips of her perfumed ears.

"Me too. Oh God. Me too," Sydney moaned. "Oh, yessss," Sydney shouted. His orgasm so intense that he nearly blacked out.

Clare and Sydney breathlessly hugged and kissed while stroking and massaging each other's neck and back. Contentedly wrapped in each other's arms, neither wanted to let go of the other. Both fantasized that this moment would last forever.

"Sydney?" Clare finally asked blissfully. "Did you say yes?" she moaned between kisses.

"Huh?" Sydney replied, still completely lost in the moment. "What do you want to know?" he wondered.

"Yes," Clare repeated. "Sydney, I want you to say yes," Clare said half sternly.

She leaned away from him, slightly arching her smooth, glistening back while placing both hands on Sydney's upper chest in order to brace herself. Clare smiled and lovingly stared directly into his sleepy, contented eyes while awaiting his response.

"Yes," Sydney obeyed.

Clare quizzically tilted her head sideways before leaning in for another brief-but-affectionate kiss. She leaned back once again and adjusted her weight so that she could surround Sydney's hard with the velvety warmth of her womanhood.

"Now say, She Sells Seashells by the Sea Shore," Clare breathlessly gasped.

"She Sells Seashells by the Sea Shore," Sydney replied as he readied himself for where he hoped Clare was about to take him.

# 13

This is getting old.

David's phone rang again the second he got into his car as he began to make his way over to the Waters' residence. The coroner at the crime scene had requested that David and the chief be on the line at the same time.

Incessant dog barking at the secluded, arborvitae, tree-lined residence gave the unfriendly next-door neighbor a good excuse to call the cops on the Waters. With a little luck, she thought, law enforcement will discover something illegal going on next door. If nothing else, answering some basic questions from the police would cause some inconvenience, she hoped.

The responding patrol officer made the grisly discovery shortly after arriving and immediately called for an ambulance and a backup. The coroner, Neil or Doc, as he was referred to, was immediately called to the scene. It was he who initiated the three-way call.

"This one is a double," Doc began after some brief pleasantries. "The male victim, I'm assuming he's the husband, took a severe blow to the side of his head with a blunt object. The body pretty much matches the identification in his wallet, but his face is unrecognizable. It's bashed in pretty good," he stated. "The female victim appears to be the lady of the house. She is strapped face down on the kitchen table with a single hole in the back of her head. It appears to be the handy work of whomever carried out the other recent murders in this town. I'll let you figure out the rest of the puzzle when you get here. Meanwhile, I have an autopsy to perform back in my office. My assistants will be here if you need anything. I'll look at these two in the morgue once you guys finish up and have them sent over to the lab," he instructed. "I'll go out on a limb, though, and say preliminarily that her brains have been scrambled. Just like the others," Doc described. "The gentleman, however, did not die from eating gas-station sushi," he said sarcastically. "He was violently attacked by a very powerful individual," he stated.

"Do either of you have any further questions at this point?" Doc asked.

"No," the chief replied. "Thanks for the info, Doc. I will talk to you a little later. You can hang up if you want," Chief instructed. "Dave, stay on the line with me for a minute."

"I'm here, Chief," Dave acknowledged. "Sounds like our serial killer is back in action. Give me a few minutes to get to the scene so I can have a good look around," he suggested. "This guy that we're looking for has to screw up eventually. I just get the feeling we're missing something obvious that will lead us right to him. I'll ask my brother to dig around and see if anyone wanted these people dead," Dave mentioned.

"This one is going to cause a shit storm, Dave," the chief added. "I'll handle the politicians and the press. Expect them both to be in a contest to see who can be the most hysterical. We, on the other hand, need to stay calm and stay focused. We'll figure it out if we keep the background noise from distracting us," he instructed.

"Calm and focused," Dave repeated in a matter-of-fact tone. "Got it, Chief," he acknowledged.

"Dave, are you okay?" the chief asked.

The chief sensed David's aloof response to the most recent murder. David wasn't his usual focused, highly intensified self. Even with an obvious serial killer on his hands, David gave the chief the feeling that he was just going through the motions. Something was obviously bothering his gifted, prized detective, and the chief thought he knew what it was.

"How's your dad doing?" the chief finally probed.

"Not great," David replied in the same matter-of-fact tone of voice. "He's recovered from surgery and starts his chemotherapy treatment tomorrow. My father will fight like hell, and won't give up easily, but he's up against a tough opponent," he admitted. "My mom, however, is worried sick about him. She is doing everything she can to hide her worries." He nervously chuckled.

David paused for a moment. The chief allowed his silence and patiently listened for him to say what he felt wanted to say next. David suddenly began to verbalize his stream of consciousness as if he were speaking to himself.

"I feel like I'm in the same boat as my mom," David finally admitted. "I think I'm doing a better job at keeping it to myself, though. I can read her worried looks and comments like a book," he sympathized. "On the other hand, I'm sure no one can detect a change in my demeanor," David bragged before snapping himself back to the moment.

"Do me a favor, though, keep reminding me to stay calm and stay focused, will you, chief?" David asked.

"Will do, Dave," the chief promised. "I'll see you in a few minutes," Chief said as he disconnected.

***

David arrived at 200 Wells Street in Chevon and found an all-too-familiar crime scene. It appeared the man put up a weak resistance effort and took a quick blow to the left side of his head. There was a defensive injury on the back of his left hand which indicated he tried to block the blow but was a little slow to react. There was a pool of blood next to his head, indicating he didn't die instantly, but once he hit the floor, he didn't move again.

She, like the other murder victims, was overpowered and strapped to the kitchen table with the same type of kayak straps that were used in the other killings. She shared the same piercing injury to the back of her head with the others who were done in by the killer. Dave could see why Doc sent his assistants to the scene. The cause of death was obvious for both victims. Evidence would be gathered and brought back to the lab for analysis, but it was another organized and, at the same time, chaotic crime scene.

David needed his brother's help in checking out the background on these two. This killing was another assassination, and there must be some thread linking the victims. He called Rick in order to break the news and to seek his help.

After a brief conversation concerning the mental state of Gerry and Mary, David got to the reason for his call.

"Rick, see what you can find out about Robert and Elizabeth Waters on Wells Street in Chevon," Dave began ominously. "There's no need for you to come over here. It's the exact same scene. The only difference is in the names of the corpses," he said.

"Not again!" Rick replied. "This is starting to get annoying," he said, stating the obvious. "Are you there now?" Rick asked.

"Yeah. Same show, different place," Dave responded. "Do some digging. See if there is anyone who might have wanted them dead. Maybe we can get together for a bite to eat later and you can fill me in. I want to stop over and see Dad tonight, anyway, so let's shoot for five at The Diner. Call me back if you need anything. Otherwise, I still have a few hours of work to do here," David advised.

"Roger that," Rick confirmed. "Let me do my thing, and I'll see you later on. I want to visit Dad as well. Maybe we can bring him some pastry. Hopefully, we can brighten his day a little," Rick explained as he disconnected.

***

Kisluks' Diner was located on Main Street in Medbury, approximately five miles from the O'Driscoll residence where Rick and his brother, David, grew up. The owner, George, had purchased four, old, sleeper-rail cars and converted them into what he named The Diner. The cars were structurally joined into a large square. The center of the square was transformed into a covered outdoor bar and patio area which featured nightly entertainment, televisions, and lawn games. The establishment was a popular night spot in town. It had a reputation for shuffling late-night patrons into the Breakfast Car for its famous omelets, home fries, pancakes, and toast after the last call was served.

George Kisluk, the owner, and Gerry O'Driscoll were the closest of friends. They had coached baseball together and against each other for over 20 years. After each game, they invariably found time to share a cold beer and tell tall tales. George was a retired high-school teacher. During his 30-year teaching tenure, he supplemented his income during the summer months by tending bar at a local banquet facility. His larger-than-life, upbeat personality garnered him larger than life tips from the many patrons that he served on a typical evening. When George concocted an adult beverage for a patron, the experience for them was like no other. It didn't matter how busy the event was. George made you feel like you were the only person in the room, and the entertainment he provided was worth the wait for everyone involved.

George knew he had a special talent for creating fun, so he set the goal of opening his own bar once his teaching days were over. What started out as a simple bar car quickly caught on and expanded to an additional breakfast car. Next, he decided to add on a lunch car, and, finally, he attached a dinner car.

The lunch car and the dinner car had some overlap with the menu choices. However, if high-priced, small-portioned gourmet food was what the patron sought, The Diner was not the right place to be. The steak was grilled, the chicken and fish were fried, and the cheeseburgers were steamed. One could get a grilled cheeseburger upon special request. The final product, however, although typically delicious, was not guaranteed as it was had it been steamed. French fries and onion rings were mouthwatering and stacked high. Soups, chowders, and salad dressings were homemade. The recipes for each were a result of George's tinkering in his private kitchen. They were held, by him and his staff, as a deep, carefully guarded secret.

Rick immediately checked the bar car on his arrival, half expecting to find his brother there. He was hoping he wouldn't. Instead, he found David sharing a booth with George, the owner, in the lunch car. Each sipped a fresh glass of unsweetened ice tea. They were engaged in deep conversation, oblivious of any outside observers.

"Mind if I join you guys?" Rick asked as he sat down on the edge of the seat next to George, opposite David.

"Rick!" George bellowed through his engaging smile as he placed him in a firm bear hug. "Dave and I have been talking about your father. He's going to be just fine, trust me," he promised. "I've known him for years, and nobody is tougher. He's going to kick cancer right in the ass and be back 100 percent before you know it."

"Thanks, Mister Kisluk," Rick replied with a laugh. "I can always count on you to provide some needed encouragement," he said. "I hope you are right! My father is a sick man. He mentioned how you stopped by a couple of times to visit with him while he was recovering from his surgery. It means a lot to him having such good friends supporting and cheering for him. I can't thank you enough for being there for him," Rick exclaimed.

"I'm here for the duration," George replied, suddenly somberly. "Anything I can do for him and your family, you guys just have to let me know. I love your father like a brother," he stated.

Suddenly, George nudged Rick to the aisle so that he could scoot out of his seat and let Rick sit back down opposite his brother in the booth.

"I have to get back to work," George announced. "Before you guys leave, come and find me. I want to send one of my famous brownies and a Bahama Mama home to your dad. Make sure you tell him I made the drink special for him," he instructed.

"Sure thing," David laughed. "He's not going to drink a Bahama Mama, though. Alcohol is off limits for him until he gets better," he stated.

"I don't expect him to drink it," George replied. He smiled and then, just as quickly, he let it fade from his face. "That's not the point. Your father will understand, though. Gerry will understand," he said as he faded away toward the bar car.

David and Rick each ordered a grilled cheese sandwich with homemade potato chips and a bowl of tomato soup. While they waited for the waitress to bring them their food, Rick pulled a notebook from his pocket and leafed through it until he found the pages he was looking for. Both struggled to focus their attention on the main reason they agreed to meet. Maybe they chose the wrong venue, but they each felt they needed a familiar setting with good friends close by. Besides, the boys were hungry, and there was no place on the planet they would get comfort food like they could at The Diner.

"What did you find out, Bro?" David asked.

"The male victim was, in fact, Robert Waters," Rick began. "He was a wealthy lawyer, and lots of people had good reason for wanting to see him dead. His wife, Elizabeth, didn't have many friends, but we didn't come across anyone yet who we feel hated her enough to have her murdered. From what we've been told, Elizabeth frequently threatened to have her husband, the lawyer, sue whomever she felt rubbed her the wrong way. The acquaintances of hers with whom we spoke, each said that they were polite to her but kept her at arms-length. She wasn't high on the list of ladies to be invited to the neighborhood-cookie swap, if you know what I mean. He, on the other hand, was the master of frivolous lawsuits. I already have a full list of targets who spent every penny they had on defense lawyers and settlement payouts. Most of these folks forfeited everything they had, not to mention what they had to borrow, in order to end his vicious legal attack. Many lives were ruined by this Robert Waters. You may want to start investigating his death by talking to some of them," Rick advised.

"I understand what you are getting at, Rick," Dave replied pensively. "The problem, though, is that the wife was the one who was assassinated. The killer strapped her to the table, just like the others, and put his signature hole in the back of her head. Somehow, I think the husband just happened to be in the wrong place at the wrong time," he said.

Rick considered what his brother had just said.

"Maybe the killer is screwing with you, Dave," Rick reasoned. "Maybe he's putting more thought into covering his tracks. There's a possibility that he wants to send us off on a wild goose chase. He could do that by whacking the husband, the real target, and then doing his signature thing to the wife," he explained.

"No." David slowly shook his head. "I think, to the killer, the husband was just like the dog in the first killing. Nothing more than a threatening animal trying to get in the way of what he needed to do. The killer is very careful, but he doesn't seem to feel any heat from us. There's no reason for him to play a phony game in order to throw us off track," he concluded. "She was the target. Not him. She has something in common with the other three. We just don't know what it is yet. I still don't believe for a minute that these killings are random. So far, the common trait is that none of the previous victims had any close friends that we could locate. See if the same is true of Mrs. Waters," he instructed.

Rick jotted a note on his pad.

"What else do they have in common, Dave?" Rick inquired. "What are we missing here?" he wondered.

"They all lived in the same town, but that must be just coincidental," David stated. "You know, birds of a feather flock together," he reasoned.

David continued to think aloud.

"I don't think it's because of where they live. I think that these people would have been murdered no matter what town they live in. It's just that the people who are attracting this murdering lunatic happen to live in a community that is loaded with lonely, elitist snobs, just like them," he said.

Rick and Dave took their time finishing their soup and sandwich. Conversation shifted from work to sports and, finally, to a golf outing planned for the coming Saturday. Neither wanted to discuss the elephant in the room that was sitting on the table, separating the two brothers.

Eventually, Rick managed to mention how he wished that Gerry was the one rounding out their foursome this weekend. And then the conversation shifted once again.

Neither could grasp nor understand exactly what their father was in for. All they knew was that he would start chemotherapy tomorrow. Based on what each had read on select websites, to them, the treatment sounded barbaric. Poisons would be injected into their father's body in an attempt to kill cancer cells. Collateral damage to healthy cells was inevitable which would steer the body to experience some unpredictable side effects. Their lack of knowledge terrified them and led to some wild speculation.

Finally, each had had enough. Dave raised his hand and asked for the check. The waitress, responding to the signal, informed him that George had covered their tab. They were all square. Surprised but thankful, the boys reciprocated by leaving the waitress an extra-large tip and then prepared to leave The Diner.

"Dave, why don't you go and head over to the house?" Rick instructed. "I'll go over and thank Mr. Kisluk for dinner and pick up the brownie and the drink," he confirmed. "I'll see you in a little while."

"That sounds good," David confirmed. "I don't know what I'm going to say to Dad," he sheepishly confided to his older brother. "For the first time in my life, I feel awkward visiting him," David admitted.

"He's still Dad," Rick replied. "Let him lead the conversation if you wish. But, in my opinion, if you have a question that you want to ask him, don't be afraid to ask it. If he doesn't want to answer, he won't. As for me, I'm going to remind him to keep his eye on the ball and hit it straight. Dad needs our support more than he needs anything else from us now. Just be there for him, Dave. And don't forget to hope, and pray, and cross your fingers, and rub a rabbit's foot, and whatever else you can think of doing that might help him. But, most of all, Dave, don't give up on him. Don't ever stop believing that he's going to beat this thing. Know that he will be back as good as new before we know it. Don't ever stop believing, Dave. Ever," he said.

# 14

Hoping, although not an ideal strategy, is sometimes the only strategy.

Mary insisted on driving Gerry to his morning appointment. She convinced him that he may not be able to drive himself home, being this would be his first treatment. The truth, however, was that she couldn't handle the thought of Gerry going through what he was about to experience alone. Mary also knew that Gerry would warp the story of what he experienced if she relied on him to recant his session once he returned from it. She couldn't handle the thought of not being able to see the process with her own eyes. Gerry, she knew, would make it sound like the whole thing was no big deal. If left to her imagination, Mary realized, she would visualize the ordeal as something approaching Armageddon.

The bottom line was that she had to see the procedure for herself. There would be no further room for debate on the issue. She had to make sure they were taking good care of her husband. She had to be available to Gerry in case he needed anything. Most of all, she felt that she had to be there to provide encouragement for her husband. Of the two, Mary was far more nervous about what the morning would bring than was Gerry. Gerry's mindset was such that he had mentally prepared himself to charge into a bloody cage match and fight to the death. Mary's task of watching the brawl from a front-row seat, being restricted to only providing dedicated care and support, was stomach-churning to her.

The two arrived at the unassuming lobby of the plain brick building after a short, quiet drive and took the antiseptic-smelling elevator down one level to the double glass-door entrance to Doctor Hearms' office. After a quick check-in, they were instructed to take the same antiseptic-smelling elevator up to the third floor where the chemotherapy parlor was located. Gerry signed in there, and he and Mary calmly waited for his name to be called.

Gerry had just started to read an article of interest from an outdated magazine, which had been carefully lined up on an adjacent-end table, when one of the nurses called his name. He stood and raised his hand as if he had just won something at a church raffle and was immediately escorted to an examination room on the right-hand side of the short hallway. The room was small but well-lighted with a window overlooking the rooftop of an adjacent building. The floor was tiled with lightly speckled vinyl squares and the white-painted walls matched the color of the dropped ceiling. There were several florescent light fixtures alternating among the two-foot by four-foot ceiling tiles, providing a bright-but-color-distorting ambiance. A sink with two, oversized, matching, supply cabinets mounted above took up the entire far wall. The cabinets were well-stocked with a variety of medical supplies. Most of which Gerry could not fathom what they would be used for.

Gerry sat on the crinkly white paper covering the examination table and blankly stared through the window at the view of the black-tarred roof and H.V.A.C. units scattered on it below. Mary sat silently in the guest chair, deep in thought, taking in her surroundings, nervously watching the door. After what seemed an hour but, in reality, was only a few short minutes, there was a soft knock on the door. In walked a woman who appeared to be in her mid-30s, dressed in light-blue scrubs, with a warm smile and a confident, take-charge look.

"Mr. and Mrs. O'Driscoll?" Nancy began. "Hi, my name is Nancy, and I'll be taking care of you today," she announced.

Gerry didn't know it yet, but he would later refer to Nancy as an angel sent from heaven to help him get through what would be a grueling ordeal. Doctor Hearms would monitor Gerry's vitals and blood counts in order to safely administer the drugs that would be pumped into his system for the next several months. Nancy, however, would be there on the front lines, in the thick of the fight with Gerry. She would look out for him physically and emotionally.

Nancy's ten-plus years of experience in treating cancer patients prepared her to be technically qualified for her position. Her five years of personally experiencing the grief associated with watching helplessly as her mother died from an aggressive form of breast cancer instilled in her a supreme hatred for the vile disease. She was fully educated about the devastating havoc that cancer wreaks on the human soul. Nancy's external demeanor was pleasant, calm, and confident. Internally, she had the intensity of a caged animal wishing to attack and rip any cancer which crossed her path to shreds.

"First thing's first, Mr. O'Driscoll," Nancy began. "I need you to get on the scale and then you can have a seat back on the exam table," she instructed.

Gerry made his way over to the upright floor scale and weighed in at 220 pounds. At six foot, four inches, he was neither overweight nor was he listed as being thin. He had lost a few pounds since his surgery but nothing dramatic.

If all goes according to schedule, it would take him six long months to finish the 12 rounds of chemotherapy necessary to eradicate his body from any rogue cancer cells. The rhythm was to be a dose every other week which gave his body a week to recover before administering the next treatment. By the time Gerry finished his last treatment, several months from now, his weight would bottom out at 149 pounds. A full-grown man standing six foot, four inches and weighing 149 pounds would, by all accounts, be considered thin.

"Next, I'm going to take your temperature," Nancy explained as she swiped his forehead with a sensor. "98.6. Very good. You pass," she encouraged. "I need your left arm please, for your blood pressure, and then I'll take your pulse."

Nancy would enter each reading into her laptop computer for her records and as a baseline of Gerry's vitals.

"Now, if you would unbutton the top few buttons of your shirt, I want to take a look at your port," Nancy calmly instructed.

Gerry mindlessly complied with her simple direction.

"It's still a little tender," Gerry offered. "I just had it put in a week ago, and I'm sore all around it. And please, it's okay for you to call me Gerry," he mentioned.

She touched the flesh surrounding Gerry's port. It was still red and swollen.

"This may sound crazy. However, if I can use the port today, you'll be much better off than if I have to tap a vein in your arm," Nancy said as she continued to gently, carefully, press the area surrounding the circular, volcano-like object pushing up from beneath the skin a few inches below Gerry's right collarbone. "It looks really good, Gerry," she assured him. "Are you okay if I use it?" she asked.

"Why not?" Gerry replied with a touch of sarcasm. "Let me guess. The next thing you are going to tell me is that this may be a little uncomfortable," he reasoned.

"Not for me," Nancy shot back with a twinkle in her eye.

Nancy had acquired, through experience, the uncanny ability to get an accurate read on her patients. In the short time that she had been exposed to Gerry, Nancy correctly read him as someone who had a fighting spirit. He wasn't, in her estimation, going to take this cancer problem lying down. She wouldn't pity him, or baby him, at least to his face. Nancy could be a stalwart coach when she needed to be. Gerry, she determined, was going to need every bit of the tough love that she intended to provide to him.

"Very funny," Gerry replied. "I will get my revenge," he promised.

Gerry stared in horror as Nancy unwrapped the specialized needle from its blue encasement and swiped his chest with an antiseptic swab.

"Whatever it is that you are planning on doing, please do not miss the target," Gerry pleaded.

"What I'm going to do is insert a specialized needle into your port," Nancy lectured. "I'll be able to draw your blood from it. We'll have your blood tested next door and the results go directly to Doctor Hearms. Once he analyzes the report and gives me the go ahead, I'll reverse the flow of the port and you'll have your drugs delivered directly into your blood stream," she stated.

"Are you ready?" Nancy asked as if preparing him for the start of a foot race.

"All set," Gerry replied as he let his mind wander from his body and perch itself high in the far corner of the room. From there, it could observe the procedure, detached from the scene unfolding below.

Gerry's upper chest was more tender than he was letting on, and he had a feeling that this procedure would be, to say the least, 'a little uncomfortable.' He took Nancy's advice on using the port, however. Gerry already had the feeling that she was looking out for his best interest. He would continue to gain more and more trust in her as time went on.

"Okay," Nancy readied as she pressed the exposed, sterile needle between her gloved thumb and forefinger. "On the count of three, you're going to feel a pinch. One, two, three, pinch."

Nancy drove the needle through Gerry's skin just below his collarbone, directly into the middle of the circled outline of his port. To Gerry, it felt just like someone was driving a needle through the skin of his tender, upper chest. He gritted his teeth from the pain but refused to flinch. A moment later, the pain began to dissipate, and Gerry's mind reunited with his body. Nancy quickly, expertly, applied a clear adhesive which kept the needle immobile and perfectly in place. The tubes dangling from the end of the contraption affixed to Gerry's chest would remain there for the next three days while the medicines were pumped into his body.

"I'm just going to take some blood samples over to the lab and then Doctor Hearms will be in to see you," Nancy said as she attached the color-coded collection glass tubes to the line leading to Gerry's port. "It takes about ten minutes or so. Make yourself comfortable," she advised.

Gerry sat silently as Mary tried to make distracting, casual conversation about current events. He didn't know what to expect next and was understandably somewhat apprehensive. The questions he asked of the various medical providers garnered such a wide range of responses that he got to the point of not asking. The routine of having Nancy check his weight, temperature, blood pressure, pulse, and blood draw were the only consistencies in the process that he would learn to rely upon.

In the coming months, if Gerry's blood work checked out, he would get his dose of chemotherapy and head down that unpredictable rabbit hole. If his blood work didn't check out, in Gerry's case, his platelet levels would, on occasion, become dangerously low; Nancy would pull the needle from his chest, and he would be sent home to continue his recovery from the previous session.

To Gerry, the days that he was denied treatment would be the darkest days of the chemotherapy process. The drugs, as barbaric as they are, had to be intravenously absorbed by his body in order to kill the cancer. If he couldn't get his dose because of the harm they were causing to his healthy cells, his odds of survival would be significantly diminished.

Finally, after what seemed an eternity.

"Good morning, folks," Doctor Hearms smiled as he stuck his head into the exam room where Mary and Gerry were seated.

The doctor listened to Gerry's heart and lungs with his stethoscope and checked him for unusual swelling of his knees and ankles. He would then ask some basic health questions before setting the day's agenda.

"Your blood looks good. Are you ready for your first session?" he asked.

"I'm as ready as I'm going to be," Gerry replied dryly.

"Okay then. Let's do this," the doctor instructed. "Just head down the hallway to the last room on the right and have a seat in one of the recliners. Nancy will be in shortly to administer the drugs," he stated. "Mary, you are welcome to join him if you would like. We should have Gerry out of here in about three hours. I'll try to circle back and see you before you leave today. If I get caught up in something else and don't make it, however, I'll see you back here in two weeks," he said. "Good luck, Gerry," Doctor Hearms encouraged as he pointed the way to the chemo parlor.

Mary and Gerry slowly made their way to the room at the end of the hallway as directed. Three patients were already there, fully reclined in soft chairs, silently receiving their treatment. Two of them were napping and never opened their eyes. The third, a gentleman in Gerry's age group, glanced over at him and offered a slight nod of the head. Gerry chose a vacant rocker-recliner along the far wall while Mary sat in a guest chair close to the door leading into the room. Moments later, Nancy approached Gerry. She was holding a clipboard and a pen.

"Gerry, I just need you to, once again, sign this document," Nancy began. "Feel free to read through it if you like. Basically, you're giving us the okay to treat you with the listed medication. It says in there that the drugs may help, but they can also do severe harm to you. Some people do very well, and others do not. There's no way of telling how your body will react until we get started. We can't, however, get started until you sign the document, saying it's okay to do so," she stated.

Gerry looked around at the other patients who were getting their treatment for whatever type of cancer each was battling. Although none of the others looked happy, they all appeared to be bravely in the thick of their private battle. Nancy was giving Gerry one last chance to back out, but he wasn't taking it.

"Give me the pen," he demanded. "It's time to get this show on the road."

Nancy took the signed document and returned, moments later, with bags of clear fluid that she carefully hung from the metallic tree next to Gerry's chair. The first drip was a saline solution which would hydrate Gerry. Once that bag was empty, she started the three-and-a-half-hour process of delivering the powerful drugs into his blood stream.

The chemotherapy parlor, on this day, was eerily quiet. The other patients were stone silent as they received their treatment. Mary felt awkward at first, just being in the room with cancer patients receiving what was hopefully their lifesaving drugs. She didn't feel like she was providing good company to Gerry, however. Mary didn't feel it was appropriate for her to be the one to break the uncomfortable silence that lingered in the room.

Finally, out the blue, Gerry announced to nobody in particular, "I have to pee."

He reached over the arm of his chair for the power cord leading from his drug tree to the plug in the wall and pulled. He stood up, a little wobbly at first, and wheeled his drugs the short distance to the adjacent restroom.

"Mary, why don't you go for a walk or something?" Gerry suggested. "Get yourself a cup of coffee. Nancy says I'm going to be another hour in here. You may as well get some fresh air," he recommended.

Mary jumped at the suggestion.

"Okay," she thankfully replied. "I'll be a half hour or so. Coffee will do me some good," she realized.

Mary grabbed her handbag and flew past the receptionist, into the hallway, and took the elevator to the ground level. The chemotherapy parlor was beyond depressing for Mary. As much as she wanted to be with her husband, offering her support to him, she couldn't bear the atmosphere. She tearfully sprinted from the front door of the building to her car, started the engine, and sat for a moment. Mary felt overwhelmed with gratitude toward Gerry for his suggestion that she take a break, but she was highly disappointed in herself for the realization that she desperately needed to get out of there already.

With her partially consumed cup of coffee in hand, Mary returned to the chemotherapy parlor a half hour later. This would be the last time that she was able to bring herself to enter the somber atmosphere of the treatment room. Going forward, Gerry would drive himself to and from his treatments. Mary could no longer bring herself to sit and watch her husband endure the three-

and-a-half-hour ordeal. Gerry understood completely. He didn't want to be there either.

Finally, mercifully, the last plastic bag of clear liquid for the day had dripped and emptied its contents into Gerry's bloodstream. The alarm on the tree that the medication hung from was chirping, calling to the nurses. The fixture noisily informed the staff that the drugs have, at last, been successfully delivered. Nancy, responding to the commotion, purposefully entered the room. Without saying a word, she skillfully disconnected the long tube leading to the medicine from the short tube that was attached to the needle in Gerry's chest.

"Is that it?" Gerry asked. "Can I go home now?" he hoped.

"Pretty soon," Nancy replied. "I have one more bag of meds that you have to take home with you."

Nancy connected a long tube leading from a miniature pump, the size of a purse, to the short tube feeding into to Gerry's port. She then loaded the pump with one more dose of the 5FU drug, locked the cover, and placed the whole apparatus into a small fanny pack that Gerry would wear just above his right-hand pants pocket for the next two days.

"Gerry, this is the last of your treatment," she instructed. "It's going to take another 48 hours to finish pumping this dose. The day after tomorrow, at exactly this time, the alarm on the pump will go off. You might as well just come in a half hour ahead of time, so it doesn't annoy you when it goes off. It's kind of loud. Anyway, just come in here and have a seat. When I see you, I'll unhook the pump and pull the needle from your port at the same time. After that, you'll have 11 days of recovery," she informed him. "We'll make an appointment for your next treatment two weeks from today."

Gerry, who was completely blindsided by the revelation that he would have to continue his chemotherapy session at home for another two days, blankly stared at Nancy. He had many questions, but figured he would find the answers to most on his own. For some strange reason, however, he felt compelled to ask what for him was the most pressing question.

"Can I take a shower with this thing?" he begged.

"No!" Nancy exclaimed. "Don't get it wet. These pumps are expensive, and you, unfortunately, are responsible for returning it in one piece," she smiled. "Oh, and one last thing before you go. Doctor Hearms called in a prescription of anti-nausea medication to the pharmacy you gave us. Pick it up on your way home and start taking it immediately. One of the clear meds that I just gave you was an anti-nausea drug, but it's going to wear off in a couple of hours. You have to stay ahead of the nausea. We do not want you to start vomiting," she warned. "In the next couple of days, if you have any severe side effects, call us immediately. Otherwise, you did great. I will see you back here in 48 hours. You are free to go."

Gerry ran the long rubber tube leading from his upper chest down through the inside of his shirt so it wasn't visible. He tucked the excess tubing inside the fanny pack containing the pump and zippered it closed. The pump made a short, noticeable, squealing sound each time it delivered some of the drug into Gerry's body. Nancy nodded approvingly when she heard the sound confirming the apparatus was functioning properly and exited the room.

Gerry lapped his tongue from the roof of his mouth back down to its normal position shortly after the first time he heard the pump working. Nothing entered his mouth; however, he suddenly had a strong taste of something metallic emanating from the back of his throat. He likened it to what he would expect if he were sucking on roofing nails. After a moment, the sensation went away, only to return at the instant the squealing sound signaled that the pump was delivering the next dose.

The repetition continued for the remainder of the day, the entire following day, and half of the third day. Each time the pump sounded, a disgusting metallic taste would be momentarily detected by Gerry's fooled taste buds.

Mary and Gerry hopped into their car and headed home via the local pharmacy. Gerry didn't feel horrible, but he didn't feel great either. The strange metallic taste in his mouth was certainly curbing his appetite. He was told it was a good idea to drink as much water as he could in order to flush his system and stay hydrated, but he wasn't very thirsty.

Gerry felt a little strange, but he couldn't describe exactly what he was feeling. It was like nothing else he had ever previously experienced, so the best he could do was say that he felt a general malaise.

Mary made a turkey sandwich with lettuce, tomato, and mustard on toast for him, and it took Gerry a solid 45 minutes to force it down the hatch. He tried washing it down with a room-temperature glass of water, but the task proved to be more difficult than expected. Gerry's mouth was suddenly so dry that it forced him to chew, and chew, and chew each cardboard-tasting bite for what seemed to him to be hours at a time.

Gerry thought about dipping the turkey sandwich in a cup of water, like the contestants do in the fourth of July, hotdog-eating contest at Coney Island, and then jump up and down as he stuffed another bite into his mouth. Mary thought that would be a bad idea, so Gerry temporarily put it out of his mind. Finally, after much angst, he managed to force down what would be his last solid food intake for the next three days.

After lunch, he made his way to his recliner, sat there, and raised his feet so he could relax for a moment.

Just as he kicked back, he felt a burning sensation on his lower abdomen. It was coming from the location where his stoma protruded into his colostomy bag. He lifted his shirt to expose the bag and discovered it to be inflated, balloon-like and full of a dark brown liquid which, from a distance, could be confused for black coffee. Gerry's severe diarrhea had begun. He rushed to the bathroom in order to empty the contents of the colostomy bag and firmly held his nose as he did.

Gerry's general malaise was intensifying by the minute. The pump, which was concealed inside of the fanny pack that he wore on his waist, was taunting him every few minutes with the squealing sound that cruelly indicated another dose of 5FU was being squirted into his body.

"I'm having some fun now!" Gerry announced. "At least I know it can't get much worse than this," he mused sarcastically.

And then the hiccups began.

As nauseous as Gerry felt, the anti-nausea pills that he was taking did their job in preventing him from vomiting. Every 20 seconds, however, for the next two-and-a-half days, Gerry's body convulsed in a loud, violent hiccup. It was difficult enough trying to sleep with the whining squeal of the pump and the subsequent metallic taste in the back of his throat that persisted every few minutes. The incessant, merciless hiccup that shook him to his bones three times each minute, however, would make sleeping impossible for the next two nights.

Gerry tried every home remedy that he could think of, which didn't involve eating something, to try to rid his body of its hiccup torture. He held his breath. He watched a scary movie. He put a paper bag over his head. He drank water from the opposite side of the glass. He hopped on his right leg while rubbing his belly with his left hand and patting his head with his right hand. Nothing worked.

Finally, Mary called Doctor Hearms for advice. Although he was sympathetic, the doctor had little to offer regarding help in trying to liberate Gerry from his hiccups so that he could get some sleep. The best Doctor Hearms could come up with was to hope the hiccups would just go away on their own. Otherwise, he genuinely hoped that everything else was okay and looked forward to seeing Gerry when he came in to get disconnected from the pump.

***

Finally, after a full 47 hours of additional chemotherapy treatment, Gerry got himself ready to head back to Doctor Hearms' office. He hadn't slept in two days. The pump, which he was told couldn't be brought into the shower, prevented Gerry from the dignity of being able to properly freshen up. His malaise was such that he had difficulty forcing himself to drink a glass of room-temperature water.

Gerry felt worse than he could ever remember feeling in his life. It was much worse than he remembered feeling while nursing the worst hangover he ever inflicted upon himself. As he was unable to accurately describe, the feeling he felt was uniquely miserable.

Mary drove Gerry to his appointment, but she patiently remained in the car and watched as he disappeared into the brick building. She feared he would fall asleep while travelling at 65 miles an hour if left on his own accord. Upon his arrival into the parlor, Gerry mindlessly gravitated to the same recliner that he occupied two days ago for three-and-a-half hours. 47 hours and 59 minutes since he last sat in the familiar seat, the alarm on the pump sounded. Nancy heard the noise from the adjacent room and wandered over to stick her head into the chemo parlor.

"Oh, look who's back," Nancy said as she approached Gerry with a warm smile. "How did it go the last couple of days?" she asked.

"I feel, *HICCUP*, like crap," Gerry replied. "The worst part is I've, *HICCUP*, had these freakin' hiccups for the past two days," he complained.

"First things first," Nancy replied. "Let me get rid of the pump for you. Open your shirt, and I'll take the needle out," she instructed. "Taking it out doesn't hurt half as much as it does when we put it in," Nancy revealed as she peeled the adhesive which held the needle firmly to Gerry's chest.

She carefully gripped the end of the needle with her right hand and lightly pressed the outer edges of Gerry's port with her left.

"On the count of three. Ready?" Nancy asked. "One-two-three," she said while quickly extracting the attachment.

Finally, Gerry was disconnected. He didn't feel any differently physically. Mentally, however, his sudden freedom from the relentless squealing of the dreaded pump overwhelmed him with a feeling of liberation that he would yearn for every other week for the next several months. Strangely, all he could think of, as he sat, untethered, was how good a hot shower was going to feel. Maybe, just maybe, he thought, it would even help to get rid of these hiccups. If only they would go away, he could get some needed sleep.

"Okay, now let's talk about those annoying hiccups," Nancy offered. "Not everyone gets that particular side effect from the drugs you are taking. Unfortunately, you got it," she admitted. "I had a patient a few months ago that had the same thing happen," Nancy recalled. "I got the doctor to change the anti-nausea medication that he was taking to a much stronger one, and it did the trick. I'll have Doctor Hearms call in a prescription to your pharmacy. Pick it up on the way home and give it a try. Let me know how it works," Nancy instructed. "Otherwise, go home and get some rest. Drink as much water as you can. It's important for you to flush the drugs from your system. Call me if you need anything else or if you have any questions. Unless I hear from you, the next time I'll speak to you will be 12 days from now. Go ahead and stop at the desk to make an appointment for your second treatment," she instructed as she moved to tend to the needs of another patient who had just arrived for treatment.

On their way home, Mary stopped at the pharmacy to get the newly prescribed, anti-nausea medication. Gerry immediately swallowed one of the pills before they even reached home. One half-hour later, he hiccupped for the last time.

"She's an angel," Gerry declared, referring to Nancy as he lumbered up the stairs to the master bedroom.

He stripped naked, ripped the colostomy bag from his lower abdomen, exposing the bright-red, protruding stoma, and hopped into a hot, steaming, shower for the first time in days.

The only time Gerry felt 'whole' throughout this whole ordeal was when he was able to shower without the colostomy bag attached to his belly. When he showered with the bag attached, he had an uncomfortable, unnatural feeling caused by the weight of his waste succumbing to the effect of gravity. Without it, he would simply wash whatever flowed out of his stoma down the drain with the rest of his body wash. If he refrained from looking down, he could pretend to be back to his old, normal self. Just like he was a couple of short months ago. Before cancer reared its ugly head and decided it wanted to be the center of attention.

Gerry begrudgingly stepped from the comfortable confines of the warm shower, dried off, and applied a new bag to his abdomen. He then tossed on a comfortable pair of oversized boxer-shorts and a tee shirt, climbed into bed, and, within minutes, was in a deep, restful sleep.

When he awoke, four hours later, he had no concept of the time of day. He simply knew he was awake and thirsty.

Gingerly, he made his way downstairs to the kitchen, all the while fighting with lightheadedness and fatigue. Gerry plopped himself into one of the wooden breakfast-bar stools next to the kitchen counter. His head was down, and his shoulders rounded. Canker sores were beginning to form in his throat, and his lips were dry and cracked. *Round one was over,* he thought to himself.

Just like in a championship boxing match, Gerry had 11 more rounds to go. Each would prove to be more difficult than the last. The accumulating effect of each blow would take its toll as the vicious brawl raged on. Gerry knew he had to focus on recovery and strength building in order to get his body ready for the sound of the next bell. Thoughts of giving up were quickly beaten back before they could further take root. There was simply no room for negative vibes.

As the fight reached the later rounds, however, it would become more and more difficult for him to brush those feelings to the side. Now, though, Gerry's simple priority was obtaining water. Room-temperature water.

Mary heard Gerry making his way into the kitchen and softly approached. She was happy he could finally get some sleep but didn't know what to expect as she turned the corner and laid eyes on him. She lightly placed her left hand on his right shoulder and bent so she could look directly into his glassy, bloodshot eyes as he slowly raised his head to look at her.

Mary could tell he still felt horrible, but this was no time for sympathy. Gerry needed a trainer and a coach right now. He needed someone to fan him with a towel, pour water down his throat, and remind him to keep his guard up just before pushing him back into the center of the ring. He didn't need someone patting his head and appeasing him with 'nice try.' Gerry would not be accepting any participation trophies. In the fight against cancer, coming in second place was fatal.

"Gerry, how are you feeling, Honey?" Mary asked.

"I feel like shit," Gerry replied matter-of-factly. "I'm really thirsty, though. I need something cold in the worst way, but the doctor says I can't have anything below room temperature. Mary, get me a cold glass of water, please. My throat is so dry!" he pleaded.

"I don't know if this is a good idea," Mary said as she poured Gerry a cold glass. "But, if you insist, here you go," she warned.

Gerry took the cold glass of water from Mary with his right hand and began to raise it to his lips. Just before he drank it, his fingertips developed a strange painful sensation which caused him to quickly put the glass down on the counter.

"Honey, I can't feel my fingers!" Gerry shouted. "I got this strange pins and needle sensation for a second, and, now, I have absolutely no feeling at all," he said as he kneaded and rubbed his fingers.

Eventually, the feeling began to reverse itself, but not 100 percent. The numbness that Gerry was experiencing in the tips of his fingers would be permanent. Depending on the room temperature as well as other minor influences, the feeling would gain and lose its intensity. But the numbness would never again leave him entirely.

"I guess they weren't kidding when they said to avoiding anything cold," Gerry realized. "What am I going to do in the winter?" he wondered. "It's kind of difficult going through the whole season without touching something cold," Gerry reasoned. "Meanwhile, Honey? Can I have a room-temperature glass of water please?" he asked.

"You are a stubborn human being," Mary teased. "One glass of room-temperature water, coming right up. How about some toast with a little jelly?" she suggested. "You haven't eaten in days. Do you think you can handle it?" she hoped.

"I'll give it a try," Gerry replied. "What's the worst that can happen?" he reasoned. "Anyway, I need to focus on building my strength."

Suddenly, Gerry glanced at some paperwork that he had left sitting on the kitchen counter. He had intentionally placed the folder in a conspicuous location so that he wouldn't forget to bring it with him when the proper time came. The documents were a shocking reminder to him of what was on the immediate horizon.

"I'm supposed to go back to work on Monday!" Gerry realized. "I get to take the weekend off to recover and, after that, Jimbo's, here I come," he said.

Mary silently toasted a couple of pieces of wheat bread for Gerry and topped them with a healthy spread of jelly. She brought him a large glass of room-temperature water which he downed while holding his nose. Water, to Gerry, still had a strong metallic taste. The sensation would ease as the cancer-fighting drugs were flushed from his system. Although the warm, metallic-tasting water would help to hydrate Gerry's body, it did little to quench his thirst. What he wanted more than anything, he was now convinced that he couldn't have. Gerry craved a cold drink. The message that he couldn't have one had been received loud and clear.

"Gerry, do you need anything else right now?" Mary asked. "Otherwise, I'm going to go and check for mail and take a short walk around the neighborhood," she said.

"No. I'm good for now," Gerry replied. "I'm just going to finish my toast and see what's on the T.V. Take your time, Honey. Thanks for making me some dinner," he said.

"Okay. I'll be back shortly," Mary said boldly as she headed toward the side door leading to the garage.

Mary left through the door leading to the garage. She reached her hand through the open window of her car and grabbed her sunglasses before heading outside into the cloud-covered but mild, dreary evening. After checking for mail, she turned to the left, hugging the curb on the side of the road. The dark glasses that she wore would conceal her watery eyes from the nosy neighbors peering through drawn curtains. But the grimaced look of her mouth and her bright red nose were in full view as she aimlessly staggered along the edge of the street, sobbing uncontrollably.

# 15

This is no time to get careless.

Gerry sat in his car for a full 15 minutes before finally convincing himself to walk the 100 yards through the employee-parking lot to the secured employee entrance at Jimbo's.

It was still early morning, and the day's first sunlight was illuminating the distant cloud cover in a beautiful, bright pink hue. "Red at night, sailors' delight. Red in the morning, sailors take warning," he recited in a quiet but clear voice. Gerry smiled, thinking about his father who never let a red sky pass without reciting the old, sailor, weather-forecasting rhyme which has been passed on through the millennia.

Days before Gerry's father lost his battle with Alzheimer's, the former navy sailor was able to clearly articulate those words as he sat with Gerry on the hardwood deck of the nursing home while staring at the evening sky. The senior O'Driscoll had no clue who the friendly gentleman was that sat beside him on that day. His memory was vivid when recalling events that occurred over a half-century ago. He could effortlessly recall the World War II sea battles in which he fought as well as the names of many of his shipmates. The recollection of the years that he spent raising his two sons, however, was erased from his memory like chalk on a sidewalk after a midsummer monsoon.

Gerry was as close to his father as his boys are to him. His father bought him his first baseball glove and taught him to play catch. His dad saved his money for weeks so he could buy Gerry a bike for his ninth birthday. Then, he taught young Gerry how to ride it. Once Gerry got a little older, he taught Gerry to play golf. The two would share a round together whenever they could for the next 40 years. And, yet, in a cruel twist, every shared memory they both held dear was completely wiped out of his father's brain.

Each time Gerry visited his father in the days leading up to his death, the elder O'Driscoll would put on an air of happiness and good cheer. When it came time for Gerry to leave, he would shake his father's hand and reassure him of another visit within a day or two. Gerry's father, with a firm handshake grip, would invariably look up and stare directly into his son's eyes. Without speaking the words, the deep, confused look in his dad's eyes conveyed to Gerry, "I know you from somewhere, but I just can't quite put my finger on how I know you or from where."

The experience would haunt Gerry for the rest of his life. Each time as he walked from his father's room to the exit door of the Alzheimer's facility, Gerry's smile would give way to large, salty tears which ran the length of his cheek and fell to the pavement below.

As Gerry swiped his identification badge against the security sensor mounted on the wall just to the right of the employee entrance at Jimbo's, he felt his father's presence. Gerry imagined him sitting right next to his head, on his right shoulder. Dignified and proud. Gerry could swear, in that moment, he heard his father speaking to him in a calm, but firm, tone of voice. He spoke directly into Gerry's right ear.

"Gerry, red in the morning. Sailors take warning," he reminded his son. "Be wary. Be smart."

Gerry pursed his lips as he contemplated the advice his father was giving him.

"I will, Dad. Thanks!" Gerry whispered as he pulled on the steel door and crossed the threshold back into the arena of Jimbo's Furniture and Firearms.

*** 

The switchboard room was located a few feet from the employee-entrance door. The secure room had multiple purposes. Incoming phone calls would be screened there and passed on to the appropriate department or individual. The operators had to be trained to answer customer questions that, in many cases, the customer could figure out on their own. Typical questions about items being in stock and how much they cost could be easily answered with a simple website query. Most times, that's exactly what the operators would do to find the answers. Questions that couldn't be answered by the switchboard-room personnel would be passed on to the appropriate department of the store.

Additionally, the switchboard was where employees would be checked in and out as they reported for work or went home for the day. As employees reported for work, they would sign out any electronic equipment needed to do their job. Portable phones, handheld computers, and in-store radios were common needs that had to be signed for and accounted for. When employees left for the day, they were responsible for returning whatever equipment they had signed out. It was the job of the switchboard-room personnel to keep track of the equipment. This was a task easier said than done.

Employees were only allowed to enter and exit the building through the employee entrance, adjacent to the switchboard room. The only exception would be if they came in the customer door as a customer on their off time. Otherwise, they passed through the corridor leading to the employee entrance and stopped at the switchboard. When exiting the building, any employee bags, backpacks, lunch bags, and jackets would be presented to the switchboard operator for inspection. Any store merchandise uncovered had better be accompanied by a receipt.

The young lady working the switchboard on this day was hired five short weeks ago. She fell under Gerry's large umbrella of responsibility but had only heard of him. She had never met him. Likewise, when Gerry approached the window to check in and say hello, he felt somewhat lost. Gerry always made it a point to meet new employees before they were on the job. Sometimes, he personally conducted a follow-up interview with the candidate. Other times, he met employees during an orientation session where he interacted with the newbies in a question-and-answer session. The person sitting behind the glass, who was entrusted with a great deal of responsibility, was a total stranger to Gerry. The realization gave him a queasy feeling. Right off the bat, he was reminded that he had absolutely no control over what has been happening in his work environment over the past six weeks. Gerry didn't micromanage, but he knew everything that was going on under his umbrella of responsibility. At least, he did until now.

"Hi there," Gerry smiled as he seemed to catch the operator off guard. "My name is Gerry O'Driscoll. I'm the long-lost operations manager here. And you are?" he pleasantly asked.

"The name is Susan," the young lady replied dryly. "What can I do for you?"

"Well, good morning to you too, Susan." Gerry replied, a little off guard. "How about if you just get me my phone? It's the one that has the number two on it. Right there on the top shelf," he politely suggested.

"Sign here," Susan demanded as she slid the clipboard with the daily sign-out log in Gerry's general direction.

"Thanks," Gerry said. "You know, it's okay to smile now and again. Especially when you answer the phone. Customers can always tell if you are smiling when you greet them when they call," he instructed. "I hope you have a great rest of the day. Okay? Be sure to treat our customers like you would like to be treated yourself."

Gerry gathered his belongings, turned away from the desk, and rolled his eyes.

"Sure," Susan shouted as she turned her back away from the entrance and returned to the paperwork that she had been consumed with before Gerry interrupted.

As Gerry continued to make his way through the short hallway toward the door that led to the selling floor, he pulled a small notebook from his front pocket. Although it was a tad old-fashioned, Gerry felt naked without it. The incredibly fast-paced environment in which Gerry existed required some sort of backup-memory system. Problems, issues, and events occurred so frequently and happened so rapidly that it was impossible to remember all of them. The important events, Gerry would make a note of. The common occurrences which he deemed routine or of little importance would never make it into the little notebook. Typically, his note would list an issue or a problem and, right next to it, the name of who he expected to take care of solving the problem. Many times, he would list himself as the owner of the problem. Just as frequently, however, he delegated the task to one of his reports. The entry would stay in his book until the issue was addressed to Gerry's satisfaction. At that point, he would either discard the page or keep it on file for future reference. He hadn't even been five minutes back into his job. Not even time to warm up a little before he made the first entry into his notebook.

'Susan! Right job fit? Improve or remove right away – Jennifer, customer-care manager,' he jotted in handwriting that only he could decipher.

The massive furniture and sporting-goods store, an hour before it opened to the public, was dimly lit in order to save on electricity. The overnight stocking crew as well as the early morning merchandising staff were used to working in such conditions. During the summer months, the air conditioning ran sparingly after customer hours. The result was a dark, hot workplace. Likewise, in the winter, the heating bill was kept to a minimum and, so, the store was dark and cold after hours.

The store environment was controlled by an energy-management system and was monitored by technicians sitting at their desks hundreds of miles away. Inevitably, there was a daily telephone battle waged between the store and the personnel who controlled the environment. Customers would complain that the store was too hot. Management would call the energy managers who would respond with sensor readings indicating that the temperature is perfect. Management would plead for some air conditioning which would get turned on once written approval was obtained from corporate. An hour later, customers would complain that the store is freezing. This would prompt another call to the energy managers. All of this was due to an attempt to save a few dollars on electricity bills. The system always makes perfect sense to the corporate managers who sign up for it. It never makes any sense to the employees on the front line who directly deal with customers day in and day out.

Gerry made his way toward the senior manager's office suite in the dark, warm atmosphere, still feeling the effects of the cancer-killing drugs. Earlier, he managed to force a bowl of cereal into his system before heading for work even though his appetite was still not good. The cup of warm coffee he was still nursing gave him a jolt of much-needed awareness.

The familiar click-clack, click-clack sound of boot metal-heel plates striking the polished, sealed concrete floor, coming from a few feet behind him put a big smile on Gerry's face. He paused and glanced slightly to his right.

"You know, you'll never be able sneak up on anyone," Gerry said without completely turning around to face his stalker.

"I'm stealth when I need to be," Steve announced, still in attack cadence. "Welcome back, brother! How are you feeling?" he exclaimed.

"I feel like shit, but I won't admit that to anyone else in this building," Gerry replied as he turned to face his colleague and dear friend.

"You look great!" Steve lied as he gingerly embraced his buddy. "I mean, other than your skin looks pasty and your lips are all cracked, and you have a kind of dazed look in your eyes. The couple of pounds you dropped gives you a healthy profile in the dim light," he said with a smirk.

"Thanks for the compliment," Gerry sarcastically replied. "So, what you're telling me is I look good in the dark," he paraphrased. "Is our fearless leader working today?" he asked, referring to Mark, the store manager.

"He's scheduled to work the closing shift today," Steve replied. "I'm guessing he'll show up at around 11 this morning and leave at around five this afternoon. Now that you're back, I'm sure Mark will go back to his ways. He has been pissing and moaning constantly about how he has had to pick up the slack because of you being out on disability. He actually worked a couple of full shifts over the past few weeks," Steve reported incredulously. "I know it's hard to believe, but it's true," he confirmed.

"I'm sure I'll have an interesting conversation with him later today," Gerry offered. "Meanwhile, I'd better see if I can get caught up on what's going on around here. I bet I have over 2000 useless emails to review. Out of those, I'll delete 1900 without even opening them. Maybe there will be 50 that are useful. The key will be figuring out which 50 are useful," he mused. "I left in such a rush six weeks ago that I never set my emails to the out-of-office setting. I can't wait to see the second and third requests sent in underlined, bold, capital letters by corporate-cubicle sitters frantically looking for me to provide some inane information."

"Don't try to do it all at once, Gerry," Steve offered. "If there is anything you need from me, just ask. I'll see you in an hour at the morning meeting. And, Gerry, make sure you watch your six today. You're dealing with Mark," he warned.

Steve often communicated in military terms and left it to those on the receiving end to figure out what he just said. Watching your six referred to the position of the number six on a wrist watch. As one looks at a watch, 12 is where you would be facing, and six would be directly behind you. Watching your six, in the military, refers to keeping an eye out for enemy attacks coming from the rear. Steve was letting Gerry know, in a not-so-subtle way, that he was dealing with someone who would feel no remorse after sticking a knife squarely in the middle of his back. Gerry had the same feeling. He kept reminding himself that it's not paranoia if it's true.

"I'll be careful. See you in a little while," Gerry said appreciatively as he headed toward his office.

Gerry spent the morning trying to reorient himself to his job. The experience overwhelmed him with a sense of bewilderment. He knew he could rely on his vast knowledge and experience to get him through the first few days, but he also knew he was rusty. Six weeks away from the daily grind had suppressed his memory. Hot topics were likely to be deemed no longer hot. Seasons come and go rapidly in retail. A frenzied workload for a holiday set ends in a flash once the holiday, or event, comes and goes. Typically, on the day after a holiday, preparations are already being made for the next holiday. If there is no traditional holiday on the horizon, the retailer will usually concoct one. Filling in the traditional holiday blanks with, 'The Biggest Anniversary Sale Ever,' or the 'Largest Markdown Event in the History of the Planet,' or, 'Our Blockbuster Friends and Family Sale' is common practice in retail. Retailers wouldn't engage in the phony tradition if customers weren't fooled by it. Creating customer urgency to purchase something that they may or may not need is a marketing art-form necessary for survival. Every retailer takes advantage of national holidays. Getting ready for Christmas is easy. Everyone knows it's coming, and preparation begins each year on December 26th for the next one. Filling in the blanks between holidays is what separates the successful retailers from the not-so-successful ones. Gerry just had to wrap his arms around where the current focus was. And fast.

Gerry also had to deal with the fact that he wasn't the same person physically that he was six weeks ago. Logistically, he had to plan for scenarios that he has never had to deal with before. He kept a backup colostomy bag handy along with the necessary accessories in case he had to change it in an emergency. He needed a change of clothes just in case he punctured the bag by accident. Even the way he dressed was different from the past. Gerry wore an oversized fleece vest zippered halfway in order to conceal the bulge that outlined his colostomy bag. Dealing with the whole process had to be mentally planned out.

Although he tried to conceal his emotions, Gerry was highly stressed and distracted by his predicament. He knew he would figure things out, but he now felt extremely uncomfortable in his surroundings. He knew his work environment like the back of his hand, but he never experienced it in his present state. Additionally, the longest he could last on his feet in his current situation was 20 minutes. Any longer, and he would surely have the need to sit and re-gather his strength.

Gerry was still weak from not only the surgeries, but from his chemotherapy. It is not uncommon for retail managers to spend six- to eight-hour shifts walking around. As a result, Gerry had to plan out his day accordingly. Accommodations for his health issues would be sparing. Retaliation for taking advantage of work accommodations would not be so sparing.

Gerry figured he would head over to the morning meeting, say hello to everyone, and begin his unfamiliar journey in an all-too-familiar setting.

Nobody on the store-opening staff pretended to be too busy to attend the morning meeting on this day. Typically, out of the 40 to 50 associates working feverishly to ready their department for the onrush of customers, a dozen would pretend they didn't hear the page for all personnel to gather for the daily words of wisdom at the morning meeting. Steve deliberately delayed Gerry in the office area to allow the troops to gather at the meeting location before the managers strolled in. The staff had been buzzing and gossiping over the past few days in anticipation of Gerry's return. Rumors of his demise were, to say the least, greatly exaggerated.

Some curiously wanted to see Gerry at the meeting similarly to how they slow their vehicles in order to rubberneck and stare at the victims of a bad car accident. The majority, however, respected and cared deeply for Gerry. They wanted to reassure themselves that he was going to be okay. The energy among the staff was unusually boisterous on this otherwise normal Monday morning. However, as Steve and Gerry approached the gathering, other than the click-clack of Steve's boots on the polished floor, you could hear a pin drop.

Finally, Steve, who strode in toward the gathering on Gerry's right, wrapped his left arm around Gerry's shoulders and pointed toward him with his right hand. The silence was suddenly broken with an eruption of applause and whistles that humbled Gerry and touched his heart at the same time. Gerry was already feeling weak. The outpouring of support he felt from the staff, however, made his knees even weaker. As the applause died down, the staff began shouting questions and words of encouragement toward Gerry. "Welcome back, Gerry!" one person yelled. "We missed you!" shouted another. "How are you feeling?" "Are you okay to work?" "We are worried about you," they called out.

Gerry smiled and held up his right hand in a gesture to try to quiet things down a little. The employees complied and fell silent.

"Steve!" he shouted dryly, looking directly at his friend. "Clearly you have lost control of this meeting. How could you let that happen?" he asked to the delight of the associates, many of whom reported directly to Steve.

"I'm thrilled to be back with the greatest staff in the world," Gerry continued. "Thank you all for your support and for your warm welcome. As far as how I'm feeling, all I can tell you is that I am doing my best to play the hand I was dealt," he assured them. "We should have all given a little more to the American Cancer Society, I guess," Gerry stated.

Suddenly, the crowd got a little bit somber as they processed Gerry's words. Gerry picked up on the mood change and broke the brief silence. The last thing he wanted was to have the meeting end on a downer. He had to recover the energy of the staff before turning them loose on the customers who were about to invade the building.

"Everything is good," Gerry announced in his strongest voice. "I'll see each of you personally in the next few days as I make my rounds. Meanwhile, Steve has some real stuff to cover with us this morning. I'm clueless about what's going on around here right now, so it's important for me to pay attention to what he's about to tell us as well. Thanks again everyone! Let's have a bang-up day. Take over for me, Steve," Gerry requested.

Gerry pointed to Steve and let his mind wander. That simple meeting exchange with the associates, something he has done thousands of times, sapped him of his energy. It was a humbling realization. The fact that he was exhausted and needed to rest was secondary to the fear he felt in the knowledge that coming back to work was going to be a major challenge for him. He couldn't go back out on a leave of absence. The lawyers at Jimbo's already notified him in writing that failure to return to work in full capacity after the allotted six weeks were up would result in termination due to job abandonment. Nobody would hire him right now. Gerry would have to inform a prospective employer that he needs every Wednesday and Friday off for chemotherapy? He knew he had to figure out a strategy to stay here at Jimbo's, at least for now, and figure it out fast.

Meanwhile, he thought his first stop after the meeting would be with Jennifer, the customer-care manager. Gerry could hide out with her in her office for an hour and catch his breath. At the same time, he could get caught up with what was happening in the customer-care world.

Gerry slowly made his way over to customer care where Jennifer patiently waited for him in her office. Along the way, several associates approached him and wished him well. Gerry fist-bumped them all with his left hand. His right hand was inside the right-hand pocket of his fleece vest, protecting his colostomy bag. He made the unfortunate mistake, a couple of weeks ago, of reaching out to shake hands with a well-wishing friend who then suddenly playfully swung his left hand and slapped Gerry in the abdomen. Not only did the blow cause excruciating pain, but it also drew a significant blood flow from the sensitive stoma where the open-handed strike landed.

Gerry learned to make many subtle changes in his mannerisms since his surgery. As he sat in the chair opposite Jennifer, who sat behind her desk, he moved his seat over to her left. This allowed him to comfortable cross his right leg over his left. A subtle maneuver with his right hand allowed him to rest his colostomy bag on top of his right thigh with his legs crossed in this manner. His coworkers noticed Gerry's behaviors but didn't understand the pragmatic reasons for them. They just assumed he was getting quirky, for some unknown reason. As a problem solver, Gerry was anything but quirky or superstitious. He had a reason for everything. No movement was ever wasted. Jennifer teased Gerry mercilessly about his pragmatism in the past. Now, however, she was just thrilled to have him back in her environment. Jennifer, like the rest of the staff, dearly missed the support that Gerry provided.

"So, what's been happening around here since my sabbatical?" Gerry asked.

"Oh my God, Gerry," Jennifer gasped. "I have six pages of notes to cover with you. How much time do I get?" she begged.

"As much time as you need," Gerry replied. "I just can't guarantee it will be all at once. Give me some of the high-priority stuff," he requested. "How are you? More importantly, how's the family?"

"You are too much." Jennifer laughed. "Everybody is good. I'm compelled to ask the same thing of you. I could lie to you and tell you how great you look. But then you'll realize I'm just bullshitting you, and you will call me out on it. From there, the whole conversation will go south," she reasoned.

"We'll end up having to start all over again later. I've seen this movie before," Jennifer bragged.

"You know me like a book," Gerry said with a smirk. "Speaking of books, I made a note in my book about your switchboard person. What's with this Susan character? Is she okay?" he wondered.

"She's second on my list of things to cover with you," Jennifer replied as she frantically flipped the pages on her yellow pad. "Gerry, Mark made me hire her. She's close friends with Mark's wife. I think Susan is the most miserable person on the planet. She's horrible. I've tried working with her. I've tried giving her extra training. I've spelled out in detail what my expectations are. She has no intentions of performing the job the way we want her to. I knew you'd be pissed about her, but I didn't know it would happen this quickly," she confessed. "I approached Mark about her last week. He is washing his hands on the whole situation. Not only is he saying the decision to hire Susan falls directly on my shoulders, but he says her job performance is a direct reflection on my ability to recruit and train the right people. Mark told me he will hold me personally accountable if Susan isn't successful. The threat was not so veiled. Gerry, this is the kind of crap we've been dealing with since you've been out. There's lots more. Help!" Jennifer pleaded.

"I got the impression, when I met Susan this morning, that either she was just having a bad day, or you were having a bad day when you hired her," Gerry said sarcastically. "Now it all makes perfect sense. Next item," Gerry said in a matter-of-fact tone as he scribbled an illegible note in his notebook next to the Susan scribble.

"Gerry, you have to keep this one to yourself," Jennifer began nervously. "Mark said he'd fire me if he found out that I told you, but I'm going to tell you anyway. Mark and Lynn have been sitting down with each of your managers in a two-on-one private setting. They are trying to get us to say rotten things about you. Things that could get you fired. Mark has the items listed on a sheet of paper, and he reads them one at a time. He'll ask things like, 'Do you agree that Gerry is not a supportive manager?' 'Do you agree that Gerry does not provide the proper direction or tools necessary to do your job?' 'Do you agree that Gerry does not provide effective feedback?' Mark goes on and on with this same type of questioning. If you don't give him the answer he is looking for, he tries to browbeat you into saying something negative about you. The conversation got heated with me because I wouldn't give in. Gerry, I don't know what Mark and Lynn are up to, but I want you to know that I didn't badmouth you. In fact, I told them you were the best manager I've ever worked with. Mark got furious when I said that. He kicked me out of his office!" she exclaimed.

"What was Lynn doing during the conversation?" Gerry calmly asked.

"She just sat there with a dopey look on her face," Jennifer replied. "She didn't say a word. She was writing on a notepad, but I couldn't see her notes."

"Did they do the same thing with any other managers?" Gerry asked.

"Yes," Jennifer replied. "Every manager who reports to you got dragged in. We were each told that if we spoke to anyone else about what they called the investigation, we would be fired," she stated.

"So then, how do you know they dragged in the other managers if you were all threatened with termination?" Gerry asked.

"We got together and had a meeting about it," Jennifer laughed. "We figured they can't fire all of us. Gerry, I know you have bigger things to worry about right now, but I don't want you to get blindsided by Mark," she warned.

"I appreciate the information," Gerry said. "Don't worry. I'll keep the whole thing under my hat," he assured.

Gerry stood up to stretch his legs and began to gather his things, signaling to Jennifer that he was heading to his next stop. Suddenly, the portable phone on Gerry's hip vibrated in its holster. Gerry removed it and stared at the illuminated screen.

"Speaking of the devil," Gerry declared.

"This is Gerry," he answered as he nodded toward Jennifer.

Gerry, with the phone to his ear, opened the door to Jennifer's office and stepped into the short hallway that led to the customer-care desk.

"Gerry, It's Mark," came the voice on the other end. "Do you have a minute? I'd like to see you in my office," he said.

"Be right there," Gerry replied as he disconnected.

The distance from Jennifer's office to the senior-manager suite typically only took a couple of minutes to cover at a moderate walking pace. Gerry, however, was in no rush to get there for this unscheduled tete-a-tete with Mark. His conversation with Jennifer confirmed his suspicions about Mark. Gerry, therefore, chose to not blow by any associate who intercepted him along the way for a quick fist bump and a warm welcome back. Gerry intelligently used the delay to simmer his blood boil back to a controlled state. Jennifer's disclosure that Mark and Lynn were conducting some sort of half-baked investigation behind his back infuriated Gerry. He kept his emotions well hidden in Jennifer's presence, but he knew if he didn't gain control of himself before meeting with Mark, he may say something that he would regret later-on.

The 15 minutes he took to gather himself worked wonders for Gerry as he entered the office area. He felt calm, alert, and ready for anything. A quick glance to the left at the human-resources office revealed to him that the lights were on, but nobody was there. Ahead of him and to the left, the door to the store manager's office was open. Muffled voices spilled into the hallway. Obviously, Mark had his human-resources sidekick in the office with him.

Gerry stopped at the pantry, poured himself a cup of coffee with a little bit of cream, and confidently headed toward Mark's office.

"Good morning, Mark. Good morning, Lynn," Gerry said unenthusiastically as he entered Mark's spacious office and took the chair against the back wall. "How are you folks doing today?" he asked.

"We are outstanding," Mark bellowed. "Gerry, on behalf of the staff, I want to welcome you back to Jimbo's. I can't begin to tell you how much I have personally missed having you here," he proclaimed while looking and nodding in Lynn's direction. "You know you have my support 110 percent as you work your way back to normal in the next few days. Cancer is a tough disease to deal with," Mark explained. "If I can do anything for you, or if there are any problems that you need my help with, please don't be afraid to ask," he spewed.

Gerry stared in stunned silence at Mark as he listened to the words being spoken. He focused his gaze on Mark's nose to see if it was getting longer but then caught himself and glanced away. His eyes wandered, and he caught Lynn staring at Mark intensely.

Lynn detected Gerry's glancing look and flashed him a warm smile. Gerry noticed a subtle roll of her eyes before she interrupted the uncomfortable exchange.

"Welcome back, Gerry," Lynn said sincerely. "If there's anything I can do for you on my end, just ask," she offered.

"Thanks," Gerry replied. "Is there anything going on around here that I should be made aware of? Any issues?" he asked.

Gerry was fishing to see what Mark would come up with. He knew Mark wouldn't call him in to a meeting with Lynn present if there wasn't some sort of major issue on the table. Typically, Lynn would be present to take notes, and Mark would launch himself into full showoff mode. It was all reminiscent of the way the male turkey fully extends his fan and struts around to impress the receptive hen. Gerry had seen this same act many times before. Although Gerry was a little aggravated that Mark was pulling this tired routine on his first day back, he wasn't surprised. After all, no matter what the circumstances, it's always all about Mark.

"As a matter of fact, there are a couple of things I want to cover with you," Mark puffed his chest as he spoke. "First, we have a lateral position available as senior manager of furniture and boats. Basically, the position is responsible for the commissioned sales teams in the building. Sales are struggling in both categories, and we need someone to take names and kick ass over there," he stated. "The job requires you to give at least 110 percent, 24/7. I want you to take the position and hit the ground running, starting tomorrow," he stated.

Gerry pursed his lips and scratched the back of his head while he let the proposal sink in. He was prepared for some sort of nonsense, so there was no total surprise with what Mark was offering.

Gerry was always amused by people who ask for more than a 100-percent effort. His mind began to wander as he amusingly contemplated the warped logic. He felt that if he gave everything he had, he was giving 100 percent. Mark was asking for 110 percent. Why stop there? Gerry silently mused. May as well ask for 200 percent or even 800 percent if a full effort wouldn't be enough.

Gerry figured he may as well have a little bit of fun with this one. See if he can get the tom-turkey to fold his fan.

"Mark, you know that with everything I do, I give more than 110 percent," Gerry deadpanned. "As a matter of fact, I think I give 120 percent on a regular basis," he reasoned. "My only concern with taking over furniture and boats is that I don't have hands-on experience in those categories. I'm going to need some training before I can have a positive impact on sales. What do you have planned for me regarding a training session?" he asked.

"Great question, Gerry," Mark confirmed. "I have arranged travel for you to one of our sister stores. You'll be working with the best for a full 30 days. We can fly you out there next Monday. I'm even trying to pull some strings for you to get one trip back home for a weekend in the middle of the training period. Don't tell anyone about that one," he bragged. "I really had to go to bat for you. Normally, you fly out for a month and train seven days a week for the full session," Mark stated. "I don't want to candy coat it though. We're expecting big sales improvements the day you return. The pressure will be on, but I think it's a great opportunity for you," he advised.

Gerry was taken aback with Mark's response. He knew Mark was a cold, self-centered individual. Still, it was difficult to comprehend how Mark could feel it was a good idea to send Gerry away for a month. Gerry concluded that Mark was trying to get him to quit on the spot. Mark was an idiot, in Gerry's estimation, but nobody is this stupid. He figured somebody must have told Mark what to do. There was no way that Mark came up with this brainchild on his own.

"Mark, you do understand that I get chemotherapy every other week," Gerry began. "On the off week, I recover to get ready for the next session. Are you suggesting that I skip my cancer treatments so that I can train for a position that I didn't seek? Do you think it's a good idea for me to be away from my doctors for a whole month?" he asked.

"I think it is necessary that you, as a senior manager in this building, respond appropriately to the needs of the business," Mark coldly responded.

"You do realize that we only have to offer you the same position level that you had when you went out on the medical leave," he stated. "That is exactly what I am doing. You are being offered a position at the same level."

"I'll keep the job I have," Gerry shot back. "If you want to discuss a different position for me once I get beyond my medical issues, I'm all ears. Right now, however, there's no way I'm going to go along with your proposal. If that doesn't suit your needs, do whatever it is that you feel you have to do, but I'm not playing along," he stated.

Gerry looked over at Lynn who was writing furiously on her lined pad. He wasn't sure what roll she had in all of this, but right now, Gerry didn't trust anyone in the room. He wasn't even positive that the phone on the conference table in the far corner of the office didn't have listeners on the other end of the line. If he was fired on the spot, he figured Mark was flying solo. Otherwise, the situation would have to be further discussed and new plans formulated.

"Lynn, make sure you put in your notes that I feel the offer is unreasonable due to the fact that I would be forced to miss important medical treatments," Gerry instructed. "Missing said treatments could be life threatening. I'm going to make my own notes on this conversation and record what I just said. I want to make sure our notes match in case the conversation comes up later. You know, like if we have to discuss it in front of 12 people whom neither of us have previously met," he remarked.

Lynn flashed a wry smile as she jotted another note on her legal pad. Gerry's not-so-subtle message was received loud and clear by Lynn. She was confident that Mark had no idea what Gerry was referring to.

"I have it, Gerry," Lynn confirmed.

"Anything else today?" Gerry asked. "Otherwise, I still have a lot of catching up to do."

"There is one other thing, Gerry," Mark began. "While you were away, Jennifer hired a fulltime switchboard associate named Susan –" he said.

"I had the pleasure of meeting her this morning when I first got in," Gerry interrupted.

"Anyway, she is struggling in her duties," Mark continued. "She flunked two corporate-test calls already. And flunked miserably. On one of the calls, the corporate caller pretended to be a customer interested in buying a two-thousand-dollar gun safe. Susan told the customer to look up the information himself online. When the customer asked to be transferred to someone knowledgeable about gun safes, she told him we don't have anyone who knows anything about them. She then hung up without even saying goodbye. The report from the corporate auditor came back stating that she was the most unfriendly operator they had ever experienced. Gerry, this falls under your umbrella. It makes you look bad. I've been trying to cover for you on this, but the big shots are losing patience," he stated.

Gerry shared the same concern about Susan's ability to perform the position to which she was assigned. He also knew that there was more to the story than Mark was revealing. He figured that he would play along for a while longer. Maybe Mark would surprise him with some form of dignity.

"I detected a little bit of an attitude when I met her," Gerry offered. "I was hoping that maybe she was just having a bad morning," he stated.

And then.

"Who hired her?" Gerry asked. "Did you say it was Jennifer? I can't believe she's that inept," he goaded.

"Unfortunately, I am going to tell you it was Jennifer," Mark growled. "She went out and made the hiring decision all on her own, the way I understand it. She didn't even ask for a second opinion. Gerry, I don't want Susan fired. I want you to fix your mistake by getting her up to speed," he directed. "And fix your mistake quickly. I was embarrassed by the findings of that audit, and I won't take kindly to having your people continuing to embarrass me like that. I hold you accountable," Mark fumed.

"The shit will flow downhill on this one," Gerry confirmed. "I am shocked that Jennifer would make such a poor hiring decision on her own like that. She knows better. A novice in this business wouldn't make such a dumb hire," Gerry stated knowingly. "She must have taken a handful of stupid pills before she conducted the interview. You don't mind if I rake Jennifer over the coals because of this, do you?" he asked.

Mark was unaware of how he was being played as the fool. Lynn was not.

"Let's be careful," Mark nervously shot back. "I don't want to make things worse. How about if you just tell Jennifer that you noticed a possible problem with the new switchboard operator? Tell her you want to help to make the situation better," he cautiously advised.

"So, what you are saying is that you want me to lie to Jennifer?" Gerry paraphrased. "Okay. I'm pretty sure I understand where you are coming from on this one," he confirmed. "I'll deal with the situation. Is there anything else today?" Gerry tiredly asked.

"No. That's it for today," Mark calmly concluded. "I'll let my bosses know that you wish to remain in your current position. I need you to get the switchboard under control right away," he ordered. "Oh, and one last thing. Just for your information, I am going to leave a little early today. Since you have been out, I have been working excessively. If you need me for anything, I suggest you get me within the next two hours. Otherwise, I'll see you whenever our paths next cross," he said.

Gerry abruptly stood, grabbed his belongings from Mark's desk, and, with a brief nod of the head, left the office. Mark's comment about letting Louis, the regional manager, know that Gerry would not take the position being offered confirmed Gerry's suspicion. This was not all Mark's doing. The play was to set Gerry up for failure, so he could be terminated for poor performance.

The commissioned sales associates in the furniture-and-boat departments were getting lazier by the day. They refused to follow up with clients and do the legwork necessary to close deals. Gerry knew he could fix the problem. He also knew it would take six months to bring in the sales talent needed to turn the ship around. Top-commissioned salespeople do not grow on trees. They are a finicky bunch who realize that they can earn a high income wherever they choose to work. The key is to lure them away from what they are currently doing and have them trust you enough to join your organization. The commissioned salespeople at Jimbo's were far from top notch. Some of them may be redeemable with training but only if they wanted to be redeemed. The commissioned sales floor at Jimbo's had to be flooded with top talent. Let the strong survive. The weak will bow out and go elsewhere.

Gerry sensed that he would be on the radar screen once he got back on the job. The mentality of the company would be to treat him like a wounded animal that needed to be culled from the herd. From the company's perspective, Gerry would, in the best-case scenario, occupy a key position and not be capable of performing at a high level. The worst-case scenario was that he would continue to be in and out of work for the next several months. The risk to the business did not support taking the chance on keeping Gerry around. Legally, it wouldn't be in the company's best interest to simply terminate his employment. Gerry could argue that he was fired because he got sick.

The course of action, which the company chose, was to see if they could get Gerry to make a mistake. See if they could get him to agree to take another position tied into turning a business around in an unreasonably short timeframe. See if they could get Gerry to set himself up for failure. They knew they had a willing participant in Mark. The regional staff didn't even have to let him in on what they were up to. The fewer people who were privy, the better. Gerry had anticipated all of this. He might be sick, but his brain was still fully functional. And he was mentally tougher than those who didn't know him could imagine.

Mark contacted Louis, his regional manager, and delivered the news concerning Gerry. More important for Mark, he wanted to have a lengthy conversation with his boss. The ploy, from Mark's perspective, was to make it unlikely that Louis will have any further need to speak with him for the remainder of the day. Sneaking out of work and not getting caught at it, was an art form as far as Mark was concerned. And he was extremely good at it. Mark had barely hung up the phone before he hastily grabbed his belongings and headed for the exit.

Lynn looked across the hall and noticed Mark's darkened office. She checked with the switchboard and received confirmation that he had left the building for the rest of the day.

She wanted to have a conversation with Gerry but knew it would be impossible with Mark around. If Mark noticed that Gerry was in Lynn's office, she knew he would barge in and pull up a chair to join in. Lynn wanted Gerry to know that she was remaining neutral. Her conscience wouldn't allow her to participate in whatever it was that Mark was up to. However, she still had bills to pay and wouldn't put herself in jeopardy for Gerry's sake. Simply put, Lynn wanted Gerry to know that she supported him, but only to a point. Her message would be subtle. Gerry would have to read between the lines, which she knew he could do. The act of inviting Gerry in for a chat, in and of itself, was the loudest message of support she would deliver.

Gerry's portable phone buzzed and sent a vibration from his hip halfway down his right leg.

"Geeze!" he said aloud as he un-holstered the humming handset and glanced at the illuminated screen. "This is Gerry," he said, laughing.

"Gerry, it's Lynn," she cheerily replied. "What's so funny?" She wanted to know.

"This phone went off and scared the crap out of me," Gerry replied. "I guess I'm still not completely back into the swing of things. Normally, I wouldn't even flinch. What's going on?" he asked.

"I was hoping you had time to stop by and chat," Lynn offered. "I didn't have a chance to ask how you were doing," she admitted. "Don't ask any more questions. Just come on over when you can," Lynn ordered.

"Give me ten minutes," Gerry replied. "I'm in the gun vault conducting an audit. So far, we look pretty good. I'll wrap this up in a few minutes. The gun guys will be happy to see me go." Gerry laughed. "They hate having me poke around up here. Especially when I find things that I shouldn't find," he said.

Gerry came to a breakpoint in his audit and headed back toward the office suite. He was feeling tired already. The day was little more than half over for him, but he was feeling the effects. Mentally, he was starting to get back into the swing of his hectic work life. The pace distracted him from being able to dwell on his medical issues. Physically, however, the story was completely different. Gerry felt lightheaded. His hips hurt from being on his feet. His lower back was pounding him with every beat of his heart. The back of his neck was sore from holding his head up. The colostomy bag felt heavier than usual on his abdomen. It annoyingly pulled on his belly fat as if it were a suction cup, weighted with a three-pound bag of quarters. Gerry also felt like he needed a nap. The problem was, he wouldn't be home for another four hours.

As he pulled on the door handle to the manager suite, he forced himself to act like he was completely energized. Gerry knew he would need his best performance as he knocked on the frosted glass window leading to Lynn's office.

"Anybody home?" Gerry shouted.

Lynn stood from behind her desk and approached Gerry with a disarming smile. Gerry held out his hand, but Lynn walked past it and warmly embraced him. She knew how cold and uncaring she came across earlier during the meeting with Mark. Gerry understood and hugged her back. He also knew that he had to be careful with what he said until he knew more about this inquisition that was going on behind his back.

The two spoke at length about Gerry's health, the wellbeing of the store from Lynn's perspective, and life in general. Gerry assured Lynn that his cancer treatments could be accommodated with creative scheduling. He did not anticipate missing any work due to chemotherapy and wanted to convey his intentions to work through it. Gerry explained how his doctors feel it is best to get back to normal as soon as possible. He explained his desire to do just that. He assured her that would fight back.

Suddenly, Lynn changed the subject to the meeting with Mark. She sensed Gerry's disdain for Mark. Deep down, she shared his feelings, but she couldn't come out and just let Gerry know. Lynn had a good job and wouldn't jeopardize it for anyone or anything. She was flirtatious with Mark. But it was only to manipulate him. As such, she came and went as she pleased. Weekends for Lynn began at noon on Friday and ended at noon on Monday. There wasn't even a remote chance that Mark would call her out or have her disciplined for any reason. Lynn skillfully played Mark for the fool that he was.

"Gerry, you seemed to get a little testy with Mark this morning," Lynn began. "Are you sure you're okay?" she asked.

"I'm okay." Gerry laughed and then changed his demeanor to reflect a serious tone. "I hope you realize that I'm aware of every detail about how we ended up with Susan in the switchboard," he revealed. "I know who hired her. I know who she is friends with. I know the whole story. What are your feelings about a manager who lies to his direct reports?" Gerry asked. "Do you find that to be a quality that is to be admired?" he probed.

"I can't answer that, Gerry," Lynn replied. "You know that I can't."

"How about the lame effort he made to try to set me up with a new position?" Gerry asked. "Why do I get the feeling he's doing something

174

nefarious behind my back?" he carefully revealed. "I can't exactly put my finger on it, but I get the feeling that Mark is trying to build a file on me. He obviously can't be trusted to tell me the truth. Should I trust him to have my best interest in mind?" he asked.

"I can't answer that one either, Gerry," Lynn muttered. "It seems you have lost some respect for him," Lynn responded with her best active-listening tone.

"Don't give me that human-resources 101, active-listening crap," Gerry howled. "I took the same class, remember?" he teased. "Lynn, you do know how Mark got his job. Don't you?" Gerry asked.

"I heard he slept with Louis's wife. I also heard that Louis promoted him to keep him quiet," Lynn blurted unexpectedly. "I don't know the details though. Do you?" She smirked.

Gerry considered the question. He was aware of the details but was uncertain about revealing them to Lynn. Finally, since she asked, he made his decision.

"There was a Christmas party at one of the local store manager's lakeside cottage," Gerry began. "I know the manager. He's a good friend of mine. Anyway, there was some heavy drinking going on. Louis was there with his wife, and he got so plastered that he passed out. The guys dragged him to a spare bedroom, tossed him on the bed, and closed the door. His wife got pissed and asked Mark if he would give her a ride home. Mark had been drinking as well, but figured he would take the risk and drove her home. She invited Mark in, and, next thing he knew, his pants were at his ankles and she was kneeling in front of him. Apparently, she has some extraordinary skills involving an unusually long tongue," Gerry disclosed. "Anyway, Mark couldn't help but capture the moment on his cellphone. Since she was more than willing to pose for some provocative photos, several were taken. Mark had a whisky rope that wouldn't quit, and the two had a sex session that lasted for hours. I'm told that our dear regional manager's wife had a pirate's smile on her face for weeks. In fact, she was desperately hoping for a repeat performance. Louis caught wind of the episode from his wife. She got pissed at him about something stupid and let the story fly after consuming a couple of glasses of wine. Louis furiously confronted Mark about the whole thing. He was probably hoping Mark would deny it. Instead, Mark confirmed everything that the wife had said and then provided some additional details about the tryst. After reviewing the picture album on Mark's phone titled *Fun Times*, the two decided it might be best to keep the unfortunate incident out of the spotlight. Mark agreed to a transfer, taking him 300 miles from Louis's wife, provided he got a promotion and a higher-paying position. The deal was struck, and here we are," Gerry concluded.

Gerry stared at Lynn who was doing a terrible job of attempting to conceal the look of horror on her face. Gerry misinterpreted her façade and attempted to clarify his position.

"The reason I have no respect for Mark is not because he got the job by banging the big boss's wife," Gerry firmly stated. "I couldn't care less about that. The reason I have no respect for Mark is because he is incompetent and crooked. Be careful with him, Lynn," Gerry warned. "Snakes don't care who they bite."

"Too much information," Lynn gasped, slightly red-faced. "Gerry, this conversation is bordering on inappropriate," she admitted.

"You brought it up," Gerry countered. "I mean, you are the one who suggested we discuss this topic. Oh, wait. I'm sorry. I don't want you to think I'm talking about anything being up," Gerry smirked. "You know, you may take it the wrong way with me discussing big things being up. As in –"

"Okay, fine," Lynn interrupted. "I'm taking my human-resources hat off. Forget the appropriate comment thing. You are right. I am the one who asked, and I guess I got what I asked for," she conceded.

Lynn allowed her blood pressure to resume normalcy. And then.

"One more question, though. Gerry, what's a whiskey rope?" Lynn asked with a puzzled look on her face.

Gerry pondered Lynn's question for a moment. He wasn't sure he wanted to answer it. He would only get himself into trouble, he thought. But then, he reasoned that since she was the one who asked, perhaps she was genuinely interested to know.

"You know how when guys drink too much and they stay hard but can't orgasm when having sex?" Gerry questioned. "The alcohol, or whiskey if you will, causes their erection to act like a piece of frozen rope. Picture what your clothesline looks like after an ice storm. Thus, the term, 'whiskey rope.' Guys have been known to have whiskey ropes for hours. It's better than Viagra!" he exclaimed. "You get it? I mean, do you understand?" he carefully asked.

"Enough!" Lynn exclaimed, red-faced. "Gerry, I think you had better get back to work. I can't take any more of this," she instructed.

"I thought I was working," Gerry countered.

"All right, I do have to go. When you called and interrupted me, I was looking at firearm paperwork. Although this session was much more fun, I have to get back and finish what I was doing," he admitted as he stood and started toward the door.

"Gerry, before you go, speaking about firearms, what is question 11a?" Lynn randomly asked. "I overheard someone talking about it the other day, and I don't know what it means," she wondered.

"It's the question that asks you if you are buying the gun for yourself on the federal firearms-purchase record form," Gerry informed her. "You can't buy a gun for someone who is not legally allowed to have one," he stated.

"Oh," Lynn replied. "Is it a problem for someone here to change the answer that a customer gave on that question?" she wondered.

"Other than the buyer, nobody can change the answers provided on the form. Any other person who changes any answer on that form should go to jail," Gerry replied sternly. "If it's an employee who changes the answer, it's grounds for immediate termination. It doesn't matter who you are. You'll be let go on the spot if you tamper with that form," he stated.

"What makes you ask me this?" Gerry wondered.

"I was just wondering," Lynn casually offered as she scribbled a note on her yellow notepad. "I don't think it was any big deal. I just felt left out of the conversation and didn't want to ask. You know, I didn't want to come off as being stupid." She laughed.

"Stop by again tomorrow if you get the chance, Gerry," Lynn offered. "I'm keeping a careful eye on you," she stated.

"I'm sure you are," Gerry teased as he turned to leave. "I'm sure you are."

Gerry looked forward to spending the next couple of hours in solitude. He usually hated sitting with piles of paperwork, conducting audit reviews. Today, however, his energy was sapped. His meeting with Lynn, although entertaining, drained him of any energy he had remaining. He slowly made his way to the storage vault and just before he swiped his badge to enter, the phone on his hip buzzed. *Now what?* he thought as he plucked it from its holster and gazed at the screen. Steve was calling.

"Steve, what's up, brother?" Gerry answered.

"Gerry, come on over to the conference room for a minute," Steve beamed. "I bought you a coffee. I figured you'd need a little jolt right about now," he stated.

"You know what?" Gerry shot back. "I could use a cup of coffee right about now. Don't tell anyone, but I'm feeling a little bit drained. I hope you had them add some extra caffeine to mine," he hoped. "I'll be right over." Gerry smiled as he disconnected.

On his way, Gerry detoured and made a quick pit stop in the men's room where he was able to freshen up a little. He glanced at his reflection in the mirror and quickly looked away. His eyes were already taking on a hollow, sunken look. Gerry's facial skin color was taking on a gray hue. The image was unmistakably his, but it was, nonetheless, difficult for him to look at his reflection. He splashed cold water on his face, took a deep breath, and marched to the conference room to share a cup of java with his close friend.

Gerry pulled open the door to the conference room and interrupted what he thought was a major meeting being conducted by Steve. 18 managers were sitting at a horseshoe-shaped table. Steve was standing at the head of the room, rambling on about the sporting clay course that recently opened in his town.

There was a large sheet cake sitting on a square table immediately to his right with writing that Gerry couldn't make out from his angle. A percolator had just finished brewing a wonderfully strong-smelling coffee. The aroma filled the room. Gerry stopped dead in his tracks as he realized what was going on. His shoulders slumped, his head cocked, and a wry smile overtook him. Gerry loved harmless practical jokes, and this one was on him.

Steve pointed in Gerry's direction and announced, "Look who's back!"

The room erupted in shouting, whistling, and applause in Gerry's honor. Each manager took turns with a hug or a handshake to welcome Gerry back with warm words of encouragement. Gerry made his way to the front of the room at the request of the hungry horde who demanded a slice of cake. The writing on the top of vanilla frosting simply said, 'Welcome Back, Gerry.' There was a purple-frosted ribbon just below, in the center of the cake, with the words, 'Kick Ass' beneath. Gerry read the simple inscription and his eyes suddenly teared and his nose dripped.

"I can't talk right now," he managed. "This means a lot to me," he stammered. "Thank you."

Steve helped Gerry to serve cake and coffee to the managers present in the room. As word spread throughout the store about what was going on in the conference room, the hourly associates organized to cover for one another on the sales floor. One by one, they took the time to make their way to the conference room where Gerry greeted them with a slice of cake. Lynn took picture after picture for a collage that she would later post in the break room for all to see.

Missing in all of this was Mark, the store manager. Nobody seemed to notice or care that he was absent. The consensus was that if he was there, somehow the event would become all about him. Steve never even informed Mark of his plan to have a cake for Gerry on his first day back.

Finally, after what turned out to be a long day, Gerry got in his car and made the arduous drive home. At times, he stuck his head out of the window, like a dog, in order to keep himself stimulated. He was tired and drowsy. As he pulled into the garage and closed the door behind him, he sighed. All he could think about was getting some much-needed sleep.

"Honey, I'm home," Gerry announced in his best Ricky Ricardo impersonation as he burst through the door to the foyer of his home.

"Gerry?" Mary responded. "How was your first day back at work? I've been thinking about you all day," she admitted.

"Everything was great, Mary," Gerry exclaimed. "It was like I never left. Oh, and they had a cake for me! A welcome-back treat. The managers are always looking for an excuse to have cake and coffee in the afternoon. Today, I was the excuse." He laughed.

"That's so nice, Gerry," Mary beamed. "I'm happy for you, Honey! It must be nice working for a company that treats their employees like family members," Mary said as she bear-hugged him like she would never let go.

# 16

Either fight or surrender.

The second and third chemotherapy sessions were, for Gerry, similar to the first treatment. Although horrible, Gerry found the routine to be strangely comforting. Like anything else, experience was helping to improve his performance. He certainly wasn't as frightened as he was the first time. And, at the very least, he felt he was doing something to offset the disease.

When Nancy took his vitals, she noted a drastic improvement in Gerry's blood pressure and pulse. Gerry was even getting used to being stabbed in the chest when Nancy accessed his port. He still felt it necessary to let his mind drift to the far corner of the room in order to witness the goings-on from a distance. But once the poking and prodding were finished, Gerry found his conversations with Nancy were quite pleasant. She seemed to take her time, marking the test tubes full of Gerry's bright red blood with the correct information in order to further the discussion they were having.

Inevitably, Nancy would leave the small exam room with her recently filled test tubes and walk them to the lab at the end of the hallway, leaving Gerry alone with his thoughts. For the most part, Gerry would stare through the soot-stained windows at the double-lane roadway to the right and the black tar-covered rooftop to the left. He never stopped wondering about how he got himself into this mess. At the same time, he realized there was nothing he could do to change what happened in the past.

Typically, 15 to 20 minutes later, Nancy would lightly knock on the door to the exam room. She stuck her torso and smiling face over the threshold while holding the door handle with her left hand and made her announcement.

"The doctor will be in shortly," she would say.

With her right hand, she would give Gerry the 'thumbs-up' sign and let him know that she would see him in the chemotherapy parlor in a little while. Gerry didn't realize it at the time, but Nancy's hand gesture was her way of indicating to him the results of his blood test. He thought her gesture was simply her way of just being generally encouraging. Thoughts of red cells, white cells, and platelets couldn't be further from his mind at this point. All

Gerry wanted to hear from the doctor was that he was doing great, the drugs are working, and everything was coming up roses. He still had lots to learn about battling cancer.

During Gerry's third visit to the chemotherapy parlor, he met a gentleman who, like Gerry, was battling colorectal cancer. Sully, as he was known, was far more experienced than Gerry in being a cancer patient, as he was already on his tenth chemo session. The two had much in common and shared stories about work and family during their three to four-hour sessions. Sully, the doting grandfather, shared pictures of his beautiful, smiling granddaughter who was a third grader at a local grammar school. Early on, he confided in Gerry the fact that she was the major motivator for him in his battle. Sully loved his wife and kids dearly, but his granddaughter's sweet smile and bear hugs melted his heart.

"You have to have a reason to put yourself through this shit," Sully spoke softly to Gerry as a sage to a novice. "Otherwise you'll find yourself in a dark place one day, and you will want to just give up. Toss in the towel. Tip your king," he warned. "When you get there, in that dark place, use your motivation to help you. Nothing anyone can say to you will give you the courage to push through when you feel you are being beaten. The courage must come from within. And you must be ready to pull out all the stops. Be prepared to go at it with teeth bared, fists clenched, and eyes streaming tears across your swollen red cheeks. Fight like hell for whatever it is that motivates you to kick the demon's ass. Otherwise, you will, without a doubt, lose your fight. You may lose anyway, but, at least if you do, go out swinging," he explained.

Gerry was still early in his treatment schedule compared to Sully. This one being Gerry's third. Although he was experiencing nausea, lack of appetite, diarrhea, and general malaise, he felt he was tolerating the chemo relatively well.

"Sully, I know you've had seven more treatments than I have," Gerry began. "Right now, I don't feel great," he stated. "But I don't feel like jumping off a bridge either. What's it like getting down to the final three treatments?" Gerry asked as he stared at the clear fluid dripping one drop at a time into the rubber tube feeding into Sully's chest.

"I have to get through this treatment, and then two more to go," Sully stated. "I can't tell you what it's going to be like for you, but, for me, if not for my granddaughter, I'd rip these tubes out of my chest and walk out of here right now," he admitted. "You know, Gerry. When I first started chemo, I was scared to death that I was going to die. After getting hit with some horrible side effects on my seventh treatment, I became scared to death that I wasn't going to die. This whole thing is barbaric, Gerry!" Sully exclaimed as he waived his

181

arm back and forth. "Pumping this shit, these poisons into our bodies to try to randomly kill any stray cancer cells that may have wandered from the main tumor seems almost crazy. Unfortunately, though, it's all we have. It's our only hope at life. The problem is, we also have to survive the treatment. We're fighting a war on two fronts. The cancer and the treatment. A hundred years from now, they will look back on the way we treat cancer today the same way as we look at bloodletting as a technique to cure migraine headaches back in the 18$^{th}$ century. They'll laugh at the pictures of us sitting here in this room and think we were nutty as fruitcakes for putting ourselves through this," he declared.

Gerry finished his treatment in the cancer center and slowly drove the side roads home. He wanted to pass by the lake a few miles from his house and maybe stop to take in the serenity he knew the place provided. He pulled into the paved lot next to the boat ramp and watched as a couple of optimistic young fishermen launched their 14-foot aluminum Jon Boat. He smiled at the memories conjured up by the scene unfolding before his eyes. Many times, long ago, he and his college roommate would grab a six pack of beer and two dozen Arkansas shiners and head out just like the two buddies on the ramp next to him. *There is nothing more relaxing than drifting for largemouth bass on a warm afternoon with a close buddy,* he thought. The biggest concern for the day is not getting hung up on a submerged tree branch and having to rig the line all over again. Otherwise, there is not a care in the world.

Gerry stayed for a while and watched the pair until they drifted around a rocky point, out of his sight. Suddenly, he was brought back to reality by the squeal of the pump resting on his lap and the subsequent metallic taste in the back of his throat. *Got to get home,* Gerry thought. *Mary will be looking for me.*

Gerry's fourth treatment, two weeks later, went off the same as the previous three. His long-term vision was to treat the whole process as a basketball game. He had completed three out of the 12 sessions. The first quarter of the game was in the books. Three quarters to go. Although the cumulating effects of the drugs were adding up, Gerry felt he was holding up reasonably well. He was losing weight and corresponding strength. So far, after a quarter of the way, he had lost 20 pounds. Gerry figured incorrectly that he didn't have much more weight that he could possibly lose. He was starting to look gaunt. In the words of his son, Dave:

"Dad, you're starting to look like a cancer patient," he recently observed.

While sitting in the examination room of the oncology office for his next treatment, Gerry got the thumbs-up sign from Nancy and the subsequent chat from Doctor Hearms. He then gathered his reading materials and made his way to the chemo parlor for his session. Nancy had just finished connecting the second plastic bag of clear fluid to the tube leading to the port in Gerry's chest when Sully gingerly hobbled into the chemo parlor and sat down. Gerry never knew Sully before he got sick, so he couldn't relate to what a healthy Sully looked like. The Sully sitting in the recliner opposite Gerry looked far worse than he did two weeks ago when they last spent time together. His skin was wrinkled and gray. He shuffled his feet while noticeably shifting his weight from one side to the other, attempting to remove the pressure from whichever foot was forced to bear it. Sully's voice was raspy as he greeted his chemo buddy.

"Gerry, how's it going, my friend?" he began.

"I'm good, Sully," Gerry replied. "How about you? How does it feel to have two more sessions to go?" Gerry encouraged. "Get yourself through this treatment and then you get the last one in two weeks. It has to be a great feeling knowing you are toward the end."

"Gerry, the last treatment kicked my ass." Sully laughed. "It's like a prize fight. Some rounds you win, some rounds you don't win. The last round I didn't win," he moaned.

"What kind of side effects are you having?" Gerry asked. "I want to know what I'm going to be in for," he said.

"It's nothing you can't handle, my friend," Sully replied, ignoring the question.

"Did I tell you about my granddaughter's third-grade recital coming up this Friday?" Sully smiled while changing the subject. "Let me show you the picture of her, dressed in her performance outfit. Have you ever seen anyone more adorable?" he beamed. "Did I ever tell you about her? How much she means to me?" Sully asked, blankly staring off into the distance.

"Yeah, you have made mention," Gerry confirmed. "You look a little tired, Sully. Close your eyes and take a short nap if you want. I'll wake you if anything exciting happens," he promised.

"The last thing in the world I want to do is close my eyes, Gerry," Sully replied. "Tell me again about the spot on the river where you caught all of those smallmouth bass. We are going to go fishing together once we get beyond this little bump in the road," he determined. "I'm getting my fishing gear ready to go. You and me. As soon as the snow melts next spring. We'll catch fish until we drop."

Sully and Gerry spent the next few hours helping each other pass the time until their session was complete. Gerry's empty bag alarm was first to sound, and Nancy skillfully loaded a pump with a dose of 5-FU and released him for the day. Sully sat in silence as his friend struggled to his feet and pulled his loose-fitting top over the fanny pack which held the pump in place.

"There! Good as new!" Gerry exclaimed as he straightened himself. "See you in two weeks, my friend. One more treatment for you. I'm happy for you, Sully!" Gerry beamed.

"See you in a couple of weeks," Sully replied as cheerily as he could. "You know, Gerry, as much as this chemo stuff sucks, it sure beats the alternative," he admitted. "You take good care of yourself, my friend. We shall meet again," Sully promised.

Gerry didn't sleep at all that night. The squealing of the pump every few minutes combined with the nausea and tingling in his fingers kept him wide awake. Finally, at five in the morning, he got up from his recliner and got himself ready for work.

The drive from Gerry's home to Jimbo's seemed shorter than normal for some strange reason. In fact, when Gerry pulled into the employee-parking lot, he didn't remember the ride. There were two different routes that he used to get to work, depending on traffic conditions. Gerry couldn't even make a guess as to which one he used this morning.

"I could use a cup of coffee," he said aloud to himself as he pulled into his usual parking spot in the employee lot.

Then, he noticed a hot cup of Dunkin Donuts coffee sitting in the cup holder of the seat console separating the driver from the passenger seats. Obviously, he had already had the same thought and stopped to get himself a cup. Gerry wondered if he paid cash or used his rewards card. "This is going to be a long day," he said to himself as he took a sip and headed toward the employee entrance.

Several employees greeted Gerry as he made his way through the store toward his office. He acknowledged each with a generic 'hello' and a wave of his hand.

Gerry attributed his difficulty in remembering their names to his lack of sleep. Although, in this instance, lack of sleep was a contributor, Gerry was starting to experience symptoms of chemo brain. Not everyone who is treated with chemotherapy gets chemo-brain symptoms. Those who do, find it to be annoying, to say the least. In Gerry's case, the drugs made him spacy. He had difficulty remembering simple things. Multitasking was extremely difficult for him. Problems that would normally take him seconds to process and produce sound solutions frustrated him. Until he was able to flush the drugs out of his system, he acted like he was a character in a Cheech and Chong movie. His symptoms lasted for only a couple of days in earlier treatments. As the drugs continued to accumulate in his body, the effect would last up to a week before subsiding.

Gerry needed all his manager skills to navigate his way through the troubled waters that he found himself facing. He relied heavily on his immediate staff to make decisions on their own when he felt he was in a fog. Gerry was able to convince his superiors that as part of their development, he was empowering his managers to make more informed decisions on their own. Luckily, they bought it. Had the upper brass known that Gerry was not mentally 100 percent, he would have been forced to resign. Meanwhile, he just had to get through the day, severe chemo brain and all. Tomorrow, he would get the pump removed and then take a nice, long, afternoon nap. He looked forward to enjoying his day off in peace.

Fortunately, for Gerry, his highly anticipated day off went without a hitch. Nancy removed the empty pump in the late morning and sent him on his way. Gerry made it home in one piece and collapsed on his bed for a two-hour nap. When he awoke, Mary served him a small bowl of homemade chicken soup with saltine crackers for his early supper. Gerry was able to swallow two-thirds of it before deciding to take a hot shower and climb back into bed for the remainder of the evening. He hadn't felt this tired since his son, David, was born. Gerry always told young expecting parents that they don't know what tired is until they experience a newborn baby in the house. "There is a baby in the house," Gerry realized. The difference, though, was that this time, he was the one who woke up every two hours, crying.

Saturday morning came quickly, and Gerry felt a little better than he did the day before. At least he was able to get some sleep now that the squealing of the pump was removed from the equation. He washed a slice of toast-and-jam down the hatch with a cup of dark roast coffee and a small glass of room-temperature orange juice. Although he didn't look forward to working the closing shift, Gerry was happy to have Saturday morning off. He was still feeling the fuzzy effects of chemo brain as well as general malaise. Mary had already been up for two hours by the time Gerry made it downstairs for breakfast.

He couldn't quite put his finger on it, but Mary seemed to be acting a little strange. There was a subtle nervousness in her voice that Gerry thought he detected. For some reason, she seemed to want to keep her distance from him. It was as if she was hiding something from him. Gerry passed it off as nothing more than his foggy imagination getting the best of him and asked.

"Honey, have you seen my tablet? I can't remember where I left it. I could have sworn I left it here on the table next to my recliner," he tried to recall. "I just want to catch up on the local news before I go to work," Gerry stated.

Mary approached Gerry, tablet in hand, ashen-faced, as if she had just seen a ghost. She sat down on the cocktail table, a few feet from Gerry, and faced him. Mary held the device close to her chest as if guarding some deep dark secret. "Gerry, you know that friend of yours from the doctor's office that you talk about all of the time? Is his first name Robert?" she asked.

"You mean Sully?" Gerry replied. "Yes, his name is Bob or Robert Sullivan. Why do you ask?" he wondered.

"Honey, there's an article in the local news about a Robert Sullivan," Mary replied. "I don't know if it's the same person," she exclaimed, red faced.

"What does the article say?" Gerry asked, eyebrows raised. "What did he do?"

"It says a Robert Sullivan was attending his granddaughter's grammar-school musical Friday afternoon when he suffered a massive heart attack. Efforts to revive him were unsuccessful, and he was pronounced dead at the local hospital upon arrival. According to the article, as soon as his granddaughter finished singing her solo, the auditorium erupted in applause. Robert attempted to stand and, in doing so, collapsed into the row of chairs in front of him. An ambulance was on the scene within minutes, but he was already gone," Mary's voice quivered.

Gerry sat in stunned silence for a moment, absorbing the news. Processing the ramifications. His eyes watered, but he was determined to fight back any tears. Although he only knew Sully for a short period of time, Gerry felt a bond had developed between them. They were fighting the same foe. Teammates, as it were, in the struggle against the inevitable. Initial sadness from the news abruptly turned to anger. In Gerry's mind, it wasn't enough for Sully's battle to end when it did. The cruelty of the opponent dealing the final death blow in front of Sully's beloved granddaughter was more than Gerry could stomach.

"Yeah, that's Sully," Gerry coldly confirmed. "He told me that he couldn't wait to see the school program. He said his granddaughter had a solo. She was so excited to perform in front of her *grampa*. Brutal, don't you think?" he asked.

Gerry tilted his head back and stared at the ceiling as if he heard a noise indicating it was it about to collapse. And then, he tightly closed his eyes. As the soft tears streamed out of the corners of his eyes and salted his ear lobes, Gerry spoke in a quiet-yet-determined voice.

"Fuck you, cancer! Fuck you, and everybody that looks like you! I'm still here, and I'm going to kick your ass," he fumed.

Mary stood and slowly made her way to Gerry's side. Although she had never met Sully, she knew his story all too well. Not only from what Gerry had relayed to her, but from what she could see happening to her husband. Right before her eyes.

"Gerry, are you okay to go to work?" Mary asked as she hugged Gerry's head and stroked his hair. "You are talking to yourself. Maybe you should take the day off," she suggested.

"No choice, Honey," Gerry replied. "I can't just take a day off. Especially a weekend day," he said as he rose from his chair. "I better go upstairs and get ready. I'm sure there are lots of big problems at Jimbo's waiting for me to solve," he sarcastically remarked. "I should be home by 10:30 tonight. We'll talk then," he promised.

Gerry did make it home at 10:30 that evening, but he couldn't bring himself to talk about Sully. For the next several weeks, he would often think about his deceased chemo pal, but he would keep his thoughts to himself.

The cumulating effects of the chemotherapy drugs were officially taking a significant toll on Gerry's body. After the seventh treatment, Gerry weighed in at 180 pounds. Soaking wet. He had already lost 50 pounds since his diagnosis, and he was far from bottoming out. Gerry was forced to stop wearing his wedding ring. His fingers were so thin, almost skeleton-like, that the band would slide off his ring finger if he held it down by his side.

One night, when he came home from work, Gerry reached his arm up to hang his coat on the hook mounted to the back of the closet door. When he did so, due to his weight loss, his pants slid all the way to his ankles. Mary witnessed the whole thing and burst into laughter. Gerry thought it was funny as well, and the two laughed hysterically until Mary suddenly switched her tears of laughter to tears of grief. Mary cried herself to sleep that night. Gerry didn't sleep at all. Instead, he stared at the ceiling all night, feeling guilty about hurting Mary's feelings.

When Gerry reported for treatment number eight, he was full of optimism. All he had to do was get through the next three days, and he would be left with only four more sessions. There was light at the end of the tunnel. The routine was as normal. Nancy was pleasantly performing her tasks in a smooth, effective manner. She and Gerry were teasing one another over who had the better football team to cheer for. He, being a New England fan and she, a New York fan. Nancy took blood samples as usual and left to take them to the lab at the end of the hall.

As Nancy returned from the lab, she passed Gerry's examination room as she typically did while he waited for the doctor. This time, however, she didn't give him her usual thumbs-up signal. In fact, she didn't give him any sign at all. She just kept walking while maintaining her straight-ahead stare.

Finally, Doctor Hearms knocked on the door and entered the examination room, taking his usual seat on the rolling stool on the opposite end of the room. Gerry read his disposition as being a little bit glum. He assumed the doctor had to deliver some bad news to the previous patient and his mood was carrying over. After some basic 'how are you feeling?' questions and answers, the doctor glanced at his clipboard and began to speak.

"Gerry, this is going to be your eighth treatment according to my records," Doctor Hearms spoke in a soft, monotone voice. "Sometimes, it starts to get a little tricky as the cumulating effects of the drugs take hold. In your case, the platelet levels in your blood are getting dangerously low. We have been monitoring it and watching as the levels have trended downward following each treatment. So far, although it has been a minor problem, we have been able to treat you. Based on where the levels are now, I'm going to have to hold off on treatments until they come back to a safer level," he said.

The revelation hit Gerry like a ton of bricks. He knew he had to get chemotherapy in order to combat the cancer. It sounded like the chemotherapy was doing more harm than good right now, and the doctor was going to stop treatment.

"Are you telling me I can't get treatments?" Gerry asked.

"Gerry, we can't take a chance on driving your platelets any lower," the doctor replied. "If you have bleeding anywhere, internally or externally, you won't be able to stop it if the platelets get any lower. Hopefully, in another week, they will be back to a level where we can administer another dose of drugs. Meanwhile, I'll have the nurse remove the port needle, and you can go. Come back in a week, and we will try it again," he encouraged.

Gerry faked an understanding smile and, once Nancy had freed him from the octopus-like tangle of tubes dangling from his chest, grabbed his jacket and drove home.

The days when he was 'kicked out' of the oncology department without receiving his treatment would be the darkest for Gerry. Although brutal, he could deal with the physical ailments caused by the chemicals. He handled the nausea, diarrhea, headaches, numbness, weight loss, sleep deprivation, mouth sores, lack of appetite, and all the other minor side effects. He did not deal well with mentally preparing himself for a round of chemotherapy, however, and being told that his body couldn't take it today.

Gerry took the news as a sign of weakness. To him, it was a battle lost. His mind was going in one direction and his body in another. The internal conflict was severe and haunting to him. His mind felt that his body was turning into a wimp. His body felt that his mind was pushing too hard and it needed a break.

Gerry's emotions shifted from severe disappointment to extreme anger. If his body wasn't going to, *Suck it up and get tough*, he thought. *We're not going to get out of this predicament alive.* Finally, he settled on accepting the situation as it was, and sadness overwhelmed his emotions. Gerry remained melancholy and withdrawn until he was able to get back into the doctor's office a week later. It became crucial for him to exorcise the negative thoughts from his fuzzy, foggy, chemo-induced brain.

***

Back in the treatment center after enduring the additional week of recovery time, Nancy stuck her hand in Gerry's exam room and gave him a 'thumbs up.' Gerry's whole outlook changed. He brightened up and couldn't conceal the wry smile on his face as the doctor entered the room to review the test results. Gerry knew he was back in the battle and couldn't wait to get in the chemo parlor. His body was correct. He wasn't turning into a wimp. His mind was the one who was clearly incorrect. Gerry came to the realization that, at this stage of the battle, it was his mind that needed to toughen up. His body was trying the best it could, but it was struggling. It was up to his mind to fight through the dangers ahead if he would win in the end.

Gerry's ninth treatment triggered the same platelet problem as he experienced going into his eighth. He was learning to mentally handle the setbacks however his body was presented with a new obstacle. Every time his treatment got put off a week, it extended the calendar timeline. Treatment number ten was pushed back into early December. It was getting cold outside. As bad luck would have it, temperatures never got any higher than freezing for the five weeks following Thanksgiving.

Oxaliplatin, one of the three main drugs in Gerry's chemotherapy treatment, and cold temperatures do not mix well. Cold, combined with oxaliplatin, can trigger neuropathy in the hands and feet. The reason Gerry had to hydrate himself with room-temperature liquids, and not reach into the refrigerator without first putting gloves on, was because of the triggered side effects of oxaliplatin combined with anything cold. The fact that he was basically walking into a freezer every morning and evening when he stepped outside wreaked havoc on his nervous system. Mentally, Gerry thought he could handle anything at this point. He just wanted to get his last couple of treatments under his belt and move along with the rest of his life. Physically, there would be another story.

## 17

She's making a list.

Gerry sarcastically belted out, *"It's the most wonderful time of the year,"* at the top of his lungs while he showered for work. Mary rolled her eyes in the kitchen downstairs, faintly listening to the a cappella performance coming from the room above.

She knew all too well of the abuse retailers were put through during the December holiday season. Not only do companies extend their hours in an absurd attempt to outdo one another, but their marketing and advertising reaches a fever pitch for the six or seven weeks involved. Many retailers, like Jimbo's, extend the mandatory work week to six ten-hour days for salaried employees with the unfulfilled promise of making up the lost time to the employee 'at a later date.'

To put the icing on the cake, customers become angry mobs of impatient psychopaths looking for someone, anyone, to feel the wrath of their self-induced misery. Enter the defenseless store employee who would be fired on the spot for sticking up for themselves against said angry mobsters.

As he toweled off under the warmth of the glowing heat lamp emanating above his head, Gerry gave the popular song one more boisterous rendition. He sang of how everyone was so incredibly happy during the holidays. His voice ascended in volume as he struggled to reach the high notes.

And then his voice gave out as he attempted the final high note, causing him to begin to cough uncontrollably. Gerry coughed and coughed while his right hand gripped the outer edge of the bathroom vanity for stability. His left hand firmly pressed against his sternum, in a futile attempt to suppress the stinging pain from within. Finally, as the coughing subsided, he bent over the sink and let loose with a glob of blood and phlegm that had filled his cheeks and the back of his throat.

"Damn mouth sores," Gerry mumbled to himself as he stepped on the scale.

The digital read which unmercifully stared up at him from between his bare big toes indicated that his current weight was 160 pounds. Gerry had lost a full

70 pounds since being diagnosed. His six-foot four-inch frame was looking more and more emaciated.

As Gerry began to shave for work, he stared into the mirror at two swollen eyes which seemed to have a faint, yellow hue to them. Gerry figured his chemo brain was playing more tricks on his perception and ignored what he thought he observed. He was thankful that he was in a recovery week from his treatments. His body was telling his mind that it needed rest. His mind forced the body to get dressed. It was time to get to work.

Gerry pulled into his normal parking spot in the employee lot at Jimbo's and cut the engine. The sun wouldn't make an appearance for at least another hour, and there wasn't even a trace of a cloud in the moonless, starlit sky. It was one of those still, cold, winter mornings when nostrils would freeze shut if one were to inhale too aggressively through them. Venus shone brightly just above the horizon, bidding a final goodnight in a spectacular blaze of glory. The outside temperature reading on Gerry's dashboard reminded him that the air he was about to step into registered in the single digits. The light snow cover from an intense squall that passed several hours ago squeaked beneath his boots as he slowly walked toward the employee entrance.

20 feet into the 100-yard distance remaining to reach the warmth of the building, pain began to set in. It was subtle at first. Something that perhaps would just go away, he thought. With each step, however, it intensified to a level that made Gerry laugh and cry at the same time. The pain was familiar to Gerry. It conjured up a memory of a clumsy, unfortunate accident that he had several years ago. Once, during a powerlifting workout at the gym, he dropped a 50-pound plate on his big toe, breaking it in two. Although he knew that no trauma had just occurred to his feet, both were experiencing the same pain, in the same intensity as he felt in the gym on that memorable day. Gerry was certain that he hadn't just broken both of his big toes, but it sure felt like he did.

The neuropathy induced by the combination of cold and oxaliplatin was causing excruciating pain in Gerry's feet as his nerves degenerated. For a moment, he felt like he couldn't walk. Therefore, he felt he had no other choice but to simply sit down in the parking lot. Gerry braced himself by placing his hands under his butt, attempting to keep his pants' seat dry. This turned out to be another bad idea as the cold pressing on his hands induced its own version of pain in the form of a severe tingling sensation in his fingers. It was as if he suddenly stuck his fingers into a wall outlet. Combined with the sensation of having just broken both big toes, he had the feeling that 'this may be a little uncomfortable.'

Gerry's mind was forced to take over at this point. His body was acting in a totally irresponsible manner. Nothing was broken. Nobody was being electrocuted. Simply stated, his nerves were degenerating, and it was causing him a great deal of pain. It was time, however, to suck it up and get inside.

Gerry struggled to get back up onto his aching feet and gingerly, one excruciatingly painful step at a time, reached the employee entrance to Jimbo's. Once inside, he sat on the nearest bench, pulled his boots off, and pressed each foot between his palms in a feeble attempt to warm them. Finally, mercifully, after 20 minutes of blowing on his hands and transferring the warmth to his feet, he was able to stand and walk with minimal pain. He gathered his thoughts and headed toward his office. The store would be open in another hour.

No customer coming through the front door is going to know or care about some store employee not feeling well or having a bad day. There are holiday gifts to buy, and there is limited time to buy them. The pressure of the season, to the customers, is enormous. God help anyone who isn't up to the task of providing superior customer service.

Steve volunteered to run the morning meeting. He had lots to cover. Extended operating hours always cause disruption with associates. Closing shifts are frequently extended for the employees who are used to getting off work at nine o'clock. Suddenly, they are required to make other arrangements for their afterhours ride home. Instead of being picked up by a family member at nine o'clock, many will have to find someone who will come to get them at midnight. Even though many of them have been through prior December seasons, Steve always felt that a reminder of what was on the immediate horizon was appropriate.

The deeper into December it gets, the busier the store gets. The busier the store gets, the more the customers will increase their ill-tempered dispositions. For most of the year, a high percentage of customers are normal, reasonable, polite individuals simply looking to purchase something they need or want. A high percentage are even enjoyable to work with and to be around. Once Thanksgiving passes, however, a good 30 percent turn into obnoxious, rude, crude, impatient zombies looking to take out their self-induced panic on anyone they encounter. Typically, their target is someone who they know cannot defend themselves against their venom. Someone who can and will lose the source of their income during the holiday season if they give any resistance in return for the crude treatment the zombies enjoy doling out. Someone like a waitress or a hair stylist or a retail associate doing their best to help find an item or ring a cash register.

Gerry observed the glazed look of many employees who stared blankly at Steve as he covered the morning's topics. The group looked beat, and the day hadn't even begun. Many of them had been forced to work a full shift on Thanksgiving while their families attempted to celebrate the holiday without them. The grudge that many held toward their employer for being required to work on that day was beginning to wear off. In some, however, ill feelings lingered like a flatulent rider in a hot, New York City cab. Gerry sensed some negative vibes and felt he had to take over for a few minutes.

"Okay, everyone, I can see it in your eyes," he playfully began. "Just a few more weeks, and we'll put the holiday season behind us. Look for the nice customers," he suggested. "They are out there. Spend more time with them if you find yourself getting beat-up by the difficult ones. If someone is giving you a hard time, it's okay to excuse yourself and take a break. Remove yourself from the situation. Let your supervisor know you will be off the selling floor for a few minutes. It's OK. Don't let someone who is in a miserable mood get to you. Above all, don't do or say something you may regret later. Every single person gets to choose their frame of mind for the day. Some people choose to be miserable. Some people choose to be happy. I'm asking you to choose happiness," Gerry requested. "Your managers are here to help bail you out if we can. Remember, you are not alone out there. Let's, everyone, get some positive energy and have a great day!" he concluded.

Physically, Gerry looked like the Ghost of Christmas Past as he spoke. Most in the group figured that if he can have a positive attitude while looking and feeling like he does, there's no excuse for me. The meeting broke with many associates feeling ashamed of themselves for their prior self-pity. If Gerry can stay positive, so can the rest of us, they reasoned.

Clare, who stood in the back row, discreetly gave Syd a firm pinch in the lower part of his butt as Gerry spoke his final words of encouragement. The two had a rare opening shift together and both looked forward to spending a full day in each other's company.

"See, don't do anything you might regret later on," Clare giggled in Sydney's ear as the meeting ended.

"Hey, Clare," Sydney softly spoke as the two walked over to the customer-service desk together. "Do you think I can get in trouble for what I'm thinking?" he asked as he pointed his left index finger to the side of his head, eyebrows raised, lips pursed, and tilted to the left. Sydney's eyes stared unnaturally up and to the right.

"Of course not, silly," Clare laughed as she picked up her pace.

"Then I think you are smoking hot," Sydney stated. "And I can't wait to get you between the sheets later-on tonight!" he exclaimed.

"Good things come to those who wait," Clare replied flirtingly.

She sprinted the final few yards to the service desk. There, she claimed the computer station furthest away from the next customer-in-line position.

"You snooze, you lose," Clare said victoriously. "Have fun on that terminal." She laughed.

Syd, having been outrun, had no choice but to sign into a terminal station closer to the head of the line. Other customer-care associates were scheduled in the coming hours, and they would fill in the locations even closer to the head of the line than Sydney. For now, however, with only the two of them behind the desk, Sydney was closest to the firing line. Until the store gets busy, the customer will invariably stop at the first available station. Clare simply took advantage of Sydney's lack of focus.

"Maybe you should get your mind out of the gutter and concentrate on your job," Clare suggested.

"Very funny," he replied. "I hope it gets crazy in here as soon as they open the doors, so your little gamesmanship doesn't matter," he mumbled.

Sure enough, from the opening bell, transactions at the customer-care desk were happening fast and furiously. As is typical, early December gets busy not only with customers frantic to find the perfect Christmas present, but also frantic to return the Christmas present that turned out to be not such a great idea. Pre-Christmas returns are not as busy as the post-Christmas returns. They are, however, plentiful.

Many customers are also painfully aware of the fact that in December, retailers become incredibly lax on enforcing their own return policies. Due to the store's effort to process as many transactions as quickly as possible, retailers will accommodate the wishes of their customers. They will offer little, if any, resistance. The philosophy brings out the best in good, honest customers. It also brings out the worst in the dishonest ones.

Clare, being in sort of a giddy mood, decided it would be a good idea to categorize her customers for the day. On top of a plain white sheet of copy paper, she scribbled three headings and underlined each. Under the first column, she chose to list the 'Naughty' customers who she would work with. This category ended up being dominated, for the most part, by men. However, some women also managed to be so designated. Most achieved the distinction simply by sneaking a peek at Clare's red-laced bra as she intentionally leaned forward to grab something unnecessary from the cubicles directly beneath the countertop which separated her from the customer. Clare's top was left intentionally unbuttoned one extra button. Teasingly, this allowing her to flirt with her chosen targets with simple, subtle, forward-bending movements. The further she reached, the deeper she bent at the waist. The further she bent forward, the more she exposed her beautiful, long neckline and smooth, firm cleavage. Most of the men she targeted turned out to be 'Naughty' by sneakily glancing at what Clare was exposing. With their eyes pretending to stare straight ahead, the 'Naughty' group focused their eyes at an extreme angle downward and to the left. Clare pretended not to notice but caught every movement out of her periphery.

Others made the 'Naughty' list in a more aggressive manner. Clare notched a hash mark next to the names of the guys and gals who took the opportunity to hit on her during their interaction. She was asked to dinner by four men. Others simply awkwardly complimented her looks while tripping all over their words. One simply stated the fact that he was a fan of beautiful butterflies. The star of the 'Naughty' list, however, was a 30-something attractive woman who invited Clare to participate in a threesome.

"My husband is going to love you!" the woman exclaimed. "By the way, so am I," she admitted in a husky, sultry voice.

Clare, however, as flattered as she was, politely declined the offer.

"Here's my card," the woman said. "Call if you change your mind. OK?" she offered while flashing a seductive smile and a wink toward Clare as she left the counter.

Clare drew a big star next to her name and listed it under both the 'Naughty' and 'Nice' column.

The list of 'Nice' customers was just that simple. Although it was possible for 'Naughty' customers to be listed under the 'Nice' column as well, double listing was reserved for those overachievers who deserved such an honor. Most of the 'Nice' customers made it there by treating Clare like one would like to be treated themselves if the roles were reversed under similar circumstances. Many smart shoppers, especially those who were looking for Clare to bend the store's rules, would offer her a candy cane or even volunteer to get her a cup of coffee once the interaction ended. Even a warm smile or words of encouragement went a long way when it came to certain store policies being ignored in order to take care of the needs of a 'Nice' customer. It was easy for Clare to overlook the time limit on a return, for example, for a customer who was being nice to her. This was especially true during this time of year. She knew Gerry would support her decisions 100 percent.

"Never aggravate a good customer," Gerry always preached. "It is much harder to gain new customers than it is to keep the ones you have," he always taught.

Clare loved how Gerry empowered his staff to make business decisions that benefitted the store and the customer. He referred to them as 'Win-Win' decisions and encouraged his staff to make them on their own.

"If we are going to make a mistake," Gerry would say. "Let's make it in favor of the customer."

Clare, however, being a normal, sensitive, human being, was likely to dig in her heels by upholding a store policy when dealing with someone whom she listed under the third category on her list.

The third and final column on Clare's list was titled 'T.F.A.' The heading was thickly underlined, and she drew three bold exclamation points after the 'A.' Unfortunately, on this day in December, lots of customers made a conscious decision to have themselves listed under 'T.F.A.' Sydney, who was working several feet away, took a special interest in those who earned this distinction.

Sydney correctly assumed that Clare was just having a little fun with the 'Naughty' and 'Nice' customers. In fact, it amused Sydney to witness what he interpreted as Clare teasing and torturing her unsuspecting targets from the other side of the counter. In broad daylight, he marveled, she had curious men chirping like male tree frogs on a warm summer evening trying to attract a mate.

However, Sydney was not amused with the people who chose to be rude, crude, and outright nasty to Clare. He surreptitiously made notes of his own regarding those who were chosen to be designated as 'T.F.A.' Clare, on the other hand, found it soothing to her psyche in the aftermath of dealing with such a miserable human being to simply list their name under 'T.F.A.' Others, like the woman who threw a t-shirt at Clare after being informed that Jimbo's has never sold the brand of shirt she was trying to get a refund on, were listed with two stars next to their names. Clare was nice enough to give store credit to the woman on two other questionable returned items when the woman pulled the third item from another bag. Sydney, however, was less than pleased with her actions and took careful note.

Gerry was in the final 30 minutes of his two-hour 'manager on duty' shift when the dreaded call came over the radio.

"M.O.D. to customer care," Clare called out.

"On my way," Gerry replied. "Is it something simple that you just need an approval for?" he hoped.

"No!" Clare tersely responded.

Gerry lumbered his way toward the customer-care desk. He could see there was a line starting to build due to Clare's customer taking some additional time. His main objective would be to remove the clog and get things back to normal as soon as possible. Gerry's patience, at this moment, was running thin. His feet still ached from this morning's parking-lot episode. His head was fuzzy and clouded from the drugs. Additionally, Gerry felt hunger pains, but at the same time, he had no appetite. Most annoyingly, his colostomy bag was heavy on his belly, and it needed to be emptied. As soon as he finished with whatever he had to deal with at customer service, he needed to get to the restroom and empty it before it burst. However, he had no idea what he was walking into.

As Gerry approached the line of customers waiting to be called to the counter, he could see the impatient body language expressed by several of them. One well-dressed gentleman, recognizing that Gerry was obviously a manager coming to solve the problem, addressed Gerry in a voice loud enough for everyone else standing in line to hear.

"If you take those boots back," he warned. "I will never shop in this store again."

When Gerry glanced at the referenced mud-caked boots sitting on top of the counter in front of Clare, he decided to pass through the security door and take a position next to Clare, behind the counter. Right away, he felt the customer was trying to pull off something seedy. Gerry intentionally positioned himself and postured with Clare to offer her support. He also wanted to give the visual appearance to the customer that he was there to help his employee to deal with the situation.

"How can I help?" Gerry asked.

"Gerry, this is Mr. Paul Kane," Clare began. "Here's his license. He would like to return these boots which he purchased from a catalog ten years ago. I don't want to touch them," she said as she held her outstretched arms facing her palms out.

Gerry visually examined the boots. The way he looked them over sent a clear signal that he too refused to touch them. They looked and smelled disgustingly horrible.

"Mr. Kane, my name is Gerry, and I'm a senior manager here," he stated. "It's nice to meet you. Now why do you want to return these boots?" he asked.

"I don't like the way they are wearing, and they have a lifetime guarantee," Mr. Kane answered in a matter-of-fact tone. "Just give me a refund and I'll be on my way," he remarked.

Gerry leaned on the counter and slid a lined pad of paper and a pen to Mr. Kane. As he did so, he spoke in a muted tone so that Mr. Kane and Clare could hear what he was saying. Nobody else could clearly make out exactly what Gerry said.

"Mr. Kane, two things," Gerry quietly began. "First, a lifetime guarantee means the lifetime of the boots, not your lifetime. In this state, the lifetime of this type of product is eight years. You yourself admit these boots have exceeded their lifetime. Secondly, you brought them here, caked in what I hope is just mud. I'm going to go with mud because I shudder to think what else might be mixed in with whatever is on them. Plus, they stink so horribly bad that I'm gagging just being near them. Here's my business card. If you would like me to consider bending the rule on the life of the boots, call me, and I'll see if I can come up with some credit for you. If I'm not here when you call, ask for Steve," he instructed. "Here, I'll write his name on the back of the card for you," Gerry offered. "Steve is my partner and will be able to take care of you just as well as I can. I'll fill him in on what you and I talked about. You aren't going to get what you paid many years ago, but I'm sure I can get you a discount on a new pair of boots. If you choose to take me up on my offer, these boots will have to be cleaned like new, inside and out. Don't even think about wasting your time by bringing them back here in this condition," Gerry instructed. "Put your phone number on the pad, and I'll give you a call if I don't hear from you within a week," he concluded.

Next, Gerry reached over and grabbed two plastic bags used to bag customer purchases. He turned the first inside out and stuck his hand inside. He then picked up one of the boots with the inside-out bag and carefully reversed the bag, so the boot was neatly secured inside. Gerry performed the same technique used by dog owners who pick up dog doo with their plastic grocery-store bags before disposing it. He handed the boot to Mr. Kane as he repeated the procedure on the second boot.

"Here you go, sir," Gerry said as he handed the second boot across the counter. "I hope you have a great day," he pleasantly stated.

Gerry looked toward the customer who had warned Gerry about not returning the old boots and offered him a subtle wink and a wry smile. He then focused on the customer who was patiently waiting at the head of the line for her turn to have her transaction processed.

"Next in line please, this register is open," Gerry announced.

"Fuck you!" Mr. Kane shouted. "I'll have your ass," he promised. "You haven't seen the last of me. I'll be back!" he said finally as he stormed away.

Gerry remained behind the counter for the next several minutes, helping to assist the next few customers. He wanted to speed up the line as much as possible. Gerry could read the aggravated expressions written all over the faces of those who had been waiting in line.

Finally, when the lines had been cleared, he figured he could head over to the restroom and make himself a little bit more comfortable.

Before he left, however, he noticed Clare's list and picked it up. Gerry observed Mr. Kane's name was boldly written under the heading of 'T.F.A.,' so he decided to ask Clare what the list was all about. He pulled her to the side, list in hand, and absorbed what was on the page.

"Clare, what do you have going on here?" Gerry calmly asked.

"Oh, that," Clare sheepishly replied. "It's just a list of my customers today."

Gerry continued to study the writing on the page and then he looked Clare directly in the eye. His chemo brain, he felt, was inhibiting his ability to comprehend the simplicity of her wordings.

"I think I get the 'Naughty,'" he said. "The 'Nice,' I would assume, is self-explanatory," Gerry reasoned, rubbing his chin. "The 'T.F.A.,' however, I don't know what that means. Explain please," he mused.

"Total Fucking Asshole," Clare unapologetically replied in a quiet-but-bold tone of voice.

She softly stared directly into Gerry's eyes as she spoke. Blinking her eyes only after he blinked his.

Gerry stared at Clare with a stunned, amused, but frightened look on his face. He certainly could empathize with the list she decided to concoct, however, it was highly inappropriate. The way she used the 'F' word, however, came of as cute, amusing, and sexy, to the point that Gerry had to use every trick he knew in order to suppress his laughter.

"Clare, I think you may want to chill on this list," Gerry spoke in a serious, matter-of-fact tone. "I don't want you to get in any trouble," he warned. "I understand why you did it. I'm sure you were just having a little bit of holiday fun. But please, no more," he ordered.

Gerry folded the page in half, crumpled it, and deposited it into the nearest trash can as he moved away from the scene.

Once he rounded the corner heading toward the men's room and he felt safely out of sight, Gerry lost it. He needed a good laugh, though. When another associate asked him what was so funny, he could only reply that he was telling himself jokes. In fact, Gerry was still cracking up, with ten minutes to go on his M.O.D. shift, when he got the next call over the radio for a manager on duty to please report to the restaurant.

"What's going on up there in the restaurant?" Gerry asked.

"There's a customer who insists on seeing the store manager," came the reply. "He's irate over the French-fries portion, and he is causing a scene."

"On my way," Gerry sighed. "Have him stand off to the side if you can. Tell him I'll be there in a couple of minutes."

Gerry took a deep breath and glanced at the staircase a few feet away from him. The restaurant was located up those stairs and across to the opposite side of the store. After almost two hours as manager on duty, Gerry was physically exhausted. His rail-thin thighs burned from their buildup of lactic acid. Gerry's loss of body mass had reduced his previously powerful legs to nothing more than skin and bone. His feet were, again, aching due to their nerve deterioration. His lungs were straining to get enough oxygen into his bloodstream in order to fuel the engine. Gerry accepted the fact that if he attempted to climb the stairs, he would probably pass out. The escalator, being all the way toward the far end of the building, would have to transport him to the second floor. The route would add a few extra minutes to his travel time, but he felt he had no choice.

While riding the escalator, he couldn't help but to check the calendar on his phone. Gerry was convinced that there had to be a full moon. *Please, God, help me get through this day,* he thought.

As he approached the restaurant, his eyes fixated on a large gentleman standing just outside of the open seating area. He was a tall man, as tall as Gerry, but at least 200 pounds heavier. The gentleman was wearing thin blue jeans that were at least two sizes too small, a red-and-black-checkered, untucked, flannel shirt, and an unzipped, black-down Patagonia vest. He wore brand new, Premium Timberland boots, loosely laced and untied. The way he folded his arms and rested them on top of his oversized belly caused the bottom of his flannel shirt to be pulled up over his navel, proudly exposing rolls upon rolls of hairy, milky-white skin straining to contain mounds of stretchmark-littered fat. Gerry did his best to un-see the unhealthy image currently consuming space in every neuron in his brain, but his attempts proved to be futile. He looked around, and not seeing anyone else who appeared like they needed assistance, he approached the large man.

"Sir, are you looking for a manager?" Gerry asked.

"Yeah," came the reply. "You da manager here?" the man asked.

"Yes, sir, I am. What can I do for you?" Gerry replied.

"How fucking long does it take for a manager to respond to a customer in this place?" the gentleman demanded. "I asked for someone five minutes ago. I own a large business myself, and if one of my employees took their sweet time like that, I'd fire his ass!" he exclaimed.

"I apologize, sir. I got here as fast as I could. How can I help?" Gerry responded, not taking the bait.

"I have a big problem. And, guess what, now you have a big problem," the man shouted as he pointed to a dish of food sitting on top of the adjacent table. "That order of fries is pathetic. I asked for more, but the idiots behind the grill are telling me I got the full serving size, and, if I wanted more, I'd have to pay for it. What kind of business are you running here?" he demanded.

"You do have a big problem, sir," Gerry replied empathetically. "It's frustrating to encounter difficult problems that are hard to solve," he stated.

Gerry used his best active-listening skills, attempting to de-escalate the emotion of the situation. Gerry was also enjoying being excessively sarcastic with the gentleman. The irony of the situation was both ridiculous and hilarious to Gerry. So far, he was getting away with it, but Gerry knew he had better not push things much further.

"It is frustrating," the gentleman replied in a suddenly calm demeanor.

Gerry's active listening had the effect of a tranquilizer on an angry mountain lion.

"What can you do for me?" the man asked. "I'm only looking for more fries, and I don't feel I should have to pay," he whimpered.

"Come with me," Gerry directed as he walked toward the grilling area. "Hey, Billy!" Gerry shouted. "I need an order of fries. My price!" he said.

Billy picked a fresh order and handed it to Gerry.

"Three bucks please," Billy stated.

Gerry reached into his pocket and handed Billy the three dollars for the fries. He then turned to the gentleman, handed him the order, and said, "Here you go, sir. The fries are on me. You have yourself a great day."

"Yeah, you too," the gentleman grunted as he turned and returned to the table where his mound of greasy food was waiting for him.

Gerry staggered from the restaurant, opened the mic on his radio, and announced.

"That's it for me! My two hours are up. Whomever is next on the M.O.D. schedule, you have the helm. Good luck," he stated.

Gerry retraced his steps toward the escalator. His mind compelled his body to retreat to his office for the remainder of his shift. He was tired and wanted to go home. As Gerry reached for the black handrail of the escalator and stepped onto the silver-grooved top step heading down, he couldn't resist a sudden urge.

He cleared his throat, and in his best and loudest holiday voice, Gerry began to croon.

*"Bells on bobtail ring. Making spirits bright. What fun it is to laugh and sing a sleighing song tonight!"*

# 18

I expect nothing less than 110 percent.

Gerry sat stiffly on the crinkly white paper covering the examination table and numbly stared through the window which was outlined in a thin layer of snowflake-patterned frost.

The late December, midmorning sun was making a valiant effort to burn through the thick, quickly moving gray cloud cover to no avail. The black-tarred roof on the building below was covered in a thin sheet of clear, glassy ice. The swirling, frigid wind effortlessly whipped drifts of snow around the roof structures as if playing a game of Ring Around the Rosie with itself. Below, cars whizzed past the reddish, brown, sand-covered snow banks lining each side of the potholed asphalt roadway. Their operators were blissfully oblivious to the plight of patients who mindlessly watched them come and go from above.

Today was the day that Gerry had officially hit rock bottom. Both physically and emotionally. Nancy weighed him in at 149 pounds. Since his diagnosis, he had lost over one-third of his body weight. Gerry felt weak to the point that if a ten-year-old child attacked him, he thought he would have no chance to defend himself.

Mentally, he was not much better. Gerry's visit with Doctor Hearms a week ago didn't go very well. Gerry was told his platelets were too low for him to receive his scheduled dose of chemotherapy. Hopefully, today, after another week of Gerry's bone marrow doing its job, the problem would be corrected.

During his examination a week ago, Doctor Hearms did not like the sounds that he heard while listening to Gerry's breathing. He had listened to the same distinct noises in the past when examining other patients in similar circumstances. Doctor Hearms determined that it would be necessary for him to confirm the reasons for these distinct signals. The doctor had to verify his unfortunate suspicions. Doctor Hearms also noticed a faint yellow hue appearing in the whites of Gerry's eyes. He didn't, however, mention his observation when he informed Gerry that he would schedule a C.T. scan in the next couple of days. He did tell Gerry that the sound emanating from his lungs was cause for concern. A C.T. scan was necessary to determine whether his suspicions would be validated or not.

Gerry, in his heart, knew that there was something else wrong. He had made the mistake of ignoring some serious symptoms many months ago. From his unfortunate error, he learned a difficult and painful lesson. As much as he tried to convince himself that coughing up blood could be attributed to his mouth sores, deep down, he knew better.

Today, Gerry would hear the results of his C.T. scan from Doctor Hearms, but he already knew what the results were. The question Gerry wanted answered referred to the next plan of attack. No matter what Doctor Hearms would tell him when he knocked on that examination room door and entered with his clipboard full of papers, Gerry intended to fight like hell. He had too much to live for. He envisioned another tropical vacation with Mary. Another round of golf with the boys. Gerry was not ready to pack it in. Not yet.

Sully's voice rung in his head.

*"The time will come when you will have to dig deep in order to muster all of your strength to fight this. Whatever your source of inspiration is, the day will come when you will have to use it."*

Gerry's wait for the doctor's knock on the door seemed to last for hours. Veritably, it was the normal time that it took for the lab to process his blood work and relay the results to Doctor Hearms. The sound of soft, muffled, murmuring voices in the hallway just outside of his door caused Gerry's heart to race and his palms to sweat. Gerry could feel in his gut that he was about to get devastating news from the doctor. One look at Doctor Hearms, who was now standing three feet away, right hand stretched in Gerry's direction, confirmed Gerry's fear.

Gerry had made his living by reading people's body language and expressions. This one was easy enough for a beginner to get right. There is a certain look given when a person is about to deliver an uncomfortable message to someone familiar to them. The look diminishes when delivering the same message to a total stranger. It's much easier to inform an employee of their job elimination if the person delivering the news has barely known the person being dismissed. The same person, delivering the same message to a longtime coworker, gets a look of dread in their eye that is impossible to disguise. Gerry recognized that same look in Doctor Hearms' eyes. The good doctor was about to say something to Gerry that he really didn't want to say.

"Gerry, I have the results of your C.T. scan in front of me," The doctor finally said after what seemed like hours of uncomfortable small talk. "I'm afraid the results are less than desirable."

"How bad is it, Doc?" Gerry asked in a soft, monotone voice while continuing to hold his stare in the doctor's general direction.

Gerry, at that moment, happened to notice that Doctor Hearms had a small piece of white tissue on his upper lip just below his left nostril. He assumed it must have been left over from a nose-blowing session and wondered to himself how long it may have been there. Surely someone else must have noticed but chose to withhold the information from the doctor. Gerry thought about telling him but figured it might be inappropriate to interrupt the conversation they were having. He weighed the plusses and minuses of telling the doctor about it, but, for the time being, he kept the thought to himself.

"The scan shows that there are lesions on your liver which were previously undetected," Doctor Hearms began matter-of-factly as he read from the report. "You have several small masses and one larger mass that appear to have recently formed in your left lung. You also have several smaller masses that were detected in your peritoneum."

Doctor Hearms looked up from his clipboard and stared Gerry directly in the eye. His expression softened as he morphed from scientist to sympathetic interpreter.

"Gerry, the chemo didn't work," he stated. "The cancer has aggressively spread."

Gerry slowly blinked his eyes. He held them tightly closed for a few moments before reopening them. As he tilted his head straight back, he was able to focus on the pockmarks of the dropped ceiling tile directly above him. His heart was beating rapidly, and his breathing was irregular.

"So, what does this mean? Bottom line," Gerry asked, suddenly focused on the words bouncing around in his head.

He needed help unscrambling this new puzzle. He also needed some encouragement. Gerry wanted to be convinced that he could overcome this newest obstacle.

"What's a peritoneum?" he asked.

"It's the membrane that lines your body cavity," Doctor Hearms replied.

He felt like a college professor suddenly put on the spot by a familiar student.

"The bottom line, Gerry, is that your chances of survival are now at around one percent," he stated.

"So, you're saying I have a chance?" Gerry responded naively.

For a moment, Gerry recalled his previous conversation with the doctor regarding odds of survival. He then quickly dismissed that thought and, instead, processed the implications of the information he had just been given.

Gerry suddenly felt the blood drain from his face as he contemplated the dire circumstance of his predicament. He instantly felt lightheaded and his vision became obscured by a black, fuzzy, imaginary shield covering his eyes. He tried to blink and then raised his right hand to his forehead in a feeble attempt to clear his view. The doctor noticed Gerry's distress and rushed over to support him from the side of the examination table. Gerry attempted to regain his balance, and, as he did so, he excitedly pointed to the small trash can on the floor a few feet away, as if asking for it. Doctor Hearms quickly retrieved the can and set it down on the end of the exam table, between Gerry's legs. Gerry gripped the outer edges of the top of the can with each hand, lowered his forehead onto the rim on the far side and vomited.

*** 

Doctor Hearms, after determining that Gerry had regained his balance and consciousness, beckoned to Nancy from the doorway. She spent a few moments, comforting Gerry with cold compresses on the back of his neck as she held his hand and rubbed his bony shoulders. There would be no need for the tubes which Nancy had, minutes ago, linked to Gerry's port in preparation for today's chemotherapy treatment. So, she removed the needle, wiped the area with a swab, and covered the wound. No additional doses of chemotherapy would be appropriate, given the circumstances.

"Doc, how much longer do you think I have?" Gerry asked when his ability to speak finally returned.

"I have reviewed your data with colleagues on your tumor team," Doctor Hearms replied sympathetically. "We all agree that you have a month. Maybe a little longer. But it could also be a little bit less. I recommend that if you haven't done so already, you should get your affairs in order," he advised.

Gerry's mind processed the data but stubbornly attempted to figure a way out of this mess.

"I've heard about experimental treatments. Are there any that might help me?" Gerry asked. "I don't want to just give up!" he desperately pleaded.

"Gerry, I can refer you if you'd like," Doctor Hearms informed him. "There are studies going on at several cancer centers across the country. Understand that these experimental treatments are administered by doctors who are more comfortable working in laboratories. It is highly unlikely that whatever treatment you get will benefit you. Maybe, the drugs they give you will lead to something that may help someone else down the road. Mostly, however, the experiments hinge on determining what kind of side effects the new, experimental drugs have on the human body. Think of yourself as a lab rat," he warned.

"Look, I don't want to tell you what you should or shouldn't do, but, if I was in your shoes, I would make every moment count. You have been through enough. Usually, these experimental drugs give people, who are in your shoes, some false hope. They can also have some horrific side-effects. You should make your own decision, Gerry. I just wanted to provide you with some of the unvarnished, gory details of what you are getting yourself into," he concluded.

"Is there anything else that you feel I should or shouldn't do?" Gerry wondered. "I think I'll pass on the experimental stuff. I'm just asking if there is anything that I should avoid due to my health," he clarified.

"At this point, Gerry, do whatever you want," Doctor Hearms prescribed. "Eat whatever you want. Drink whatever you want. If you feel you can do something that you want to do, I am in no position to advise otherwise. Nancy has a folder full of information for you. Take it home and read what's inside. There is information on hospice care, a note from me to your employer requesting a medical leave of absence, an end-of-life checklist, and other documents you may find useful," he offered.

Doctor Hearms stood and sympathetically placed his hand gently on Gerry's emaciated shoulder. He hated this part of his chosen profession but was optimistic that someday, perhaps in his lifetime, conversations like the one he was having with Gerry would be a rarity.

"Gerry, I'm sorry we didn't get the outcome we wanted. I'll say a prayer for you," Doctor Hearms promised.

Gerry stood, wobbly at first, and regained his composure. If nothing else, Gerry was committed to maintaining his dignity. He straightened his clothing and combed his hair with his bony fingers. Nancy embraced him in a warm bear hug, handed him the folder she had prepared for him, and gave him some final words of encouragement.

"Gerry, you did everything you could have done," she tearfully assured him. "Sometimes, this happens. Don't be afraid to call me with any questions that you might have. I'll do anything I can for you," she promised. "The hospice nurse who is referenced in the folder is expecting your call. She is a wonderful person and will take great care of you. God bless you, Gerry."

There was no need to schedule a follow-up appointment, so Gerry blew a kiss and waived to the receptionist as he passed the window at the front desk for the last time. The receptionist smiled and returned the wave, still oblivious to what was transpiring. For one, final time, Gerry entered the antiseptic-smelling, dank elevator and pressed the button for the ground floor. He had no further need for an oncologist.

On the ride home, Gerry gave serious thought to not telling anyone about his predicament. Mary, he correctly assumed, would freak out. Gerry was not mentally ready for that scene, but, in the end, he felt it would be unfair to her if he kept her in the dark for too long. His mind was conflicted, racing.

As he got closer to home, Gerry decided to pull into the parking lot at the nearby lake. He had spent so much peaceful time there over the years, and, at this moment, Gerry needed a few more moments to reflect. He also felt the need to formulate a game plan.

Gerry took his usual parking spot facing the ever-changing beauty of the now-frozen surface of the kidney-shaped pond. He smiled at the sight of a young child seated on a Flexible Flyer being pulled across the ice with a jigging rod in each hand. To Gerry, it seemed like yesterday that he was that child being pulled along on his own sled. "Come on, Dad, faster!" he would command from the rear while his father struggled to transport Gerry and a second sled full of ice-fishing gear to their favorite spot. Gerry's smile turned to laughter at the vivid memory of his father slip-sliding across the ice. Flailing his arms like the scarecrow who had just been lowered from its post to the ground by Dorothy.

Gerry's mood got somber as he fast forwarded, catching glimpses and snippets of a wonderful life that was soon to be cut short, way too soon. Suddenly, his eyes swelled, and tears flowed. Gerry allowed himself a few moments to privately sob. He vowed to get it all out of his system. Gerry would not allow himself to make things worse on his family by being weak in his final days. He wanted them to remember him as a person of dignity and fortitude. There may be some tears, but he vowed to quickly turn them to smiles.

Gerry's conversation with Mary went just as expected. Her emotions ranged from fear to anger to sorrow. Mary didn't trust Gerry to be factual with his story, so she spent a full hour on the phone with Nancy and Doctor Hearms. She had good reason to not trust him. Gerry intentionally kept his tell-tale symptoms of the spreading cancer to himself. He didn't want Mary to worry any more than she already was. He never told her that he had a C.T. scan scheduled due to the doctor's suspicions. He certainly didn't tell her that in his upcoming appointment with Doctor Hearms, he would get the results of the scans.

In Gerry's mind, worrying didn't do anything positive for anyone. Mary, at first, was furious with Gerry for keeping her out of the loop. After her conversation with Nancy, however, Mary changed her attitude.

"He was just trying to protect you," Nancy assured Mary. "Don't be mad at him. Enjoy whatever precious time you have together. You know, as a nurse, I try to not get too emotionally attached to my patients. In Gerry's case, I couldn't help it. He is a wonderful human being. I've been crying all day. Take good care of him, please," she begged.

That night, Mary finally fell asleep at approximately four o'clock in the morning. She was awakened an hour later by the serenade coming from the master bathroom.

Gerry was singing his favorite Christmas carol, as loudly as he could, over the blast of the hot, steaming shower as the water pelted the fiberglass at his feet.

Mercifully, the racket ended as Gerry stepped out of the stall to dry himself.

"Gerry!?" Mary shrieked. "What are you doing?" she demanded.

"Just getting ready for work, Honey," Gerry cheerily replied.

"What?" Mary asked incredulously. "Gerry, please tell me you are not going to work," she pleaded.

"I'm going in to inform them that I have to take a leave of absence," he replied. "I have a company life-insurance policy," he said. "There are extra funds for my beneficiaries if I die while employed. Honey, I know how these people operate. They are going to do everything they can to try to screw you out of that money. You should trust me on this. I'm going to go in to inform them that I will be going out on a short-term leave due to my health. Doctor's orders," he stated.

He continued to get ready. Just like he always had.

"This won't take long. I'll be home by lunch time. We'll get something to eat at the Diner," Gerry promised. "I have to tell you that I feel pretty good today," he continued.

And then, as if surprised.

"Why don't you see if you can get a little sleep?" Gerry suggested. "You look tired," he observed.

Gerry felt an odd sense of relief as he made his final commute to Jimbo's Furniture and Firearms. For the past couple of years, he dreamt about his retirement. He wondered how much healthy time he would have to do the things that he truly enjoyed.

He often said, "If I could get 15 years of healthy retirement, I'd sign up right now. I'm not trying to be greedy; all I ask for is 15 years."

Gerry yearned to spend those years traveling and playing golf with his family and friends at the club. Someday, hopefully, there would be grandchildren to take to the park. He dreamed about how he would watch them play sports or perform their recitals. He would be so proud, attending their graduation ceremonies. Maybe, one day, Gerry would even write a book about them.

In his heart, Gerry felt the cause of his cancer was, in some way, related to the high stress environment in which he had spent his adult life making a living. So many of his colleagues and peers, some of them dear friends, had succumbed to cancer. Gerry, however, always assumed that cancer was something that happened to other people. It would never happen to him, he thought.

The sudden realization that he had days, not years, left in his life recalibrated his sense of time. Wasting an hour of his precious time on something foolish would equate to wasting a month in his new way of thinking. He would give Mark and Lynn as little time as he possibly could. He would tell them only what they needed to know. Not even one syllable more. As he pulled into the employee-parking lot, Gerry was pleasantly surprised to see Mark's car already there. Even though the salaried employees were still required to work a six-day, 60-hour work week, Mark continued to be a master of manipulation when it came to his schedule.

"This may go quicker that I thought," Gerry said to himself as he stepped out of his car and onto the icy pavement.

Gerry wasted no time seeking out Mark. He made a beeline to Lynn's office where he correctly figured Mark would be hanging out.

"Good morning, everyone," Gerry unenthusiastically announced as he poked his head into Lynn's office. "Since I have both of you, do have a few minutes for me?" he asked.

"Not right now, Gerry," Mark replied. "I'm in the middle of something important," he coldly replied.

"When then?" Gerry insisted.

He knew there was no way Mark would agree to an impromptu meeting. Mark, being the control freak that he was, had to be the one to schedule any such get-together. Subtle power-plays always created a great opportunity for Mark to show off in front of Lynn. Gerry knew that Mark wouldn't let this chance go to waste. He also knew that since Mark was in the building early, he probably had plans to sneak out. There was no way he would push the meeting into the afternoon.

"I'm sure I can squeeze you in for a few minutes," Mark bellowed. "How about in a half hour?" he suggested.

"See you in a half-hour," was all Gerry said as he ducked out of the room.

Gerry spent the next 15 minutes at his desk, going through some of his personal belongings. He stuffed a couple of pictures and some of his favorite pens into his briefcase. He didn't want to make it look like he was permanently leaving, but he did want to take some of his cherished possessions. The rest, he would leave intact for his replacement to toss into a trash heap. The various company awards and recognition certificates which he had been presented with would be useless to Gerry in his next assignment.

He left his briefcase on the end of his desk for easy access and took one last stroll around the selling floor. He enjoyed the peacefulness of the pre-opening environment. Normally, as part of his early morning walk through, he would make note of observations that required immediate attention. A missing sign here, an empty peg hook there were all issues that were worthy of a short note in Gerry's little notebook. Today, however, Gerry was taking one final pleasure cruise.

As horrific as the job could be, it comes with a lot of laughs. Gerry chose to remember the laughs and laugh at the horror. In retrospect, situations like the one with the French-fry guy, were hilarious to Gerry on so many levels. *Good times,* he thought. *Good times.*

Gerry returned from his walk and knocked on the door of Mark's office. He caught Mark's eye through the narrow, vertical glass window and requested permission to enter. Mark waived him in before returning his attention to the notepad on the desk in front of him. Upon Gerry's entrance, Mark turned the pad face down and grinned at Lynn who had joined him there a few minutes prior to Gerry. Lynn ignored Mark's exchange and, instead, greeted Gerry. She sensed that Gerry had something significant on his mind and knew that Mark did not have the same intuition.

"Gerry, how are you feeling?" Lynn asked, genuinely concerned.

"Thanks for asking, Lynn," Gerry responded, looking directly at her. "I'm not feeling all that great. In fact, that's the reason I asked to meet with you two –" he confirmed.

"What's the matter?" Mark interrupted. "Are you looking for a day off or something?"

"Actually, kind of," Gerry quickly replied.

The tone of Mark's question made Gerry angry and put him on edge. He took his time unfolding the document he was about to share in order to take a deep breath and gain his composure. He would make this quick.

"I have to take a leave of absence effective immediately," he began. "My doctor feels it is crucial to my recovery that I not work for at least the next six weeks," he stated.

Gerry unfolded the note from Doctor Hearms stating as such and handed it to Mark. He produced another copy and handed it to Lynn.

The tips of Mark's ears turned crimson red as he read the contents of the note from the doctor. He sipped his coffee and turned his head to face Lynn who was also studying the document. Mark, on one hand, was happy to have Lynn present. She would help him to quell his anger in the event his response raged out of control. On the other hand, he wished she wasn't present so he could unleash a barrage on Gerry that he would not soon forget.

"You're kidding!" Mark bellowed. "You're taking a leave of absence? At this time of year?" he incredulously asked.

"Yes," Gerry deadpanned, correctly assuming the question being asked was not rhetorical.

"We are all working six-day work weeks," Mark fumed. "Christmas is next week. Holiday gift returns are hectic as hell the following two weeks. Inventory is two weeks after that. To boot, you still haven't fixed the problem with the woman in the switchboard. I told you weeks ago to fix that screw up. And now you're pulling this crap?" he demanded.

"Yes. I am," Gerry stoically responded.

"Everybody knows you can get a doctor to write whatever note you want," Mark pressed on. "You had him get you out of work at the busiest time of the year? The selfishness of this stunt is epic," Mark declared.

Mark's anger brought him to his feet. He glared for a moment in Gerry's direction and then turned his attention to Lynn.

"Lynn?" Mark pleaded. "Please tell me we can deny his request. This is so wrong," Mark whined.

Lynn pretended to consider Mark's plea.

"Mark, these are his doctor's orders," Lynn informed him in a tone so frigid that her breath was practically visible as it clashed with the hot air coming from the other corner of the room. "At a later date, you can pursue whatever avenue you choose. Today, however, we should wish Gerry a healthy recovery and make arrangements to cover his shifts," she suggested.

Mark disgustedly slammed the document onto his desktop and returned to his chair. He sat quietly staring at the sheet of paper, hoping against hope that he would find a mistake. Maybe he could deny Gerry's request on a technicality. A misspelled name. An incorrect date. A missing signature. There must be something irregular on the note.

Mark spent what seemed like an eternity scrutinizing the page. He found nothing. Finally, he held the paper in front of his face with both hands and peered over the top. Staring directly into Gerry's tired, green-and-yellow eyes, he uttered a simple sentence.

"Just go," he said.

Gerry stood and turned to leave Mark's office. He didn't say another word. As he lifted the handle to open the solid wooden door with the glass insert, he heard Mark speaking to Lynn.

"I'm assuming you'll handle the paperwork and change his work status in the system?" Mark spoke as if Gerry wasn't still present.

Mark couldn't resist the opportunity for one final dig. There was no need for him to give Lynn instruction on handling H.R. protocol. She was fully aware of her responsibility. Even if there was a need, it could have waited until Gerry left the room. Gerry pretended not to hear. He wouldn't dignify the comment with a response. The brief exchange solidified the thought that it was okay for Gerry to remember Mark precisely for what he was.

Gerry returned to his desk. As he grabbed the handle of the briefcase which he previously staged for a quick escape, he heard a door slam behind him and detected light footsteps coming in his direction. Gerry turned to look and was quickly embraced in a soft, firm, bear hug. No words were exchanged. Lynn's velvety cheeks pressing against the side of Gerry's head felt good to him. He needed a hug.

Although he was slightly surprised by the provider of his sudden comfort, Gerry was fully appreciative of the gesture. When Lynn loosened her grip and leaned away from him, Gerry could clearly see the emotion in her eyes. She then simply leaned forward, kissed Gerry on the cheek, and turned away. Gerry heard her sniffles as she quickly walked the narrow corridor and firmly closed the door to her office behind her. Gerry blew a kiss in Lynn's general direction. It was a gesture that she would never see.

Then, briefcase in hand, he made his way toward the employee entrance and left the building for the last time.

# 19

A day for giving.

Steve nervously checked his watch. It was coming up on four o'clock in the afternoon, and Jimbo's Furniture and Firearms was still bustling with last-minute shoppers. His wife had Christmas Eve dinner scheduled to begin at six o'clock sharp. Family and friends would start arriving at 5:30 for cocktails and caroling without him. Steve had warned his wife that she was cutting it close since the store didn't close until five o'clock. In the unlikely event that every customer was cooperative, the earliest he could get the store shut down was 5:30. That meant he had no more than a half-hour to get on the road and travel home. Steve's wife wasn't hearing it. Appetizers would be served at six.

Many other employees unfortunate enough to be scheduled to work the Christmas Eve closing shift were in the same predicament as Steve. Every step he took, an associate reminded him of the obvious.

"It's Christmas Eve, and I have a family event to attend. Make sure we get out on time," he heard again and again.

Today, because the store would be totally abandoned, a senior manager was required to be the closing manager. Christmas Day was the only remaining holiday in the calendar year that Jimbo's would remain closed. Every other day, the store operated on a 24-hour basis. Typically, the overnight stocking manager would take charge once the store was closed to the public. Since there would be no overnight shift on this night, extra steps were necessary to ensure that the building was secured.

Firearms had to be removed from the selling floor and locked in a secure vault. The store had to be thoroughly walked in order to make sure nobody was hiding. Every year, retailers report incidents of 'breakout.' Criminals hide in a remote area of any given store and sit quietly while everyone leaves. Once enough time has passed, the criminals will grab the targeted items and quickly exit through an emergency fire door to an awaiting escape vehicle. The thieves can execute the planned maneuver in minutes. If not properly secured, firearms would be a highly targeted item. Otherwise, electronics are easily fenced on the street in the black market. It was the senior-manager-on-duty's

213

responsibility to take the necessary precautions to prevent a breakout from happening.

Once the guns and money have been secured, and after triple checking to determine that no person remained hidden in the building, it would be Steve's responsibility to plug his special code into the alarm panel. In doing so, he would be allowed two minutes to vacate the premises as the internal motion detectors along with the perimeter alarms would be activated. The alarm company then sends a callback signal once they have determined that everything is properly functioning, and the system is being monitored. At that point, the senior manager is relieved from his responsibilities and can safely go home.

Since Gerry was out on a medical leave, and Mark unsurprisingly pulled rank and left to go home several hours ago, Steve would have the helm. No matter the pressures coming from home, Steve would professionally execute his duties. There would be no cut corners. No procedure or duties would be forgotten or rushed. When Steve raised his glass to toast his guests this evening, it would be with a clear conscience that he properly carried out his mission.

\*\*\*

Steve glanced back at his watch as the minute hand struck 12, and the hour hand pointed accusingly at the four.

"The witching hour," Steve said to himself. "Please let this year be different," he pleaded with palms pressed together in front of his chest. His fingers pointed directly at the ceiling where his eyes were fixated.

No sooner had he lowered his gaze than he heard the first frantic call on the radio.

"M.O.D.? This is Clare up at customer care."

"Yes, Clare. It's Steve," came the soothing reply.

"Some idiot just puked all over the floor up here," Clare reported. "He's passed out on the carpet, and his drunken friends are trying to drag him out by the ankles. You might want to get up here," she advised.

"Right on cue," Steve replied. "I'm on my way."

On his way to ground zero, Steve contacted the maintenance associate on duty and prepared him for his upcoming task. The associate was fully trained in cleanup operations and understood what was necessary to accomplish the mission. The area would be sealed like a crime scene and the spill would be dealt with like the toxic waste that it was.

Steve, in his 30-odd years of experience, has never worked a Christmas Eve where the store wasn't invaded by obnoxious patrons who have been imbibing at office parties since noon. Come four in the afternoon, they stumble into retail stores, not knowing or caring that the store would be closing in an hour. Typically, these drunken derelicts were the most difficult when it came time to close. They attempt to linger for as long as possible, oblivious to closing announcements. Inevitably, one of them would step over the imaginary line and justify a call to the local gendarmes for reinforcement. Once there was a cop in the building, the miscreants would head for the exits as if someone yelled 'fire' in a crowded theatre.

At ten after four, a mere 50 minutes until closing, Steve hoped it would happen soon. 52 hourly associates and six other salaried department managers were counting on him to get the place evacuated on time. Each of them had family and friends awaiting their arrival before the holiday celebration could begin.

By the time Steve got to the scene of the passed-out drunk, his friends were in the process of carrying him to the front door. Steve intercepted the group just as they reached the front foyer.

"Do you guys need any assistance?" Steve offered. "I can call for medical help or a police officer if you need it," he declared.

"No. We're good," replied a young man who was decked out in a Santa hat and fake beard. "We don't need any help. Our friend here just had a little too much eggnog. We're bringing him home now," he stated.

"Can I get his name?" Steve asked. "I have a form I have to fill out. Name, address, and phone number would be nice," he politely requested.

"His name is Mister Grinch," the fake Santa replied. "He lives on Mount Crumpit."

The two buddies struggled to lift the dead weight of their limp friend into a shopping cart so they could roll him out to their waiting vehicle. Steve steadied the cart so that it didn't tip over and send its hapless rider tumbling to the concrete floor. The fake Santa realized that Steve was being helpful, and a hint of humility overtook him for a fleeting moment.

"Have a Merry Christmas, okay, Mister?" he offered.

"Be careful," Steve cautioned.

With that minor incident in his rearview mirror, Steve turned back to eyeball any busy spots of the store where he could allocate additional staff. He already had closing procedures in action. Ten certified firearms associated were in the process of securing firearms in the gun vault. Jennifer was busy closing unstaffed cash registers and securing tender to the vault room. She

215

would keep ten registers open until 4:30. From that point, registers would be closed based on customer traffic.

Steve resumed his perimeter walk of the showroom when his radio sounded.

"M.O.D., I need your help in fishing!" came the frantic call.

"This is Steve," he replied. "What's the matter?"

"Some asshole just grabbed a 'Ready to Fish' fishing rod off the rack, tied on a hook, and baited it with a rubber worm," the associate began. "He dropped the worm in the trout pond, and our 15-year-old brown trout attacked it like he'd never eaten before. There's blood and water everywhere," he described.

"Can you save the fish?" Steve asked.

"Not a chance," came the reply. "When they pulled him out of the water, the struggle caused the hook to rip him up pretty good inside. He stopped flopping around the floor already. The only movement is from his gills trying to get some oxygen into his system," he stated. "These idiots think the whole thing is funny."

"I'll be right there," Steve replied. "Don't confront the customers," he cautioned. "I'll deal with them."

Steve quickly headed toward the direction of the trout pond to see what was going on. The call from the associate came over the general in store broadcast so any employee with a headset could hear the conversation.

"Hey, Jennifer? Are you listening to this?" Steve asked.

"Yeah," Jennifer replied. "I have been listening."

"Get the police on the line. Tell them what happened. Maybe we can have one of them to talk to these guys," Steve instructed.

"I am way ahead of you, Steve," Jennifer declared. "The dispatch told me that there was an officer close by. He should be here any minute," she stated. "In fact, look who just walked through the door. It's your buddy, Mike. I'll tell him where he can find you," Jennifer said as she moved to intercept the officer at the entrance.

When Steve arrived at the scene of the crime, he was horrified. The fishing associate wasn't kidding when he said there was blood everywhere. Obviously, the fish had been allowed to flop all over the polished concrete floor, fighting for its life, until it could fight no longer. No attempt had been made to try to save it.

The giddy, obnoxious, drunken fishermen were taking turns posing for pictures with the now-lifeless trophy fish. Steve halted his approach and allowed each to have his turn in the limelight. He wanted to give the approaching police officer enough time so they could meet the group simultaneously.

216

"Who came up with this bright idea?" Steve finally demanded as he interrupted the group. "I have to explain to Officer Mike over here which one of you is going to be held accountable for this. Do I have to have security review surveillance footage or do some of you get leniency for cooperating with the police?" he wondered.

The group stared at Steve. He returned their pathetic look. And then.

"Why don't you talk among yourselves for a minute and figure out what you want to do?" he suggested.

Suddenly, the group grew quiet. Steve signaled to Officer Mike that he wanted to have a word with him.

"Thanks for coming, Mike," Steve quietly began. "These guys are causing quite a disturbance as you can see. If you can just make them go away, I'd appreciate it. I can't really press charges for anything that would be worth the effort. If you scare the crap out of them, I'll be happy. Maybe convince them that it would be a good idea for them to pay for the fishing gear they used. We'll deal with the dead fish," he stated.

"No problem, Steve," Officer Mike replied. "I'll take it from here," he said. "Hey, how's the family? Good? Tell them I said Merry Christmas."

"Merry Christmas to you too, Mike," Steve wished his longtime friend. "I hope you get some time off in the next couple of days. Spend some time with the kids," he suggested.

Officer Mike stood in front of the group of four and began speaking to them in his best, no-nonsense, police-officer tone of voice. On one hand, he was annoyed about having to deal with this bunch of disrespectful clowns. On the other hand, he had public safety to consider.

"The manager here is nice enough to not press any charges for the damage you caused," Mike said as he pointed toward Steve. "As long as you pay for the equipment you used, he's letting you go. On the other hand. I want to know who is driving? I can smell booze from here. Which knucklehead got behind the wheel and chose to drive the rest over here to cause trouble?" he pointedly asked.

The previously raucous group of young men looked at each other and said nothing at first. Finally, the one still holding the fishing rod looked at Officer Mike with glazed eyes and meekly replied.

"We don't know how we got here," he said.

"All right," Officer Mike angrily commanded. "Let's go, everyone! We'll settle this at the police station. Two of you are riding with me. The other two will ride in my partner's car. He's waiting outside and is the type that gets extremely impatient. It would be a real bad idea to keep him waiting much longer. I do not want to hear another word from anyone," he commanded. "Come on, let's go. MOVE!" Mike ordered.

Officer Mike turned to look at Steve as he ushered the group of revelers to the exit. He flashed a smirk and a nod in response to Steve's thumbs-up signal. The small gathering of onlookers dispersed as the troublemakers were enjoying their walk of shame with Officer Mike. Others, who may have been so inclined to cause their own disturbance, suddenly thought better of it. The vision of spending Christmas Eve at the local police station was sobering for the like-minded inebriated celebrants who observed the spectacle from a distance.

Steve checked his watch. At 20 after four in the afternoon, the atmosphere in the store was now calm, respectful, cheerful, and business-like. Steve hated seeing the fish being killed, but, in retrospect, things like this were expected to happen. He had bigger things to worry about right now.

Steve aggressively delegated store-closing tasks and refocused himself as captain of the ship. The maintenance associate had both spill scenes cleaned and under control in no time. So far, the closing of the building was smoothly running and on time.

Steve tasked one of the fishing associates with gutting the 15-year-old, ten-pound trout. He then had the guys in the restaurant pack it in ice. Steve decided it would be a good idea to drop it off at the local soup kitchen on his ride home. At least some folks who were not so fortunate would enjoy a fresh trout dinner this Christmas Eve. The detour might cause him to get home a little later than expected, but, to him, it was worth the trip.

Along with the fish, Steve gathered any edible leftover food from the restaurant and purchased some canned goods from the stockpile. An hour from now, while he was on his way to the soup kitchen, he would concoct some outrageous white lies. His wife was going to kill him for getting home so late.

At exactly 4:30, Steve opened the mic connected to the store's paging system. Management had gone to great pains to implement internal communications systems in order to minimize obnoxious, annoying pages. There is nothing more aggravating to a customer than being subjected to constant interruptions over the store's loudspeakers. At some retail establishments, the perpetual stream of paging seems to never end.

"Manager, take a call on line one."

"Jeremy to the customer-service counter."

"Manager, you still have a call holding on line one."

"Sally to the office."

"Manager, you still have a call holding on line one."

It can go on like this all day. Some retailers haven't yet figured out that internal radios and phone systems make for a much more enjoyable customer-shopping experience.

At Jimbo's, pages were rare. Everyone in the massive store stopped what they were doing and listened as Steve's voice went over the airwaves. "Attention, Jimbo's shoppers. The time now is 4:30. In order that our valued employees can go home and enjoy the holiday with their families, we will be closing our last register today promptly at five o'clock. Please make your final selections and bring them to our checkout lanes. Cashiers are waiting to process your transaction quickly and efficiently. Thank you for shopping with us today. Have a good night," he stated.

The store was predictably emptying out. One more closing announcement would be made at 4:45 for the benefit of those customers who thought the previous page was nothing more than a bluff.

Steve made his way throughout the selling floor. He stopped briefly to thank each associate for their hard work and extended his hand while wishing each a Merry Christmas. Even those who didn't celebrate appreciated the gesture and wished him a Merry Christmas in return. In the retail world, Christmas is usually a paid day off. Everyone involved, in one way or another, has a Merry Christmas.

Finally, Steve stopped at every cash register and thanked each cashier. They are the folks who deal with every purchaser. Some customers are pleasant, others are not so pleasant. The cashiers and customer-care associates are tasked with always maintaining their professionalism. No matter the disposition of the customer.

Clare was his last stop. She was busy preparing her workstation for closing when Steve approached.

"Thank you for your hard work today and every day, Clare," Steve said, holding out his hand. "I hope you and yours have a Merry Christmas. Do you have any special plans tonight?" he asked.

"Sydney is coming for dinner later on tonight," Clare smiled as she responded to his question. "He was lucky enough to get the day off. He said he had something to do later this afternoon, but it shouldn't take long. My mom is expecting him at around eight o'clock. She is so happy that I finally found such a nice guy," Clare gushed.

"Well, I hope you have a great night. Tell Syd I said Merry Christmas," Steve requested. "I'll see you the day after the holiday. Be ready," he warned. "It's the busiest day of the year."

***

Christmas Eve at the O'Driscoll residence was as festive as ever. Gerry was having some good days and some bad days. Mostly bad days. As the cancer continued to spread throughout his body, he would endure intense, rapid flare-ups of excruciating pain. His body was becoming more and more opioid-tolerant, making the pain medication he was taking less effective. Today, however, he, so far, felt okay in a relative way.

Rick and Dave came by early with their wives. Mary invited her sister and brother-in-law. The couple who lived next door also stopped by to partake in the festivities. It was all Gerry's idea. He begged Mary to treat the day as if nothing unusual was going on. He didn't exactly have the energy to jump up and dance around the house. He did, however, have a strong desire to spend a special day with those closest to him.

Mentally, Gerry couldn't have been more uplifted.

*This,* he thought, *was going to be the best Christmas Eve of his entire life.*

Gerry didn't have much of an appetite that evening, but everyone else in the O'Driscoll home sure did. The three pounds of shrimp cocktail that Mary served as an appetizer was devoured in minutes. The main course of ham, broccoli and cheese, roasted potatoes, and green bean casserole was likewise being consumed at a furious pace. Gerry politely picked at a few morsels but, instead, chose to enjoy living vicariously through his ravenous offspring.

The O'Driscoll household was full of laughter and love that evening. Shared stories of Christmas long ago highlighted the memorable feast. The infamous story of the Batman cave was shared from two perspectives. First, Gerry detailed the intense pressure he was under to assemble and decal the 'ten-thousand pieces' that came in the innocent-looking box with the cool picture on the cover. Gerry could be prone to exaggeration, but nobody challenged his claim of a ten-thousand-piece count on this night. The story of him fumbling with tiny plastic pieces and vague instructions on how to assemble them was just too funny for anyone to question the fuzzy details. He recalled starting to put the toy together when the kids finally went to bed at 9:30 on Christmas Eve. The attachment of the 'Bat Searchlight' decal was the final task for Gerry that night. He completed it at 4:45 on Christmas morning. Just in time for little Rick and Dave to take over and start pretending to be Batman and Robin a half-hour later.

Rick, who was eight at the time, and his younger brother, Dave, had an entirely different perspective than Gerry. Both boys remembered how ecstatic they were to see the toy for the first time. Dave recalled waking up and charging out of control down the carpeted staircase leading from the upstairs bedrooms to the living room in his onesie pajamas, oblivious to the potential danger of slipping in his vinyl footie soles and breaking his neck in a head-over-heels tumble.

The sizable plastic cave, Bat-mobile, Bat-helicopter, and Bat-boat had been carefully placed in close-proximity to the multicolored, lighted Christmas tree. The young boys immediately got busy exploring their new toy. They instantly imagined scenarios in which the Caped Crusader and his loyal sidekick would chase down the most colorful, evil villains in Gotham City. Rick and Dave, in their youthful exuberance, couldn't hide their unbridled appreciation directed toward their newly found special hero, Santa Claus.

Once the boys finished telling their side of the story, Dave opened a bottle of Dom Perignon champagne that he had been saving for such an occasion. The bottle made a loud, deep, pop sound, signaling to the group that something special was about to happen. A chorus of 'oohs and aahs' filled the room while Dave positioned the bubbling bottle at the center of the table and counted out the long-stemmed glasses. Dave poured half of a flute for everyone, including Gerry, and raised his glass.

"To Santa," were the only words he managed to articulate as his eyes teared.

"To Santa," everyone else repeated as they clinked their glasses and tilted them in Gerry's direction.

After the toast, Mary made her way back into the kitchen where she could have a moment to herself. The scent of the evergreen candle burning on the stove top along with the Christmas music playing on the countertop stereo gave her a warm feeling inside. She didn't want the evening to end, but realized it would be over all too soon.

Mary ran hot water over the long, sharp carving knife that she would use to serve Gerry's favorite dessert. Gerry didn't know if he could eat any, but he still requested the Oreo-cookie-layered, vanilla-and-chocolate ice-cream cake that he's been craving for months. He flashed a broad smile in Mary's direction, encouraging her to not waste any time in her preparation. Since the chemotherapy stopped, he was able to eat and drink cold things. Gerry didn't have much of an appetite, but he was determined to share a piece of cake with those he loved.

As Mary hummed along with the background music and pulled the Christmas dessert dishes from the China cabinet, Dave felt a buzzing in his left pant pocket. He ignored it the first time. However, a few minutes later, he felt the same relentless buzz on his left thigh. Begrudgingly, he subtly dug his left hand into his pocket and retrieved his cellphone to see who was bothering him. The large white lettering on the phone's illuminated screen simply spelled 'CHIEF.' Dave could touch the green dot to answer. Temptingly, he could touch the red dot to ignore. He thought for a second, took a deep breath, and touched the green dot.

"Chief?" Dave spoke softly as he rose from his chair and walked to the living room for privacy. He stood on the exact same spot where he and his brother discovered the Batman Cave on Christmas morning many years ago. "So nice of you to call to wish the O'Driscoll family a Merry Christmas," he said wishfully.

"Dave," the chief began solemnly. "I'm sorry to bother you. I really am. He's back, Dave! I thought he moved away like so many of these madmen do. It's been so quiet that I feel we let our guard down. It's the same guy, Dave. I need you to get over here right away. You have to see this," he said.

"Same guy?" Dave asked. "What do you mean it's the same guy?"

"It's the same hole in the back of the head," the chief replied nervously. "This isn't a copycat. It's him! He struck again. I'm staring at the latest victim right now, and it's not a pretty sight. Plus, he's starting to talk to us. He's teasing us or something. I can't explain. Just get over here," he ordered.

"Text me the address. I'll be there as soon as I can," Dave unenthusiastically replied.

The thought of leaving his family celebration nauseated him. Ironically, he knew his father would be the most understanding of the group. Gerry knew all too well the feeling one gets when having to forego a holiday celebration for his job. Dave just didn't want to break the news to those gathered that he had become a chip off the old block.

"Do you know where your brother is, Dave?" the chief asked. "He's not answering his phone. It must be turned off," he reasoned.

"Haven't seen him." Dave didn't try to hide his fib. "If I do, I'll let him know you're looking for him."

"It's okay, Dave," the chief said. "I hope he's just spending time with your Dad. Dave, I'm sorry about this. Merry Fucking Christmas, huh?"

"Yeah," Dave replied. "Merry Fucking Christmas to you too," he wished.

Dave broke the news of his imminent departure to one family member at a time in hushed tones. Each reacted with steely glares followed by a hug or a handshake. Finally, he approached Gerry, who was attempting to shovel a spoonful of ice cream into his gaping mouth with marginal success. Somehow, it appeared to Dave that his father's skin had taken on a deeper shade of gray in the few minutes it took to speak with the chief.

On the other hand, Gerry's perception level had grown inversely proportionate to his energy level since his illness struck. He attributed it to additional side-effects from the chemotherapy. Gerry claimed to have a newly acquired sense of smell equivalent to a blood hound. He said he could hear faint sounds that he never could before. He perceived and processed minute body-language that he never noticed in the past. Still looking straight ahead, he struggled to swallow the last bit of frozen ecstasy still swirling over his stimulated taste buds. He sensed Dave's presence along with the vibes he was projecting. Gerry knew Dave was about to tell him something. He also knew exactly what it was and how Dave felt about the whole situation. Before Dave could open his mouth to speak, Gerry cleared his throat.

"You have to go. Don't you?" Gerry asked.

"Yeah," Dave sheepishly replied as he took his father's right hand in his. "I got called to work. There's been a crime committed in the next town, and the boss wants me there right away," he stated.

"It's not like I never missed out on family get-togethers because of work," Gerry spoke encouragingly. "I missed out on so many picnics and ball games and birthdays and every other thing that I've lost count over the years. I'm just grateful we had some time together tonight, Dave."

Gerry managed to clear his throat and with tremendous effort, he swallowed.

"You want to know something?" he asked. "I think this is the best Christmas I've ever had. I'm getting a little bit tired anyway. How about if you go fight crime, and I go fight my pillow?" Gerry suggested.

"You're the best, Dad," Dave said as he pressed his left hand on top of his father's right. "Merry Christmas! I love you, Dad."

"Right back at you, Dave. I love you too," Gerry said. "Now, go on. Get out of here! Catch this guy. Will you?" he demanded.

*** 

Dave revved the engine of his performance sedan and sped toward the address in Chevon that the chief provided. He was fuming about having to leave his family on Christmas Eve. He briefly glanced at the mirror above the visor in front of him and caught a glimpse of his own reflection.

"I blame you!" he said aloud to himself.

For months, Dave has been struggling to piece together what little evidence he had and solve this murderous crime spree. The chief was right. For some reason, the murders had suddenly stopped. Dave and his team had grown complacent. They figured, incorrectly, that the murderer had either moved on or somehow wasn't able to continue his practice. Maybe he was in jail for some unrelated offense. Possibly, he was dead. Whatever the reason, things had quieted down, and Dave was lulled into complacency. The killer struck when it was least expected. Dave left his guard down and was struck with a solid blow to the chin. The pain of it all pissed him off.

He was still hot under the collar when he arrived at and caught his first glimpse of the crime scene.

"Dave, I'd like to introduce you to Paul Kane," the chief said disgustingly as he motioned his right hand toward the lifeless corpse. "I think he wants to wish you a Merry Christmas, but we haven't been able to get a single word out of him," he snarked.

Dave ignored the chief's futile attempt to make a joke and barely acknowledged his presence in the room. He was in no mood for humor. The room where the murder appears to have been committed reminded him structurally of the room where his family was enjoying spending Christmas Eve together.

At first sight, the scene before his eyes was both horrific and confusing. An act of extreme violence occurred a short time ago, in this very room. While Dave was greeting and hugging family members and wishing each a Merry Christmas, the bloody victim lying face down a few feet away was facing a cold-blooded killer.

"This is a little different," Dave mused as he bent at the waist, hands on his knees, to get a better look at the body.

Paul Kane was bent over, face down, on top of the breakfast bar located in the rather large kitchen of the modern two-story home. The same type of kayak straps as in the other murders were used to immobilize the victim to the granite countertop. This time, however, the middle of one strap was wrapped tightly around the neck of the corpse. The ends of the strap were then secured to the oven handles of the gas range located directly across the room. Each of the victim's arms were individually secured by a second and third strap in a similar manner and tied off to a solid handrail directly behind him. His feet were left untied to support his weight if the victim wished. Now, however, they simply dangled to the floor slightly bent at the knee.

With the victim's head tightly pulled forward and his arms tightly pulled backward, there wasn't much movement the victim could have accomplished without inflicting major pain on himself. Judging from the strong stench of stale booze still emanating from the victim's clothing, the murderer would have had little difficulty overwhelming his clumsy opponent. The single, three-inch open wound just below the victim's left eye indicated there may have been a blow delivered early in the encounter. In all probability, it was all that was needed to incapacitate Paul Kane. Lastly, curiously, a narrow slit had been cut into the victim's pants on the backside middle seam. A work-boot, from the toe to just before the heel, was sticking out of the hole in the back of his pants.

The boot's upper was still bulging against the fabric inside of the victim's soiled pants.

"What do you make of this, Chief?" Dave pondered.

"He's screwing with us, Dave," the chief replied angrily. "This is the first time he has decided to send us a message. We need to figure out what he's telling us. He has a boot sticking out of the guy's butt. It's like he's got him crapping a boot. What the hell does that mean?" he demanded.

Dave processed what the chief was saying as he continued to examine the victim. He walked over toward to the bloody, lifeless head of the corpse to get a better look at the taut straps that were grotesquely stretching the neck from the top of the limp shoulders.

"Don't flatter yourself, Chief," Dave deadpanned. "I don't think he's talking to us at all," he reasoned.

"Of course he is!" the chief barked. "I've seen the same thing before. This isn't my first rodeo, you know. The killer gets cocky and starts playing with the detectives. They leave strange messages. Like they are playing a game. Eventually, the messages get easier to figure out, and we trace them right back to the source. That's when we nail him, Dave. That's exactly what's going on here. I don't want any more murders. No more additional messages. This is the only one we need. I need you to figure out why this dead guy is posing like he is shitting a boot!" he exclaimed.

"Nah," Dave murmured, obviously offhandedly dismissing the chief's thesis. "First of all, he's had plenty of chances to communicate with us if that was his intent. I don't think he knows or cares about us. Nothing here indicates to me that he wants to send us a message. He's leaving clues. But he's not talking to us. The clues are unintentional," he stated.

"Okay then, genius. What's with the boot?" the chief asked.

"The victim isn't crapping a boot," Dave scoffed. "The killer isn't talking to us. That boot isn't coming. It's going. That old, muddy boot is being shoved up his ass. The murderer is talking to the victim. Not us. Why is he sticking that boot up his ass? I don't really know just yet. What I do think is that the murderer must have been pretty pissed with this guy if he allowed us to find him like that. If the toe of the boot was facing in, I would say it's the murderer's foot going up the victim's ass. It isn't though. It's the upper that's going in first. The murderer is making it look as if he's sticking this specific boot up the guy's ass. Why though?" he wondered.

"Interesting take on the same picture," the chief calmed stated as he processed Dave's interpretation. "I hadn't really thought about it that way," he admitted.

"The murderer is so pissed with this guy that he chose to let him be found like this," Dave softly spoke, as if he were talking to himself.

He then slightly raised his voice as if speaking to a room full of students.

"This isn't a random killing," David declared. "These two have interacted before. Where? How?" he wondered. "At least, in this case, we have something to go on, Chief. The killer just left us a breadcrumb. This might turn into his first big mistake. He let his anger get the best of him this time. I need background information on the victim over here. Maybe he randomly met the killer this afternoon at a Christmas party and pissed him off over something. The thing is, it's the same killer as the others. Nobody else knows about the hole-in-the-back-of-the-head thing. There's been nothing in the press about the method used in these murders. There must be some common thread tying all the victims together. This boot thing is something to follow up on. I'll have my brother provide some information on this guy. I'll fill him in later tonight and get him started," he planned.

The chief looked weary.

"Just figure this out, Dave," the chief begged. "I can't take much more of this shit. By the way, I thought you said you didn't know where your brother was. That's what you told me when I called you earlier," he remembered.

"You mean when you called and interrupted my family dinner?" Dave asked. "When we were trying to spend a little time with Dad on his last Christmas? That call?"

"Yeah," Chief replied. "That call."

"I couldn't see him at the time while we were speaking, so I didn't know exactly where he was," Dave replied sarcastically. "Without all of the facts, I didn't want to assume anything and risk providing you with bad information."

"Dave, I get it," the chief empathized.

He could sense the stress Dave was dealing with on all fronts. Sympathy was not one of Chief's strong suits, but he was a skilled supervisor. The last thing he wanted was for Dave to blow up, and he was getting the feeling that he was close to doing just that.

"Why don't you wrap up and get out of here for the rest of the evening?" the chief suggested.

"I need a little more time before cleaning up," Dave said assuredly as he slowly abandoned his sarcastic demeanor. "Did the guys already interview whomever found the victim?"

"Yeah. His wife discovered the body," the chief replied. "She was at a different Christmas Eve party than him. I hope she took a cab home because she was blasted when the guys spoke with her. She said she didn't touch anything because she didn't want to get blamed for his death. What does that tell you? Anyway, last I heard, she was passed out on the sofa in the living room. Good luck getting anything out of her tonight. If a bomb went off next to her, I doubt she would even flinch. Stop by and see if she's more coherent tomorrow. You're wasting your time trying to talk to her right now," he stated.

"Got it," Dave confirmed. "I'm still going to stick around a little longer while our friends from the coroner's office do their thing. I'll see you tomorrow. Or the day after that?" he asked.

"Yeah, I'll talk to you tomorrow," the chief confirmed. "I need to get out of here myself. I've seen all I need to for now."

Dave spent the next couple of hours with the detectives who were on duty when the call came in. They were the first ones to arrive at the crime scene and secure the premises. To a man, they were infuriated by the cruelty of the crime. Nobody deserved to be murdered like this. Particularly on Christmas Eve.

They vowed to redouble their efforts to catch who was doing this. None could fathom the sort of monster they were dealing with. He must be a hardened, career criminal used to animal or child abuse, they concurred. Perhaps the murderer himself was brutally abused as a child. The monster had to be older, experienced, and unusually cruel with few or no friends. For certain, if he did have a job, it involved hours of solidarity. No way could this be a social human being. Their expressed collective thinking and observations silently opened Dave's eyes to an entirely different perspective. Perhaps they weren't viewing the picture with the intent of the artist. Maybe, just maybe, there was something else to all of this. Whatever was the situation, the other detectives surely had narrowed their thought processes. Dave would let them pursue their own trail. He had other ideas in mind.

# 20

There is nothing to be afraid of. You have to go sometime.

Gerry placed his ball on a tee, with the arrow below the logo perfectly lined up toward the distant target, and swung through the ball. As his right shoulder brought his chin up during the follow-through of his controlled, balanced swing, his eyes picked up the flight of the ball. Gerry marveled at the beauty of the white ball sailing against the backdrop of the cloudless, blue sky above and the greenery of the tree-lined, deep-green fairway below. Even the birds couldn't help but to applaud the effort. A brilliantly colored, bright red cardinal perched on a tree high above the tee box made three high-pitched chirps followed by ten long, crisp, loud whistles in appreciation of the shot.

Gerry carefully placed the head cover back on to the business end of his driver and returned the club to the slot allocated for it in his golf bag. While he strolled along the fairway, preparing to hit his second shot, he thought about the one he had just hit. It wasn't the longest drive he had ever hit. Nor was it the straightest. It was, however, perfectly placed on the right side of the fairway, giving him an excellent angle to the green on this slight dogleg left, 18<sup>th</sup> hole.

Gerry left himself 150 yards to the flagstick. There was big trouble to the left of the green in the form of a water hazard which wrapped around the entire length of back as well. To the right of the green was a deep, ominous pot bunker. The apron in front of the green was clear of any trouble. There was nothing for Gerry to worry about as long as he hit his approach shot straight. He knew he could get there with an eight iron, but it would require a full swing with perfect contact. Gerry didn't think he could muster the strength to pull of that kind of shot. Fatigue was setting in from the earlier holes of his round. He, instead, decided that it would be wise to take one more club. Instead of hitting a full eight iron, Gerry would take a three-quarter swing with a seven iron. He pulled it from his bag, cleaned the grooves on the face of it with a tee, and spoke to it.

"Okay, seven iron. It's you and me. This is it. I'm about to hit my approach shot to the final green on the last hole. I'm going to play this ball slightly back in my stance, so it flies low. It's crucial that we keep it below the influence of the shot-altering wind which is swirling at the tops of the trees. I will take a three-quarter controlled swing and strike the ball in the exact center of the clubface. It is going to land on the front of the green, ten yards from the flagstick and run up to the hole. I have executed this same shot thousands of times before. Let's finish the round on a high note," he envisioned.

Gerry stood over the ball as planned and hit the shot exactly as he visualized. The ball flew low with a slight hint of a draw directly at the pin. It landed perfectly, ten yards from the flag. Due to the modest degree of draw spin that Gerry put on the ball, it started rolling dead center toward the hole. Gerry watched his ball roll with exhilaration, thinking that he had a chance to hole-out for an eagle!

His exhilaration quickly changed to fear, however, at the thought of the possibility that he had just hit his last shot of the round. With the sweat-stained cord rubber grip of his seven iron tightly squeezed by both hands in front of him, he twisted and contorted his body from side to side in a feeble attempt to apply body language to the ball. He feverishly began shouting instructions to the ball as if it could hear or understand his orders.

"Don't go in!" he demanded.

"Kick right!" he ordered.

Gerry planned and hit the shot exactly the way he wanted to hit it, but he suddenly became horrified with the reality of the consequences. He wasn't ready to end his round. Gerry wanted to take that final stroll up the fairway to the 18th green. Once there, he would accept his fate and tap in for a birdie. But not like this. Not this way.

"Please don't go in. Please!" he pleaded.

As luck would have it, one of the players in the previous group made a spike mark on the green, directly in Gerry's line. Just as his ball was tracking inches from the hole, it struck the clump of loose grass left by the inconsiderate player before him and veered to the right. The ball stopped rolling less than an inch from the right lip of the cup, still visible from the fairway, 150 yards away.

"Wow, that was close," Gerry said to himself. He wiped the sweat from his brow, relieved as he guided his seven iron back into his bag and began his walk to the green.

Gerry felt a little silly at the thought of how he reacted when he thought the ball was going to go in. Surely, when he gets to the green and taps in for his birdie, he won't have the same reaction. He would draw on what he just experienced to help him when the time comes for his last shot. Inevitably, he realized he will, at some point, have to take that last shot. He just felt so much more confident and serene now that he had the chance to feel what it was like to come so close to holing out.

Gerry's mind wandered as he slowly walked the final 150 yards to the green. He thought of the shots he took on the previous holes during his round.

Most of the shots played on the first couple of holes were fuzzy in his memory. In fact, he could hardly remember any specific shots at all. He remembered, though, for the most part they were not well-planned or executed. Being early in the round, however, he recalled them being played with tremendous enthusiasm. Oblivious to hazards or traps or sucker pins, he recalled generally playing those shots with reckless abandon.

The middle part of the round found him playing power shots. Some of the shots he took, however, were ill-advised. Gerry didn't always pay attention to the advice he was given from others who had previously hit similar shots. Many times, the shots he stubbornly took worked out great. Other times, the ball had no sooner left the face of the club when he wished he could take it back for a do-over. Those shots were the worst to deal with since they often involved either a miracle recovery shot or a sideways chip to get the ball back in play. Sometimes, the ball was so off target that it was futile to try to find it. There would be no other option than to take a penalty shot and play another ball. Gerry learned to avoid those costly errors in the later part of his round. In the middle of the round, however, mistakes led to knowledge.

The final holes in the round were played with smoothness and expertise. Gerry often wished he had the experience and knowledge in the middle part of his round that he had in the final part of the round. Conversely, he also wished he had the strength and exuberance toward the end as he had in the middle. Either way, the combination would have been tremendous. During the final stretch of his round, Gerry seldom took a shot without carefully planning and visualizing the outcome. Before he struck the ball, he considered his ability, internal and external factors, possible dangers involved, and desired outcomes. He learned to love and appreciate the round he was playing. Gerry chose to take nothing for granted and enjoy every remaining shot.

Most importantly, Gerry learned to love and appreciate everyone who played in his group. Some of those with whom he shared his round brought more enjoyment than did others. In fact, for some in his group, Gerry would gladly absorb any penalty shot they had to accept due to their unfortunate landing in a hazard. He knew those players would do the same for him if the opportunity presented itself. For them, Gerry would do anything in his power to help or advise. When the people closest to Gerry hit a poor shot, he felt as horribly as if he had hit the errant shot himself. Conversely, when they hit a fantastic shot, Gerry was happier than he would have been, had he struck it himself. But in the bigger scheme of things, Gerry truly believed that all who shared his round with him were responsible for making it as special as it turned out to be. Had he played alone, his round would have been meaningless.

*＊＊*

Shortly after Dave excused himself for the evening on the night before Christmas, Gerry experienced one of the intense and rapid pain flare-ups that had become more and more common. He had been experiencing them in greater frequency over the past several weeks. Skillfully, Gerry hid the frequency of these occurrences from everyone, including his doctors. Sometimes, the pain would originate in his lower back and then spread to engulf his entire torso in one massive, intensely painful spasm. Other times, the pain flared from just below the ribcage, in his abdomen.

Frequently, the pain started out dull and then sharpened to the point that Gerry couldn't breathe normally. It gave him the sensation that he was bursting from within. At its highest intensity, Gerry felt that if he could just muster one good burp, the pressure would be released, and the pain would stop. Unfortunately, burping didn't help. It wasn't gas that was causing the pain.

Usually, to help matters a little, Gerry would swallow a pain pill or three. Mercifully, shortly thereafter, the pain would gradually subside.

This time, however, the intense pain stubbornly persisted. In fact, as hard as it was to imagine, it intensified to the point that Gerry couldn't stand it any longer. He did his best to hide his discomfort until the last guest had departed for the evening. However, he hadn't been able to utter a single word in over an hour. Finally, when it was just Gerry and Mary in the house, he took a shallow breath in order to inflict minimal additional pain on himself and slowly spoke as he exhaled.

"Mary, Honey, take me to the hospital," he gasped. "I can't take this any longer. I need them to take the pain away."

"Gerry, what is it?" Mary asked. "Did you take any of the pain pills that the hospice nurse left for you?"

"I took four of them, over an hour ago," Gerry admitted. "The pain is getting worse, Honey. I can't do this anymore. I'm sorry," he said as his voice trailed.

One look at Gerry, who was now curled into the fetal position on his favorite recliner, told Mary all she needed to know. Gerry's face had lost another shade of color as the blood continued to drain from his already-gray skin. He helplessly looked into her eyes and then breathed a quiet moan as he glanced away.

Mary had seen enough. She quickly put on her winter coat and helped Gerry get into his. Although she knew Gerry would spend the night in the hospital, Mary didn't bother to take the time to pack an overnight bag. Mentally, she had been preparing herself to make this drive with her lifelong soul mate. She had to be strong for Gerry now that the time was here. The fact that it came so quickly, and on this specific night, added to her loathing of the cruelty inflicted by the beast. She would have her revenge one day, she imagined. Dance on the grave of this insipid disease. Now, however, Gerry was in pain, and she needed help to comfort him.

***

Mary parked in the valet space closest to the automatic sliding doors of the emergency entrance of the hospital and sprinted toward the front desk. On her way, she carelessly slipped on a small patch of ice that had formed on the sidewalk and performed an awkward, helicopter arm-pirouette in order to regain her balance. Gerry managed a smirk and polite applause at the performance Mary had just given for his perceived benefit. Mary, who was not equally amused, disappeared inside the building and then just as quickly returned with a wheelchair yielding orderly. Gingerly, the threesome managed to position Gerry into the wheelchair. As the orderly pulled the chair through the curb cutout and up the ramp to the sidewalk, he spun Gerry around in a direction that faced him toward the southern sky. Before he could continue the rotation and wheel Gerry toward the glass doors leading inside, Gerry held up his right hand and asked him to stop for a moment. Thinking there was something else wrong, the orderly obliged and moved toward Gerry's left to engage him.

"Are you okay?" he asked.

"I just want to take a couple of breaths of fresh air," Gerry reassured him.

The pain was still as intense as it was when Gerry left home. His body was screaming for mercy, but his mind wanted to enjoy one more of life's pleasures.

"Please, just give me a moment if you will," Gerry asked.

"Gerry, you can take all the time you want," Mary said as she took his exposed right hand in her fur-lined, mitten-covered left.

"What a waist of space," Gerry muttered, barely but clearly audible.

"Honey, what's a waste of space?" Mary asked curiously. "Gerry, what are you talking about? Are you okay?" she wondered.

"Orion's Belt," Gerry pointedly answered. "Look at it, Mary. Isn't it beautiful?" he asked as he raised his left arm and pointed to the three brightly illuminated stars perfectly aligned to form the waistline of the ancient warrior. The distinct sparkles of light interspersed with hundreds of others that were less visible in the cloudless sky.

"You know, I've seen those three stars thousands of times in the past, but never have they looked so gorgeous to me. I feel like I could reach out and touch them," Gerry marveled. "I wonder what it would be like to be able to talk to the people who first noticed their pattern thousands of years ago. People who are now long gone from here. Maybe their souls still exist among those very stars. What do you think, Mary?" he asked.

"First, I think that's the worst joke I've ever heard," Mary lectured while wiping a single tear that had rested on her upper cheek. "I can't believe I fell for it again! Secondly, yes, it is a spectacular view, Honey," she confirmed.

Mary reached her left arm around Gerry's shoulders and gently pressed her left cheek against the right side of his forehead. She planted a gentle kiss on his cold, gray, right cheek. Mary couldn't tell if Gerry was smiling or grimacing, but either way, she thought he appeared to have a peaceful look in his eyes.

"I'm so happy we got to share this moment together, Honey," Mary whispered. "Thank you for taking the time to point out the heavens. Come on, I'm getting cold. Let's get you inside."

*** 

David was up and about very early on Christmas Day. In fact, he didn't sleep very well due to the latest murder adding turmoil to his already-cluttered mind. After gulping a strong cup of Cuban-style coffee, he relentlessly convinced his wife, Gina, to take a stroll around the neighborhood. Dave needed to clear his head and the cold, crisp winter air would help him to do just that. The young couple fondly recalled how great it was to spend some time with David's family on Christmas Eve. Gina expressed to him how much she looked forward to spending Christmas Day with her family. They agreed that it was great to see Gerry having such a nice time the night before. Gina came clean by letting David know that after he left the party, Gerry seemed to quickly lose stamina. She said that by the time she left the gathering, he was sitting quietly alone in the corner of the family room. They each passed it all off as something to be expected after the excitement of the day. Surely, he just got a little tired, they reasoned.

Rick's phone buzzed on the nightstand next to his side of the bed. He reached over, picked it up, and glanced at the screen. It read six o'clock in the morning, and his brother, Dave, was calling. The two had spoken on the phone for over an hour at around midnight, just a few hours ago. David had already filled him in on everything he had seen at the crime scene. What could he possibly want at this hour?

"Merry Christmas again, Dave," Rick unenthusiastically greeted his brother. "Didn't I just get off the phone with you?"

"Yeah, you did," Dave answered. "Merry Christmas one more time to you too. I just got off the phone with the chief. He wants us to get over to the crime scene this morning. The guy's wife isn't being all that cooperative. She wants us to do whatever we have to do and get out of her hair as soon as possible. It sounds like she woke up with a tremendous hangover and flipped out on the guys who were left to keep an eye on the house. We should get over there and sniff around a little bit. See what we stumble on. Can you meet me there in an hour?" he asked.

"Yeah, I can get there," Rick replied.

As he answered Dave's question, he glanced over at his wife, Julia, who was awakened by the phone call.

"Hopefully, we can be back by noon," Rick declared. "Julia's family is planning a big Christmas dinner this afternoon. I would hate to miss it," he stated.

"I'm in the same boat, brother," David replied. "You may want to send her a little earlier and meet her there. You never know what kind of day this is going to be."

"True that!" Rick said. "I'll see you in a while," he confirmed as he disconnected.

Rick quickly showered and shaved before deciding to toss on a pair of jeans and a flannel shirt. He peeked outside through the open blinds at what appeared to be a typical cold, December morning. Even the forest green leaves on the rhododendrons beneath the window had a shriveled, freezing look to them. They had involuntarily assumed the curled, shrunken, embarrassed appearance that the freezing temperatures will cause. The puny leaves were barely a quarter of the size that they would boast when the warm summer breeze takes over, months from now. Just before Rick pulled his jeans over his boxer shorts, he pulled the elastic waistband of his underwear just below his navel forward with his thumb and fixed his stare at his pee-dog warmly nestled below.

"Shrinkage," Rick said to Julia. "It happens throughout nature. It's God's way of telling us that cold weather sucks!" he lectured.

\*\*\*

By the time Rick arrived, David had already been at the house where the murder occurred for a half hour. The scene was a little surreal to Rick who missed out on the excitement of the day before. The kitchen, where the body was found, was relatively neat and clean. It appeared to him as if nothing unusual happened there. The body had been removed, and the pool of blood that gathered from the victim's head wound had already been cleaned. Whatever physical confrontation the victim and the murderer engaged in was minimal. If the victim had a chance to fight back, he didn't do a very good job of it. It was almost as if he passed out drunk on the countertop and never knew what hit him.

Rick glanced around the corner of the kitchen doorway to the living-room area. There, his brother, Dave, was engaged in a conversation with a middle-aged woman who appeared to be sipping on a large, clear glass of Alka Selzer. When David saw his brother approaching, he extended his hand to the woman, stood, and excused himself.

"Totally useless," Dave informed Rick as he glanced over toward the victim's wife. "She has absolutely no idea about who or why or how this happened," He declared.

"Great," Rick replied sarcastically. "Let me have a look around. I'll see if she's okay with me poking around in his laptop. Something tells me she's going to tell me to get lost, but it's worth a try," he reasoned.

"Before you do that, get a load of this," Dave offered. "I was poking around in the kitchen. They keep a wicker basket on the far countertop for miscellaneous crap. You know, spare change, gum, Chapstick. That kind of thing. Anyway, I found a business card from a Gerry O'Driscoll. Jimbo's Furniture and Firearms. On the back of the card, in Dad's handwriting, it says, 'Boots.' And then he lists Steve's name right under it."

"Who is Steve?" Rick asked.

"I think it's the guy who Dad works with," Dave answered. "Not the store manager. He is some other guy. I can't remember his name, but I don't think Dad is too fond of him. This 'Steve' guy is Dad's partner and friend. I think," he stated. "I remember Dad telling me to ask for Steve if the people at customer care couldn't find his briefcase when I went to pick it up for him. It must be the same guy," he reasoned.

"Did you ask the victim's wife about this?" Rick asked.

"She had no idea what it was about," Dave replied. "She said her husband never told her when he planned to go to Jimbo's. She said if her husband bought another gun, she would be pissed." He chuckled. "There's a large gun safe in the basement, by the way. The wife has no idea how to open it. I'm staying out of that part, though. See if you can get one of the locksmiths to crack it open. You never know what we might find in there," David declared.

"Maybe we should call Dad," Rick suggested. "He can tell us for sure who 'Steve' is. With any luck, Dad will even remember meeting the victim. God only knows how long ago it was, though," he realized. "This is a bizarre coincidence. Even though everyone around here shops at Jimbo's, this is the second time someone who interacted with Dad was murdered."

"Well, at least we know where Dad was last night," David chuckled, embarrassed that he had ever let the thought of his father as a suspect enter his mind. "Even if we didn't know where he was, I think we can safely assume that he couldn't violently attack someone," he awkwardly continued. "Maybe we need to find out where 'Steve' was between six and seven o'clock last night," David decided. "It's already after eight o'clock, Rick. Why don't you give Mom a call to wish her a Merry Christmas and see if Dad is awake? If he is, we'll put him on speaker and cheer him up a little. Maybe he can give us some insight on the dead guy. See if he remembers giving out his business card," David declared.

Rick retrieved his cellphone from his left pants' pocket. Normally, on Christmas morning, Mary would call both before this hour to wish a Merry Christmas and invite the boys and their wives for breakfast. The boys always looked forward to a large serving of French toast casserole served with a locally produced maple syrup that was out of this world. There was always a large bowl of fresh fruit salad, juice and coffee, and boisterous conversation. The boys were fully aware that this year would likely be a little different. Dad was feeling lousy, they figured, and Mom would want him to get the chance to sleep in if he was able to.

Since the boys still hadn't received a call, Rick rightfully assumed that the breakfast wouldn't happen this year. He stared at his phone for a second, wishfully thinking that it would ring at any moment and the invitation he longed for would be extended. Suddenly, as if telepathically, the screen of his phone illuminated. It was Mom calling.

"Merry Christmas, Mom!" Rick answered. "You're running a little late this year," he teased.

"Oh, Rick," Mary's voice sounded alien to him. It was as if she was speaking through a voice-distortion device. "Rick, I'm at the hospital with your father. I think you should get over here, right away," she advised.

"What do you mean, Mom?" Rick replied. "Is he okay? What's going on?" he asked.

"Just come," Mary replied. "I'll explain when you get here. He's on the top floor. In the hospice ward. Would you call your brother for me? He needs to be here as well," she explained.

"Dave is with me now," Rick assured her. "We'll be right over," he stated.

"Hurry," Mary instructed just before she disconnected.

***

David and his wife, Gina, stepped out of the elevator on the top floor of the hospital and looked around. The floor was eerily quiet for a hospital. There were no nurses or doctors bustling around with charts in hand, darting from room to room while ignoring some of the nonstop loudspeaker pages, changing direction, and charging full speed toward others. There were no gurneys lining the spacious hallway beneath flashing red lights mounted above double-sized doors. No empty carts or rolling medicine stands waiting to be dragged into duty at a moment's notice appeared before them.

For a brief moment, they wondered if they had mistakenly wandered into an abandoned section of the hospital, or one that had been recently closed for renovations. It appeared to them that the patients' rooms were all located in the relatively short hallway to their right, so they headed in that direction. Several steps into the walk, they were startled by the appearance of a woman who suddenly stood from behind a desk which was neatly tucked into a nook of the otherwise mundane hallway. She was dressed in a cream-colored sweater with red-and-green trim, black pants, and black, soft-sole walking shoes. The only indication that she was part of the hospital medical staff was the stethoscope which dangled from around her neck. The woman had a relaxed, pleasant look on her face and warmly smiled as she greeted them.

"Hi. My name is Lindsay," she said. "I'm the nurse on duty. Is there something I can help you with?" she softly asked.

"Uh, yeah," Dave stammered. "My name is Dave O'Driscoll. This is my wife, Gina. I'm looking for my father, Gerry O'Driscoll. Do you know what room he is in?" he wondered.

"Pleased to meet you," Lindsay replied as she extended her hand. "Follow me. I'll take you to his room," she invited.

Lindsay led the way to Gerry's room which was only a short walk along the brightly lit hallway. She stopped at the doorway leading to his room and turned to face the couple. Lindsay's left hand was outstretched in a welcoming manner indicating that they would be entering the room without her.

"Your father is resting comfortably," Lindsay informed them. "Feel free to make yourselves at home. If there's anything I can do for either of you while

237

you are here, please let me know. I'll do everything I can to make your time here as comfortable as possible."

That said, Lindsay quietly turned and walked away, back to her station.

There was a short hallway at the entrance to Gerry's room with a door on the left leading to a spacious restroom. A tan-colored curtain, which could be mistaken for a shower curtain, was drawn closed at the end of the brief hallway. David pulled the right side of the shield open just enough to see the rest of the room behind it. Although he had no reason to not trust Lindsay, he was comforted once he was assured that he was in the right room.

The room was spacious and cheerily decorated with an area rug covering the middle of the otherwise cold, naked-tile floor. There was a small sofa against the far wall, a small dinette set with two chairs in front of the picture window, several comfortable armchairs, and a television mounted to the wall on the opposite side of Gerry's bed. Gerry was on the hospital bed, feet slightly raised, and his torso elevated in a sitting-up position. Some would refer to his posture as being in a zero-gravity position as it imitates the body positioning astronauts assume as they blast off into space.

Gerry's eyes were closed. His hair was neatly combed, and his face was as smooth as a baby's bottom indicating that he had somehow recently shaved. He had a docile, calm look on his face. David had the impression that he was almost smiling. Rick and Julia were already there and were seated at the table in front of the picture window. Mary stood from the chair next to the head of Gerry's bed when she saw her son and daughter-in-law and moved to greet them. Dave leaned what he was carrying against the wall beneath the television in order to free his hands and embraced his mother in a long, comforting hug.

"Is he sleeping?" Dave asked in a whispered tone as he gestured toward his father.

"No," Mary replied in a normal tone of voice. "He appears to be out, but I wouldn't call it sleeping. Lindsay says he can hear everything. He can't respond or talk. In fact, he can't even move a muscle. However, she claims he's fully aware of what's going on around him. You'd never know it by looking at him though," she admitted.

"Mom, what happened?" Dave demanded. "When did he get here? How did he get here?" he asked.

"Late last night," Mary began. "After everyone left the house, he told me he was in a lot of pain. He admitted later that he had been hiding it all night. He was hoping it would go away, but it just kept getting worse. The pain pills weren't doing anything to help the situation. Finally, he couldn't take it anymore," she described. "Once we got here, it seemed like he was doing okay for a few moments, but once he got in to see the doctor, all hell broke loose.

He was doubled over and could barely breathe. The doctor gave him something stronger which helped his pain subside, and then they ran some tests on him. Your father's organs are shutting down," Mary revealed. "The doctor was less committal, but Lindsay said it would be a matter of hours before his body totally shuts down. It's good that you are here to be with him," she sobbed.

David tightly hugged his mother and wept. He knew his father was sick. He realized that the time was coming when Gerry would no longer be around. David had been silently and privately preparing his mind for the inevitability of this moment. And, yet, now that the time was here, he found himself woefully unprepared.

After a few dark moments, David came to his senses and realized one thing. His father wouldn't want him to be like this. Gerry would want David to be like David and keep him company as he prepared for his big journey. David felt his father unselfishly give him the strength he needed to get through the day.

"Mom," David began in his normal, strong tone. "He looks so peaceful though. Dad actually looks pretty good if I do say," he realized.

"The doctor gave him some kind of fentanyl concoction for his pain," Mary revealed. "I don't know or care to know exactly what it was. All I know is it took away his pain. Lindsay says if he starts to stir, she'll give him another dose. She didn't think it was going to be necessary though," Mary stated.

Mary took David's hand as if he were a child and lovingly gazed at her husband. She did her best to smile through her tears and spoke softly.

"About an hour ago," she recalled. "A wonderful elderly gentleman appeared from nowhere and asked if he could give your father a nice shave. The man said he was a retired barber who volunteers to stop by as often as he can for just such an occasion. He gave your father one of those old-fashioned shaves," Mary described. "He had a coffee mug full of shaving lather in one hand and gently spread the cream over Dad's face with a soft, fine brush with his other hand. The man even pulled out one of those old straight-edge razors with the faux-ivory handle and sharpened it by stroking it on a thick leather strap. He was incredibly careful and gentle with every swipe of the blade against your father's skin. I bet it's the best shave he has ever had. Afterward, the gentleman perfectly combed Dad's hair, shook his limp hand, and left. What a nice thing for him to do!" Mary exclaimed.

"It sure does sound nice," David confirmed as he tossed his used tissue into a nearby trashcan and turned to face Gerry.

"Hey, Dad!" David loudly announced as he moved toward the head of Gerry's bed. "It's Dave. How are you doing?" he asked. "You look pretty good.

It's okay if you don't talk. I know you can hear me though, so it's useless to pretend that you can't," David warned as he slightly retreated.

"Hey, Dad. I brought you a Christmas present. Look!" David excitedly exclaimed as he retrieved the packages that he had leaned against the far wall. "It's that new driver that you said you saw in the golf magazine. Remember?" he sniffled. "You said you wished that you would get the chance to try it out," David reminded Gerry. "Well, here it is! I also got you a dozen of your favorite balls. You know what I'm talking about! It's a box of the balls that you are too cheap to buy for yourself. I agree with you that they are expensive for balls, but since its Christmas Day, I figured you were worth it. Anyway, I already made a tee time for us. I took care of all the details. All you need to do is show up. I can't wait, Dad! We're going to have a great time. You will be hitting those balls long and straight with that new driver. Just get a little rest for now. Okay, Dad? You deserve a little rest," he said.

Gerry tried to speak to his son, but the words wouldn't come out. He tried to move his hand to waive his acknowledgement, but he wasn't even able to twitch a single muscle in his now-useless body. In default, he let his mind abandon ship and allowed it to wander to the upper far corner of the room. From that vantage point, his mind could witness all that was necessary for him to see.

*That poor bastard,* Gerry thought to himself as he simultaneously surveyed his motionless body and each family member. *Look at what the doctors are doing to him now,* he mused as he witnessed his body struggle for air. His chest rising and falling ever so slightly.

Gerry felt a deep sense of sorrow that his body wasn't cooperating enough to communicate with his loved ones. He wished he could tell the love of his life, one more time, how much he loved her. He yearned to give his boys one more dose of fatherly encouragement. His mind was screaming at his insubordinate body to finish the task at hand, but it was to no avail. As willing as the mind was, the body was indifferent to its demands.

Time was suddenly passing quickly for Gerry's mind. Events were beginning to blur together in a single, concurrent event. The only audible sound in the room was coming from the television. The broadcast of the Pope delivering his Christmas homily was playing in a continuous loop. *"In Bethlehem, we discover that God does not take life, but gives it,"* the Pope reassured the O'Driscoll family. Dave and Rick stood next to each other, holding hands, with their opposite hand, each tightly held the hand of their spouse. The four stood silently, head bowed, in silent prayer as they listened to the Christmas celebration.

240

Gerry's mind was suddenly distracted by a flash from a bright light. He stared intently at the source until the images of beings emerged from the kaleidoscope chaos in the distance. There, just beyond Gerry's perceived arm's length, stood the unmistakable profile of his father. He stood statue-like, staring straight back at Gerry. As Gerry's mind closed in for a better look, his father grinned, reached into his pocket, and bent from the waist. He then placed a white ball on a brown tee exactly two inches above a perfectly manicured, deep-green grass tee box. The haze and confusion in the background of Gerry's intense stare cleared, revealing the most beautiful golf course that Gerry had ever imagined. As his father straightened, he rested his left hand on the end of his driver with his palm facing down. The head of his club was on the ground a short distance in front of him, forcing him to stand in a posing position as if someone was about to take his picture. He slowly moved his right hand so that it hovered above his left and turned it, so his right palm faced up. With the back, fingernail side of the middle and ring finger of his right hand, he began tapping the watch on his left wrist as if to signal to Gerry that it was their tee time. His hand didn't move. His arm didn't budge. Just his two fingers moved up and down, tapping his watch. 'It's time, Gerry,' his father motioned.

Gerry's mind quickly shifted back to the room and focused on his motionless body below. Mary sat holding his left hand with her left and raised it to her lips. Her right hand was firmly pressed on Gerry's chest so she could feel the slow, irregular beats of his failing heart. Gerry's breathing was becoming shallow and labored. Each breath his body managed to take was more difficult than the last. Mary rose from her chair and kissed Gerry's forehead. She then pressed her right cheek against his, so her lips were lightly touching Gerry's right earlobe. In a soft, whispered tone that only he could hear, Mary spoke to her husband for the last time.

"Gerry, Honey, if you can hear this, you're dying. It's okay to go. You were the best husband and father ever. I will love you forever."

Gerry's facial expression remained the same. His eyes were closed but not tightly closed. Almost like he was squinting to see something out of his range of vision. His mouth was tightly closed and angled back, forming the appearance of a slight grin. His lips were narrow as if they were being sucked inside away from view. Gerry listened to Mary and yearned to respond. He couldn't begin his journey without telling her how much he loved her. Gerry had to let her know that he would save a soft beach chair for her, but he would insist that she take her time before joining him. The fact that his useless body wouldn't allow him to do so frustrated him. Instead, the best he could do was to take a shallow breath. As he exhaled, he managed to slowly but deliberately inflate his throat, from just above his Adam's apple to just below his chin. For a moment, it appeared as if a balloon had been inflated inside his mouth, beneath his jaw. And then, just as suddenly, it was quickly deflated. A single tear formed in the corner of Gerry's right eye and quickly ran down his smoothly shaven cheek. It finally came to rest on the bottom of the pillow which comfortably propped his head.

Gerry's mind was not only observing the goings-on in the room below, but it was consumed in deep thought.

*For the life of me,* his mind pondered. *I can't remember something of significant importance. When I putt, do I inhale or exhale while bringing the putter back? Conversely, when I bring the putter forward to strike the ball, do I exhale or inhale? As I stand here on the 18th green, about to hole out and finish my round, I need the answer to this question. I'm not sure I can make this last putt without knowing,* he thought.

Gerry's body was not so consumed. He took one final, labored, deep breath, causing his chest to rise and held it there for a moment. Gerry then slowly exhaled, and as he did so, he brought the blade of his putter forward and tapped in his birdie putt. His round was complete.

In that same timeless moment, his conscience and his soul simultaneously exited the brightly lit hospital room at light speed and became part of the beyond.

Mary anxiously pressed her hand against Gerry's chest, waiting to feel the next heartbeat. But it never came. She pressed the button on the signal device to alert Lindsay that her assistance was needed. Lindsay promptly appeared in the doorway, took one look at Mary, and instantly knew why she had been beckoned. Lindsay gently pressed the end of her stethoscope against Gerry's chest, glanced up at the clock on the wall above his head, and simply announced, "He's gone. Please take your time, everyone. My condolences to all."

The O'Driscoll family stood in silence and hugged one another for comfort. Each took one last moment to take Gerry's hand, pat his shoulder or kiss his forehead as they offered him final words that he would never hear. Rick led them all in a prayer, parts of which were memorized from scripture and other parts which he made up as he went along. The words he spoke were soothing. They reassured those who were closest to Gerry that his agony has finally ended. Mercifully, there would be no more pain for him. No more mental anguish. No further fear of the unknown. Gerry's fate has been sealed. He was certainly now in a better place.

"Even though his physical presence will be dearly missed, his spirit will be with us forever," the O'Driscoll family promised one another.

242

# 21

Does quid pro quo mean anything to you?

The day after Christmas, in the brick-and-mortar retail environment, is arguably the busiest day of the year. The sales figure posted does not compare to that of Black Friday or even the Saturday before Christmas. When combined with the return figure, however, the total transaction number for the day can be staggering. In a store the size of Jimbo's, register banks had to be segregated and designated as 'return only' registers. Bins would be positioned to separate and quickly facilitate the process of preparing the returns for resale. Customers would be greeted and directed upon arrival into lanes designating the type of return that they wished to have processed. Those with receipts were herded into the fast lane. Customers without receipts were placed in the 'Bad Boy' lane where their patience would be tested along with the patience of the store associates. Sometimes, the research necessary to process their return would be simple. Other times, it would not.

Many, who refused to take the direction given to them upon their arrival, stood in the wrong line. They would subsequently be directed to the correct lane once they reached the front of the line which they incorrectly chose to stand in.

Any customers who simply wish to take advantage of post-holiday savings and buy something quickly breeze through the registers which are designated 'for purchase only.'

The day can best be described as 'organized chaos.' The store appears to be totally out of control due to the extremely large volume of customers combined with the number of various transactions that take place. When properly executed, however, the day runs relatively smoothly.

Steve, as the opening manager, handled the early morning meeting. His steel toe and heel boots clicked loudly on the concrete floor as he marched to the employee gathering assembled at the meeting area. One could almost hear a bugle blaring in the background as he took his position toward the front of the assembly. George C. Scott himself couldn't have struck a better profile.

Associates standing at attention toward the rear, believing that they were out of sight, mocked a weak salute.

"I'll be brief," Steve began. "I hope all of you had a wonderful holiday. Now it's time to take care of business," he declared.

Steve continued to stress the customer-service requirements of the day. During the delivery of his missive, he carefully detailed the scenarios that the associates were certain to encounter and how to deal with each of them. He then conjured up some of his favorite military colloquialisms in order to drive home his point.

"Today, it's all-hands-on deck," he announced in honor of the fine men and women of the navy, marines, and coast guard. "Anyone who wants extra hours on this day is welcome to speak to their manager. We scheduled everyone today. Any extra effort that you are willing to give to us is much appreciated," he confirmed. "It's not going to be an easy day," he cautioned as he waived his right index finger. "Today, it's balls to the wall," he firmly commanded.

Steve was fond of using that frequently misinterpreted Air Force expression. He once got in trouble for uttering it at a meeting and enjoyed explaining the origin of it to the ignorant.

The throttle of a fighter jet, back in the day, was topped with a ball. The shape helped the pilot grip the lever to give better control to the plane's thrust. The throttle was located next to the pilot. Its position is reminiscent to the way a stick shift is conveniently spotted in an automobile. Pushing the throttle forward accelerates the engines, giving the pilot more power and speed. Pulling back on the throttle does the opposite. The dashboard, if you will, had the appearance of a wall full of gauges and instruments. The wall was located directly in front of the pilot, just as a dashboard in a car is positioned.

When the squadron commander orders, "Balls to the wall," he is instructing the pilots to push the ball on the throttle toward the wall in front of him. In other words, he is commanding them to engage in 'full throttle.' When Steve explained the expression to Lynn while he was seated in the human-resources office attempting to defend himself for using such an expression, he asked a simple question.

"Why in the world would someone direct a man to place his genitals against some sort of wall?" Steve asked. "Doesn't the thought of that sound a little silly to you?" he wondered.

Lynn furiously kicked him out of her office before answering the question and asked him to go about his business.

Today, however, Steve finally ended the day after Christmas morning meeting with a simple command.

"Time to lock and load, people!" he ordered in deference to his army buddies. "Let's do this," he said as he clicked his heels and marched off to attend to his duties.

Many in attendance that day would later swear that they heard the unmistakable sounds of high-pitched pipers playing in the background as Steve marched off into battle.

The store hadn't been open more than 15 minutes when the loss-prevention staff nabbed the first shoplifter of the day. People who steal for a living are also fully aware that the busiest day of the year makes for a very profitable day. The key is in not getting caught. Time is money for a shoplifter, and any time spent being processed by store detectives and subsequently by the local police is very time consuming.

This enterprising individual was digitally recorded purchasing an expensive sweater, dropping it off in their car, returning to the store, and placing another one in the same bag. He then attempted to return the second one using the original bag and sales receipt. Unfortunately, for him, he got to spend the remainder of the morning with the police. By the time he was able to get back in the game and use the same technique at a different store, half of the day was wasted.

Shoplifters plan on being inconvenienced now and again. It's all a part of doing business. Little, if anything of consequence happens to them via the legal system. The fact of the matter, however, is that it is difficult to earn a solid living from the police station. There isn't much to steal there. Getting caught shoplifting the day after Christmas, though, is due to pure carelessness and bad planning.

From the instant the doors opened to the public, Jimbo's was packed with customers. Every sales associate was doubled or tripled up with people looking for assistance. Every department manager was engaged in helping to solve an unusual problem for a customer. The cash registers were humming nonstop with both sales and return transactions. As Steve would say, every pilot from the get-go was operating in a 'balls to the wall' manner.

Just as Steve finished with a problem customer at the service desk, he was interrupted by a radio page from Lynn. The day after Christmas was typically a quiet day for the human-resources department. Even though every associate was working, they were all too busy on the selling floor to think about reasons to complain in the human-resources office. Usually, Lynn would spend the day after Christmas with Mark planning the upcoming layoffs.

Some of the additional seasonal staff that had been hired would be kept on the payroll through January to help with taking inventory. Inventory occurs the second or third week of the month of January, and those who were most productive are frequently asked to remain on staff until it has been completed. Those employees who were either not very productive or not very reliable will be let go in the first wave of layoffs. The day after New Year's Day is typically their last day. Any excuse, however, given to an overworked manager by an unproductive employee, will be used to cull the herd immediately.

Since Lynn and Steve were on different paths today, it was highly unusual for her to interrupt him. Especially given the fact that it was such a busy customer-transaction day. Steve thought he detected that Lynn's voice sounded a bit shaky. As if she was nervous about something.

"Steve?" Lynn asked. "Are you available to come to my office?" she wondered.

"Now!?" Steve questioned incredulously. "I'm up to my ass in alligators over here!" he exclaimed. "Can it wait?"

"Steve, I wouldn't ask you to come if it wasn't important," Lynn quietly assured him. "Please, as soon as you can. Okay?"

Lynn sounded differently to Steve. She wasn't her usual confident, bordering on cocky self. It was almost as if she needed Steve to be with her. Like she wanted his company for some reason. It wasn't like the usual beckoning when she needed Steve to perform some sort of task for her.

"All right," Steve replied. "Give me a few minutes. I just want to let Jennifer know so she doesn't start looking for me," he said.

Steve signaled to Jennifer who was engrossed in a conversation with her own problem customer. He tried to indicate that he needed to see her for a second. Jennifer, however, was in full blown 'I'm busy, don't bother me' mode, and she shot an evil look Steve's way. Steve shot back his own 'this isn't my idea' look. The two of them had communicated without words for years. In fact, sometimes words got in the way. Jennifer, as soon as she was able to free herself, put down the daggers and approached him.

"Steve!" Jennifer demanded. "WTF? I feel like I'm a one-armed wallpaper hanger with a jock itch right now. What's the matter?" she asked.

"I don't know," Steve replied. "I'm busy myself. Lynn asked me to meet her in her office. She says it's very important. I'm not sure if her sidekick, Mark, is with her or not. She didn't say. Maybe they're going to can me," he snickered. "We reload our vacation accrual next week for the upcoming year. You know how Mark can get. Nobody deserves vacation time except for him," he laughed.

"They better not!" Jennifer snapped. "God knows that Mark isn't going to help out around here. Even though he should have his butt out here right now, helping us take care of customers. The problem is, though, he wouldn't know a customer if he fell over one," she declared. "All right. Let me know when

246

you finish your cake and coffee with the human-resources department. I can use your help back here where the customers roam."

"I'm sure you can," Steve shouted as he headed toward the office suite.

Jennifer barely heard him above the background noise of the bustling store.

Steve hurried through the managers' office door and made his way to the human-resources wing to the left. He knocked on Lynn's door, turned the unlocked handle, and let himself in to her office. Lynn was sitting behind her desk, alone in the room, and appeared to have been crying. Steve knew Lynn to be a strong woman. He had never seen her upset before, and the look on Lynn's face confused him at first. He couldn't determine if maybe she had caught a terrible cold and was simply blowing her nose or if she had something irritating her eyes. Regardless, he was relieved to see that Mark wasn't in the room with her. Steve didn't feel like dealing with Mark right now. He didn't have the time for foolish games. The store was busy.

"What's going on?" Steve asked, concerned. "Are you okay?"

"Steve!" Lynn began boldly. "Have you spoken with Gerry lately?" she wondered.

"As a matter of fact, I have," Steve answered confidently. "Gerry called me on Christmas Eve. It had to be around three o'clock in the afternoon. He just wanted to wish me a Merry Christmas. We joked a little about how whacky the customers get after four o'clock, so I know it had to be around three that we spoke."

"Get ready," he said. "They're pounding cocktails as we speak. The nutcrackers will be in to see you soon," he kept teasing.

"I sent him a text message yesterday just to wish him and his family a Merry Christmas, but he didn't respond. He was probably busy with family. You know how that can be," Steve reasoned.

"Gerry passed away yesterday," Lynn blurted as she stared directly into Steve's eyes. "His wife called a half hour ago and spoke with Mark. I happened to be in his office when the call came through. Mark had her on speakerphone, so I heard the entire conversation. Gerry's wife specifically asked that you be informed. She said Gerry would want you to know."

Steve heard the words, but he had difficulty comprehending them. The room seemed to close in on him and then, just before crushing him, expand back to normal size. The thoughts running through his mind combined a mixture of anger, sorrow, and grief. For a moment, he was frozen, trying to decide what to do next.

Lynn abandoned her human-resources façade and stood crying behind her desk. Her arms hung limp by her side. She and Steve had tolerated one another since they began working together several years ago but were never trusting of one another. Steve, seeing Lynn's distress, likewise stood from his chair and approached her. The two hugged and exchanged words to comfort one another for the next half hour as if they were brother and sister who just learned of the passing of their father.

Steve finally left Lynn's office and slowly made his way down the hallway toward his own private area. He had no choice but to pass Mark's office along the way. Just before he got to Mark's office, he couldn't help but hearing Mark, apparently talking on the phone, in his typical loud and boisterous tone. He was speaking with a store manager from a neighboring Jimbo's store located a couple of hundred miles away. The two were yucking-it-up about the impending January layoffs. They compared notes and stories about how much they savor the looks on the faces of the associates who get the axe. Each tried to outdo the other in describing the looks they get from the employee being let go compared to the look an animal makes just before being shot. Mark and his buddy were just having a hilarious, madcap conversation when Steve's frame appeared in the open doorway. Seeing Steve, Mark held his hand over the mouthpiece of the telephone receiver and stared at him.

"Do you need something?" Mark asked annoyed.

"Lynn says you need me for something," Steve replied coldly.

"Oh, yeah," Mark replied as he waved Steve into his office and motioned for him to have a seat.

He then pulled his hand away from the mouthpiece and said to the manager on the other end of the line.

"Let me call you back in a couple of minutes. I've been asked to tell one of my managers about something that happened. It's what we talked about a little while ago. I'll call you in a little bit." Mark chuckled as he placed the handset back on the phone cradle and returned his gaze toward Steve.

Steve sat in the chair opposite Mark and blindly stared directly at him. Although Steve knew what it was that Mark was going to tell him, Mark had no way of knowing that Lynn had already given him the news. Steve didn't need any further confirmation of how he felt about Mark. Still, he was angry enough to allow Mark to, once again, show his true colors.

"What did you need, Mark?" Steve bluntly asked.

"How is it out there?" Mark asked in reference to the sales floor.

"Typical day after Christmas," Steve deadpanned. "Busy as hell. How is it going in the office? You as busy in here as we are out there?" he wondered sarcastically.

"Yeah. Straight out!" Mark replied without taking the bait. "It's been one thing after another. All day," he described. "Steve, I've been asked to relay some information to you. I'm not quite sure how best to tell you, so I guess I'll just say it. Gerry's dead. I've been sitting here heartbroken all morning thinking about him. I know how close you guys were, and I felt it was best if you heard the news from me," he offered.

"I already know about it," Steve coldly replied. "Is there anything else for me or is that it?" he questioned.

Mark was annoyed. Not because Steve had already learned about Gerry. He was furious about having his conversation with his buddy unnecessarily interrupted.

"Yes, that's pretty much all I needed you for," Mark admitted.

"All right then. Well, I have got to get back to work. Nice talking with you," Steve said as he rose from his chair, turned his back, and left the room.

Mark, once Steve had left the room, lifted the handset from his desktop phone and called his manager buddy several hundred miles to the southwest to continue their boisterous conversation.

Word quickly spread throughout the store staff about Gerry's demise. Some reacted with surprise. Most with a deep sadness. To a person, however, even those who barely knew Gerry expressed the respect that they had for him.

The day which had begun with a fully engaged and energetic staff had suddenly been deflated. The employees went about their business in an efficient, professional manner, but their enthusiasm disappeared. An unmistakable dark cloud hung everywhere one looked.

When Clare heard the news from Jennifer, she openly wept and retreated from her station at customer service into the backroom. Sydney followed her into the back and tried to console her, however, it was to no avail. Clare felt incredibly sad. It was as if a member of her own family had passed. Syd offered a hug and kind words to her. He hated to see her cry and would do anything to help her feel better. In fact, Syd was getting an anxious feeling deep inside at his inability to cheer her up. He was like a caged animal watching its offspring being harmed. He wanted to help but felt powerless to do so.

Sydney tried to relate to what Clare was feeling. He wished he could share her state of mind so he could understand how to help ease her sadness, but there was nothing there. He was close to Gerry. In fact, he and Gerry had many deep, personal conversations. If there was anyone who could be considered a father figure to Syd, it would be Gerry. Sydney vaguely remembered how he felt when his father died many years ago. He tried to conjure some of those feelings now. Surely, he would have some remorse at the passing of Gerry. Maybe not as intense as the feelings he felt when his own father died, but at least a portion. Yet, to his confusion, he felt nothing at all. He had no hurt feelings. No sadness. No remorse. Not even a sense of loss. Gerry's death had absolutely no impact on his brain.

249

***

Sydney patiently waited in the sitting area next to the managers' administrative assistant. The office hallway was active with so many department managers hustling in to pick up packages or print copies of documents for their customers. Mark's office was only ten feet away from where Syd was sitting, but with the door tightly closed, Sydney had no idea what was going on in there. All he knew was that Mark called Jennifer and instructed her to send him to the office.

Sydney didn't mind being pulled from his workstation on a day like this. The store was extremely busy, and customers were getting more and more impatient as the day wore on. Jennifer wasn't happy about having one of her most experienced associates pulled from his duties. Although she protested, there was no other choice but to send Sydney back to the manager's office. It would be insubordinate of her to flat-out refuse, even though it would have been the right decision for the customers she served.

Once there, the administrative assistant asked Sydney to have a seat. She informed him that Mark wished to speak with him and would be with him shortly. Sydney was invited to make himself comfortable. If there was something that he needed, she would see what she could do for him.

Finally, after Sydney endured a full 20-minute wait, the door to the store manager's office swung open and Mark appeared in the doorway. Unimpressed, Sydney glanced at Mark who then flashed a broad grin in his direction.

"Hello, Sydney," Mark warmly bellowed as he extended his right hand. "Thank you for taking time out of your busy day to come and visit with me."

Mark accentuated his appreciation in an over-the-top tone of voice. He wanted to make sure that Syd knew how grateful he was to have him stop by for a chat.

"Come on in," Mark beckoned with a wave of his right arm. "Close the door behind you and have a seat," Mark instructed Sydney who was still a little confused about being beckoned to the office in this manner. "How about something to drink?" he offered. "I have soda, water, and all kinds of juice. All nice and cold in my mini fridge over here. Which one would you like?" Mark asked.

"Cold water would be great," Sydney replied. He had been on his register all day and was genuinely thirsty. "Thank you," he said as Mark handed him a cold, clear plastic bottle.

"There's a dish of wrapped chocolates over there," Mark pointed. "There, on the conference table. Help yourself," he offered. "And please, make

250

yourself comfortable. I just wanted to invite you here today to ask you a couple of questions. I'd like to get your feedback on a few things," he stated.

"My feedback?" Sydney asked. "Why would you want my feedback?" he wondered.

Mark ignored his question.

"You know, Syd," Mark began. "I've been hearing some great things about you. You're one of our most experienced and knowledgeable associates," he complimented. "There's a bright future for associates like you. How does that sound so far?" Mark teased.

"I guess it sounds good," Sydney confirmed. "What do you have in mind?" he suspiciously asked.

"Let me be more specific. And direct," Mark suddenly became more serious. "I think, based on what I've been told about you, that you have what it takes to be placed in our management-training program. How would you feel about doubling your salary?" Mark needled.

"You mean, instead of 12 dollars an hour, I would be making 24 dollars an hour?" Sydney asked, still skeptical.

"Well, not at first," Mark clarified. "After successfully completing the management-training program, however, that's exactly what I mean. If you are interested, and meet my requirements, the preprogram-qualification process can begin immediately," he declared.

Sydney thought for a moment and considered the proposal that Mark was making. He was certainly somewhat flattered by the attention he was suddenly getting. Jennifer and Gerry had always encouraged Sydney, and both expressed their appreciation for his contribution to the team.

Mark, however, until now, had barely spoken to him. Sydney was a little surprised that Mark even knew who he was. Never mind the fact that he seemed to be suggesting a proposition to him that could provide some much-needed additional income.

Spending his entire career in retail was not something Sydney envisioned for himself. Instead, he hoped he could, one day, be a system engineer or maybe a software developer. Making big bucks in Silicon Valley would satisfy his desires and long-term goals on many levels. Still, for the time being, doubling his pay sounded like something that he would have to be crazy to pass up.

"This all sounds great," Sydney confirmed. "What would you like me to do? How do I proceed?" he asked.

"Great! Super!" Mark exclaimed. "Let me explain," he excitedly began, rubbing his sweaty palms together. "It isn't necessarily 'what' I would like you to do as much as it is 'how' you need to go about doing it. You see. If you want to be a manager, you have to start acting like one," Mark lectured as he stood from his chair and leaned on the conference table a few feet away. "Here, Syd. Have a piece of chocolate, and I'll explain what I mean," he offered. "As managers, we set the rules for the hourly associates. More importantly, we enforce those rules. It is impossible to be too strict when dealing with people who work under us. The more we bend the rules, the less respect we get. Therefore, rules cannot be compromised under any circumstances. The challenge for you, Sydney, is to show me that you can separate yourself from the hourly employees. You must prove to me that you can create that impenetrable barrier between you and them. Between us and them. Do you understand what I mean?" he questioned.

"I think so," Sydney replied. "So far, I think you are asking me if I could supervise my peers," he paraphrased.

"Good," Mark confirmed. "Let's start with a real-life example. One that you might be familiar with. Prove to me that you can build that barrier and act in the best interest of the business," he requested.

"Okay," Sydney agreed.

"Are you familiar with this list of names?" Mark asked as he handed Sydney a piece of paper that he pulled from a folder on his desk.

The page appeared to have been previously wrinkled. As if it had been removed from the trash.

Sydney didn't have to stare long and hard at the sheet of paper before he realized what it was. This was the list that Clare was having some fun with a few weeks ago. The reason he did stare long and hard was to gather his thoughts. He had already murdered one of the people on the list, and a couple of other names staring back at him from the page were in the same queue. If Mark was on to this fact, surely there would be a police officer in the room. It must be something else, he reasoned. Whatever it was that Mark was getting at, however, Sydney sensed danger. He felt it would be best, at this time, to plead ignorance and see where the conversation led.

"I can't say that I am familiar with it," Sydney said as he handed the sheet back to Mark.

Mark held the sheet of paper to the side in his left hand and pointed toward it with his outstretched right. Reminiscent of one of the models on "The Price is Right."

"This is a list of names that one of your coworkers at customer care put together," Mark declared in a matter-of-fact tone.

"In one of the columns, your peer categorizes some of our beloved customers as, if you'll excuse my language, total fucking assholes," Mark shuddered. "The list was brought to my attention by another one of your coworkers a few weeks ago. The coworker who brought it to us has already given a full statement. She was highly offended and has filed a serious complaint with our human-resources department. The associate, in her statement, says that you were working that day. In fact, she says you were right next to the associate who compiled the list. Do you remember now?" he sneered.

Sydney could feel beads of sweat forming on his forehead as he contemplated his next move. He would have a hard time continuing to deny that he knew anything about this situation, but maybe he could minimize what he did claim to know. Either way, he didn't like how the conversation was going. Mark was playing Sydney for stupid, and he knew it.

There were several other associates around that day who knew what Clare was up to. Nobody acted offended by it. Sydney didn't hear anyone voice their displeasure. Who would rat her out, he wondered? Was there another associate who harbored hard feelings or perhaps jealousy toward Clare? Clare was attractive and extremely popular not only among the customer-care associates, but throughout the entire store. At least, that's what Sydney thought. It would have been easy for someone who, for some reason, wanted to harm her to pluck the paper from the trash and turn it in to Mark.

Regardless, Sydney couldn't rewind the clock. What was done, was done. If someone else did fill out a statement, Mark would need someone like Sydney to confirm the story. Corroborating statements would work better for Mark than single, random statements. There was no chance, however, under any circumstances, that Sydney would do anything that he thought would harm Clare. Other than his mother, there was no person on Earth who Sydney cared for as much as he cared for Clare. Sydney felt he had to play along a little longer. He had to stall for time so he and Clare could figure out a defense plan.

He stared at Mark and rubbed his chin with his right hand as if in deep thought.

"Maybe a little," Sydney said. "I remember Gerry holding a piece of paper and telling Clare that he was going to throw it away. It was some sort of list. I think. The store was busy, if I remember correctly, so I didn't get much of a chance to see what was going on," he bluffed.

"You know, Sydney," Mark lectured. "That's the reason Gerry had absolutely zero respect in this place. He just couldn't stay on the manager side of the barrier that I explained to you earlier. You have a great opportunity in front of you, Sydney. Prove to me that you can operate on the manager side. Separate yourself from the rank and file and show me what you've got," he inspired.

"How?" Sydney asked.

"I need you to fill out your own statement of what happened," Mark directed. "Tell us how your coworker referred to our lifeblood as 'fucking assholes.' Write about how deeply offended you are by not only what happened, but by what could potentially happen in the future if no further action is taken. You have the opportunity to rise above the rest and show me the kind of leadership you can provide for this organization!" he declared.

"Like I said," Sydney stammered. "I didn't really see anything like what you are describing. I didn't feel offended because I didn't know what was on the list or what each column meant," he revealed.

Mark pondered Sydney's position. He tried his best to empathize with the young man but had difficulty comprehending how anyone could try to protect someone else's wellbeing. Especially if doing so could inhibit advancing his own interests.

Instead of continuing to try to understand, Mark decided on a new tactic.

"You know, Sydney," Mark spoke softly in a fatherly tone. "When I was a young man in a similar situation as the one you are in right now, I had to make a decision. I asked myself a simple question. Am I comfortable being a low-level employee or do I want to better my life and be somebody? I decided I wanted to be somebody special. I understood what my manager was asking of me," he fabricated. "Even though I had absolutely no knowledge of the situation my manager was referring to, I knew exactly what he wanted me to do. I took a pen and paper and wrote the best statement ever written. I demanded strong action be taken to rectify the situation. I signed and dated the statement even though I had to make up everything that I wrote. As you can see, I am now where I am. Proud and true," Mark boasted. "How about it, Sydney? What's your destiny?" he asked.

Sydney's mind was spinning furiously. Mark was asking him to fabricate a statement that could be used to discipline Clare. But why, he wondered? What did she ever do to him?

There was no question that putting that goofy list together was not the best idea that Clare has ever had. It was funny though, he recalled. When Gerry saw it, he asked her to get rid of it. He didn't want to see Clare get into any trouble. Did Gerry turn Clare in, Sydney wondered? No way. Impossible, he concluded.

Sydney had heard stories about how Mark sometimes targets his employees seemingly out of nowhere and terminates them. Some say he does it to set examples and impose a fear factor on the remaining staff. Others theorize he targets certain employees in order to sabotage a department manager who might have crossed him. Without Clare, the customer-care desk will not run nearly as smoothly as it does now. Clare is one of the best employees the store has. Jennifer would be screwed at this time of year without her. One strategically placed termination could make Jennifer's job and life miserable.

As seasonally tired as Jennifer was, losing one of her best employees would toss a significant wrench in her works. Unavoidably, it would result in Jennifer being required to pick up additional shifts. Jennifer is required to do whatever it takes to keep the customer-service department operating properly. If she lost a key player, she would simply have to work longer hours. That's just the way it works.

Jennifer was always perceived by Mark as being much too dedicated toward Gerry. She wasn't 100-percent cooperative when Mark was calling in managers one at a time, attempting to build his case against Gerry. Mark had Gerry in his crosshairs and still felt the sting of not getting off the shot.

Unfortunately, for Jennifer, she picked the wrong horse when she decided to do what she felt was morally correct. The horse she chose died coming down the home stretch. The time had come for her to pay off her debts. Now that Gerry is permanently out of the picture, she has nobody to protect her. What better time than now for Mark to make it clear to her who the boss is? Collateral damage, in the person of Clare, is insignificant to Mark when considering the bigger picture. She is nothing more than a lowlife, hourly employee to him. Jennifer is Mark's new target, and he is a skilled marksman. He won't be cheated out of taking the shot this time.

"I need some time to think about this," Sydney finally revealed. "I really didn't see anything, and I'm not comfortable just making up a story. Can you give me a day or two to think about this?" he asked.

"It's now or never," Mark replied. His tone was as cold as the blowing wind outside. "How badly do you want to get ahead? That's the bigger question," he barked.

"I can't do this right now," Sydney declared.

"Get back to work, then," Mark ordered. "You have been in here way too long."

"What about the manager-training program?" Sydney questioned. "Can we talk about it again?" he wondered.

"I said go!" Mark ordered. "Don't approach me. If I'm interested in talking to you further, I'll call you," he directed.

Sydney stood and turned toward the door. Before he opened it, he heard Mark lift the handset on his phone and call Lynn. He instructed her to drop everything and report to his office right away. Mark's tone of voice was angry and demanding. Sydney, for a second, was certain that the anger was a result of the conversation that he had just engaged in. It seemed a little over the top to him, however.

It was difficult for Sydney to imagine that Mark was that enraged over his refusal to write up a false statement. He assumed that Mark was simply angry with Lynn about something else and was calling her in to clear the air.

When he opened the door and stepped into the hallway, his thinking changed. Seated next to the administrative assistant, sipping on a cold bottle of water, waiting to see Mark, was Clare. She had a puzzled look on her face when her eyes met Sydney's. It was a 'what's this all about?' expression. Clare didn't appear to be frightened or nervous. Just curious. Sydney, however, quickly processed what was happening and began moving in her direction to give her a fair warning about what she was walking into. He desperately needed to speak with Clare, but the look on his face was misinterpreted by her. There was crucial information that he had to relay to her before she went in to speak with Mark. Unfortunately, just as he took his first step toward her, a loud, boisterous, joyful voice boomed from directly behind him. It was intentionally loud enough for the entire office suite to hear.

"Clare!" Mark bellowed. "So nice of you to join me on this busy day," he laughed as he spoke. "And look who's right behind you! It's Lynn, coming to join us. Come on in you two."

He excitedly waived his arm, inviting them to follow him.

"I must be one lucky guy to have the pleasure of you two lovely ladies coming to visit with me on a day like this," Mark beamed. "Have a seat, Clare. Would you like something to drink? More water, or a soft drink?" he offered.

"Lynn, close the door behind you. Get Clare whatever she wants to drink," he ordered as he took his position behind his desk.

Sydney was horrified. He wasn't sure of what was going to happen in Mark's office, but he assumed the topic of Clare's silly list was going to come up.

Sydney started formulating best-case and worst-case scenarios in his mind. The best that could happen, he thought, is that Clare gets a slap on the wrist and told to refrain from making any similar lists in the future. The worst that happens is Clare gets fired, he dreaded. Sydney rationalized that even if she does get fired, they still have each other.

Maybe they won't get to work together any longer, but that could turn out to be a good thing, Sydney reasoned. Clare can get another job in a heartbeat. Maybe their work schedules can be arranged so that they can spend even more time together than they do now. Clare won't have to suffer any long-term consequences from this. Although it will be a shame, Sydney figured if Clare gets terminated, it would be Jimbo's loss. Not Clare's. His emotions calmed at the thoughts, and he methodically returned to his workstation at the customer-care desk.

Sydney approached Jennifer and informed her that he would like to take advantage of Steve's offer at the meeting this morning. He would like to offer his services by extending his work day. Sydney offered to work the remainder of the day until closing. Jennifer was thrilled to have him volunteer. The store was still swamped with customers. She needed all the help she could get. With Mark pulling Jennifer's help away from the selling floor in order to attend meetings, she was having difficulty keeping up with the busy customer flow. Sydney's offer was a relief to Jennifer. It was a gesture that she wouldn't forget. If there was a pecking order that Jennifer kept, Sydney, by bailing her out on the busiest day of the year, just moved several rungs toward the top.

***

Mark rested his folded sweaty hands on top of the manila-folder which was lying flat in front of him. He laughed hysterically at the jokes he delivered while making idle, ice-breaking small talk. Clare, sitting opposite from Mark, politely smiled in response to his animated performance. Lynn sat stone-faced slightly behind and off to Mark's right, in an armchair against the side wall of the office. She stoically stared at the yellow-lined notepad balanced on her lap. The end of her pen was tightly clenched between her teeth. Occasionally, during Mark's comedy show, she would jot something on the pad and then stare at his profile. The tooth marks on the ocean-blue cap to Lynn's pen were clearly visible to Clare from where she was positioned across the room.

Finally, mercifully, Mark decided to get to the crux of the matter.

"So, Karen," Mark changed gears. "I bet you're wondering why I really asked you to come on over to talk with me today. Aren't you?" he assumed.

"Karen?" Clare asked. "Don't you mean Clare? Or is it someone else you wanted to see?" she hoped.

"Did I say Karen?" Mark guffawed. "I meant Clare. Of course, I wanted to see your smiling face today. How funny is that?" He laughed. "Let's start over. Shall we?" he suggested unapologetically.

Lynn pulled the pen from her mouth and faintly shook her head from side to side while rolling her eyes. She flipped the page on her pad to a blank sheet and made a subtle note to herself. Next to a large bullet point at the top of the fresh page, she scribbled, 'mark as whole.'

It was a comforting reminder that she considered Mark to be an ass hole.

Mark instantly regained his composure after his gaffe and took a moment to gather his thoughts. Since he was always under the impression that anyone invited to share in his presence was in total awe of him, he felt no further need to feign humility.

"I'm sure you already know, Clare, that part of my job as store manager is to look into a variety of situations that sometimes arise," Mark lectured. "It's actually for the good of everyone when I investigate possible policy violations and correct behaviors that are not company approved. Am I making sense to you so far?" he asked.

"Yes," Clare replied. "I understand that you have to enforce the rules," she paraphrased.

"Exactly!" Mark exclaimed. "You know, Clare, you have the reputation of being extremely intelligent," he beamed while pointing his index finger in Clare's direction. "I can see why," Mark declared.

After gaining a sign of agreement from Lynn, he continued.

"If rules are strictly enforced, everyone benefits. Each employee can be assured of fair, consistent treatment. It's a major component of my job to make sure that everyone in this building is adhering to the letter of the law. Can I count on you to help me make sure that everyone is following the rules?" he wondered.

"You have my commitment," Clare pledged.

Nervously, Clare looked toward Lynn who was nodding approvingly as she jotted something on her notepad. Mark remained silent for a moment, allowing Lynn time to memorialize the verbiage. Finally, Clare broke the brief silence.

"Is that it?" Clare wondered. "Can I go now?" she asked impatiently.

"Not just yet," Mark smirked. "You see, something has come up that actually involves you," he stated.

Mark opened the folder that was laying on his desk and removed the formerly wrinkled piece of paper from within. He then reached across his desk and extended the paper toward Clare who, in turn, reached forward to grasp it.

"Do you recognize this?" Mark simply asked.

Clare stared at the list she had made. Her mind swirled as she recalled the day that she composed it. Internally, she smiled at some of the naughty and nice names and frowned at some of the others. Clare could have sworn the paper was tossed in the trash, though. How did Mark get it, she wondered to herself. More importantly, what was he planning to do with it? Mark's question seemed rhetorical to her. Obviously, it's her list. It's written in her handwriting. It would be difficult for her to credibly state that she doesn't recognize it. May as well just admit the truth and move along, she decided.

"Yes," Clare confirmed as Lynn furiously scribbled more notes in the background. "I made that list a few weeks ago. It was a busy day," she recalled.

Mark held the list at arms-length and, for show, he pretended to read the contents. He peered over the top of the page and stared directly into Clare's eyes.

"I think everyone can agree on what 'nice' means," Mark stated as he retrieved the sheet and studied it intently. "Naughty, could be open to interpretation. Would you confirm to me what you meant by 'T.F.A.'?" he asked.

Clare thought for a moment. Obviously, Mark had already done some research about the list. He probably knew the answer to the question he was asking. There was no sense lying about it, she reasoned. The day she put the list together, nobody seemed all that concerned about it. In fact, Gerry told her that it was best to just throw the thing in the waste basket so she wouldn't get into any trouble. Clare was having a hard time figuring out what the big deal was.

Mark probably was going to give her a lecture and a written warning, she thought. Clare figured she might as well hurry up and get this session over with. She didn't care to spend any more time with Mark than was necessary.

"It means total fucking asshole," Clare calmly stated.

From there, not only did Clare wish to change the subject, but she had a genuine, important question to ask. This simple question was disturbing to her in its nature, and the answer could have monumental repercussions.

"If you don't mind my asking, how did you get that thing?" Clare asked chillingly.

"I can't tell you exactly," he immediately replied.

Mark glared menacingly at Clare, making her suddenly uncomfortable.

"What I can tell you is that, sometimes, people who you may think are friends, are actually anything but," Mark advised. "Every single person with whom you worked on that day has been in here to talk to me about how offended they were by your callous actions. I have statements from your coworkers, in this folder, detailing how horrified they were by what you did. Do you feel it is okay referring to our precious customers as 'T.F.A.'?" he scolded. "What would you do if the roles were reversed?" he asked. "If you were the store manager, and a customer-care associate referred to our dedicated customers in such a derogatory manner, how would you handle it? Your fellow customer-care associates are filing complaints left and right. All are demanding an apology," he declared.

The thought of Sydney turning on her hit Clare like a ton of bricks. Nothing else Mark said got through to her. Her brain froze at his first sentence.

*Why would Sydney do this to her?* Clare silently wondered.

She was genuinely falling in love with Sydney. Now, Clare felt that she had been fooled into thinking that he was falling in love with her as well. This whole charade, however, that she was now deeply engrossed in, pointed directly at Sydney being the instigator.

The more she thought about it, the more upset she was getting. Her position at Jimbo's was secondary to her right now. Emotionally, she was overwhelmed with the realization that all indicators led to her to conclude that she had been betrayed by Sydney.

Clare fought back the tears that were beginning to well in her eyes. No wonder Sydney had that look on his face when he emerged from Mark's office and saw her sitting in the waiting area. He had the unmistakable look of a little boy who got caught with his hand in the cookie jar. Why else would Sydney be in Mark's office, she realized. Now, Mark was rehashing what Sydney had just complained about? Concerning her?

She became determined to not let Mark's words get to her.

"What's going to happen?" Clare asked directly.

"That's going to be up to you," Mark advised. "Depending on how cooperative you are, decisions will be made. What I hope you will do is apologize to your fellow associates who were so highly offended by your actions. In writing, I'd like you to state exactly what you did. State how you labeled our customers in such a derogatory manner. Apologize to them. State how you offended your coworkers by using foul language to classify our guests. Not only apologize to your peers, but state clearly that you will never do such a thing ever again. I think it's important that we all know how sorry you are for your actions. It is especially important to all of us that you will pledge to not repeat those actions going forward. Don't you agree?" he asked.

"Yes," Clare agreed.

Her mind was still consumed with the disappointment of how drastically Sydney turned on her.

"I'll do what you want," Clare surrendered.

"Great," Mark encouraged. "Lynn, get Clare a pad and a pen so she can write her apology. Clare, go ahead and write everything down. You'll be more comfortable sitting at the table in the corner. Take your time. It's important that you are thorough," he instructed as his voice trailed off.

Clare sat with Lynn at the conference table and began writing. The more she wrote, the angrier she became with Sydney. It wasn't so much the fact that she got in trouble at work. She was furious about having the feeling of betrayal. Every indicator led her to assume that Sydney, for some reason, turned her in.

Clare decided it would be best for her to write the apology letter that Mark was looking for and get back to work. She would straighten things out with

Sydney when she returned to the customer-care desk. Clare looked forward to the verbal beating she would lay on him. There were plenty of other fish in the ocean, she realized. Sydney, by turning on her, was playing with fire. And, this time, he was about to get burned.

The angrier she became, the faster she wrote. Finally, she aggressively capped the tip of the pen that she had been using, tore the completed sheet from the legal pad, and extended it toward the opposite side of the table.

"Here you go. Finished," Clare declared as she handed the lengthy statement to Lynn who quickly passed it on to Mark.

"This looks good," Mark complimented. "It states clearly what you did. How sorry you are for doing it. It acknowledges how you realize the enormous harm you caused to our customers and staff. I like it!" he exclaimed. "The only thing left for you to do is sign and date it for me," he casually reminded her.

Clare obliged by signing the bottom and dating the page. Lynn made the document official by signing it as a witness and confirming the date and time. Lynn then handed it back to Mark for a final review.

"This looks very thorough," Mark calmly stated. "I want to thank you for being so cooperative, Clare. You have been extremely helpful to me," he confirmed.

Mark carefully placed Clare's statement inside of the folder which held the other documents related to the case. He closed the folder and shoved it to the corner of his desk with the back of his right hand.

"Now, what I want to inform you of," Mark coldly began. "Is that based on your admitted decision to refer to our customers in such a vile manner, I'm dismissing you from your position here at Jimbo's. I would like to wish you all the best in your future endeavors. Lynn will help you to clean out your locker and walk you to the door," he explained.

Clare felt the blood drain from her face as she listened to Mark's words. The realization that he had been leading her along the entire time silently enraged her. Mark had every intention of firing her the moment Sydney walked out of his office and she walked in. Tears formed in her eyes, but she wiped them with the backs of her fingers and struggled to suppress the tears that tried to replace them.

Clare was as angry as a hornet that just had its nest carelessly whacked with a broomstick. She needed to calm herself, but right now, she simply didn't want to. She told herself to say something. Anything. Maybe it will help, she thought.

"I thought you said it was important to apologize so we could go forward," Clare snarled.

She was regaining her composure, but it didn't come back all at once.

"Can't we work something out?" Clare calmly asked.

"The decision is made, and it is a final one," Mark immediately replied. "Now, get out," he ordered.

Lynn escorted Clare to the employee break room where she could gather her personal belongings and empty her locker. The familiar, embarrassing exit escort was noticed by several other employees who happened to be nearby. Word spread quickly throughout the store. It was like a brush fire in a meadow after a six month-long drought. By the time Clare had turned in her security badge, which had already been deactivated, and left via the employee entrance, the entire store population had heard what happened.

Not everyone knew exactly why Clare had been fired. Mark and Lynn were clever in their response to any questions regarding her sudden departure. Covering legal liability issues was their major concern. Mark, however, was highly skilled at leaking coded tidbits to the general staff. When fear is a manager's major motivator, it is crucial to let the masses know what could happen to them if they too step out of line.

Word of the dismissal reached Sydney at about the same time as it did everyone else. Even though it was the worst-case scenario, as he had projected, his mind was at ease knowing that he and Clare still had each other.

Sydney waited for a while, and then he asked for permission to go on his meal break.

He had two major tasks to accomplish before he left to go home at the end of the night. First, he had to call Clare. She must be dying to hear from him, he reasoned. Surely, she would understand that he would only be able to call and talk to her once he was able to take his meal break. Reaching out to her would be his top priority. Secondly, he had to see if he could get his hands on that list that got Clare in trouble. Mark and Lynn had already left for the evening. Maybe he could snoop around to see if Mark left it on his desk. Sydney didn't want to chance having someone see the names on it and put two and two together. He had already killed one of the T.F.As. and didn't want to disqualify any of the others from having their opportunity to be pithed due to him being nervous about getting caught.

Finally, Sydney was able to break away from his workstation and make his phone call.

Clare's phone went straight to voicemail. Sydney thought it was odd but decided to give it a few minutes and try again. Maybe she was in the shower and had her phone turned off, he thought.

Meanwhile, on his way to have his meal in the break room, Sydney ducked into the manager suite and quickly closed the door behind him. The entire office area was dark and deserted. Several department managers were on duty, but they were all on the busy-selling floor, dealing with customers. The office area was eerily quiet. Sydney realized that he would have to act fast.

He had a plausible excuse ready to be delivered in case someone walked in on him. Sydney was in to see Mark this afternoon, he would say, and he lost the pen that his mother gave him for Christmas. He was hoping to find it in Mark's office.

However, when Sydney attempted to push the door handle down, he discovered that Mark's office door had been locked. Fortunately, the cheap lock was easily compromised by sliding the blade of his pocketknife in the door's gap and pulling it forward and down, releasing the latch.

Once inside, Sydney quickly moved to Mark's desk using only the indirect lighting coming through the window of the door for lighting. Mark had left the folder containing the paper directly in front of him. Sydney fished around with his right hand and felt what he hoped was what he was looking for. He grabbed onto the folder and slid his body over to where he could better use the light from the door to see what was inside. Luckily, he hit pay dirt. Without hesitation, he removed the single sheet of paper, placed the folder back on Mark's desk, and crawled back to the door.

Sydney calmly listened intently for a few moments and then quietly opened the door to Mark's office and left. With purpose, he quickly left the office-suite area and continued toward the break room. As soon as he got there, he again tried to reach Clare. Once more, her phone went directly to voice mail. This time, however, he left her a message to please call him as soon as she got this. He needed to speak with her, he messaged. Sydney was sure that the two of them had a lot to talk about.

When his break time was over, Sydney returned to his station at customer care and carried on as if nothing unusual had happened.

Another two hours passed since Sydney had left his message for Clare. He was busily working behind the customer-care desk but had his phone with him in his right pocket. He had it on vibrate so he wouldn't get in trouble if it went off. The truth of the matter was, however, that he would risk getting himself in hot water in order to speak with Clare. He was getting anxious about not hearing back from her and was wondering if something had gone wrong.

And then, finally, after what seemed like an agonizing eternity, Sydney's phone buzzed. It wasn't a ringing buzz, however. It was a short, text-message buzz. Sydney finished the transaction he was working on, wished his customer a great day, and turned his register light off. He informed the associate on the register next to him that he needed a quick break. She smiled and told him to take his time. She would happily cover for him.

Sydney walked into the backroom area, and, as he did, he removed his phone from his pocket. He could see that the text message was from Clare, and, at first, he was relieved to hear from her. Although he didn't know what had taken so long for her to get back to him, he was sure she had good reason for the delay. In any event, he was happy to see that she did reach out to him. He couldn't wait to see what she had to say.

All of that changed when he read the text message.

"I CAN'T BELIEVE YOU TURNED ON ME LIKE THAT. I'M SO EMBARRASSED AND HURT. WHAT A FOOL I WAS TO TRUST YOU. DO NOT ATTEMPT TO CONTACT ME ANYMORE! CLARE."

# 22

We'll play the next round as a twosome.

David was running a little late as he cruised his performance sports car along the smooth, tree-lined drive. There were no leaves on their limbs which left the mighty oaks and symmetric maple trees fully exposed. It was as if they had just stepped out of the tub after a refreshing morning shower.

Engraved granite stones, barely visible from behind the trees, blended with the color of the exposed bark as chameleons do in a rainforest.

A gray squirrel scurried three quarters of the way across the road in front of David's car. Suddenly, for no apparent reason, it stopped, froze, and stared directly at the approaching vehicle. Sensing impending doom, it decided to hurriedly retrace its steps back to the safety of where the crossing was first contemplated. David never saw the furry hair-brained daredevil, but he did feel a soft thud, which was immediately followed by another soft thud, reverberate through his super-sensitive steering wheel. Although it was unmistakable as to what had occurred, David never flinched. His focus was to steer his car to the end of the approaching cul-de-sac as quickly as possible and find the nearest parking spot. Time was of the essence on this cold, dreary, late December day.

The frigid temperature outside turned David's nose a bright shade of red as he approached the passenger-door handle of his hastily parked car. Before he lifted the handle to open the door, he pushed his sunglasses up toward the bridge of his nose. The base of the frames settled barely above the freezing skin of his upper cheeks. He sensed the upper frame with the wiry hairs on his brow.

With his right hand still on the open door, he reached his left hand into the warm vehicle. Gina grasped it with her right hand and used the assist to modestly step out of the car. David's mind was numb. Maybe it was due to that ill-advised fourth martini he had the night before. Or perhaps it was due to the sleepless night he spent watching episode after episode of *The Twilight Zone*. Whatever the reason, he needed a hug from his lovely wife.

"I don't want to be here, and I don't want to do this," David quietly whispered in her ear. "I love you, Honey," he said as he led her toward the brick building a short distance away.

David pulled on the heavy, oak-stained door and followed Gina into the chapel. An organ played softly in the background as if warming up for the inevitable ear-busting notes to come. The couple made their way to the seats just off to the right-hand side of Gerry's casket and greeted Mary. She had been stoically seated there, barely moving, for over an hour. The medication she took was working wonders to keep her from totally melting down. David and Rick embraced one another in a long, brotherly exchange of mutual support.

Friends and relatives filed in and expressed their condolences to the family before choosing their seats. Some knew the family. Others knew Gerry through work or pleasure but did not know the rest of his family. Steve and Jennifer introduced themselves as representatives of Jimbo's. Moments later, Lynn simply introduced herself to the boys as a coworker of Gerry. She hugged Mary and expressed her feelings of respect before taking a seat behind Steve and Jennifer. Clare silently sat by herself several rows behind Gerry's family. She stared straight ahead, oblivious to Sydney's presence a few rows back.

The priest read from scripture and offered his kind, comforting words before blessing the casket with holy water. He then sprinkled incense on a small piece of hot charcoal which slowly burned in a copper-colored vessel and muttered prayers as he circled Gerry's body. Along his journey, he wildly waved the ghostly smoke-spewing urn, symbolizing Gerry's ascent to the heavens.

The smell of the burning incense nauseated Sydney. It also sparked a slight feeling of deeply suppressed sadness that he had difficulty recognizing. In turn, he took a deep breath and ignored his suddenly uncomfortable sensation. Sydney knew it was right for him to pay his respects to Gerry by attending the service. Beyond that, his only desire was to leave the somber gathering as soon as possible.

Rick stood from his chair and moved next to the casket facing the gathering. He wanted to express his gratitude to those who took the time to come to pay their respects to Gerry. He offered comforting words of optimism that he knew Gerry would want expressed. Rick spoke fondly of the wonderful childhood he shared with his brother, David. How Gerry was a terrific family man. The best husband and father anyone could ever ask for. Rick expressed how much his family would miss having him around. He bemoaned the fact that David and he would have to play their round of golf as a twosome from now on. But that Gerry would want them to carry on without him.

Rick invited everyone to a lunch in Gerry's honor to be held at Kisluks' Diner immediately following the ceremony. He then reached into his coat pocket and unfolded a single sheet of paper.

"My father asked that I read this today," Rick stated as he cleared his throat. "I'll do my best," he said as he held the page over his face as if studying it.

Once he gathered himself, he began.

"My dear family and friends. I asked Rick to share this with you today being that he is my oldest son. Ideally, he and Dave would read it together, but I don't think that would work out very well. From the bottom of my heart, I want to thank you all for attending this morning. Thank you for supporting each other. It means a lot to me. Some of you might be feeling a little sad today. It's understandable, but I'd prefer it if you turn that frown upside down. You see, I've known for some time that I was fighting a difficult battle. I didn't need the doctors to tell me that the treatment wasn't working. The pain I endured over the past several weeks was excruciating. I just couldn't handle it any longer. I'm sorry if I let anyone down. Don't think that I lost the fight. I didn't lose. In the end, I grabbed it by the collar with two hands and pulled it over the cliff with me. Call it a draw. Cancer sucks. Sorry for my bad language, Father. I'll be sure to ask the big boss for forgiveness when I see him next. Anyway, cancer cuts too many lives way too short. My plan was to someday retire and spend time traveling and golfing with many of you here today. Instead, I'm flat on my back in a wooden box. If I only knew in advance. I hope you can find it in your heart to participate in cancer fundraisers. Run a benefit road race. Spend an hour at a cancer walk. Donate your recycle cans. Every little bit helps. There are a lot of geniuses out there who need money in order to find the answers to some complicated questions. I also hope you spend a few moments this morning reflecting. Life is not forever and is not to be treated as a dress rehearsal. Spend your time wisely. And for Heaven's sake, be respectful of one another. I hope you all get a chance to have a cold one on me at the Diner this morning. I literally paid the tab, so you'd better take advantage. It's the last drink I'll ever buy for you. Tell some funny stories at my expense. God only knows you all have something ridiculous to share about me. Cheer each other up. Leave today with a smile on your face and a fond memory in your heart. You'll only hurt my feelings if you don't tell a good story about me. You never know, I might be there, listening. We don't really know for sure what happens once we leave here. Do we? I believe I will see all of you one day on the other side. Take your time joining me, though. Until then, I leave you with my enduring love and affection. Gerry O'Driscoll."

David tugged on the handle to the massive, solid, oak doors and entered the foyer of the huge building. The oversized electric heater above him blew hot air on a downward angle, like a hurricane, but it felt good to him. He purposely wasn't wearing his hat or gloves. The short walk from the parking lot to the front door, however, was enough to chill him to the bone.

David uncharacteristically arrived 15 minutes early for his scheduled appointment. So, he decided to shop around a little. He recognized a few of the faces from Gerry's service, but no one seemed to recognize him. Less than a week had passed since the funeral. The numbness from his loss still lingered in David's head, but he was beginning to get back to a normal lifestyle. Fighting crime was a good way to distract him from his grief.

Spending time retracing his father's steps, in the environment that he spent so much of his time, wasn't helping matters, however. David felt his anger building at the thought of speaking with the store manager. He knew he had to suppress his feelings if he intended to gain any information from this character. Gerry never said too much about him, good or bad. Mary, however, made it clear to David and Rick that she loathed the way Gerry was treated by him.

"This should be interesting," David quietly said to himself.

***

Mark lifted the handset from his office desk-phone and dialed Lynn's extension. There was no answer. Panic-stricken, he depressed a button on the upper right side of the phone to make a general, storewide page.

"Lynn, please report to the office," Mark's voice boomed.

His voice reverberated throughout the massive enclave. Associates stared at one another with a puzzled look. Mark was strict about keeping pages to a minimum. He also didn't have the reputation of letting on to the associates that he was in the building. He neither wanted to give the impression that he was available to them, nor did he want them keeping track of his coming and going. His bellowing, like an elk looking for a mate, amused the staff. If nothing else, it provided some comic relief on an otherwise dull day.

Lynn returned to the office area from her brief bathroom break and made a beeline into Mark's office. He stared at her from behind his desk with a look of total relief.

"Where did you go?" Mark demanded.

"I had to use the bathroom," Lynn casually replied. "Why? What's up?" she asked.

"I got a call from some local detective," Mark nervously replied. "He says he'll be right over to talk to me about a case he is working on. I don't know why he wants to talk to me! I didn't do anything," he pleaded.

"Did he say what he wanted to talk to you about?" Lynn probed.

She kept a serious look on the outside, but inside, she was totally amused by Mark's paranoia.

"He didn't," Mark answered. "I need you to be here with me," he ordered. "If I start saying something that I shouldn't say, make sure you interrupt me. Just sit tight right next to me. He'll be here at any minute."

Mark had no sooner finished giving his instructions to Lynn when he heard a loud knock on the outer door leading into the manager suite. Mark's administrative assistant started to make her way over to the door when it cracked open, and a head popped into view.

"Is this the manager's office?" David asked the woman who was approaching him. "I'm looking for a person named Mark. I was told he is the store manager."

"Yes," she replied. "This is the managers' office. Is Mark expecting you?"

"Great," David declared as he fully entered the hallway. "He is expecting me. My name is Detective O'Driscoll. Would you tell him I'm here?" he politely requested.

Mark, who had been listening to the conversation, instructed Lynn to go out and meet with the detective and escort him into the office. Lynn had only met David once and that was at Gerry's funeral. David looked completely different to her on this day. He understandably seemed to be more relaxed. Still, she recognized him immediately. Not wishing to rehash a bad memory, Lynn simply reintroduced herself as the human-resources manager. David, in turn, vividly remembered Lynn from the service. He pretended not to, however, and warmly took her offered hand. He casually stated it was nice to meet her as well.

As Lynn escorted David toward Mark's office, she wanted to make sure it would be okay if she was present for the meeting. David assured Lynn that it would be perfectly acceptable for her to be present. In fact, he made mention that he thought he might have some questions for her as well. On top of that, David had a sense that Lynn possessed a decency that was going to be sorely lacking in the rattlesnake den that he was about to step into.

"Mark, this is Detective O'Driscoll," Lynn announced as she introduced David. "He has a few questions that he would like to ask us," she stated.

"Welcome, sir," Mark said as he extended his right hand. "Did you say Detective O'Driscoll? We used to have someone by that last name who worked here," he declared.

David politely shook hands. He was immediately unimpressed.

"Do you know a Gerry O'Driscoll?" Mark asked as he took a seat behind his desk and nervously folded his hands across his chest.

"Never heard of him," David deadpanned. "It's a common last name. Maybe we are related somehow," he suggested. "Is he married? Does he have any kids?" David began questioning.

"I think he was married," Mark replied. "I'm not sure if he ever had any kids, though. It never came up in conversation," he stated.

David subtly raised an eyebrow.

"How long did you work together?" David calmly continued.

Lynn sat in the same seat on the side wall that she usually occupied during Mark's daily associate interrogations. She was both horrified and impressed by David's seemingly innocuous ice-breaking questions. There was no doubt in her mind why David was asking them. There was also no doubt that Mark would unwittingly expose himself to David as being the total fool that he was.

She thought for a moment about interrupting the conversation in order to change the subject per Mark's earlier instructions. Instead, Lynn allowed David to continue. Mark was already beginning to expose his true colors to David. There was no helping him now even if she wanted to. The fact that Lynn didn't care to help him was moot.

"We were together for a little over three years," Mark bragged. "We worked day and night, side by side. I spent more time with him than I did with my own family," he embellished.

Beads of sweat were conspicuously forming on Mark's upper lip.

"And you don't know if he has a family?" David laughed approvingly.

David couldn't resist. His next questions were for his amusement only.

"How come he doesn't work here anymore?" he wondered.

"Sadly, he recently passed away," Mark informed him dejectedly. "We all miss him dearly around here. Don't we, Lynn?" he asked, nodding his head approvingly.

Lynn slowly nodded in agreement as she stared at Mark with daggers in her eyes.

"Did you go to the funeral?" David instigated, having noticed Lynn's disdain. "I bet you had a lot of good stories to tell at the after party. Especially since you guys spent so much time together," he assumed.

"Unfortunately, I couldn't make it," Mark said. "I put in so many hours around here that I wasn't able to break free. Anyway, what can I help you with today?" he asked.

David caught Lynn's eye. She quickly looked elsewhere.

"I'm working on a Christmas Eve murder case," David began. "The victim had been given Mr. O'Driscoll's business card. On the back of the card was written 'Steve – Partner.' From what you are telling me, I guess I won't be able to talk to Mr. O'Driscoll. Before I talk to Steve, though, I'd like to ask you a couple of questions about him," he stated.

"Sure," Mark answered, relieved that he wasn't the subject of the inquiry. "What can I tell you?" he wondered.

"Can you tell me about Steve's background?" David asked. "I'm curious to know what his home life is like," he stated.

Mark stuttered and stammered over the question. He had absolutely no idea about Steve's life outside of Jimbo's. He never cared enough to ask him.

"Steve has an extensive retail background," Lynn interrupted. "He is the consummate professional. He's always willing to help those in need. Steve has the reputation of being a wonderful family man. He'll do anything for his wife and kids. Just a great guy is the best way that I can describe him!" Lynn informed him.

Mark neither confirmed nor denied Lynn's opinion of Steve. He meekly sat in silence, waiting for the next question that he hoped would not be as difficult for him to answer.

"Were either of you working on Christmas Eve?" David asked. "More importantly, was Steve working?" he wanted to know.

"Lynn and I worked until around noon," Mark replied. "Steve was the closing senior manager. The store closed that night at five o'clock. I'm going to guess he was out of here by 5:30," he stated.

"Do you know if he went straight home?" David asked.

"Funny you should ask," Mark replied. "One of my little spies was telling me Steve was supposed to be at some Christmas party and got there late. I guess his wife, or someone, was pissed at him for not being there on time. He probably left here and went out to get a beer or two. It's understandable after working a full day on Christmas Eve. We deal with all kinds on that day. I bet he just had a bad day and decided to blow off some steam before going home," he reasoned.

"Is Steve here today?" David asked. "I'd like to talk to him."

"No. Unfortunately, he requested the day off," Mark replied. "Would you like me to call him at home?" he volunteered.

"No thanks," David replied as he stood from his chair. "Is it common for a manager to write another manager's name on the back of his business card? Do you think Steve ever met the customer?" he asked.

"Mr. O'Driscoll probably put Steve's name on the back as a contact in case he wasn't here to take the customer's call," Mark replied. "Steve is probably aware of the situation or Gerry never would have referenced him. I don't know why Gerry gave this customer his card. I'm sure Steve can clarify for you whatever he was told. Are you sure you don't want me to call him?" he offered.

"No," David confirmed. "I would like to see his office area though. Is it possible for one of you to show me where his desk is?" he requested.

"Lynn will be happy to," Mark instantly replied as he stood and extended his hand.

Lynn, who hadn't volunteered to do so, faked a smile in Mark's direction and stood.

"Nice meeting you, Detective. If I can be of any further help, just let me know," Mark said.

"You'll be the first person I call," David assured as he quickly shook Mark's hand and turned to leave.

Lynn escorted David down the hallway to Steve's desk area. Adjacent to Steve was the empty office space previously occupied by Gerry. David couldn't help but notice the performance awards that his father left mounted on the wall. He smiled at the thought of Gerry leaving them there for someone else to dispose. He knew that his father was proud of his career accomplishments. In the bigger scheme of things, however, David realized that the awards meant little to him at the end.

David noticed a work photo still propped on Gerry's desk facing the empty chair. It was a snapshot of Gerry along with a random group of associates, none of whom David recognized, dutifully pointing their index finger toward the sky. Apparently, the group had attained number-one status in something important. The blank picture frames that were abandoned in the center of the desk confirmed to him that his father took other photos of pleasant memories home with him on his last day.

"Do you mind if I sit in Steve's chair for a minute?" David asked Lynn. "I just want to get a feel of the environment where my father spent so much time," he revealed.

"Please do," Lynn assured him. "Do you mind if I pull up a chair and join you?" she asked as she wheeled an adjacent chair from across the aisle. "You know, David. We really miss your father around here. He was going through so much toward the end. Gerry was an inspiration to many of us who worked with him. You are lucky to have had him as your father," she stated.

"That's nice of you to say," David replied. "My father spoke fondly of you. He said you two had some interesting conversations. My father admitted that you got the best of him on many occasions. That's not easy to do," David laughed.

"I'm surprised he admitted it," Lynn smirked. "We did test each other's convictions now and again," she fondly recalled. "You know, David, it was interesting to me, watching you play with Mark just now," she said. "What was that all about?" she probed.

David continued to poke around his father's desk, seemingly disinterested in Lynn's query.

"You're not all that fond of him. Are you?" David asked as he leaned back in Steve's chair.

"What makes you say that?" Lynn nervously replied.

"I noticed the way that you were looking at him back there in the office." David grinned. "It's part of my job. I think I got my 'powers of observation' from my father. I swear he could read people's mind," he marveled.

"My take on your relationship with Mark is that he likes having you around. It comforts him to have a smart, attractive personal assistant in the room with him when he needs support. He requires your presence in order to distract attention from his misgivings. He looks at it differently, though. The way I read things, Mark doesn't believe he has any misgivings. To him, you are his trophy or a status-symbol. Someone that he can prop up to show off in front of others," he observed.

Lynn stared in amazement at David as if he were rearranging tea leaves on the desk in front of her and relaying their meaning. She knew that what he was describing was accurate but didn't like hearing it out loud. For an instant, she considered asking him to stop, but then she thought better of it and remained silent. David correctly interpreted her look of curiosity and confirmation and continued to describe the uncomfortable.

"You, on the other hand, see right through it all," David revealed. "Although you can't stand him, you tolerate the situation for some reason. You are okay with being his trophy. Maybe you get some special privilege that others don't get. You put up with him for some overriding reason, but you don't feel good about it. One day, you'll arrive at your breaking point. My read is that you are approaching that time as we speak. When that day comes, he will regret having used you the way he did," he anticipated.

Lynn could not hide her feelings. David was spot on and she didn't like the fact that she was accurately perceived by him.

"How am I doing so far? Would you say that I am over the target yet?" David asked.

His smugness was both annoying and charming to Lynn.

"The apple doesn't fall far from the tree. Does it?" Lynn shot back. "Are you sure Gerry isn't whispering in your ear right now?" she wondered.

Lynn wanted to be angry with David for being so presumptuous, however, the accuracy of his account was troublesome to her. Was it that obvious, she silently wondered? Or, is David simply that good at reading people?

Additionally, she was having a difficult time being angry with someone who just described her as smart and attractive. Lynn found David's words to be extremely flattering. In fact, she wickedly allowed her mind to drift for a moment while she basked in the compliment that had just been paid to her.

As much as Lynn suddenly wanted to continue with the conversation, she felt it best for all involved if she ended it. At least for now.

"Anyway, it was nice seeing you again," Lynn admitted. "Stop by for coffee any time you are in the neighborhood," she politely invited.

Lynn stood and wheeled her chair back to where she had retrieved it from. She then pivoted around and re-approached David.

"I really should get back to work, if you don't mind," Lynn admitted. "Come on. I'll show you to the door," she offered as she turned away and slowly began to lead the way.

David stood, and, as he did, he subtly reached with a tissue in hand and scooped up a half-eaten cough drop which had been left in a glass tray on Steve's desk. He stuffed it in his left pocket and circled around to the front of the desk to join Lynn.

On their way to the door that separated the office area from the selling floor, Lynn and David passed Mark's open door. Out of his periphery, David observed Mark's enthusiastic wave from his desk chair. David didn't bother to acknowledge him. In fact, he pretended to not notice the gesture as he continued walking. His eyes stared straight ahead until he reached the door at the far end of the hallway.

"Thank you for your hospitality today," David said as he held out his hand to Lynn. "And thank you again for the nice words about my father. The wound is still deep. Your words were comforting to me. If I feel the need to speak with Steve about that business card, I'll be sure to stop in to say hello," he promised.

"I look forward to it." Lynn smiled as she opened the door to the sales floor. "You have a great day. Don't be a stranger," she said as she closed the door behind him.

Lynn was still glowing as she heard Mark call out to her. She pretended to not hear his beckoning. Instead, she continued walking to her office and closed the door behind her as she entered. Lynn needed a little peace and quiet right now. More than that, as she sat at her desk and lifted the handset to her phone, she needed total privacy.

Before leaving Jimbo's, David took a final stroll around the lower level of the selling floor. He passed by the customer-care area, and Jennifer noticed him right away. She felt David had a striking resemblance to Gerry and was quick to point it out when she approached him.

The two spoke off to the side of the customer-care counter for an extended period. Jennifer, who had been close to Gerry, imagined she was talking to her former boss when he was still in his youth. The similarities to her were haunting. Even the sound and tone of voice were reminiscent of Gerry.

As the two spoke, they had a perfect view of what was transpiring behind customer care. Sydney was busily working. He waited on customer after customer in almost a frantic pace. The look on his face, however, was stern. Not only did he not look happy, but the scowl on his face gave the impression that he was extremely unhappy. Even angry.

"That guy was at my father's funeral," David interrupted Jennifer mid-sentence. "He also helped me when I came in here to pick up Dad's briefcase a while back. He seemed to me to be a great guy. What's his name again?" he asked.

"Sydney?" Jennifer replied. "Yes, he was there at the funeral. He didn't come to the lunch afterward, though. Your father was a strong influence on him. Almost like a mentor. You see, Sydney's father died when he was a young boy. Although his mother is a wonderful person, the death of his father left him with a huge void. Gerry had many fatherly conversations with Sydney. He confided in Gerry on many personal issues. Whenever Sydney needed advice of any kind, personal or professional, he would ask to speak with your father. Syd misses your dad in the worst way," she described.

"Is that why he looks so pissed?" David asked. "Or is he always like that?"

"I'm sure it's a part of it," Jennifer stated. "That, plus his girlfriend recently dumped him. She used to work here at customer care right beside him. For a reason that I can't get into, she left us and him at the same time. He's still struggling with the whole thing. Too bad Gerry wasn't here right now to help him get through a tough time. I guarantee you that your father would help him to get his head straight over the whole thing," she confirmed.

"I believe I saw his ex-girlfriend at the funeral," David confided. "Beautiful young lady. She was there alone if I remember correctly. Was that her?" he wondered.

"Yeah," Jennifer confirmed. "That was her. She won't even talk to Sydney anymore, and it's killing him. He had better get over it, though. Life goes on," she admitted.

"I actually had the pleasure of speaking with her after the prayer service," David casually mentioned. "Clare was her name, if I remember correctly. She approached me. After offering her condolences, she spoke with me at length. We talked about lots of other things as well. She is one very bright, observant, young lady. Mature beyond her years. In fact, if she wanted to, she could make an excellent detective one day." He smirked.

"I agree." Jennifer laughed. "I think Clare can do whatever she puts her mind to. Plus, whatever she does decide to do with herself, I know that she will do it extremely well. I can see why Sydney over there was hurt when she abandoned him," Jennifer reasoned.

"Sometimes, when you get involved with a heartbreaker, you get your heart broken," David chuckled. "He'll be okay. Just give him a little time," he encouraged.

And then.

"What's the matter with the young lady working next to him?" he asked, nodding toward the customer-care desk. "She's kind of cute. Maybe Sydney should get back up on the horse and ask her on a date," he suggested.

"That's Samantha," Jennifer replied. "We call her Sami. It's funny you say that. She has been hitting on Sydney since the day Clare left here. I've had to call her into the office to tell her to stop flirting with him." She laughed. "For whatever reason, though, Sydney isn't interested in her. Maybe he'll change his mind someday in the future. Now, however, he's still struggling to get his mind off Clare," she said.

"I'll wave to him as I leave," David mentioned as he checked his watch. "I don't want to interrupt his work. Please let him know that the family appreciated his presence at the funeral. It was nice of him to come and pay his respects," he said.

"Will do," Jennifer replied. "It was great seeing you, David. Give my best to your family," Jennifer said as she hugged him. "Stop by again," she invited.

David waived to Sydney and gave him a thumbs-up signal as he passed the customer-care counter on his way to the front door. Sydney was in the middle of a customer transaction but managed to return the wave. His expression stayed the same and he quickly returned to the task at hand.

As soon as David stepped into the parking lot, he took his phone from his pocket and reached out to his brother.

"Rick, I just left Dad's store," he began. "I know this might sound a little crazy, but I think we have to look into what Steve was up to. Apparently, he worked here on Christmas Eve but didn't go home after work," he advised.

"Where did he go?" Rick asked. "How did you find out that he didn't go home?" he wondered.

"I spoke with the store manager and the human-resources manager," David said. "The store manager strikes me as being a real loser, so I don't even know how reliable he is as a source. However, according to what he told me, Steve left work at around 5:30 on Christmas Eve and was supposed to go to a Christmas party at his home. According to him, Steve got to the party late and there was no legitimate excuse for it. Nobody is sure of where he spent the time between when he left work and arrived home. Wherever he was, it was around the same time that the murder occurred. As far as Steve having contact with the victim, I didn't find out for sure if he ever had any contact with him. Maybe if you run some phone records, we can get answers?" he hoped.

"I'm way ahead of you on that one," Rick replied. "The victim did call the store a couple of days before Christmas. Dad wasn't there, obviously. Maybe the guy asked for Steve. Do you think it's possible that the victim pissed Steve off enough on a phone call for him to whack the guy before going home?" he asked.

"I know," David reasoned. "It does sound a little farfetched. According to Lynn, the human-resources manager, Steve is a levelheaded family man. She says he's the type of guy that's always there for others. You never know, though. People snap for weird reasons. Especially during the holiday season. I grabbed a half-eaten cough drop from Steve's desk. Maybe we can match some D.N.A. with what was taken from some of the victims. It's worth a shot," he reasoned.

"Was that the Lynn who came to the funeral?" Rick asked. "Is she okay to talk to about this?"

"Yeah. That's her," David replied. "She is the one to talk to in Jimbo's. I don't trust the store manager even a little bit. He oozes sleaze. She, on the other hand, strikes me as being as bright as she is attractive. I won't mind if I have to visit with her again," he admitted.

"Careful, Dave," Rick cautioned. "Remember, you have a wife already."

"Yeah, don't worry," David said. "Just because I'm on a diet doesn't mean I can't read the menu, though. Anyway, I'll get the lozenge to the lab and see if we get lucky on the D.N.A. You never know unless you try," he stated.

"I hear you, Bro," Rick confirmed. "It's worth taking a look at, but I get the feeling we are barking up the wrong tree," he sensed.

"Maybe," David replied. "For some reason, though, I'm getting the feeling that we are in the right neighborhood. I can't put my finger on why I'm getting this feeling. I just am," he revealed.

David paused for a moment as he unlocked his car door and sat inside. He pressed on the ignition and then returned to his thought.

"Hey, Rick, have you ever read about when our ancestors first started walking upright? Thousands of years ago?" David asked, seemingly out of the blue. "The hairs on the back of their neck would stand up when they sensed danger. The sensation saved a lot of hunters and gatherers back then from being eaten by oversized cats. Anyway, the longer I stayed in that store, the more the hairs on the back on my neck stood up," he admitted. "I can't get the feeling out of my head."

# 23

A simple job for simple people.

Steve arrived for work much earlier than normal on this otherwise typical Friday morning in late January. The busy holiday season was mercifully in the past. Inventory, having been completed over a week ago, was now nothing more than an unpleasant memory. Jennifer had been given the task of heading up the inventory process since Gerry's position had not yet been filled. Mark delegated the monstrous task to her in hopes that any problems encountered could be blamed on her incompetence, possibly leading to her ultimate demise. Unfortunately, for him, Jennifer had been well-trained. She executed the counting process flawlessly, leading to a formal commendation from Moses Horwitz, the corporate director of asset protection.

Contained in the widely circulated electronic memorandum sent to Jennifer, Moses expressed his interest in being able to show his appreciation for a job well done in person. He indicated to Jennifer that his hopes were to visit the store in the coming weeks. Preferably sooner than later if his schedule allowed.

This revelation put Mark on edge, to say the least. To him, the best visits by anyone in the asset-protection arm of the business were those which never occurred. The same principle applies to tax delinquents who do not feel comfortable having I.R.S. agents attend their children's birthday parties.

Typically, once inventory has been conducted, salaried employees get a chance to catch their breath. Sales slow to a crawl in January. People are paying down over extended credit-card debt from the holiday season. In the northern part of the country, it is too cold and miserable outside to venture out on a shopping excursion. Although the lack of sales contributes to a whole new set of problems, managers can at least get back to a five-day work week.

Usually retail stores engage in a spring clean-up program. Cleaning, consolidating space, and filling in the empty shelves with new product consumes much of the associates' time. Many of the employees who are, at last, being scheduled minimal hours are relieved to have survived the end of year layoffs. Long-term employees invariably complain incessantly that, due to the afore-mentioned layoffs, they are required to complete additional tasks without being afforded additional pay.

The fact that a major reduction in sales results in a major reduction in scheduled man hours never seems to resonate among the troops. The situation can cause friction between management and hourly personnel. Good managers who understand the perspective of the hourly staff are easily able to overcome the friction through communication and direction. Poor managers allow the negative feelings to fester and often come to a boiling point. In a situation where the general manager is a poor leader, it is not uncommon to have one department happy and productive and another unproductive and miserable. Such was the case at the Jimbo's where Steve and Jennifer were employed as managers and Mark was their designated leader.

Late in the day on Wednesday, two days prior, Steve received a call from Moses. He requested a private meeting with Steve early in the morning on Friday. The meeting would take a minimum of two hours, he was told. Plan to be prepared to begin promptly at five o'clock. The nature of the meeting and, for that matter, the fact that there was to be a meeting in the first place, was to be held confidential. Nobody was to know about Moses being in town unless he, Moses, approved it. Steve, although he had never met Moses in person, was aware of his reputation. Moses could and would be ruthless when crossed. Steve assured Moses that no information would be leaked by him to anyone. He knew better.

Moses Harry Horwitz, director of asset protection, had been a close friend of the Johnson family for years. Like many who were hunting buddies of one of the founders of the company, Moses was able to land a highly paid, extremely powerful position within the organization. As director of asset protection, he was, as the title indicated, responsible for protecting the company's assets. In a nutshell, Moses protected those assets from being lost or stolen.

Internal, or employee theft at Jimbo's, accounted for the largest chunk of the company's losses due to stealing. The same is true for most retailers. It is why retail companies enact so many employee-related policies and procedures. Each time a new stealing technique is uncovered, the targeted company will invariably enact a policy to combat it.

External or shoplifter theft, is also a large contributor, but not the major focus of the asset-protection personnel who work in the store environment. Apprehending shoplifters can be an expensive and dangerous proposition. Laws in many states protect shoplifter rights over the rights of the retailer. To offset losses due to shoplifting, most retailers simply raise prices on goods and services that their honest customers are forced to pay.

Paper shortage, or procedural errors are also prevalent in the organization. They too must be monitored and controlled through operational audits. Losses due to carelessness in following proper procedure are just as costly as are losses that occur through shoplifting. All losses of assets directly hit the company's bottom line, and it was Moses's job to minimize them.

Moses also had full responsibility in controlling the firearms business at Jimbo's. Any time a firearm was brought into inventory or taken out of inventory due to a sale or other legal transaction, a significant number of forms had to be meticulously filled out. Accuracy in controlling the firearm inventory was something that Moses took very seriously. He expected perfection.

*** 

Steve entered the small conference room in the manager's office suite and sat in a chair at the far end of the table, facing the door. A few moments later, he heard the outer door leading to the sales floor open. He listened to the voices suddenly coming from the direction of the office hallway and found himself to be slightly confused. Steve could swear that there were two separate voices, as they both spoke at once, but the sound was eerily similar. It was almost as if someone was standing in the corridor talking to himself.

When Steve rose from his chair and walked to the conference-room door in order to greet his guests, he understood why. Steve, having been noticed, was immediately approached by a gentleman who appeared to be in his mid-60s. He was a thin, almost gaunt, gentleman of medium height. His hair was gray, and his complexion matched his hair color. Although he looked like he should be wearing a size 38 regular blazer, it appeared that the one he was wearing was a size 42 long. He wore a collar stained, white, cotton, button-down dress shirt that required both a tie and ironing. Neither were applied. As the gentleman got close enough for Steve to shake his outstretched hand, the smell of cigarette smoke overwhelmed him. It wasn't the smell of someone who had moments ago smoked a cigarette and the lingering smell followed him inside. This gentleman smelled like an ashtray.

This early in the morning, it was all Steve could do to keep his composure. "Are you Steve?" the gentleman asked.

"I am," Steve managed through a short breath. "And you are?"

"Moses Horwitz," came the reply. "So great to finally meet you in person," he conveyed. "This is my brother, Jerome. Corporate director of human resources," Moses said while gesturing to toward the man standing behind him.

Jerome, like his brother, was a longtime friend of the company founders. He had been the director of human resources for decades. When Jerome joined the company, he had no related experience. Through the years, however, Jerome grew into the responsibility of looking after what the company considered to be its most valuable assets. These assets were otherwise known as employees.

Jerome was also of medium height but boasted a much larger upper body than his brother. He appeared to be in his early 50s, but it was difficult to gauge his age through the fake spray on tan that he wore on his face. Jerome's hair was cropped, making it difficult to determine what color it was. It appeared to be light brown if allowed to grow out. The blazer he wore was a 48 regular, and he filled every bit of it. The fact that he wore it open and unbuttoned was not because he was making a fashion statement. Jerome wouldn't be able to button that blazer if preserving his life depended on him doing so. The right sleeve of the garment rode up on his thick forearm as he reached his hand forward in order to greet Steve.

"Hello, Steve," Jerome said as he vigorously shook Steve's hand. "Thank you for coming in this early to meet with us," he cheerily stated.

"My pleasure," Steve politely replied.

Steve glanced back and forth at the brothers, moving his head from side to side. Jerome was speaking, but if Steve closed his eyes, he would never be able to tell which one of them was doing the talking. Although the brothers didn't look alike, their voices echoed one another. The similarity gave him an eerie feeling.

"What can I help you gentlemen with this morning?" Steve nervously asked.

Steve was experienced enough to assume that when the corporate director of asset protection, along with the corporate director of human resources request your presence in an early morning meeting, it must be bad. Steve, initially, was not overly concerned about meeting with Moses. Now that his brother was in the mix, however, his mind began wildly speculating. Although Steve knew he hadn't done anything illegal or unethical, it didn't mean someone hadn't accused him of something that he would now have to refute. He suddenly feared that this was going to turn out to be an extremely unpleasant day.

"Come in and sit down," Moses calmly instructed.

Steve was careful to look at who was speaking so he could correctly follow given instructions. Moses was calling him into the conference room to begin the meeting.

"The reason my brother and I want to speak with you is due to a concern that we have about accurate completion and storage of firearms paperwork," Moses began. "It has been brought to our attention that you may have been instructed to break the law by someone. We want your help in getting to the bottom of the revelation. Are you willing to answer some questions for us?" he asked directly.

Steve froze. The last time anyone asked him to do something wrong with gun paperwork was the time Mark asked him to fudge an improper answer to one of the questions on the federal form. Steve, however, didn't report the incident to anyone other than Gerry. And that was in a casual conversation, several weeks ago. Steve assumed that Lynn was in the room with Mark when the improper directive was given, but she never mentioned anything about it to him. Lynn never asked him if he was uncomfortable about what Mark was asking of him. In fact, Steve was pretty sure that even if Lynn was in the room, she wouldn't understand what Mark was asking him to do. Maybe there was something else that happened, he thought.

"Sure, guys," Steve replied. "I'll answer anything I can for you. Off the top of my head, I can't think of anything like that happening but, I will cooperate to the best of my ability," he assured them.

"Great," Jerome replied. "Let me just close the door so we can have some privacy and we can get started," he said as he gently sealed the room from any outsiders and turned to take his seat opposite Steve.

*\*\*\**

Louis Feinberg scrambled his way through the employee entrance and quickly made his way to the office area. Even as the regional manager, he jumped when he got the early morning phone call from Jerome asking him to get to the store right away. Louis had a four-hour drive from his office store to the location of the surprise meeting where the brothers were beckoning him. He made it there in three-and-a-half hours.

During his drive, Louis frantically tried calling Mark who neither answered his phone, nor returned the missed calls. Louis didn't know the purpose of the visit, but he did know that having the Horwitz brothers in one of his stores, unannounced, was not a good thing. He was further aggravated by not getting a prior heads-up that the brothers were planning a special visit. Surely, the trip wasn't arranged at the spur of the moment. It was preplanned. For some reason still unknown to him, the details had secretively been kept from him.

Louis realized that he would have to quickly get over his hurt feelings and become more welcoming, however. It was imperative that he show how much he supported the entire organization by fully cooperating with the corporate visitors. The Horwitz brothers are not to be messed with. Even by someone on Louis's level in the hierarchy.

Louis entered the manager suite and noticed Mark's office door was open and the lights were on.

*This is a good sign,* Louis thought to himself. *Mark is probably in his office, entertaining the brothers. Making them feel welcome,* he pictured.

He breathed a sigh of relief, thinking that the reason Mark didn't answer his calls was due to him being tied up with the two visitors. Louis peeked his head into the open office and saw Moses sitting in Mark's chair, behind his desk. Jerome was seated at the small conference table in the back corner, poring over papers and documents.

Not only was Mark not in his office, but there appeared to be no sign of him.

"Hello, gentlemen," Louis shouted as he knocked on the open door. "To what do I owe this pleasure?" He forced a phony, nervous laugh and offered his outstretched hand.

"Hi, Louis," Moses casually looked up and replied.

Jerome offered his own halfhearted wave from the back of the office.

"Nice to see you again," Jerome deadpanned. "I've been meaning to call you to meet us here today, but I forgot. It was probably just as easy for us to call you when we got here. Don't you think?" he asked, looking for agreement.

Louis did not agree. He hated surprises like this. They never ended well.

"You are always welcome, at any time," Louis replied confidently.

And then, uncomfortably.

"If you don't mind my asking, what's on the agenda today?" he asked.

"We have some questions for your store manager," Jerome stated. "Where is he, by the way? His schedule says he is supposed to open today. He wasn't at the morning meeting with the staff. Here, it is midmorning, and I still haven't seen him," Jerome informed him as he glanced at his wristwatch to make sure it was still morning.

The gesture was not overlooked by Louis.

Louis felt his blood begin to boil. He knew of Mark's habit of playing games with his schedule. He also knew that Mark seldom put in a full work-week, so it shouldn't be much of a surprise that he was missing in action this morning. The fact that Louis never did anything to correct Mark's bad behavior may come back to haunt him on this day. Of all the days for Mark to decide to come in to work late and leave early, this was not it.

From the brothers' perspective, Louis not knowing where his store manager is could turn out to be a very embarrassing moment for him. It may give the impression that Louis didn't have a tight control on his operation. Louis had two choices. He could either think quickly and make up a story, or simply tell the truth.

He made the obvious choice.

"I spoke with him earlier," Louis fabricated with confidence. "He said he was making a recruiting visit this morning. Mark is always proactive when it comes to anticipating open positions in his staff. He should be here shortly," he bragged.

"No problem," Moses replied. "We have plenty of time. Our return flight isn't until tomorrow afternoon. Plus, I haven't had a cigarette in a half hour. I'm going outside for a smoke or two," he confirmed.

Moses stood and reached into his pocket to check on his cigarette inventory. After checking his watch and making a few calculations based on the number that remained in the pack, he made his way to the office door.

"I'm going to take Jennifer with me," Moses announced. "I want to thank her for the outstanding job that she did in conducting the recent inventory here. That woman has a bright future in this company," he declared. "Make sure you take great care of her, Louis. I'll be paying careful attention," Moses ordered.

"Do either of you care to come with me?" he offered.

"Too cold out there for me," Jerome replied. "I do need a bathroom break, though. I'll catch up with Jennifer a little later. I want to thank her myself. What a terrific asset she is to our organization. You must be very pleased, Louis," he beamed.

"How about if we all meet back here in a half hour?" Jerome suggested.

"Sounds good," Louis agreed. "Take your time. I'm going to get a cup of coffee myself and settle in," he admitted.

The brothers left Louis to himself, and he immediately closed the office door behind them. Panic stricken, Louis tried again to reach Mark's cellphone.

Finally, in the middle of the fifth ring, it stopped ringing. A moment later, on the other end of the line came a raspy, groggy voice.

"Hello?" Mark answered as he cleared his throat.

"Mark!" Louis screamed. "Where in the fuck are you?" he demanded.

"Huh?" Mark fuzzily replied. "Oh, Louis? I'm home. Why do you ask?" he wondered.

"Aren't you supposed to open the store this morning?" Louis asked incredulously.

"Oh, yeah," Mark confirmed. "My wife took a personal day today from her school-teaching job. We have been having some serious marital problems lately. She decided to take a long weekend and made the three-hour drive last night to stay with her sister. She's complaining about me having to work all day Saturday so she figured she would spend a couple of days with her family before coming back on Sunday." He yawned. "I took the opportunity to howl a little last night, but I'm regretting it now. I got home kind of late. Boy, does my head hurt," Mark admitted. "Boss, you know how smoothly my store runs. No need to worry. Everything will be fine until I get there," he assured.

"I'm not worried about the store people," Louis sneered. "The Horowitz brothers are in your store. Right now!" he revealed. "They called me early this morning, and I drove up here to join them. We are all here. In your building. Without you!" Louis exclaimed. "Get your sorry ass in here right away. And when you do grace us with your presence, tell them you were out recruiting this morning. I had to make up a lie to cover for you, and it was the best I could come up with at the time," he stated.

"How long are you going to be?" Louis demanded.

"Give me 45 minutes," Mark moaned. "I just need a little time to get my act together. I saw the memo Moses sent to Jennifer, but I can't believe they came here today. It's Friday for Christ's sakes. Don't they have weekend plans?" Mark complained. "Nobody works a full day on Friday in corporate," he declared.

"Are they looking at anything else or did they just come to visit with Jennifer? What am I walking into?" Mark asked once his head started to clear.

"They are looking at you," Louis revealed. "I don't know why. Maybe they want to promote you and give you a big raise," he said sarcastically. "You never know. Just get here," Louis demanded.

When the brothers returned from their respective breaks, Louis was sipping on a large cup of coffee. He had moved from Mark's office to the large conference room adjacent to Mark's space. He stared intently at the screen of his laptop computer, too engrossed in his work to pay any attention to the returning visitors. Upon the brothers' entry, the smell of cigarette smoke overwhelmed the room. Louis looked up from a screen full of unread emails. He found himself unable to ignore the sudden aroma and began to engage them in conversation.

"Moses!" Louis exclaimed as he feverishly waived his right arm back and forth, attempting to circulate the air. "How many cigarettes are you going to smoke today?" he innocently asked.

"I'm down from three packs," Moses replied nonchalantly. "Now that I'm in my 50s, I figure it's time to cut back a little," he said.

"You look like you're in your 60s," Jerome scoffed. "And cutting back one cigarette every six months isn't going to get you anywhere," he lectured.

"Mind your own business," Moses ordered. "Who asked you?"

Voices were getting louder.

"Anyway, Louis, where's your store manager?" Moses interrogated. "I'm starting to get a little aggravated. How long are we going to have to wait for this guy?" he wondered.

"Sorry I brought up the smoking thing," Louis replied. "Mark should be here any minute. I spoke with him when you were out. He's on his way," he informed.

"Okay, good," Jerome said. "I'm going to go and get my things out of his office. I'll be right back," he stated.

"I'm coming with you," Moses said. "I have a few things in there that I'm going to need as well. I think it's best if we all meet in here," Moses indicated with a broad wave of his hand. "The room is bigger, and we can all spread out," he gestured.

"Hold down the fort, Louis. We'll be back in a few minutes," Moses requested.

The brothers left the conference room together and made their way over to Mark's office, next door. Although the distance was short, Louis overheard the two sniping at each other as they made their way. Jerome was landing some solid shots at Moses for his smoking habits. Moses was landing equally damaging blows regarding Jerome's rather rotund physique.

Louis felt a strong urge to step in between the two. For one thing, the barbs were getting nasty. Additionally, Louis wanted cooler heads to prevail if they were going to have a conversation with Mark. The last thing Louis wanted was having to deal with two angry Horwitz brothers in a closed-door meeting with his prized store manager.

Louis quickly jumped from his chair and followed the brothers into the office next door. He had to attempt to at least try to get them to calm down. If he got lucky, he could even get them back to the good mood they were in earlier this morning.

When Louis got to them, the two brothers were standing nose to nose, hurling insults at one another. Arms were flailing and neither appeared to be backing down. Louis felt that if he didn't intervene, they would surely come to blows at any moment. Instinctively, he wrapped one arm around Jerome and the other around Moses and squeezed both tightly.

"Boys, boys!" Louis interrupted. "Please, calm down. You're disturbing my coffee break!" he exclaimed. "Moses, why don't you come with me. I want to show you a fish mount one of the department managers has on the wall above his desk. It's a beauty," he suggested. "Jerome, I'm going to show your brother something just down the corridor. We'll be within shouting distance if you need us," he assured.

Louis walked Moses the 20 feet or so, past Gerry's empty office space and toward the afore-mentioned mounted fish.

Moses, for the most part, had begun to settle down. It was as if someone had slipped him a Prozac and it had kicked in. He was laughing and smiling while imagining the ferocious battle the fish must have waged with the angler who caught it.

For his part, Louis was relieved. He became more and more relaxed as Moses's mood changed back to what it was before he and Jerome nearly came to blows. Louis felt it necessary, however, to keep the brothers apart for the time being. The last thing he wanted was to trigger another outburst.

Meanwhile, Jerome was keeping himself busy in the conference room by catching up on emails that he had been copied on. There was always something going on company-wide that needed his review or input.

Finally, out of the corner of Jerome's eye, he detected a lone figure standing in the conference-room doorway. Jerome gathered himself for a moment, wondering how long this person had been watching him. He looked up and turned his head to look directly in the direction of the door. There stood, in Jerome's impression, a disheveled individual who appeared like he had just rolled out of bed. The person stared directly at Jerome, with a frightened look on his face, as if he had just seen a ghost.

"Can I help you with something?" Jerome politely inquired.

"My name is Mark," he stammered. "I'm the store manager. We have met before on a few occasions. It's nice to see you again, Jerome," he said.

"Oh, Mark," Jerome bluffed.

Although he has, at one time or another, met every store manager in the company, Jerome didn't remember Mark. Especially as he appeared to him now.

"Of course," Jerome confirmed. "It's nice to see you again. You look a little different to me since the last time we met," he admitted. "Anyway, come on in. Have a seat. We have a few things to cover with you," Jerome revealed.

Mark inched his way inside.

"Excuse me for a second. I just have to let my brother know that you are here," Jerome stated.

Jerome stood and stuck his head over the threshold and into the corridor. He looked toward the door leading to the sales floor on the right, and then toward the managers' office area to the left. The corridor, and the entire office area, were void of all store personnel. Nobody wanted to give the brothers the impression of having free time on their hands. Time that could be spent on the sales floor taking care of customers' needs. Everyone knew that if the brothers wanted to speak with someone, they would ask. Otherwise, look busy. And stay out of the office.

The voices Jerome recognized coming from around the corner at the end of the corridor were obviously those of his brother and Louis. Although he couldn't see them, Jerome could tell by the laughter he heard that the two were engaged in a pleasant conversation. He hated to interrupt, but he also wanted to get started.

"Hey, Moses! Hey, Louis!" Jerome excitedly called out. "Come back. Mark is here, and he can't wait to see you guys!" he exclaimed.

*\*\**

Moses, as director of asset protection, took a position at the far end of the conference table. Jerome, director of human resources, sat on the same side of the table but at the opposite end. Louis, the regional manager, sat between the brothers on the same side of the table. On the other side, directly across from Louis, Mark stiffly sat facing the panel of the three executives.

The brothers attempted to ease Mark's obvious discomfort by engaging in banal small-talk but it was to no avail. Finally, nobody could take it any longer, so the brothers decided to get to the meat of the matter.

"So, Mark," Moses spoke while shuffling some papers in front of him. "Do you consider yourself to be an expert when it comes to local and federal firearms regulations? Are you confident that as a seller, you conform to the rules and conditions required of you?" he asked.

"110 percent," Mark enthusiastically replied while nodding in Louis's direction. "I know every regulation like the back of my hand. Nothing slips by me. Nobody is on top of the firearms business any more than I am. I can say with confidence that I am the best there is," Mark bragged.

Moses listened. Stone-faced.

"Are you familiar with this form?" Moses asked as he passed a piece of paper to the center of the table.

Louis intercepted the document, took a brief glance at it, and then passed it across the table to Mark.

"Looks like a federal form 4473," Mark said, stating the obvious. "Every customer is required to fill one out when they want to buy a gun. How am I doing so far?" he asked with a cocky hint of sarcasm.

Louis, detecting the cockiness coming from his store manager, subtly swung his right leg upward and delivered a solid blow to Mark's upper shin with the toe of his shoe. Jerome, not oblivious to the shenanigans taking place under the table, simply smirked and pretended to not notice.

"That's right, Mark," Moses confirmed condescendingly.

He didn't hide his disdain for the lack of respect that Mark decided to show him.

"Let me then ask you a slightly more difficult question, if you will," Moses declared. "Do you see anything unusual about this specific form? Would anything strike someone, as skilled as yourself, as being a little odd?" he asked, slightly annoyed.

Mark studied the form and could see an obvious discrepancy with the question that asks the customer if the gun being purchased was for the individual who was filling out the application. The question, on the date of purchase, had been answered 'No.' He also saw that the answer had, on a later date, been changed to 'Yes.' The change was dated and initialed by the customer who originally applied for the purchase. Although the initial transaction was extremely sloppy, the correction on the form made it a legal transaction. The fact that the incorrect answer wasn't detected on the day of the sale was highly problematic. The correction of the error, however, was acceptable.

Mark wracked his brain, trying to think of why this corrected error warranted questions from the three executives. He came up blank. This type of mistake, although unusual, is not unheard of. When it happens, it is simply dealt with through proper corrective procedures.

Mark, for a change, figured he may as well just tell the truth and go along with the flow of the questioning. At least for now.

"It looks like the customer checked the wrong box when he answered question 11a," Mark replied. "It also looks like he came back and changed his answer several days later. Other than that, I don't see anything unusual," he stated.

"When something like that happens," Moses said, at first wondering out loud, and then turning his focus directly toward Mark. "Would it be appropriate to simply change the answer on the form for the customer?" he wondered. "Let's say we noticed the problem the day after we sold the gun to the customer. He already has the gun at home or wherever. But we notice that he is telling us by the answer on the form that he is not buying the firearm for himself. Maybe he's buying it for a felon. Or a terrorist. Or some other whack job. The customer is, by his answer, admitting to us that he isn't buying the gun for himself. But we sold it to him anyway. In the scenario that I described, it could be stated that we sold the gun illegally. We can lose our license to sell firearms if we sell them illegally. We would go out of business if our permit got pulled. Do you think we should simply change the answer for the customer and hope for the best?" he interrogated.

"No," Mark replied.

He changed his demeanor. He became serious and respectful.

"Of course not," he confirmed.

"Do you think it would be a good idea to instruct one of your employees to change the answer for a customer?" Moses casually asked. "You know, just fix the error and don't tell anyone about it?" he wondered.

Mark realized where this conversation was going. His brain was now as clear as the numerous shots of 'Few Gin' that he swilled the night before. Being skilled at setting up unsuspecting victims of his own interrogations, he was painfully aware that he was now in that same seat which he had placed so many.

Mark remembered instructing Steve to do just what Moses described in his questioning. Panic was setting in. Mark wiped his forehead from the beads of alcohol-infused sweat that were forming and did his best to come up with a quick defense strategy. This whole incident happened weeks ago, and he reasoned that the only other individual who would know anything about it was Steve. At least, as far as he could remember.

It would be his word against Steve's, Mark assumed.

Why would Steve wait until now to bring this up, though? Something didn't make sense to Mark, but he didn't have time to figure it all out. Moses was waiting for a simple answer to a simple question. Mark's default strategy was always to deny any wrongdoing. Never tell the truth when a lie will better suit the situation, was his motto. The strategy had served him well to this point. There was no sense changing now, he reasoned.

"No. That would be a horrible idea," Mark stated with conviction.

"Why would that be a horrible idea?" Moses asked.

"Because," Mark stammered, "directing a subordinate to break the law would be the same as actively breaking the law myself," he foolishly admitted.

"Did you ask someone to change the answer to that question?" Moses looked directly into Mark's eyes. "That form. That customer. Did you instruct someone to fix that answer to question 11a?" he pointed at the document.

"No!" Mark shouted defensively. "Absolutely not –" he exclaimed.

"Phew! Thank God," Louis loudly interrupted. "For a minute there, I thought you might have done something horrible, Mark," he aggressively continued. "I can't tell you how relieved I am to hear that you had nothing to do with this." Louis nervously nodded his head vigorously toward Mark in a gesture of approval.

Louis folded his hands on the table in front of him and silently looked at each of the brothers in turn.

"Is there anything else, guys? Are we finished –" Lois finally asked politely.

Neither brother was amused.

"I'm not finished," Moses interjected. "I have statements from multiple people stating that you did instruct someone to break the law," he barked at Mark.

Louis felt he had a clear picture of what happened. Mark was backed into a corner. He tried to offer a life line.

"Do you still want to stick with your answer, Mark?" Louis asked, red faced.

Mark felt that he was much too savvy for Moses's unsophisticated trick. There was no way Moses had multiple statements, he assumed. In fact, Mark frequently used the same ploy when springing a trap on an unsuspecting employee whom he targeted. He would bluff them into thinking he had all sorts of evidence of something and trick them into admitting wrongdoing. Sometimes, the employee hadn't even done anything wrong, and he could get them to admit to an offense. He wouldn't fall for this one, he silently mused.

"I did nothing wrong," Mark calmly stated.

Now that Mark perceived Louis's support, he once again felt emboldened.

"You see!" Louis exclaimed.

Louis' shoulders were shrugged, almost touching his earlobes. His hands outstretched.

"Mark didn't do anything wrong," Louis concluded. "Let's wrap this up! There's nothing more to see here," he stated.

"I'm not convinced," Moses seethed.

The room fell silent for a moment as each of the contestants plotted their strategy. Louis and Moses were at odds. Their opinions, thus far, were miles apart from one another.

"Well," Jerome finally interrupted. "In my opinion, there doesn't seem to be any need for further questions. He says he didn't do anything wrong," he concluded.

"Stop!" Moses shouted angrily. "We are not finished," he barked while pounding the table. "Mark, leave the room," he ordered. "Just get out. We'll call you if we need you. Otherwise, just go back to whatever it is you have to work on," he said dismissively.

Mark gathered himself and left the conference room as quickly as he could. The three executives at first sat in silence, glaring at one another. Once they knew they had complete privacy, a major food fight broke out. Each had a different opinion based on their own interest. Nobody relented.

"I have statements from Lynn, the human-resources manager, as well as from Steve, the senior manager who was ordered to break the law," Moses tersely stated. "Their statements are corroborating. Lynn was sitting right next to Mark when he asked Steve to change the customer's answer. Steve wasn't the one who brought this to our attention in the first place. Lynn reported it. We didn't even talk to Steve about the whole thing until this morning," he revealed. "Steve cooperated with us, but he didn't want to at first. He said if he tells the truth, it will probably cost him his job. Steve believes that nothing will happen to Mark and that he will be retaliated against for speaking. Mark needs to be fired!" Moses opined. "He is going to cause us to lose our license to sell firearms if we don't take action," he declared.

"Mark is innocent," Louis retorted in a matter-of-fact tone.

Louis defensively folded his arms across his chest, signaling that nothing would convince him otherwise. The thought of Lynn making a statement against Mark puzzled him, however. Louis thought that the two of them were tightly woven. He could certainly see Steve bringing something like this to light, but Lynn? According to Moses, Steve sounded reluctant to confirm the incident had occurred. Something didn't make sense to Louis.

"I don't believe the statements," Louis decided. "If you want, I can investigate this further some other time. Now, however, I think it is best that we just let it go," he concluded.

"This is risky, legally," Jerome added. "Mark obviously isn't going to admit to any wrongdoing. If we term him, we might be slapped with a costly lawsuit. Those statements won't hold up against a good lawyer," he reasoned. "We have to be careful."

"I'll tell you what else is risky," Moses continued. "Leaving an obviously corrupt manager in charge of one of our stores is risky. He is dirty!" Moses declared. "This guy is going to cost the company a massive loss if we continue to allow him to make decisions on his level," he stated.

Moses attempted to calm himself. The more he thought about the situation however, the more worked up he became.

"What's wrong with you guys? Can't you see what's staring back at you? It's right in front of your nose?" he frustratingly pleaded.

"I still say we do nothing," Louis stoically replied.

"I think we have to give it some time before we make a final decision," Jerome reasoned. "I'm not comfortable firing him today. I'm also not comfortable with the decision to simply allow him to continue to run this store. I want to meet with the legal staff back in corporate and get their take on it. Tomorrow is a travel day for us, so I'll arrange to meet with them on Monday. Meanwhile, let's suspend Mark with full pay for the next several days," he decided. "Louis, I want you to let Mark know that he is suspended pending further investigation. Tell him we anticipate getting back to him in four days. Are you guys good with this?" he asked. "If not, I am forced to agree with

Moses. We'll just terminate his employment today and deal with any legal consequences as they might arise," he concluded.

The room fell silent. Each considered the compromise.

"I can live with it," Moses muttered. "How about you, Louis?"

"Sounds like I don't have much of a choice," Louis replied reluctantly. "I'll call him in now," he offered.

Realizing that he may have succeeded in getting himself in hot water by firmly resisting the will of the brothers, Louis felt the need to offer an olive branch to Moses.

"Would you gentlemen like to join me for dinner, or do you have other plans tonight?" Louis wondered.

Moses was still hot. Jerome was the most comfortable of the three.

"Let's head back to the hotel," Moses said to Jerome. "I have some calls to make, and I need a little privacy," he declared. "Louis, if you want to meet for dinner, pick us up at 6:30. Otherwise, we'll talk again in a few days," he concluded.

Moses and Jerome gathered their belongings and, in full view, paraded their way toward the employee exit. The store associates, like slithy toves, nervously reappeared from their hiding places. Each wished to catch a reassuring glimpse of the visitors' departure.

Collectively, they felt safe, knowing that they had survived the surprise visit of the corporate director of asset protection and the director of human resources. Once secure in the knowledge that the brothers had departed, the associates confidently returned to their mundane duties like a zebra returns to eating and frolicking, oblivious to the pride of lions feasting on a fresh kill on the outskirt of the herd.

Louis paged for Mark to return to the office. Mark was already fully aware of the brothers' exit, having witnessed it himself. Although he felt slightly uncomfortable with them leaving without saying goodbye, he assumed that he was off the hook. There was no way severe disciplinary action would be doled out without the director of human resources present. At least, that was what he thought to himself.

Confidently, Mark strode into the office and entered the conference room where Louis patiently waited.

"Did you want to see me, Boss?" Mark casually asked.

"I do," Louis confirmed. "Close the door and have a seat, Mark."

Mark closed the door as he was instructed and decided to take the lead.

"You know, Louis, I'm not very happy about the accusations being made about me," Mark began. "I think someone tried to go after me, and I'm not going to take it lying down. If you are going to storm the bastille, you better make sure you get the king. I think Steve tried to storm the bastille," he said, resuming his cockiness.

"There's plenty of time for that later," Louis confirmed. "I'm not positive myself as to who started this whole thing. Let's make sure we know who the culprit is before you go after anyone," he instructed.

"Who else could it be?" Mark asked. "He's the one I told," he stopped short.

Mark was not sure if Louis caught his confession. He hoped not as he continued on the offensive.

"I mean, he's the only one who might know about this. Or something. Anyway, I think he's the instigator. I don't like him in the first place, so there's no harm in getting him. Do you want to place an over and under bet? I say he doesn't last more than a month," Mark defiantly estimated.

"I'm taking the under," Louis laughed. "Meanwhile, the brothers are going back to corporate to have some meetings. They decided to suspend you for a few days. You'll be fully paid. They just want a couple of days to determine what, if anything, should be handed down as far as discipline," Louis delivered the news in a straightforward manner.

"You don't think they are going to take any action against me, do you?" Mark asked incredulously. "Is this just some kind of show?" he wondered.

"I don't think it is a show," Louis replied. "But I don't think any severe disciplinary action is going to be taken," he consoled. "I can see a whack on the wrist coming for you in the future. I don't think you have anything major to worry about as far as your job goes, though," he said reassuringly.

"So, what's next?" Mark asked, suddenly concerned. "What do I do now?"

"Just sit tight and relax," Louis instructed. "I'll call you in a few days. As soon as I hear from them, I'll contact you. Take some time for yourself. Enjoy the paid time off. Think of it as a surprise mini vacation. I'm going to tell your staff that I gave you some well-deserved time to spend with your family. A thank you for all the long hours and hard work that you have put in over the past couple of months. They'll understand. I'm sure it will be a morale boost to them knowing that I gave their beloved leader a token of my appreciation," Louis boasted.

"Sure thing, Boss," Mark said. "Thanks for the gesture." He laughed. "I'll talk to you in a few days. Leave me a message if I don't answer. I promise I'll call back next time," he kidded.

***

295

Mark left without saying a word to anyone in the store. He knew that Louis would take care of any communication that was necessary with the staff. Steve and Lynn were each told separately that Mark was taking a few personal days. The remaining managers were called into a meeting and were told about the extra compensation days that Louis felt Mark deserved due to his hard work.

Louis noticed, but misinterpreted the odd looks being shot back and forth among the meeting attendees. Nobody cared about not having Mark around for the next few days. In fact, they felt they could be more productive without having to endure his incessant distractions. The overt, puzzled looks on their faces reflected their thinking that either they were being lied to, or their regional manager was a genuine stooge.

On his drive home, Mark decided that since his wife was off visiting his sister-in-law for the next few days, it would be a great opportunity for him to have a little fun. He changed his navigation and headed to a topless bar located in the heart of the city. The establishment's highway billboard directed travelers to take the next exit to experience their world famous 'Lunch, With a View.'

Mark ate, drank, and tipped the dancers until he finally ran out of money at around 7:30. Feeling tipsy, and reeking of stale perfume, he fumbled for his car keys and confidently took to the highway.

Halfway to his destination Mark realized that the reason other cars were flashing their lights and honking their horns at him was because he still hadn't turned on his headlights. He thought to himself that maybe he should have refrained from giving each horn blower the middle finger. The more he considered it, however, the more he finally concluded that the other drivers should have minded their own business. Each, he finally decided, deserved to be on the receiving end of his mini display of road rage.

When Mark finally pressed the signal button on the sun visor to open his garage door, he breathed a huge sigh of relief. All he had to do now was to pull into his parking spot without running anything over, and he would be in the clear.

Slowly, carefully, he edged his car forward, all the while checking the distance from the side mirrors to the frame of his two-car garage. Depth perception was currently not one of Mark's strengths. He got out of the car, determined that he was not far enough forward to safely close the garage door, and tried again. This time, he succeeded in safely reaching his destination.

Mark pressed a doorbell-type button mounted to the unpainted interior wall and watched while the garage door closed behind him. As he waited for it to completely close, he couldn't suppress the self-realization of how much his clothes stunk. Combined with the stench of booze on his breath and the red-

and-blue glitter covering his clothes, he felt grateful that he didn't get pulled over by a state trooper on his ride home. Mark felt confident in his skills to lie and deny, but even he felt it may have been difficult talking his way out of this one.

Still, after a fleeting moment of reflection, he couldn't suppress a toothy grin. Once again, he came out on top. The only thing he may do differently the next time would be to bring more cash with him. He could still be out having fun if only he had planned his evening a little better, he mused.

And then, things became curious, to say the least.

Mark was certain he hadn't left any lights on when he left the house to go to work. As he stood frozen inside the hallway leading from the garage, not only did he notice that the kitchen light was on, there was also a noise coming from the same direction. Mark was having difficulty processing the sound he was hearing. Although it was a familiar sound, it was out of place, given the circumstances. It sounded to him like silverware falling to the floor.

He didn't think anyone was home. His wife's car wasn't in the garage. Did she come home a day early and leave someone to watch the house while she ran out to do an errand, he wondered?

"Hello?" Mark called out as he removed his coat and hung it on the rack. "Who is there?" he asked as he slowly approached. Mark's voice trembled.

"Come on in," came the clear, firm response.

Mark thought that he recognized the voice but couldn't, at first, associate it with a person. It was someone he knew, but not well enough to immediately make the connection.

Cautiously, Mark approached the kitchen where the light, voice, and sound were originating. There, to his amazement, sat Sydney at the kitchen table with two spoons placed end to end. Ignoring his visitor, Sydney continued lining up the forward spoon with an empty water glass and pounding the rear spoon on which it rested with his leather-gloved right hand. As the spoon being flipped into the air gravitated toward the glass, Sydney applied body language, attempting to direct it to land squarely inside the glass. Time after time, the spoon missed its target and noisily flopped onto the tabletop.

Mark's presence didn't seem to have any effect of Sydney. He knew Mark was there, but he continued his compulsive quest to make a perfect spoon flip. Out of the corner of his eye, Sydney noticed that Mark had moved to the opposite side of the table and appeared to be glaring at him. Grudgingly, Sydney moved the spoons and the glass out of his way and slid his backpack closer to him.

"How's it going, Mark?" Sydney asked dryly. "How was your day?"

"How did you get in here!?" Mark demanded.

"Someone left the sliding door to the back deck unlocked," Sydney deadpanned. "It's a good thing, though. Kept me from having to break in," he calmly mentioned.

"What do you want?" Mark stammered.

Sydney glared at Mark. He was clearly annoyed with Mark's intrusive questioning. Since their last conversation, Sydney learned to not trust the sincerity of Mark's inquisitions. He no longer felt any need to directly respond to what was being asked. Mark was not in charge of this interaction, Sydney decided. Sydney was. And he was getting angry.

"Are you aware of the murders that have been happening over in Chevon?" Sydney casually asked. "There has been a bunch of them," he mentioned in an offhand way.

"Yes," Mark answered in a condescending tone. "I have heard about them. Why do you ask?" he aggressively demanded.

"I'm the killer," Sydney disclosed as he began emptying the contents of his backpack onto the table.

Mark stared wide eyed at Sydney. He was stunned. He realized that Sydney wasn't confessing because he wanted Mark's help to rehabilitate. Certainly, Sydney wasn't confiding in Mark like a sinner to a priest.

Mark realized what was going on but was having difficulty processing a plan of action. He recognized the fact that he had just unwittingly wandered into a 'fight or flight' situation, but he also realized that he was still highly inebriated. Therefore, he knew he was severely handicapped in any interaction requiring physical balance and coordination.

Before he did anything, however, Mark figured that it would be worth trying to talk his way out of the trouble he suddenly felt he had stumbled into.

"Very funny, Sydney," Mark nervously chuckled. "You had me going there for a second," he kiddingly admitted. "We both know you wouldn't hurt a fly. Seriously, what do you want? What can I help you with this evening?" Mark said in an attempt in to strike a friendly tone.

"Actually, I'm not kidding," Sydney soberly explained as he stood and gravitated toward the end of the table.

Sydney pulled the ends of his driving gloves tightly toward his elbows, like a baseball player does as he enters the batting box. Instead of a bat, he grabbed the tent stake from his backpack with his left hand and the hammer with his right.

"For some reason, I take great pleasure in killing people who piss me off," Sydney coldly admitted. "People like you." He pointed at Mark with the end of the tent stake. "Don't let my looks or demeanor fool you. I am a cold-blooded killer. And you are my next victim," he stated.

Mark realized that there would be no talking his way out of this. He could attempt to flee, but in his drunken state, he knew he wouldn't get far. Simply giving up wasn't a good option, either. The only thing left for him to do was to fight, he thought.

Mark could tell that his adrenaline was pumping by the way his hands uncontrollably shook. The more he thought about it, however, the more his drunken logic convinced him that someone of his stature and prestige could easily prevail in a physical confrontation with someone as lowly as Sydney.

Mark's initial fear turned into bravery as he made a tight fist with his right hand and, without warning, threw a haymaker punch directly at Sydney's nose. Sydney saw the slow, awkward blow coming just in time to attempt to duck out of the way. He wasn't, however, able to completely avoid contact. Instead, he bowed his head forward and down so that his nose was pointing toward his own chest. The full force of the blow from Mark's fist landed squarely on the crown of Sydney's head. A sickening sound of shattering bone was quickly followed by a guttural howl emanating from the diaphragm of Mark who had just obliterated every bone in his hand.

Sydney, briefly, saw bright flashes of light before his eyes as if a swarm of fireflies momentarily interrupted the bout. He placed the hammer on the kitchen counter to free his right hand and vigorously rubbed the top of his head. Satisfied that he was okay, Sydney quickly made a fist of his own with his free, right hand. Timing his movements to face Mark, who was busy gingerly dancing in circles while holding his limp right arm with his left, Sydney delivered a short, quick blow directly to Mark's left eye socket. The force of the punch knocked Mark to the floor where he sat propped against the far wall. Stunned, bloody, and staring straight ahead.

"I give," Mark slurred. "You win. I can't take anymore. Just leave me alone. I won't say anything to anybody. You can trust me to keep a secret," he reasoned as he struggled to get himself back on his feet.

Mark pressed the small of his back against the far wall and leaned his head back until it too was supported by it. Blood flowed from a deep cut just below his left eyebrow. Combined with his now-swollen shut eye, the blood flow obscured his vision on that side of his face. The adrenaline rush had worn off as did his unwarranted surge of bravery.

The last thing Mark would ever see was the metal tent stake that Sydney now held inches from his right eye. Mark gripped Sydney's left wrist with his left hand in self-defense, fiercely attempting to keep the stake away from the intended target. Sydney pushed a little harder, inching the pointed tip toward Mark's right eye. Mark tried applying additional resistance pressure by placing his right forearm on top of his left hand. His right hand was broken, limp, and useless, but he desperately tried to keep the point of the stake from hitting its mark. Sydney brought his right arm over to his left in order to allow him the ability to apply additional pressure with both hands. The added force was overwhelming for Mark.

Frantically, Mark pushed forward, away from his body with all his strength. However, he gained no distance against Sydney who still maintained half of his power in reserve. Lactic acid built in Mark's triceps to an excruciatingly painful level. He couldn't hold Sydney off much longer. Panic set in as he realized he was defenseless against Sydney's superior strength.

"Sydney, please stop," Mark pleaded. "Please!"

Without warning, Mark suddenly released his pressure against Sydney's hands, causing the tip of the tent stake to lurch forward, deeply into his right eye. Sydney pulled back on the stake and retreated to where he had placed his hammer on the countertop. He would need it to complete the task at hand.

Mark, who was now totally blind, took an angry, wild swing with his left clenched fist in the general direction of where he thought Sydney stood. Sydney easily sidestepped the clumsy attack. In perfect timing, he swung the hammer forcefully downward, in a windmill motion, and delivered a powerful blow to Mark's wrist with the hammer's head.

Due to his blindness, Mark never saw the blow coming. Nor did see the next blow in which the head of Sydney's hammer landed squarely on his left temple.

The full force of the blow penetrated Mark's skull, dropping and killing him instantly.

Sydney wriggled the hammer free from where it had become lodged in Mark's head. He took his time washing the bloody tent stake and hammer with dishwashing liquid and warm water. Carefully, he used the dish towel that was hanging nearby to dry his implements and returned the wet towel to its holder. The same way as he had found it.

After loading his belongings into his backpack, he pulled on the freezer door of the refrigerator and reached for a few pieces of ice from the tray beneath the ice maker. With his left hand, he applied the cubes directly to the egg that had grown on top of his head. He howled at first from the pain of the contrasting cold against the heat emanating from his contusion. After a few minutes, however, the ice numbed his pain, and he could feel the swelling begin to subside.

Before he left the blood-drenched kitchen, there was one more thing he felt compelled to do. Sydney garnered a few more cubes from the freezer and sat at the kitchen table. He placed the two teaspoons end to end and slapped the one closest to him, flipping the other into the air. Finally, after several tries, he landed the acrobatic spoon directly into the center of the water glass.

"My work here is done!" Sydney gleefully exclaimed as he gathered his belongings and turned off the lights.

Finally, Sydney slipped out through the same sliding glass door that he used to enter the home and quietly disappeared into the darkness of the cloud-covered, moonless night.

He had worked up an appetite and looked forward to picking up a bite to eat before heading home for an uneventful evening alone.

# 24

What I did last night. What she said last night.

David hurriedly slid to the end of the bench where he was seated and quickly stood. He had to pee like a racehorse and couldn't hold out for another minute. Like a dancer, he pirouetted between tables and navigated his way to the nearest water closet. While he was away, Rick flagged down their waitress and ordered two more of 'Mr. Kisluk's famous frozen tequila drinks' as he so aptly put it.

It had been another long week for the brothers, and a casual Friday evening spent with their wives was having a positive, therapeutic effect on them. The dull pain still lingered from Gerry's passing, but time was helping to slowly fade their grief.

Invariably, the conversation between the brothers drifted to the murders that remained unsolved in Chevon. The murder in Red Bush a couple of weeks ago appeared to be unrelated to the crimes which fell under the jurisdiction of David and Rick. The killing in Red Bush, although violent, didn't have the same execution style to it as the Chevon murders. There was no single, precise hole drilled into the back of the skull like every victim in Chevon. It just seemed like a brutal brawl where both landed blows, but the one delivered to the loser was fatal.

Detectives in Red Bush were under the impression that the victim either was followed home by the murderer or brought him home in the same car. There was no indication that the home had been broken into.

Evidence taken from the victim indicated that he had been out drinking somewhere and likely angered his murderer while in the bar. It was suspected that he was in a strip joint and may have somehow crossed a dancer's boyfriend. Perhaps jealousy played a part in the crime. Detectives were showing the victim's picture in every local topless bar to see if anyone remembered him patronizing the spot. To date, they were having no luck.

David's time spent in the restroom, staring at the wall while making his bladder gladder allowed him some private time to think. He was having difficulty forgetting about work and focusing his attention on his tablemates.

He couldn't refrain from tossing his thoughts out there as he returned to the table.

"You know, Rick," David said as he returned from the restroom and slid onto the bench toward Gina. "I've been thinking about Dad's former boss getting whacked a couple of weeks ago. Do you think it was the same killer as we have been chasing?" he asked as he downed a generous gulp from his fresh drink.

"It's possible," Rick answered. "I don't think it's the same guy though. Our killer seemed like he wanted to send us messages the last time he struck. From what I hear, the killing in Red Bush was the result of a brawl. Dad's boss, by all accounts, was not liked by many and hated by most. I bet he was out drinking with one of his so-called buddies, and they got into an argument once they got to his house. I'm just happy it didn't happen under our watch. We have enough to worry about," he said.

"I am..." David started to speak, but he suddenly stopped and placed his right hand over his forehead and slouched against the back of the bench. "Arrrgh," he moaned as he attempted to raise his left arm but couldn't.

David dangled his motionless arm by his side as if it were dead. His mouth hung open and his face turned a bright shade of red. For a minute, he stopped breathing. His body froze as if posing for a portrait and stiffened.

"David!" Gina screeched. "David, what's the matter?" she pleaded, looking first to him and then to Rick and Julia who looked on from across the table.

"I think he's having an aneurism," she declared, frightened to death.

"Ow," David suddenly managed, still leaning his head straight back, eyes closed. "No. It's not an aneurism," he moaned. "M.T.Q.," was all he could mutter.

"M.T.Q.?" Gina asked, still terrified by the look on the face of her husband.

"Margaritas Too Quick," Rick deadpanned. "You know, brain freeze," he chuckled. "Dave, I told you to go easy on those things. God, I can't take you anywhere," he observed.

"You are shut off!" Gina declared. "I'm ordering you a glass of pineapple juice in a sippy cup. See if you can handle it like a big boy!" she said as she raised her hand to get the attention of the waitress.

"Oh, man," David said as the severe, dull pain began to fade from above his eyebrows. "That was brutal," he described, blinking his eyes furiously.

It took a moment for him to gain his senses.

"Anyway, like I started to say, I'm glad we don't have to deal with the murder in Red Bush. I only met Dad's former boss that time I went to check on Steve," David recalled. "I felt like I needed a shower after talking with him.

The guy was sleazy. I hate to say it but, maybe he was why the hairs on the back of my neck stood up when I was there that day. If he treated people outside of work the same way he treated the people that he worked with, something had to give at some point," he concluded.

"I never met him, but from what I've been told, the guy had plenty of enemies," Rick confirmed. "At least it looks like we were able to clear Steve in all of this. Come to find out, he was helping at a food shelter on Christmas Eve," he said for the benefit of Gina and Julia. "He volunteered his time after working all day at Jimbo's to feed some homeless people. We were looking at him as a potential suspect in a gruesome string of murders. Dave even figured a way to check his D.N.A. against some random sample left at one of the crime scenes. I think it's safe to assume that Steve didn't have anything to do with any of the killings," he confirmed.

Rick had enough of the work talk that David insisted on bringing into the conversation. After all, it was his night off. He preferred spending the evening clearing his head and engaging in something more casual. Unsuccessfully, he attempted to change the subject.

"Are you sure Dave can't have another drink?" Rick sheepishly asked Gina.

"No more drinks," Gina ordered.

She glared at Rick and then turned her stare toward David who was doing his best to act normal. Gina suddenly realized that she was being overly dramatic and figured it would be best if she calmed herself.

"I am curious, however, to know how close you guys are to catching the murderer?" Gina peacefully offered. "I know you can't name names, but how much longer before you make an arrest –" she wondered.

"I feel like we are back at square one," David interrupted. "We have limited evidence. The killer is methodical and incredibly clean. What little evidence we have will hopefully be useful in convicting him once we figure out who it is. The problem is that the evidence alone won't lead us to the killer. Rug fibers and clothing fibers can possibly be matched once we find the guy. What we have, though, is so common that there is no chance it will, on its own, lead us to who brought it to the murder scenes," he said.

"How will you find him, then?" Julia asked. "What's the next plan of attack? People are nervous around town. The murders seem to be so random that everyone is afraid they could be the next victim," she stated.

"He's going to screw up," David revealed as if talking to himself. "He's going to confide in someone close to him whom he feels he can trust with his little secret. So far, nobody knows what he has been up to. Except him. That's going to change," he explained. "He is going to tell somebody and that somebody is going to tell us. I can feel it in my bones. It's going to go down just like that," he confidently declared.

All four considered the possibility.

"Do you guys get many tips?" Gina asked.

"We get calls every day," Rick replied. "Most of them are screwballs who think they want to be cops," he scoffed. "Once we ask how the victim was killed, the tipsters quickly cave. 90 percent come up with shot or stabbed." He laughed. "This murderer has a unique signature that he leaves on the body. So far, nobody has given the right answer. So far," he said.

"We've been sent on a few wild goose chases that turned up nothing. I'm ashamed to say the best lead we thought we had was Steve's name on the back of Dad's business card. That one turned up nothing," Rick continued, frustrated. "I hate to just sit back and wait, but that's pretty much all I can do right now. Knowing David, though, I'm sure he has other ideas brewing. That's why he has his role, and I have mine." He nodded toward his brother.

"Something tells me I'm going to be back at Jimbo's asking questions in the near future," David revealed. "I can't put my finger on why. Maybe it's because I'm still thinking about Dad. Who knows? I just get the feeling that there was someone there who wanted to get to know me better," he offered an impish smile as he spoke.

"Anyway, thanks for buying dinner, Rick. It was great! Good night, Julia. See you Monday, Rick?" David asked as he slid from the bench as put on his coat.

"I didn't remember offering to buy," Rick said as he reached for his wallet. "But, yeah, I'll see you Monday. Good night, Gina," he said with a toast from his water glass. "Be safe tonight. Both of you!"

*** 

Sydney gathered the leather folder sitting on top of his desk along with the pertinent reports and memos that he had printed and headed to the large conference room for his first manager meeting. He was excited to be part of the management team even though he still felt uncertainty about his ability to succeed in the role.

Jennifer, upon accepting the tremendous opportunity to fill Gerry's shoes as senior operations manager, immediately looked to Sydney as her replacement. She assured Sydney that as his supervisor, she was there to support him in his new role. Jennifer convinced him that she would guide and continue to develop him until he was completely competent on his own accord. Sydney's success would translate to her own success, she explained.

Now that Mark was no longer the store manager, the culture of the store had changed dramatically. Instead of being managed with fear and intimidation tactics, employees were being led with support and direction. In just a few short weeks, morale in the organization soared. Productivity skyrocketed as did the overall performance of the business.

The new store manager, Tina Weymouth, was the driving force behind the metamorphosis. Jerome Horwitz felt Tina would be a good replacement for Mark. He strongly recommended that she be promoted from her position as senior merchandise manager at the Jimbo's located next to the corporate office. Louis was in no position to argue against the wishes of the director of human resources. He offered her the position and made the change effective immediately.

Tina was an experienced retailer in her late 30s who navigated her way upward through the ranks at Jimbo's by outworking and outsmarting her competition. If there was a sales goal, she exceeded it. If there was a company-wide contest, she won it. If there was a difficult project to be executed, she did it. No matter the task before her, Tina found a way to not only complete it, but she made sure she stood out as completing it better than anyone else. Associates under her umbrella loved working with her. Nobody ever felt they were working for Tina. They all felt that as part of a team, they were working with Tina.

She loved to compete and, more than that, she loved to win. Her winning attitude was contagious. It drew the most positive and optimistic candidates to her fold. Those on her team who became less motivated than their teammates invariably ended up deselecting themselves. Employees with bad attitudes didn't fit in with her group. Self-declared victims were not allowed on Tina's team. The more everyone got to know her as the new store manager, the more respect they gave her.

Sydney looked forward to participating in a meeting conducted by Tina. He was told that she had a simple rule in meeting protocol: 'You can say anything you like. Just say it nicely.'

Sydney took a chair next to Jennifer in the crowded conference room. The department managers, having attended Mark's meetings for the past couple of years, were used to being lectured for an hour or so about whatever came to his egotistical mind. They would pretend to listen intently while taking fake copious notes of the supposed brilliance being uttered from his wet, swollen lips. Instead, however, each of them wasted meeting time by doodling in notepads and checking their watches, frivolously wishing to hurry the time away.

Tina was different. Her meeting agenda was distributed to the staff two days in advance. It was expected that all attendees would be prepared to discuss all topics as they pertained to their department. Sydney quickly learned that meeting participation was mandatory. There was no place to hide when it was his turn to speak. And he had better get used to having his position challenged on the topic being discussed. Tina was an expert in determining whether a manager could maintain the courage of their convictions or not.

The final topic on today's meeting pertained to staffing levels. Each manager was asked to give a brief synopsis of how strong they felt their current staff was compared to what they anticipated four weeks from now. How many open positions are there presently and how many openings does each manager expect in the short-term?

Tina, knowing that Sydney may struggle with this topic, called on him to go last. Sydney reported that he had a full staff presently, and he wasn't expecting anyone to leave in the immediate future. He also reported that he felt his staff was experienced and strong. Sydney informed Tina that although customer care recently lost a top performer, a qualified cashier was transferred to fill the spot. The new customer-care associate was doing a great job learning the ropes. The expectation was that she would soon be a good replacement.

Jennifer was happy with the way Sydney conducted himself in his first meeting. She leaned toward him and quickly whispered as much once Tina took the floor to wrap up the meeting.

"You did good, kid," Jennifer said. "Real good."

Once the meeting was adjourned, Sydney gathered his belongings and exchanged a few pleasantries with some of the other managers. He felt good about himself for the first time in a long while. Sydney was beginning to consider staying in retail for the long term. The pay was good, and it could get much better if he performs. Having Jennifer as a boss was an added-bonus for him. She was firm but fair. Plus, she made the job fun for Sydney.

Jennifer credited Tina for the new management style and culture in the building. Sydney felt that he could still maintain his computer studies by taking online courses. He no longer felt he was in a hurry to get settled in another career. He was still young and figured he had a long way to go before succumbing to the pressure of making a final career choice.

The only thing missing in his life was that he no longer had his best friend to talk to. Sydney missed Clare in the worst way.

Before Sydney left the meeting, Tina shouted to him that she wanted to see him in her office before he headed back to his department. Jennifer was asked to join them. The not-so-subtle invite prompted much obligatory teasing from the other department managers who were now Sydney's peers. Their verbal jabs ranged from 'teacher's pet' to 'you're in big trouble now' and encompassed every other taunt imaginable.

Red faced, Sydney walked out of the room like a dog with its tail between its legs and entered Tina's office. The last time Sydney was in the store manager's office, Mark was trying to trick him into turning on Clare. Sweat started to bead on his forehead as he recalled the unpleasantness of that day.

"Great job participating in today's meeting, Sydney," Tina beamed. "I thought you made some valid points about the upcoming advertising event. Plus, I was pleased with your understanding of your staff. Do not be afraid to consult with Jennifer or me as you continue to grow in your new position," she added.

"Thanks," Sydney replied, glancing back and forth from Jennifer to Tina. "You two have been great so far. It's nice to know I have your support," he admitted.

Tina moved to the real reason for the meeting with Sydney and Jennifer.

"I want to ask you two about Samantha," Tina began. "I believe she goes by the nickname, Sami?" she asked.

"What about Sami?" Jennifer asked. "What did she do now?" Jennifer wondered out loud.

"It isn't so much about what she did recently," Tina replied. "It's more about what she was doing in the past," she said. "I wasn't here more than a few days when she asked to see me in private. Apparently, she had some sort of special arrangement with Mark. She would provide him with real or imagined information about goings-on in the store. In return, he was giving her all sorts of special perks. Sami filled me in on the preferential treatment that she has become accustomed to. Plus, Mark finagled the system in order to add an extra dollar per hour to her wage. Did either of you know this was going on with her?" Tina asked. "Sami wants to know if this deal is still on, now that Mark is no longer with us," she casually informed them.

Jennifer glanced at Sydney who stared straight ahead with a puzzled look on his face. Before he could try to answer Tina's question, Jennifer broke the silence.

"Mark had informants throughout the store," Jennifer began. "Nobody knows for certain who they were other than the individuals themselves and Mark. I suspected that he was using Sami, but I didn't let on about it," she admitted. "For one thing, I have more important issues to worry about. For another thing, there was nothing I could do about it. I certainly couldn't complain to Mark. Like everyone else in this building, we all just learned to live with the situation. It's one of the reasons nobody trusts one another around here. I can't prove it, but I would bet the house that the reason I lost one of my best customer-care associates was because of Sami. I think she turned something stupid in to Mark and he made a huge deal out of it in order to get rid of a good person. Mark was probably trying to get back at me for something else, so he used one of his little spies to dig up some dirt on one of my top employees. Like I said, people are still leery of one another around here," Jennifer confessed.

Jennifer's revelation hit Sydney like a ton of bricks. He didn't realize that Jennifer was so aware of the goings-on around the store. Sydney had never been a part of closed-door manager meetings where sensitive information was being shared. Information that was necessary to understand individuals' motivation for doing things that otherwise would appear to be irrational.

Sydney now understood that it was Sami who spearheaded the gathering of information which lead to Clare's firing. Clare, he surmised, was fired so Mark could make Jennifer's job more difficult.

Additionally, the termination removed Clare from the scene so Sami could try to put the moves on Sydney. The minute that Clare was fired, Sami started relentlessly asking him to take her out on a date. She was, now, finally getting the message that he wasn't interested, but it took a while.

Sydney's mind was now clear as to what happened. The conversation that he was listening to enlightened him. It also angered him. Sami was the reason that he lost Clare.

"I think I have a good understanding of what was going on," Tina confirmed. "It sounds like I still have a lot of work to do when it comes to restoring people's trust. Anyway, I informed Sami that I do not operate like Mark did. Not only do I not use informants, I find the practice abhorrent. I believe in openness and honesty. If someone makes a mistake, I want to discuss it, correct it, and move along. Employees should not be afraid to come to me with a problem," she stated. "Sami, however, does not seem all that comfortable with my approach. She is used to getting special treatment and privilege. And, I am here to tell you that she liked her elitist status. When I informed her that those days are over, she didn't take it well. Sami is used to being above everyone else," Tina declared. "The main reason I am filling you two in on what I learned from her is that my instincts tell me that she is not going to stay with us much longer. Syd, you mentioned that you were not anticipating any open positions in the coming weeks. I beg to differ. As soon as we finish here, head on over to human resources and tell them you want to have some screened applicants sent your way," she instructed. "You are going to have to fill Sami's position sooner than later," Tina warned.

Jennifer spun as if looking for someone or something.

"I'm surprised Lynn isn't in here with us now." Jennifer laughed. "I don't ever remember having a meeting with Mark without Lynn sitting over there taking notes," she described.

"I have a tremendous amount of respect for our human-resources partners," Tina stated. "They are here to support us in our effort to manage this business. However, they are not here to tell us how to run the store. If I feel I need their input on something, I'll invite them in. Otherwise, I won't interrupt them from carrying on their important duties. If that sounds different than what you are used to, so be it. It will take some time before we all get used to one another! Right, Sydney?" she said instinctively.

Tina sensed that the conversation was slightly above Sydney's understanding. She could tell that he was having difficulty following along and felt it necessary to bring him into the discussion.

"I'm new to this manager stuff," Sydney replied. "I think I can handle the changes. But yeah. Right," he confirmed.

"I know you can handle it," Tina encouraged. "Okay. That's all I have for you today. Is there anything else that I can help either of you with? Otherwise, you are dismissed," she informed them with a broad smile.

***

Jennifer led Sydney into the human-resources suite and showed him how to put in a request for screened applicants. The two of them then headed in opposite directions.

Jennifer had follow-up reports to complete and submit which were requested during the manager meeting. She still felt slightly awkward about taking over Gerry's desk and office area. Time, she knew, would erase the uneasiness. Gerry, she told herself, would want it that way. Jennifer would sometimes find herself channeling Gerry for the rest of her career. Especially when decisions were difficult and consequential.

Sydney made the trek across the store to his office behind customer care. Although the department was running smoothly, he could have sworn Sami was scheduled to still be there working with customers. And, yet, she was noticeably absent. Maybe she had to use the restroom, he thought as he greeted the rest of the staff and made his way to his office.

Sydney immediately noticed the sealed envelope sitting on top of his compulsively organized desktop. He didn't even have to open it to know what was inside.

Sami's resignation letter was short and direct. She apologized for not giving proper notice. Sami explained that she had accepted an offer from another company, and she wanted some time off before starting her new position. In closing, Sami made one last pass at Sydney.

"If things don't work out between you and Clare, give me a call," Sami wrote.

Sydney glared at the letter and reread it in anger. He didn't care about her resignation. He also didn't care that she basically walked off the job without giving two weeks of notice. He would figure out a way to fill her scheduled shifts. What infuriated him was what he perceived as her taunting him about his lost relationship with Clare. If her intention was to rub salt in Sydney's still-open wound, she succeeded beyond her wildest dreams.

The next couple of hours were spent at his desk, reviewing applications and, with Jennifer's help, reworking the customer-care schedule. Fixing the schedule was time consuming, however, the work was necessary in order to accommodate the needs of the business. Some of the staff volunteered to pick up extra shifts. Others made deals where they would work one of the crucial openings in exchange for another day off, causing another ripple effect.

Sydney glanced at the clock on the wall. His stomach was telling him that it was getting late in the day. One adjustment that Sydney was still getting used to was no longer being paid as an hourly associate. Being on salary meant not having to worry about working overtime. He had already put in a ten-hour day, but he wasn't finished with what he felt he needed to accomplish. Sydney had to decide on whether he should get a bite to eat and stay another couple of hours, or just keep at it and work hungry for at least another hour. His stomach won out.

"I'm going to go and grab something to eat upstairs in the restaurant," Sydney announced to his staff at customer care. "I'll be back in an hour," he said as he waved and flashed the peace sign in their general direction.

On his way to the restaurant, Sydney felt his cellphone buzzing in his pocket. His first instinct was to ignore the call. He wished to have some time alone to sit and enjoy his supper. He then decided to see who was calling.

*It could turn out to be something important, one never knows,* he thought to himself.

Just before the phone went to voicemail, he managed to dig it out of his pocket and glance at the screen. At first, he thought his mind or someone else was playing a cruel trick on him. He would soon find out. The call appeared to be coming from Clare.

"Hello?" Sydney nervously answered. His hands were shaking.

"Syd, it's Clare," she calmly announced. "I wanted to call and congratulate you on your promotion. I was surprised to hear you took the job, but if it's something you want to do, I'm happy for you," she said pleasantly.

311

Clare was taught to smile when speaking on the phone. Sydney sensed her smiling at him in the tone of her voice.

"Thanks!" Sydney replied.

He couldn't believe he was hearing Clare's voice again. Sydney missed Clare to the point where he, at times, felt physically ill just thinking about her. He did everything he could to train his thoughts from bringing her into them. As soon as something or someone reminded him of Clare, Syd would go into a funk of depression. His appetite would evaporate and take with it all motivation to move any other part of his body.

Although he yearned to speak with Clare, hearing her voice over the phone was having the effect of restoring that empty feeling. It was another reminder to him of how much he missed her. Instinctively, he started to feel suspicious about getting a call from her, seemingly out of the blue.

"How did you hear about it?" Sydney asked, attempting keep the conversation going.

"Sami called me the other day," Clare replied. "We had a lengthy conversation. She told me lots of things. She said she was the one who handed my list over to Mark. She was making extra money as a spy for him, so when he asked for something that he could use to fire me, she had to produce," she revealed. "Sami also told me that since she had the hots for you, by getting me out of the way, she felt the door would open wide for her to be with you. The problem was, Sami said you wouldn't play along," she teased, laughing.

"Do you believe her?" Sydney asked, cautiously.

He was beginning to sense that the conversation was taking an unexpected change in direction. Sydney felt that he needed to gather his composure. Clare was seemingly sounding like her old self to him. She was almost toying with him, he sensed. It was as if she was talking to him like nothing had happened between them.

Sydney would not allow himself to get dragged into false hopes only to be crushed again, he reasoned. Hearing Clare's voice could turn out to be nothing more than a nostrum. Still, Sydney decided that he would go along with whatever it was that Clare was peddling. At least for now.

"Did she mention anything about the new store manager?" Sydney asked. "Does she still like her job now that Jennifer got promoted and I'm her new boss?" he wondered.

"She said she was going to walk out today," Clare replied. "If she's still there, then I don't believe anything she had to say. If she did quit, I guess she was telling me the truth about everything. Did Sami quit today?" she asked.

"Yeah," he replied in amazement. "She left a resignation letter on my desk and left without saying goodbye to anyone."

"Then, I guess I believe what she told me," Clare stated.

Clare suddenly stopped talking. She wasn't sure what she wanted to say next, but she was hoping Sydney would break the silence for her. Sydney, however, not only remained silent on the other end of the line, but he couldn't figure out what would be best for him to say, either. In the situation he was in, Sydney felt that whatever he offered would only further mess things up for him. Therefore, he kept quiet. Each listened to the other's breathing for what seemed like an eternity, until, finally, Clare broke the silence.

"Syd, I'm sorry," Clare blurted. "I should have never doubted you. You just had a strange look on your face when you walked out of Mark's office that day, and I took it the wrong way, and I wasn't feeling good, and I can make all kinds of excuses," she rambled as her voice trailed off into muffled sobs.

Clare sniffled and attempted to speak through her emotions, but forming words became difficult for her, given the sudden state of mind she was in.

"Sydney, please forgive me. I miss you so much," she said. Her voice quivered. "I promise I'll never refuse to listen to you again. I'll never doubt you," she managed before turning the phone away from her.

Sydney removed the phone from his ear and stared at it as if he were trying to figure out a magic trick that had just been performed in front of his cynical eyes.

Could this sudden change of fortune really be happening for him? He has been miserable since the day Clare abandoned him. Sydney's feelings haven't been hurt like this since the death of his father many years ago. He allowed Clare into his inner self and, when she left, it tore a piece of his heart out. He yearned to have her back in his life. She made him happier than anyone has ever made him feel. Sydney has never been in love with anyone and wasn't quite sure about how it felt. One thing he did know was that Clare made him feel wonderful and exhilarated. He wanted to be with her every second of every day. He wanted to share his life and everything else that he possibly could with her.

The thought of holding Clare in his arms again suddenly made him feel incredibly warm inside. Caring for her was all that he thought about. If feeling how he does about Clare is love, then so be it. Sydney confirmed to himself that he was madly in love with her. For the first time in his life, he was ready to throw caution to the wind and dedicate himself to having a relationship with another human being. There were so many ideas and experiences that he longed to share with Clare. He would be an open book to her if he could. Sydney's existence would dramatically change if only he could manage to have Clare in his life once again.

"Clare, of course I forgive you," Sydney finally shouted. "I have missed you more than words can describe," he said. Then, he thought of the ramifications of what he was telling her. "Does this mean we are back together?" Sydney pleaded. "Can I come by later to see you?" he sheepishly asked.

"I want that in the worst way," Clare replied.

"Before you do, though, I just have one more question for you," Clare said tauntingly. "I already know the answer, so you had better tell me the truth. Otherwise, if I think you are fibbing, everything is off," she teased. "I just have to hear you say it to me. Loud and clear in your most truthful, honest, sincere voice," she instructed.

Sydney was grinning ear to ear at Clare's silly request. He knew she was going to ask him if he had started dating someone else.

Or perhaps she was going to ask him about missing having sex with her. Those would be easy questions, he thought to himself.

Maybe, though, she was going to ask him if he loved her. Sydney prayed that she would ask him that question. What else could she possibly want to hear him tell her, he finally reasoned? Clare would ask him if he loved her, and he would shout his answer, as if from the mountaintops, as loud as he could, that yes, he does love her. He has always loved her. Sydney would announce the news for all within earshot to hear. And he always will love her.

First, however, he would have to play along with Clare's impish request. He would have to pretend to be caught off guard by her glaringly obvious question and immediately blurt out the unmitigated truth. A truth that was shared between them but, until now, never fully committed to.

"Okay," Sydney placated. "One question for all of the marbles. I'm ready. Let's have it," he chortled.

"Sydney, did you murder Mark?" Clare asked.

CPSIA information can be obtained
at www.ICGtesting.com
Printed in the USA
LVHW020834040121
675397LV00007B/513

9 781645 757191